The Well-Kept Secret

The Well-Kept Secret

David Brooks, Ph.D.

ISBN: 978-1484989142

To Avery, Clay, and Olivia,

and to the hundreds of my history students who have sat and listened and helped me construct *The Well Kept Secret*

Table of Contents

Chapter One

The Butterflies Scatter

They swarm me thickest when I have given up hope. Since we were kids, Nelson had always refused to walk with me when they get like this, and so my twin brother now walked far ahead. He understood completely that in this moment of my darkest sadness I would not deny these yellow and orange beauties what was theirs. As I turned the corner and started up the Professor's street, the sight of his familiar house brought a sudden rippling shutter of comfort. The startling kindness of this sight released one reluctant tear and sent it cascading down through the sweat of my face and into the folds of the ridiculous party dress I was wearing. It was a tear of shame, and it humiliated me even more than the earlier events of this horrible day. They were flipping and dipping all around me now, thicker than I had ever seen in my life. It was as if they would not be denied their final feast. Two miles of walking in this heat, combined with the light, airy fabric of my party dress, had apparently glazed me to absolute butterfly perfection. My mom and her mother before her had both whispered to me their secret, that when we were alone it was okay to let them feed on our sweat, and ever since I had always let them in. They had been with me this summer when I had dived insanely down the secret well. They had been with me this afternoon when I had let myself slip away and surrendered to leaving college and this town forever.. They had been with me an hour ago when I had been brutalized by the man who was now after us. They had been there through every darkening stage of my life and now they were here to say good-bye. They were welcome. Others would not ever know the comfort that their scratchy clinging and bobbing wings had brought. But to these yellow-wings, and to nothing else on our planet, even fully sunken, I was somehow still worth something. I would let them savor my sweat until they had their fill. They were convinced there was something valuable still in me. They knew me better than I knew myself. They knew my well kept secret.

Only in Alabama do the Octobers swelter like this. As we approached the Professor's house, I shook my fluttering escorts off and tried to billow them out of this dress. Only one or two remained hidden with me, and they had earned the right to stay. I covered myself up with my cowboy hat as Nelson and I bounded up the four dusty wooden steps that rose to the Professor's porch amidst a loose cloud of eight or ten of the most persistent yellow butterflies at varying distances from me and my twin brother Nelson. By this point in our lives, and we were nineteen, Nelson and I had actually seen the peeling blue paint of this front door many times. When we had been kids we had often visited this door and these butterflies with our Daddy. Our father and the Professor had debated and solved the world's problems for hours in the study while we twins played hide-and-seek out back or, most fun of all, built oversized and cleverly constructed forts in the living room out of the Professor's zebra-skin blankets and antique furniture. Once we were discovered, the Professor would always laugh and wave away my father's objections and instead would encourage more and more outrageous construction techniques and secret rooms in our fort. The Professor's old grizzly-hide rug was usually the roof of the main fort room. This small dusty house seemed to us to contain an unending supply of exotic furniture and big bulky African carvings. Professor Flanagan O'Shea was our godfather and now we desperately needed his help. He had, with much flair we were told, taught historical linguistics here at the University for thirty-eight years until his retirement the previous spring. Several decades back, Professor O'Shea had even taught our father, Mike Stuart, and the two had over the years developed a very strong friendship. The Professor had been flattered to be asked to be our godfather, and I always got the feeling that long ago he had promised himself that he would watch over us in a way that would be extraordinary. And that is exactly what he did on this night that would change humanity forever.

Nelson looked nervously back over his shoulder and quickly and firmly rapped the doorknocker with four sharp cracks. It had been our father who had insisted that while in college Nelson and I should visit the linguist from time to time, which we had most certainly not done at all. A house that had been a delightful playground for children's games had been—until this afternoon—met so far this semester by our blank teenage disinterest. Yet one thing that Nelson and I remembered most about this house was that without fail the Professor had always served a bowl of Reese's Cups—a childhood tradition we had always enjoyed while the older men dominated the conversation. These candies were very, very good.

Now was our chance, I thought as I waited on the porch, *to score points with Dad, to stall on the studying for tomorrow's medieval history midterm exam, to figure out this insane book, to hide from the crazyman, and to get some candy in the process*! It had been months since I had experienced the sensation of joking, and for a fleeting moment I found that I had missed it. My first months of college had been a real-life nightmare for me.

We looked at each other impatiently as we waited in the silence of that late afternoon. "The Professor knows everything," I remember Nelson and I saying at the same time. Nelson impatiently rang the doorbell with his free hand. We both thought, "We're used to thinking the same thing."

Finally, Professor O'Shea slowly opened the door, and though he at first seemed a bit groggy, he immediately burst into a broad smile when he recognized us. "Haley! Nelson! What a pleasure!"

Apparently he had just woken up from a long nap. As we expected, the Professor was very glad to see us and even gladder to see the heavy book that

Nelson was carrying. He looked straight at it and only occasionally looked away as he greeted us.

Before he could follow up on his inquisitive eyeing of the book, I blurted out, "Professor, we are in big trouble. Can we come in?" Looking up from his examination, a bit alarmed, he nodded and stepped aside. We moved quickly into his foyer as he closed and locked the door. We had always been amazed at the security seal that seemed to surround this house, and as he locked his front door we were comforted by the same old hissing sound that seemed to seal the front door permanently closed. I just said, "Nice security system, Professor."

The Professor looked at us a bit sideways, paused, and simply said, "If you are in trouble, then follow me." He led the way through the house and downstairs to his den. Before he spoke again he carefully sat down in a huge leather chair.

It felt so good to be back in this room. His oversized downstairs den had long ago lodged in my mind as the most interesting and exotic room I have ever been in. It was here that I had sometimes whiled away the hours of our visits by imagining the Professor to be an exciting secret agent instead of what he was, a boring professor. The walls were flanked on two sides with floor-length windows that were covered by large, billowy curtains. These were made of what appeared to be an almost-sheer, faintly-embroidered fabric which I had always imagined had been made in some tiny village somewhere in the Middle East. The fabric moved easily and silkily when the Professor had the windows onto his garden open, as they were on this scorching October afternoon.

The ceiling was my favorite. It was draped with crocodile netting, all over it, which fell off the ceiling only in the corners, giving the impression that the Professor could capture us any time he wanted to! The lighting was also very unique. Lamps were placed behind each of the four heavy leather chairs and behind each of six small tables, illuminating only the space behind and above this furniture. The impression, then, with the flip of the one wall switch, was of a flood of indirect and soft lighting.

The floor was now covered with something that had been added since our childhood. It was an enormous polar-bear rug, a real hide, that had the softest fur I had ever felt. But it must have been fake, because it was almost thirty feet long, covering the length of this comfortably large den. But as I sank down into it and ran my fingers through the luxurious fur, it didn't feel fake at all. What was odd was that now that I was older, I began to suspect that some of the stuffed animals in the room were actual species that were completely extinct. The dodo birds in the corner, for example, weren't they extinct now? As I looked around, I even suspected that actually all of the specimens in this den were extinct. The room was also overflowing with elaborate mirrors, exotic upholstery fabrics, and unidentifiable artifacts from every corner of the globe except our own. This had been a child's paradise and was now a college freshman's new refuge. This was the right place to be as the sun began to set on this day and on my old life.

The Professor, who apparently only sat in his own chair, had been rummaging through his tobacco pouch. Finally the pouch seemed as organized as he thought it should be and he reached for the remote to turn off the CNN that apparently constantly ran as background on his huge cracker-thin plasma HD TV. But his motion was arrested by the story that was airing. At the Vatican a religious conference between the Catholic Church's Holy Father, the principal Rabbi of the Temple of Jerusalem, the Anglican Church's Archbishop of Canterbury and the Buddhist religion's Dalai Lama was just getting underway. The reporter was saying that many other world religion leaders were also in attendance, notably the Patriarch of the Eastern

Orthodox Church, and the highest spiritual authorities of Japanese Shinto and Indian Hinduism. Some TV evangelists were even there.

"The breaking news," the reporter was announcing, "was that the proceedings had apparently been interrupted by the unexpected but very welcomed arrival of the Imam of the Kaaba, the Muslim cleric responsible for the central Islamic Mosque at Mecca toward which all devout Muslims pray five times a day."

And so for the first time in human history, the leaders of every single world religion were together in one room. "With every major world religion now represented at this nine-day conference," the on-the-scene reporter explained, "this unprecedented meeting is giving hope around the world that an accord could be reached between the great world religions." The reporter added that some in the crowd outside St. Peter's Basilica were even prayerful that "the seeds of a unified world church might come out of this meeting." But he quickly "discounted such ideas as unlikely given the strained dialogue that had characterized this opening day of the conference."

The Professor snapped the power off. "Apparently they could not even agree on the seating chart! A unified world church would take rather a miracle, would it not?" he chuckled.

"Now, what is so pressing? Where did you get this book?" He looked at us a bit accusingly. "Did you and your brother steal this book, Haley?"

The Professor turned his attention to the book Nelson had carried in. "Hand me the book right now, Nelson." He immediately began turning the pages much more carefully than we had. "It is written in Anglo-Saxon, and it is very rare," he said under his breath. His voice began to strain with a deep excitement. "Old English may be the term you are more familiar with."

As he opened a second section, he quickly looked up into our eyes. "This is not Anglo-Saxon, how could I be so wrong? It is Old Norse rune, the language of the Vikings!"

He looked back at the first section and his brow wrinkled uncontrollably.

"Absolutely fascinating. Let me see another section. Yes, I thought so. This appears to be a work of early Middle English, a Middle English story working as a frame for a series of Old English narratives that are inserted within the larger story. It starts in Middle English, then goes into Old English, and then goes back to Middle English many times. There are also passages in Old Norse, Old Welsh, and Medieval Latin.

His expression fought off any real possibility that we were criminals. "Surely you two have not robbed a museum? What exactly is going on here?"

Nelson seemed disappointed by the Professor's tone. "Well, Professor, we've had a rather wild day. It's a little hard for even us to believe what really happened. I guess we need to tell you the whole story so you can really understand the meaning of this book. Here it is in a nutshell:"

"This afternoon, about an hour ago, Fitzy here was on the roof of our house like she is almost every afternoon these days, doing the same thing she always does. She just sits up there alone. And you may remember, Professor, that Fitzy's one cool but creepy party trick has always been that her sweat is apparently irresistible to butterflies. Of course mom has the same bizarre affliction." He shot an exasperated look at me.

Nelson had always called me "Fitzy" ever since I could remember. My middle name, Fitzarthur, had apparently been an opportunity too tempting for an annoying twin brother to pass up, and I had grown up used to his pet name for me. I kind of liked it.

"Shut up, Nelson, Mom says it's just the chemistry of our blood." I added in my mind, *I think it's strange but it is also neat. I like to feed them and they love our sweat!* "Mom says it doesn't really *mean* anything. It just is."

Nelson looked at me with one eye half-closed and continued to explain to the Professor what had happened: "Anyway, just like she used to do when she was a little girl here at your house, Professor, earlier this afternoon Fitzy had climbed out her bedroom window and was up on the roof of our tiny rental house letting butterflies feast on the sweat of her hands and arms. Anyway, believe it or not, Fitzy then turned to find a man with a stocking over his head rushing at her! He grabbed her and put her into a crushing, dangerous headlock and dragged her across the roof and back into her bedroom. The butterflies scattered." I sat silently as Nelson recounted the horrible story he heard me tell the police when they arrived.

I broke my silence and continued Nelson's account, "Once in my bedroom he then gripped me by both shoulders and I remember he smelled foreign; both his breath, which was horrible, like dead fish, and his sickly-sweet cologne were totally new to me."

"This attacker said something like, 'Where is the bloody book, Ayley?' He roared this in a thick English accent as he pulled back his fist and rammed it hard like concrete into my stomach. As he reared back to hit my slumping body again, I heard Nelson coming up the stairs with his buddies. At this point I blacked out and my head hit the dusty hardwood floor of my bedroom with a thud."

The Professor was totally stunned.

I continued, "After few minutes I heard Nelson ask, 'Fitzy, are you okay'?"

I went on, "When I came to, I was lying on my bed with Nelson leaning over me, stroking my face with a wet washcloth that was way too hot. His friends had come over to study for our medieval history midterm which is tomorrow at eight in the morning."

Anyway, I explained to the Professor, "His friends were now gathered around me like it was the bed scene from *The Wizard of Oz*. There were also two officers of the campus police in the hallway. Nelson was explaining to the older one, who was taking notes, that we were students here and that our home was in Lexington, Kentucky. The younger officer was squatting and examining the smashed and splintered doorframe of the door to my bedroom, which had apparently been kicked in. The front door of our dirty, dark rental house was also smashed in and was in a similar condition."

The Professor interrupted. "Haley, are you alright?" He stood up, walked over, and pressed the back of his hand on my forehead.

"I really don't know, Professor. It was like a bad dream."

"Well," he said, sitting down again, "I need to hear every last detail of what has happened to you two during the last hour. Tell it all to me, and leave nothing out. Can you do that?" Sometimes the Professor could sound very official.

"Okay, Professor if you want me to. Anyway, right when I regained consciousness in my bed Nelson asked, 'Who was that man'?"

"How would *I* know?" I answered as I sat up with much more ease than I had been expecting.

"Professor, I might as well tell you and Nelson something at this point. I don't want to tell you this but I can't hide it anymore. On the roof this afternoon, right before the attack, I finally made the decision that I am going to drop out of college and go back home. I am so confused and lost in all my courses. I hate accounting even though it was Dad's major. My classes make me feel hopeless and really so nervous that I am constantly near throwing up. This first freshman semester has been horrible." I added, hoping to avoid the looks that I knew were coming, "The decision is really a great relief and I am planning to pack up and go back to Kentucky in the morning."

Nelson and the Professor sat in silence and said nothing. Nelson was my roommate and must have known this was coming for weeks, and the Professor had also had conversations with my Dad. Dad had apparently informed the Professor that this first semester was not going well at all for me. I hoped that all three of these men understood the stress I had been under up until the point I made the decision to drop out.

I broke the silence. “So, anyway, back to what happened. I tried to get up and Bart, Nelson’s friend, asked ‘Should you be sitting up’?”

Nelson interrupted, “Let me tell this part. You won’t do it justice. Fitzy then snapped rudely at my friend, ‘Why shouldn’t I sit up? I feel perfectly fine.”

Fitzy was even ruder to the policemen. “Hey officer," she said as she snatched the hot washcloth from her forehead, "if you’ve sent for a doctor, please cancel the order. I feel great, and we can’t afford any more bills.” Her tone was so angry and shrill that the younger officer didn’t even bother to object, but appeared to just give up on her, looking annoyed.”

I glared at Nelson at this point.

Nelson intentionally did not look at me and tried to continue, but I cut him off. “As the officer put one finger in his ear, turned toward our small kitchen, and radioed to cancel the ambulance, I saw Bart look down and judge me cringing there in my bed. Then he shot a look at Nelson that screamed, “Your twin sister is a real piece of work.” Neither boy said anything.

I continued, “At this point the older of the officers, a husky man with a bushy mustache and a crisp blue polyester uniform, stepped up and rubbed his temple. He looked like he was racked with guilt over the exhausting interrogation that I was about to undergo. But strangely, I began to be aware that the officer was peering knowingly at me, as if he knew me or something. He nodded his head, and said, “I’m Sergeant Thackerson of the Campus Police. Honey, can you tell me what happened?”

I looked into his badge and read his nameplate blankly. *Thackerson. I’d never seen this man before. And though he had never met me, he looked at me as though he knew I had just given up on school.*

I began with my story. “I was on the roof when that man that we all saw…”

Nelson and his friends nodded supportively and expectantly. I was not sure, but I thought they were making fun of me.

I scowled at them and continued, “Well, out of nowhere I guess he grabbed my throat, from behind, and began to strangle me. He drug me across the roof and into here. It really hurt. I think he meant to kill me.”

This realization shot another spike of fear through me again as I sat on the Professor’s polar bear.

Nelson continued with the story, “Fitzy lay back down on the bed. She continued, almost spitting now, “And he knew my name. He knew my name was Haley. He called me ‘Ayley.’ He had a nasty English accent and wore a black stocking mask. It was ribbed. I guess he was average height and build, but strong and mean! And I remember he wore a black leather jacket. Before he hit me I think he said he wanted ‘the book,’ then he hit me really hard, then I guess you two came in and saved me.”

Sarcastically, I added, “My heroes! Too bad you couldn’t have beaten him to a bloody pulp so I wouldn’t have to sit here and wait for him to come back for me!”

The Professor interrupted again with a concerned tone, “I assume they have caught the guy by now?”

We both shook our heads nervously and the Professor at that point realized for the first time why we were really there. We needed sanctuary.

I continued, “As I was laying in the bed, being leered at by all those strange men, Nelson finally began to sense how scared I really was, and he responded to the tension with his usual inappropriate humor: he said something like, ‘The dude definitely dropped you like a bag of dirt, Fitzy. But the guy took off like a bat as soon as he saw us, slamming Bart here pretty bad’!”

The Professor was looking at Nelson disapprovingly at my description of Nelson's insensitivity to what was really a very brutal attack. I continued, trying to make Nelson look as bad as he deserved, "Nelson smiled teasingly at Bart, but this playfulness evaporated as they both realized again that this criminal was still around, desperately searching for whatever book this was that he wanted so badly."

Nelson added, "Well, no one in the room knew anything about the man, and no one knew anything about whatever book he was after. The Sergeant stated, "Ma'am, earlier today another crime took place, and I suspect they are related. This morning a man was attacked while riding his motorcycle, and he had a black leather jacket stolen, as well as his black helmet and his black racing Honda. You can't miss it, it's real loud."

Bart volunteered, "Hey, I heard a motorcycle, a really loud one, start up right after this happened." The others agreed they had been annoyed by the thunderous sound, too. I hadn't heard anything like that.

I resumed the story, "After Sergeant Thackerson finished taking my statement, the officers and Nelson's friends began to leave my bedroom. On the way out, the police said they would be cruising the neighborhood for a few days."

Nelson interjected, "At that point Fitzy lost her mind and went off on the policemen. She said, really, really, loud, 'Yeah, right, I feel so safe!' I couldn't believe it."

I looked embarrassed and explained, "Well, I did say that, and then the police left my room with two frowns on their faces, pulling the door as closed as it would go in its demolished condition." I added in my thoughts, *at that point somehow I had done it again. I had pushed away yet another person who might have helped me.*

Knowing I was looking like a horrible girl to the Professor, who had always been so nice to me up until today and who had always seemed in some way to admire me, I tried to justify my outburst. "But Professor, here's how that ended. Abruptly, the door opened again and Sergeant Thackerson stormed back in. His pot belly shook with the animation of his body as he rudely barked out his instructions. He ordered everyone out into the hallway so that he could speak to me alone. Not knowing what else to do, Nelson and his buddies left my room, escorted by the younger officer, who also seemed very ticked off at my little comment about not feeling safe. This younger cop's veins in his forehead and in his neck were now flared up pretty good."

"The older officer walked over to the bed where I was now sitting up again. I fisted the peach-colored afghan on my lap as the young officer jammed the front door closed completely, leaving me alone with this man and only the sight of a few hungry butterflies flipping around outside to comfort me."

"He leaned down, almost squatting, with his hands on his knees. His bushy mustache was only inches from my whitening face and his eyes were bloodshot and bulging. His breath stunk of cigarettes and coffee. Then he spoke."

"Missy, you've been through a lot today, and you have every right to snap at anybody you want. But you gotta know one thing. I'm not one to allow people to beat up little girls. I'm gunna find this English fella who tried to kill you. I'm gunna chase him down, And I'm gunna kill him. I'm not just sayin this, I swear to God, ma'am, I'm gunna kill him personal. You don't worry 'bout a thing. This conversation never happened, right, ma'am?"

I looked straight at the Professor. "I stared into the bulging eyes of this strangely confident campus cop, and he stared back into mine as the butterflies fluttered on outside. I slowly began to nod obediently as Sergeant Thackerson with some effort stood back up straight, patted me on the shoulder a bit awkwardly, and walked away. He violently jerked the door open and swaggered out. The South is definitely a very interesting place for a girl to live."

I continued recounting the events to a very concerned godfather. "The others came back in, and they were a little shaken up, mainly embarrassed that they could not or had not stopped the police from pushing them around. I lied to them and told them that the officer just cussed me out for being rude. That's sure what he should have done. But it's sure not what he did. Nelson's friends said their goodbyes and left with sudden awkwardness."

I resumed, "Professor, at that point I think I began wigging out. I kicked Nelson out and went into my bathroom and after a few minutes of showering and dressing, I stepped back out of my room into our shoebox living room. I was in the same black jeans with studs and a faded black tee shirt that I had worn all day…"

Here Nelson interrupted, "You mean all month."

I ignored that. "…and I shuffled a bit off-balance to our tiny kitchen to stare into the completely empty refrigerator. Nelson sat on the sofa, with his back to me, and seemed to be becoming excited. 'Look what the FedEx man left for us this morning with Stephanie next door. She just now brought it over while you were in the shower. Come in here and take a look'."

Haley continued, "But of course, Professor, I did not do what he said, since I make it a point to never do what Nelson tells me to. Instead, I just leaned on the kitchen doorframe smirking at the back of Nelson's head. Despite years of him annoying me, I have to admit how great Nelson has turned out to be as a student. Everything seems to come so easily to him. Even the events of this afternoon seemed more of a challenge than a threat to him, and somehow he never feels any of my sense of impending tragedy. You know Nelson's full name is Peter Nelson Stuart, but "Nelson" fits perfectly, doesn't it? His grades were always good in high school, well, better than good, and now that we attend the University, he stands out even more in his classes as one of the most interested and gifted students. The fact that Nelson has one deep olive left eye and one very light, Scandinavian blue right eye has made him all the more popular here at college."

"I'm just a colorful guy," Nelson chimed in. His eye color had never hindered Nelson much at all, and in fact had really only served to ground him in the humility that made people like him so much. His disarmingly goofy personality, the irrepressible kindness that radiated from his face, and his razor-sharp wit resulted in one simple truth: everybody loved Nelson.

I continued, "Professor, we now have to tell you about what we did for summer vacation, because that was where we found this mysterious book. In England I had such a relaxing and interesting time. I loved the strange smells, the new insects, the exotic accents, and especially the fish and chip stands that were everywhere. Most of our twenty days had been spent wandering the streets of the local town, Ashingdon, or the grounds of the estate, which our sweet Uncle Spencer had called 'Thursdale' in a most aristocratically British accent."

Nelson added, "Now our trip to England, *that* had been a blast. The property was about twenty acres, which is large for England. On one of our daily walks, Uncle Spencer had informed us that one acre that was the highest summit, nestled far out of view at the rear of the estate, was already our property. He walked us up to a vacant lot at the top of a hill. In her will, apparently, my mother's Aunt Rose had expressly granted us this small windy hilltop. It was actually just a big rock. Go figure."

I wanted to do this part. "Uncle Spencer told us 'She even granted you mineral rights and all that.' Uncle Spencer had said with a smile suggesting how unpredictable his wife had been. He finished, 'and she insisted that the tract in question stay in the blood family forever'."

Nelson explained, "Uncle Spencer had said with one of his winks, 'She was quite insistent.' I thought this was strange since I had been told that the rest of the land would, after Uncle Spencer's passing, go to Mom, and then, presumably one day, to us twins. I had already noted several times on this vacation that the English could be quite odd."

I continued, "Nelson and I loved touring the Tudor-style, diagonally-mowed Thursdale. It seemed like a museum, especially since the grounds included ruins that Uncle Spencer said dated from the eleventh century. The butterflies of summer were out, creating strange figures with their outlines as they flipped through their air and followed me around. I wondered to myself how many generations these yellow and black beauties had been ornamenting this estate. It seemed pretty clear that they must have been flitting through these woods for over a thousand years, perhaps a million. But they had evolved so far over these ages, into such delicate and efficient creatures!"

I looked directly at the Professor. "It all started when one yellow-wing flittered over and landed on the ledge of an old well that was near where the lawn sloped sharply upward into deep forest. From this well I could see our summit off to the right, far in the distance. The butterfly crawled off the ledge and down into the well. I remember walking over to look down the curious old well only to see dozens of butterflies, apparently drinking the water far below. This was strange because it was exactly what they usually do to me. I let some butterflies land on me and I craned my neck to look down the well. Unlike American church wells with smooth sides and strong protective iron gratings, this well was ancient, large in diameter, wide open, and I guessed it still worked. As I bent over, I could see the rough, uneven rock far down one side of the well. In this position I felt a pang, a shock of recognition that I found very exciting. I let myself play with this strange sensation for over a minute. As this feeling passed, I peered down as hard as I could, and clearly saw in the water below the reflection of the clouds and the butterflies and myself, looking back up. 'There's treasure here, I'm sure of it!' I echoed to Nelson, and, laughing aloud at my silliness, pulled my head out and bounded to catch up."

"On our daily strolls, though, I would stop at my well, my little secret. I always sat on its edge, and looked very deep down. And as the days passed, the nostalgic flutter I had felt at first blossomed into a deep feeling of belonging. I soon discovered that on a sunny day, through the butterflies who seemed to swarm this well, I could always see my reflection down at the bottom, but somehow, I thought, my reflection here looked richer and fuller than any other mirror I had ever seen. And the sun had certainly been shining brightly every day; England was experiencing a drought, the worse one in anyone's memory, according to Uncle Spencer. About fifteen feet down, I judged, was the water, and it seemed lower than the day before. I wondered how deep it was, and if there were Roman pennies or some other treasure at the bottom."

"One day, as I was watching the yellowtails float to the wet rocks near the waterline, I saw an irregularity at the bottom that fascinated me. One of the sides of my well was gone. In my imagination, it was as if the water had dipped below the top of a tunnel running away at a right angle at the bottom of the well. But if this were the case, only the very top of the mouth of the opening was above the level of the water. I showed Nelson, who dismissed it as a simple irregularity in the construction of this well. But I kept my eye on it."

"The following day, the day before we were to leave England, I came back and the water level was even lower. I could see the irregularity at the bottom of the well wall, and it appeared to me to be twice as big as the day before. When I peered down, I saw myself plainly in the distance, with the bright light of outside silhouetting my falling blond hair. *My grandmother must have looked down this very well, and my mother, too*, I thought to myself."

"Then I had an idea. I went over to a nearby garden and picked a pretty white daisy. Walking back to the well I twirled the daisy between my fingers, even as I swung my legs over the edge of the well so that they dangled down the shaft. Then I popped its head off and threw the stem away. I held the flower out and let it go. The daisy head fluttered downward, flipping and twisting, and finally landed silently in the water far below. It floated there, half-submerged on the surface. It didn't move. Then I brought over a few stones as big as my fist and began plop, plop, plopping them into the water so that the flower would be pushed over a little each time. After several trips to get rocks, the experiment worked. The daisy disappeared beneath my irregularity, now clearly a ledge of some kind. My arms went all goose bumps and I made myself a plan. I would have done it right that second except I needed Nelson to haul me back up and I needed a big flashlight in case I was right."

Here I had the Professor's complete attention. "The next morning, the day of our departure, I woke early and set my plan in motion. It had rained hard all that night and the drought appeared to be ending. At first I was alarmed by the rain, but then I decided it wouldn't really affect my big idea. I began packing for home but left one clean outfit out. I stuck my head into Nelson's half-opened bathroom door and told him as he was brushing his teeth to meet me at the well in five minutes for a surprise. In my jeans and a tee shirt that I had taken from Nelson's laundry basket without asking, I went down to the kitchen and borrowed a big black flashlight. I loaded fresh batteries and rolled the flashlight up in a yellow lawn leaf bag so that the plastic wrapped around the light many times. Then I stuck this entire assembly down the front of my pants. It was very cold on my thigh. I walked straight to my well and looked in."

"Not too much to my surprise, the water level had risen dramatically, and the indention, which in my imagination had become a tunnel, was now invisible far below the surface. But I would do this. I had promised myself. Nelson came out and began walking toward me. I yelled, 'Use this bucket to pull me back up'!"

"Before he could process what I had said, I braced and let myself fall. The water shocked my senses, but I was soon dog-paddling normally. Nelson had reached the rim of the well, and was looking down. 'You are a dingbat. You do know that? Uncle Spencer is going to kill you'."

"'Shut up, Nelson, and lower the bucket. I'm going to explore that tunnel. I'll be back. I know you're going to tell Uncle Spencer, so go ahead. I have a waterproof flashlight down my pants. By the time you get back I'll be back too.' And before he could even open his mouth to start, I disappeared beneath the surface."

Nelson explained, "I did not want to alarm Uncle Spencer with something that was either fine or a disaster that no one could do anything about, so I just waited, gazing down that well at a twin sister who has always been dangerously impetuous. I hoped that trait would not catch up with her someday."

I resumed, "I took a huge breath and down I went, lowering myself quite a few feet and using the wall to feel my way down. Feet first I went down and down, but found no break in the wall. Knowing I would need plenty of air if I did find and follow a tunnel, I had no choice but to let myself rise to the surface."

"I'm coming up," I called as I grabbed the rope firmly and pulled it until all its slack was out. After some very unladylike grunting I made it back to the ledge and scrambled out onto the grass. It was clear what I needed to do, and it was just as clear that Nelson would not allow it, so I kept quiet until I had all my strength back. Looking over at the shape of the well, it seemed quite easy. The crank was behind the well, not over it, and the bucket lay on the grass, so I had a clear path. Without thinking it all the way through, I stood up and took off running before Nelson could react. He was speechless as I sprang up onto the ledge and threw myself up into the opening position of a perfect swan dive. As I started down, I took a huge breath and made my body as rigid as possible. I sliced like a jet into that water and through time and space I dove deep down my wishing well."

Chapter Two

The Frisbee Treatment and the Swan Dive

The Professor had settled fully into his overstuffed chair by this point in my tale and I could tell he was fascinated by what I was relating.

He requested calmly, “Go on, Haley.”

I continued, “As my momentum began to subside, I violently kicked downward and began to feel the wall in my upside-down position. Suddenly, the wall vanished. The indentation was actually a tunnel, one that ran up-hill at an angle! I entered the tunnel so that I was head-up again and followed it upwards. After holding my breath for a ridiculously unsafe amount of time, I finally broke the surface of a pitch-black pocket of air.”

“There, wherever ‘there’ was, I dog-paddled for a minute gasping, spitting, shivering and completely disoriented from dizziness, cold, and from being surrounded by pitch-blackness. I gasped a few more times and then felt for a ledge or something. I found one. With shaking muscles I hoisted myself up out of that dangerously cold water so that I sat shivering in the fetal position on a sort of rim. After only a few seconds my ambition began to overtake the iciness that was gripping my body. Taking out my flashlight and unwrapping it, I regained enough composure to wonder whether there would have been any air at all in here if the last few days of low well water had not let fresh air in. Suddenly I realized how little air I must have. Abruptly it came to me that this was a stupid thing to have done, and I began to worry that I may not ever get out, alive or dead.”

I still had the Professor’s full attention. “I snapped on the powerful flashlight and found myself in what felt like a crypt, almost Egyptian. This space was a small, obviously man-made room with stone walls and a stone ceiling. At several places the stone had collapsed inward spilling earth that seemed as old as the stonework. Mud had trickled through the cracks of the rock cascading downward leaving the effect of ancient dried mud waterfalls all over this room. The smell of earth was overwhelming, but in a way it was sweet and pure. How someone could have built this room utterly escaped me. It appeared that an entire half of the room, the far half, had collapsed more recently, and it immediately struck me again that this was not a safe place."

"At that point I remember thinking that maybe the new air of the past few days or my movements will bring it all down. On the one remaining wall hung a very strange object whose shadows caught my eye. On a high stone shelf there sat a boxy shape covered in what appeared to be candle wax of many colors. There were mounds and mounds of candle wax on top of the object so that it appeared to be a labor of many years. I could not even guess at the size of the contents of this waxy chunk. Just then, I heard a rumbling and before there was any time to think another part of the far wall collapsed, and part of the ceiling. With my heart pounding I stood up on the ledge, walked boldly through the dust over to whatever it was, and gently tried to lift the waxy object, which I found to be quite heavy. With a quick motion, I took it in both arms, walked back through the dust to the opening, and plunged into the water. The object floated immediately to the surface, bringing my small frame along with it. By the faint glow of the flashlight now lying on its side, I saw the rest of the room begin to collapse, and I took a deep breath and was gone."

"As I swam down through that pitch darkness, I knew my only chance to save this heavy chunk of wax was if Nelson had stayed put and had lowered that bucket. If the wax cracked, then the whole thing, once it filled with water, might sink like a stone. I also understood that if I did not swim strongly, the wax would pull me back up to the cavern, where I might all too soon be visiting my ancestors. But I made it all the way down and through the turn, and soon broke the surface of my well, the waxy thing pulling me up behind it. I quickly heaved the waxy thing into the waiting bucket. As I did this it cracked in half."

"'Crap! Pull it up! Now'! I yelled through chattering teeth."

I explained, "I immediately felt the bucket begin to lift. A few seconds later I felt a powerful and painful slap of the rope on my head and shoulders. The force of Nelson's throw told me how he felt about my little stunt. After struggling with a rope climb that was far more difficult than I ever expected, I sat dripping on the grass, panting, and looking out of the corner of my eye at the cracked waxy box glimmer in the sunlight. It was beautifully colored with hundreds and hundreds of streams of wax, made up of many shades of red and yellow and green that I had never seen before. These were very exotic, muted colors. As my head began to clear I thought the object would make a very cool historical centerpiece in one of Uncle Spencer's rooms. Maybe it could be easily melted closed so it was fixed again. Uncle Spencer was just walking over to see what the commotion was, and was very displeased and very disappointed with me at the story he heard. Of course, I left out the part about the collapsing room, but I told Nelson as soon as we were on the plane."

Nelson added, "In the bright daylight we began to understand that the thick wax appeared to be only some kind of protective cover. After Uncle Spencer tugged it a bit, the wax broke neatly into two halves. As he slid one half of the waxy box off of its contents, two small red candles tumbled out onto the grass. With one half of the casing removed, the contents were clearly revealed. Professor, the wax had protected the ancient book you are holding."

Nelson continued, "'Remarkable condition,' Uncle Spencer had said. 'This wax must have kept moisture out for centuries'."

"He pulled the other half of the wax casing off and placed it on the ground by its mate. Holding the book, Uncle Spencer fondled the beads on the cover. 'It is indeed a strange and ancient book. It might have belonged to your ancestors. How extraordinary'."

I spoke again. "Uncle Spencer, who had little interest in history except perhaps the history of tennis, quickly volunteered to have the heavy book shipped to America as a souvenir of our visit to England, since, as he pointed out, 'This was a book of your people, not mine. I married into your bloodline'."

"Anyway, it turns out that this huge book had arrived at our house via FedEx and the package was brought by our neighbor to our door right after the attack. Nelson had shredded the brown paper from the package by the time I crushed down next to him into our cheap vinyl sofa. I snuggled into it. The package, as I expected, contained the strange leather-bound book that Uncle Spencer had promised to send along. It was only at that point that I finally put the two together: the criminal had been after this book! Crap! But why? And how in the world did he know anything about it?"

I continued, "So the book that both Nelson and I had almost completely forgotten about had arrived. The package contained only the book and a brief note from Uncle Spencer. Here's the note, Professor.

"Enjoy! Sorry for the delay. We lost track of the book for a bit but finally found it, in the room of one of our employees. Apparently, he had been trying to read the foreign gibberish! The soft toff! Actually, we discovered over time that he had been embezzling from us. The staff had warned me not to hire this one, and as usual they were more perceptive than I! He has been let go. Hope all is well and you are enjoying University.

Yours truly,

Uncle Spencer

Nelson said, "At that point I suggested we leave the house right then."

"And for once I couldn't agree more with my twin brother. We then discussed whether to leave the book or to take it with us. We both agreed that if we left it, the attacker most likely would come in and get it and we'll be done with him. I told Nelson that it was only a stupid ancient book. It was not worth our lives."

Nelson explained, "I agreed. But on the other hand, I told Fitzy that the book must be extremely valuable for the dude to fly across the Atlantic after it. I guessed it must be worth a fortune as an antique. I told Haley that it was her call, but what finally sold us both was the fact that Mom and Dad need the money in a bad way."

Since Nelson usually called me by my childhood nickname, "Fitzy," unless things were really formal and serious, I paused for a while to think.

I finally said, "I think we should go someplace safe, look it over, and then decide. Let's go. There's still plenty of daylight."

"Let me change this green shirt," Nelson said, "since I was wearing it when the stalker ran by me. And you definitely need to disguise yourself. He'll spot your black sweatsuit look from all the way across the Commons. Get in there and put on some of your old 'babe' clothes--you know, blend into the sorority life?--I know you still have some party clothes squirreled away somewhere."

"I thought a disguise was a very safe idea, considering getting Nelson harmed was the last thing I ever wanted for this day. Yet I had a longstanding habit of always disagreeing with my brother on principal. So I didn't budge from my spot on the sofa. After he left to change, I called over my shoulder absently, "This looks like a butterfly." I fingered a simple design that adorned the cover of the volume. It was a very curious design: four vertical marks, then two to their right, then one, forming a triangle, then one, then two, then four, forming another triangle. The two triangles, pointing at each other, did form something of a butterfly shape. The strangest thing was that where the two points of the two triangles almost touched, the mark there seemed to be in the shape of an hourglass. All these fifteen dimples were silver against a pure black background. I opened the dusty tome and let my guard down enough to be somewhat amused by the utter gibberish that was the writing in this exotic book. Yet on another level something deep in me stirred as I peered hard into the text."

"At that point my heart ballooned and stopped as I realized I was not alone. I suddenly felt someone breathing behind me, imperceptibly blowing the hairs of my neck. I looked over my shoulder to see the splintered front door strangely open.

"Nelson, come here," I called calmly. He walked into the room as I looked back down at the book. There was no movement in my body as I just sat still. I sat quietly, hoping that Nelson's tone would set me free of this vague and growing grip of fear. Had I imagined that breath? Was the broken door causing a draft in here that I had never felt before?"

"Any idea?" Nelson asked as he reached over my shoulder and flipped to another section written in the same impenetrable writing.

"Latin?" I ventured, trying to resume normal breathing.

"Actually," I added decisively as I was getting up, "let's talk about this later." When I turned around, there was Nelson, wearing a sports coat and a huge knitted rainbow Rastafarian cap complete with sewn-in dreadlocks. He looked hilarious, but at the same time he was surprisingly a very convincing Jamaican. I stepped into my room and in less than one minute stepped back out wearing my one form-fitting cotton party dress, and a curvily-contoured cowboy hat. We walked out of that house, me carrying the book. With the lock still broken, we didn't have to slow down to lock the door. We set out for the Commons, which is the acres and acres of beautiful lawn and oak trees at the center of campus."

I continued. "Without discussing it, once we approached the library we both headed for its main lower entrance. In order to do this, we had to cross two lanes of traffic separated by a landscaped median. As we began to cross, we both heard the distant thunder of a motorcycle roaring toward us. Nelson looked over at me sharply and barked, 'Act natural!' But by that time I could barely hear him."

"Way up the street the black bike was cruising slowly toward us, its rider systematically turning its head, searching both sides of the street. The helmet was black, shiny and reflective, like the angular Honda itself, and its black visor concealed the identity of the rider completely. It was horrifying. I felt light-headed but Nelson's hand on my elbow helped bring me back. By the time it reached us we had nonchalantly crossed the street and were reaching for the doors and stepping inside the library. I remember thinking that the huge book was so conspicuous, but then, thankfully, we *were* entering a library. My body was working automatically, with very little consciousness. Without looking back, we let the library door glide closed behind us, shutting out the guttural roar completely. Or had the engine been switched off?"

"Nelson had been in the library much more often than I had, so he led the way, which was fine with me. Blood must have rushed back to my brain in the relative safety of the circulation department because suddenly my body became hyper-ready for action. First, Nelson almost ran to a corner staircase and took three steps at a time up to the fourth floor. Then, with both of us trying to act like we weren't winded, he led me through many stacks of books to a service elevator marked 'library use only.' It stood empty and open. We hopped on and Nelson tugged the metal gate closed and pushed the B2 button. Darkness closed around us as we creaked downward into the closed stacks area of the lower basement of the library. We stepped out of the elevator and took off running, me with my cowboy hat in hand, Nelson, up ahead, with the heavy book in both hands, dreadlocks flying behind. Through the dim light and shadow, under stacks of yellowing bundles of newspapers towering over us, we ran full out the entire length of the library. At the end of the building Nelson took several wrong turns down dead-end aisles before he found what we knew must be there: another staircase. We slipped up this employee's staircase, thankfully not running into a soul. I put on my hat again and we stepped out, as though we were not breathless at all, behind the second floor librarian's desk by the photocopy machines. Unseen and alone, we ambled through the second floor lobby and finally left the building through the seldom-used second floor entrance. Our book did not set off the library sensor alarm. We both felt pretty certain that no Englishman who had just arrived from Britain could possibly know about this obscure library entrance on the Commons side of the library. Safe on the Commons, where no motorcycles were allowed, we were able to relax a little, at least for now. We had certainly not been followed, and hopefully, we had not even been recognized."

"Ahead, we saw one sprawling oak tree that stood alone in the middle of the lawn, far from the others. I remember having a strange reaction, an instant identification, with that massive, solitary oak. I somehow suspected that though it was alone, it was not lonely. We approached it, sat down in the shade of the tree, and opened up the book again."

Nelson stared hard at the final pages. "I don't think it's Latin, and I don't even think that the language of the middle section is the same as the language of the end section. That's very weird." I have to admit that I was also mildly curious.

Nelson blurted, "I have a great idea: let's go visit the Professor!"

So, squinting into the motes of the late-afternoon sunlight, I said, "you know what, Bob Marley? I agree. No criminal could know Professor O'Shea is our godfather or that that's where we've gone, and so it's the perfect place to try to make some sense of this situation before we go back to the police.

"I'm glad you see it my way. You know, you don't look half-bad when you leave your sweat pants at home," Nelson teased.

"I had brushed my long reddish-blond hair for this disguise, and in the rays of this late-afternoon sun I suspected that, thanks to this get-up, I must be noticeable again to the boys. This tight dress had been a mistake. And of course I had not planned on going to your house, Professor, but there was no going back to the house now." I was suddenly very embarrassed.

I hurried back into the story, "Anyway, we began to cross the main Commons and we took turns carrying the heavy book under the stately oaks. I liked carrying it because I could cover myself up by holding it against my chest."

"Nelson saw several people he knew. To my frustration, he stopped to visit with everyone, including our next-door neighbor returning home. Nelson excitedly told every friend we met that they were going to see Professor O'Shea to get to the bottom of this mystery. My brother can be a real idiot, Professor."

Nelson continued, "Fitzy, tell him about the incident with Steve. Oh, she won't, but I will. As we emerged from under the oaks onto an immense lawn, halfway across the Commons, I pointed out to Fitzy a few guys throwing Frisbee far ahead."

"As we walked briskly toward your house, Professor, I explained to Fitz that those guys are conducting what is known as 'the Frisbee treatment'. It's a classic college tradition."

I blurted in, "Professor, I must admit that I had immediately recognized one of the boys as Steve, a guy from my medieval history class." I added in my mind, *a very perfect guy who I had actually noticed quite often. I had even sat close to him some days out of curiosity. I liked his wavy blond hair, so wild that it was almost an afro, which set off a very white smile that he was not afraid to show. Thinking about him had been a welcome escape during the lectures.*

I continued, "We had said "hey" a few times, and I remember that Steve had been the one to explain *actually, he whispered it* the answer to a question I had asked him before class early in the semester. I had asked him what, exactly, medieval history was. He had explained to me *whispering for some reason* that "medieval history" was history from 476 A.D. until 1450 A.D.

"Why those dates?" I had asked.

He continued, *leaning in very close* "Medieval history is the period of history starting from the fall of Rome, which ended ancient history in 476 A.D., until the Renaissance kicked off modern history about 1450."

"*Thanks," I had mouthed.* "Steve had even allowed me to copy his notes once due to one of my many absences from class. From what I had gathered from my analysis of his notebook, he was a somewhat quiet junior, pre-med, with unbelievably meticulous notes and extremely high grades."

Nelson continued, "The treatment works like this. When a particularly cute girl walks across the Commons, the guy on the far end of the field heaves the Frisbee directly at her. It flies smoothly straight for the target, and another guy chases it furiously, running smack into the girl, filled with apologies and introductions—girls are not supposed to know about this—our secret, right?"

"Actually, Professor, I was not really listening much to Nelson, and instead was wondering why it had to be this hot in October. As Nelson was absently lecturing, I did, however, notice a projectile frisbee, a big one, apparently on a collision course directly for us. I also noticed Nelson's friend Steve careening toward us at a furious rate. Nelson noticed none of this."

"The simplicity is elegant," Nelson lectured to the Professor. "In the worst case, you get some prime tactile contact with a beautiful girl; in the best case, she accepts your apologies and agrees to let you buy her lunch. College definitely rules."

I continued, "At this point Nelson looked up, but too late. Steve, who had been zeroed in squarely on me, found that at the very last moment I deftly sidestepped the onslaught, sending Steve crushing into Nelson, both of them landing in a pile, Steve's arm slightly bloody, my butterflies scattering."

"You almost hurt my book," I scolded, as I stepped over the pile of manhood. "I'm sorry," he said, reddening as he recognized me from class. "They put me up to this, and I didn't know it was you; your hair is, uh, different; uh, nice. Nice outfit."

"As Steve was brushing himself off he gestured to the hilarious laughter across the Commons. 'I never should have listened to those jerks.' He blasted the Frisbee off side-armed, sending it straight and sure and moving at terrific speed, back toward the crowd of unsuspecting hecklers. While he did this I pulled the book up over my chest and crossed my arms around it. One of the hyenas was beaned squarely in the back of the head. 'Hey!' we heard in the distance."

Nelson interrupted, "Steve then said, 'You're really quite coordinated,' through a laugh as he finished removing most of the dead grass from his clothing. Then you should have seen it, Professor. Steve looked into Haley's face for the first time and they both appeared to jolt a little as their eyes met. It was very awkward!

This set me to thinking. *My eyes were definitely my best feature, and I was aware of the shock friends later reported on first seeing them. Guys have always commented on the thin, almost imperceptible ring of deep blue that encircles my olive irises. The effect was made so startling, I had postulated over years of staring into the mirror, by the flecks of yellow that lightened the impression while the deep olive set a serious, romantic mood that one boy had said "made him fall through time."*

Nelson and others had always insisted that I was devastatingly pretty. I never believed that for a minute. They would counter that if I wasn't gorgeous, then how did I become Homecoming Queen? Well, I knew the answer to that. I was the queen because I was always nice to the underclass students. I was friends with dozens of younger girls and would always take the time to hear their problems and to guide them if I could. And I would just visit. It was this openness and kindness to the younger half of the high school that earned me the votes to win queen, not any particular physical attractiveness. Or at least that was how I saw it.

I had definitely been nice to Steve on the quad. I smiled for Steve, a big, inviting smile, a smile so long absent from my face that I felt a sensation of chapping as my taut facial skin framed my eyes one more time. Apparently, my smile went over well with Steve, because it was obvious that something had dangerously interrupted his breathing. He definitely appeared not to be breathing.

Suddenly I realized that I was not talking and that the Professor and Nelson were looking at me, waiting for me to go on. I continued, "Well, to save this moment from becoming even more awkward, I explained to Steve, 'I had agile ancestors.' I said this, almost closing both eyes in a glare at him, and then walked off, my book pressed to my chest. 'Come, Nelson'."

"Nelson, who had been brushing himself off while sitting on the lawn, got up, scolded Steve that he had 'invented the frisbee treatment,' and ran to catch up with me as I was walking on." But I was already moping again, sure I could never have a guy of Steve's caliber, or any other guy for that matter. I did not speak any more, and Nelson, who is used to my sullen moods this semester, didn't even try to make conversation. It was actually in this mood of that I climbed the stairs to your house, Professor."

At this point, I turned my face toward the closest of the open floor-length windows to meet an unexpectedly cool garden breeze which had filled the curtains and which was stirring the heavy pages of the open volume.

"So, can you actually read any of these languages?" I asked, half distracted.

The Professor reddened a bit and puffed, "Well actually, the preponderance of modern cognates together with my extensive personal lexicon, in conjunction with my understanding of the basic syntactic and semantic constructions of the western Indo-European languages usually results in adequate translation."

"Then that would be a 'yes,' Professor?" asked Nelson with his usual half-smile.

From over his glasses Dr. O'Shea countered dryly, "That would be a 'yes,' Nelson."

The Professor continued, "Just give me a minute to retrieve a few reference books that can help me with the more obscure passages." I suspected that retirement may have been hard on him, and now, for the moment, he was in his element again.

As the Professor left the room, I could feel a change beginning to come on. The Indian summer of the South was drawing to a close as the humidity that hung like a worry over the South began to stir. Perhaps, I thought, there was a new front moving in. Whatever the cause, as the sun dipped toward the cooling pine forests to the west, the baking weight that had been constant for months began in this early evening to sharpen into a crispness that I deeply welcomed. Every few minutes the chilling promise of true autumn wafted in through the drapes, and I found this new coolness strangely exciting.

Chapter Three

Rexy the War Dog Takes Her Place

"Now let me see this magnificent volume," said the Professor, as he finished carefully arranging, in alphabetical order by editor, a dozen or so dog-eared books. They were placed on a shelf that was in easy arms-reach of his big leather chair. Our book seemed to be bound quite well considering how large it was. The only thing that adorned its thick brownish-black cover was the strange butterfly design.

The Professor spoke as he ran his fingers over the cover of the book, "Thanks to your library tactic, I believe we can be absolutely certain that you were not followed and that we are perfectly safe as long as we stay here. I suggest that the best approach is to begin reading the book immediately to try to get some clue as to our next step."

We both nodded in complete agreement.

"Well, here goes," said the Professor with a grin. As he opened the first page the spine made a cracking noise that seemed to trouble the Professor very much. He forced himself to say, "The fading penmanship is round, upright, and deliberate, and it seems to be written on superior vellum, which means parchment."

He looked up at our stares and added, "That is, paper. The opening page here, yes, is written in Middle English."

The Professor looked the first page over more closely than before, from the bottom to top, then from top to bottom. After a prolonged silence, he announced, "It's definitely early Middle English, and I am very intrigued."

Slowly, in a deep and musical voice that came, we supposed, from decades of university lecturing, he began:

On a miserable gray winter's afternoon in the ninth year of the reign of our King William Rufus, I began the longest night of my life. O my sons and daughters, we all, in the course of our daily lives, wait for our personal breakthrough to overtake us and reshape our destinies. We wait for the hand of our Lord to reach down and guide our steps. I leave the following record to inform my offspring of the course of this mighty night, and the knowledge I gained over the course of this evening through fourteen biographies of my ancestors, revealed to me one at a time, as the night grew long. During this long night I was offered a clear view of those from whom I had sprung: my eight great-grandparents, my four grandparents, and my two parents, none of whom I had known at all before this night; as indeed, I had not known myself. Although it feels strange to write it down, the truth is, all my life, as the rootless orphan that I was, I had been kept a secret from myself.

I read these fourteen stories with urgency because I had been warned that only the knowledge contained in these booklets could save me from the perils of this night, and only these chronicles would lead me to my destiny and to my final salvation. Into this one book that you hold in your hands I have compiled these fourteen booklets, each introduced and concluded by me in turn, in the order and manner in which they were presented to me, in hopes of recapturing the power of this night for you, my descendants. Read this book well, for as you will see, the soft promise that was sunrise brought a very new day for all those of our blood.

"Remarkable," said the Professor. "He is writing to his progeny, that is, descendants, whom he apparently does not know. The book is a frame story, a chronicle written in early Middle English containing fourteen Old English biographies. I need to make some phone calls right now to some friends of mine--professors of history, linguistics, archaeology, and literature--whose lives this book is about to turn upside down."

Nelson interrupted his motion to get up out of his leather chair. "This was found on our family estate and it's personal to us. There is a madman out there somewhere waiting to attack us. Could we read a bit more before the media blitz?" Nelson was deeply interested in this book, and I knew it felt good for him to share something with me for the first time in many weeks.

The Professor looked at Nelson's excited eyes, and then into my deeply sad eyes. I got the feeling that the Professor sensed that for me this distraction was of unspeakable importance as I prepared to leave college. I found out years later that the Professor had spoken to my father during the preceding week, and the two had discussed the best approach to my situation. Dad had been very concerned. Now that the opportunity of this evening was upon us all, the Professor told himself that he would seize the promise of this night. No matter what the cost in terms of sleep, money, or time, my godfather did his very best to watch over me this night. He simply said, "Then let us resume."

Shuffling into the cold on this blistering afternoon, three days following the Day of St. Scholastica, I clung tightly to my cloak in a desperate attempt to escape the cutting wind that brought so much pain to me. I had layered up nicely: first, my braies and my linen shirt were against my skin. My braies were secured by my braiel, which held my empty purse and also supported my hose, one loose stocking for each leg. These undergarments, my braies and undershirt, were covered by my long linen overshirt, then my knee-length woolen tunic, covered by my heavy woolen cloak. I was wearing everything I owned, but I began to fear that it would not be enough to win against this ferocious winter day.

Nelson interrupted, "Professor, have any idea when this is?"

"I have every idea, Nelson, but I did not want to interrupt the narrative. As I read to you tonight, I will not elaborate or explain anything. If you want clarification, however, just ask. I taught Anglo-Saxon England for thirty-eight years and have written eleven books on the subject." He sniffed.

"Now, to answer your question, in the eleventh century, years were usually counted from when the king took the throne; the setting here, then, was the ninth year of King William Rufus (1087-1100), who took the throne after his famous father, William the Conqueror (1066-1087). In other words, the year is 1096."

The Professor explained, "During this period of history dates within years were reckoned by saint's days, and St. Scholastica's day fell and still falls on February 10. That puts the action of this afternoon on the thirteenth, one day before a saint's day with which I'm sure you hopelessly romantic young people are already familiar. Of course, prior to the 1380s, there was no association whatsoever between the idea of romance and the observance of St. Valentine's Day; it was Chaucer who suggested that relationship, centuries after the 1096 scene before us. In February near London, there would have been only about nine hours of daylight, as opposed to July, which has over sixteen. That would put it about three in the afternoon. Now, back to February 13, 1096, at 3 p.m."

Stumbling over the roots and stones of the road, I carefully peered through my frozen, ice-encrusted eyes for signs of any threat that might take form in the flurries of snow. Various friends at the guildhall had warned me that dragons, sprites, fairies, leprechauns, and Satan all lurked in the forest, waiting to strike, especially as night began to fall. As I crunched through the silence of this new-fallen snow, my mind from time to time slipped carelessly into weakness that would imagine terrifying shrieking man-monsters crouched in the sides of my vision, breathing more and more roughly, tightening up their muscles for their delicious kill. I had to keep my mind hard against the visions of my fear. Lord, protect me on this road.

But against such demons, very real and very dangerous, I knew that I had no defense. Therefore I tried to plan for those threats that could be overcome with mortal hands and a quick mind. I knew wolves and robbers were ahead; of this I had no doubt. Early this morning I had left Watling Street, the heavily-travelled road from London to Canterbury, and even on such a busy road, where I had traveled with several strangers for mutual protection, we had already had to defend ourselves against both wolves and thieves. And now they had gone their way and I traveled completely alone.

And I knew the danger was even graver if I encountered a man of the local sheriff, bishop, or knight. Any one of them in a bad humour could have fined me for any number of offenses, and unable to pay, I would be subject to forfeiture of my wergeld status. The Normans who now rule England call wergeld 'frankpledge,' but the two are the same: money paid by my master at the guild as a bail payment for a crime before any crime is committed. Its payment constitutes freedom for a peasant like me, and without this guarantee of money I would have no legal protection.

At this point Professor O'Shea went to a closet and brought out a creaky metal easel that he set up in one corner. He left the room and came back soon carrying a huge, stiff, styro-board map of medieval England. It almost touched the alligator netting on the ceiling. I noticed that in tiny print on a corner it said *U.S. Senate use only* and it looked like it had been used quite often. He delicately sat back down, took a powerful laser pointer out of his shirt pocket, and fired the laser at the map.

We turned to look at the map. "This is Watling Street, a medieval road that connected the length of England from northwest to southeast, and here are the cities of London and Canterbury." He would refer to this map whenever Nelson and I asked about places.

The Professor resumed:

> In other words, I could have easily become a slave, although the fashion among the Normans of late had been to prefer enserfment—being legally bound permanently to the land because of debt—to enslavement in order to save the expense of the upkeep of slaves. While most officials would have applauded my bravery in traveling alone to Normandy to join the Holy Crusade led by Robert, the great Duke of Normandy, there was no certainty in this day.
>
> For the past month in London, the talk of the town had been the thousands and thousands who were taking up the banner of God against the infidels who were blocking the Holy Land from good Christians. Though few in London were heeding the call, the talk from merchants was that Normans and Frenchmen of high and low station were gathering in droves in centers such as Flanders and Normandy. After much deliberation, I had come to a decision. I would offer my services to Robert, the great Duke of Normandy, and would surrender my fate to God. But do not think I deluded myself; I fully understood that should I prosper long enough to discover Robert's company before their departure for the Holy Land, and should I survive the years required for this journey to Jerusalem, as a faceless and nameless foot soldier in the throng, I stood virtually no chance to survive the many battles. My goal was not a glorious return, but glory in the life to come. After all, I had nothing left to live for in London, and Pope Urban had promised full absolution of all sins for any man who died in this great Crusade.

The Professor looked up and said, "Fascinating. While I cannot be sure whether this young boy is a real historical character, certainly those whom he describes are the real actors of the eleventh century. Pope Urban II, Robert, Duke of Normandy, and King William Rufus of England, for example, are the people whom I have been lecturing about here at the University for the past thirty-eight years. So even if the main characters in this book are fictional, all those whom they encounter will be actual, memorizable history. Got that, kids?

"We have it, Professor."

"Then let's resume with the poor boy's narrative."

Yet these threats huddled quietly at this point in the late afternoon because my body knew a deeper truth: the spikes that the wind was stabbing into my flesh were very dangerous. Each crunching stomp onto the snow brought both of my pin-pricked feet another step toward a level of frozenness from which they might never return. The bread I had brought from London, five days behind me, had lasted until this morning, and the stomach crunches of hunger had come and had almost passed away by now, leaving a generalized weakness that I knew might well be no match for this cold.

Sadly, even the onset of frostbite could not mask my true and deepest ache, the pain that washed over all my other troubles and drowned them. The face of my Emma, a beauty I could never see again, haunted every stumble, every wince, every pang of fear. The Crusade was the only escape from the torment brought on by my certainty that we could never be together again. The wind whipped the knot in my cloak apart, which broke my thoughts for a moment of full consciousness as my cracked hands worked the rough wool back into place. Without the security of the main road and the benefit of fellow travelers, the terrors of the night would fall all too soon.

Five days out of London and alone in the forest of Essex, I knew the risks were very real, and counted myself fortunate to be in possession of such a stout staff. I had been informed of a cheap boat fare to Normandy from Maldon on the Channel in Essex, and so I had chosen this direction, one obviously not heavily traveled from London. I had borrowed a large knife from the guild and had fashioned this magnificent staff weeks before in preparation for the beginning of this journey.

Do not be impressed, though; I was certainly not a member of the renowned swordmaker's guild of London at the young age of nineteen. No, I was their servant boy. I sharpened the swords, cleaned the cesspools when they became full, and was used as the sticking doll for the noblemen who would come in to pick up their new swords. Before paying, these lords would insist on trying their swords out immediately on someone who could fight. So the masters chose me to learn every parry and thrust known in Christendom.

In the gray barn behind the guild they taught me the techniques of a wide range of fighters, so that the swordsman who came in to collect his custom-made sword would have someone to test it on in the manner in which he was accustomed to fighting. I had strict instructions to determine instantly his style and preferences, and to duplicate them eighty percent as well as the customer. Therefore, the nobleman always got a good fight, always won, always went away happy, and of course always tipped me for a good try.

The Professor interrupted with his capped teeth broadly smiling, "How delightful! I am enjoying this translating immensely! I am trying my best to maintain an entertaining tempo, while at the same time translating as closely as I can the exact meaning into language that will be accessible to you children. It is a thrilling and difficult challenge, perhaps the greatest challenge of my career as a linguist! I will meet the challenge!"

Nelson and I looked at each other with a knowing *would ya get a load of Dr. Dorkerson here?* look, but we were both happy he was so excited.

He began again,

Yet the masters made very clear to me with their insults and their spit that I would never be a master sword maker. They guarded their monopoly of the production of swords very jealously, and the men of the guild would physically attack anyone reported to be producing weaponry of any variety. Once, they traveled twenty miles outside London and threw, one at a time, one hundred burning torches into the house of a suspected sword maker. While the masters made swords, they also dabbled in battle-axes, knives, and the bow and arrow, all of which I was required to know, on horseback and on foot, very well or "it would be out in the street with you." It was made equally clear to me that I would likewise never be invited to attempt the seven-year apprenticeship that was a prerequisite to becoming a master.

No, I was only "Boy," an orphan, a nameless servant who was required to remain silent unless spoken to. The lazy guild bookkeeper, though, named Aelfsige, taught me to read and write well enough to keep his books "in those times when he is unable," which turned out to be almost always, due to his affection for the ale. They had not noticed when I borrowed the knife to make my quarterstaff, and, after an uproarious laugh, they flatly denied permission for me to depart for Normandy and the Holy Land. So in the middle of the night, with only my clothes, my burlap bag of food and some flint and steel for starting fires, my cloak, my purse, and my quarterstaff, I left that guild forever.

The staff was equally my height, just thick enough for my fingers to touch as I gripped it. It was hard and green and still a bit damp, affording a superb grip. Yet I knew that I was even more fortunate to have Rexy by my side. Why Emma had insisted I take the dog had never been clear to me. I explained that I could not feed even myself; I explained that owning a dog like this--a large female with black snout and pointed black ears--so obviously imported, suggested a social rank to which I should not pretend; I objected that Rexy might go into heat and would attract wolves; I objected that the dog would draw undue attention to me. As usual, Emma did not listen to one word I said.

As I trudged on down the frozen trail, the act of thinking about Emma, though it racked me with pain, was also the only pleasure I could offer myself, and it was wonderful. Though I had resisted it earlier on the trip, I began to grant myself this luxury more liberally as the first horrifying hints of dusk began to present themselves to me.

I had first seen Emma watching me the previous spring, while I was busy with my Saturday afternoon employment as a trainer of dogs for Lady Wallington, the Lady of Surrey. Alone far from the manor house, I was to teach basic commands such as stay, sit, fetch, come, heel, and kill. I must say I was an excellent dog trainer. After the third Saturday that the Lady Emma, daughter of the Lady Wallington, watched me from a fence some distance away, I perceived that the highborn girl was mocking me, and I conceived a plan to gain mild retribution.

For the past three months I had been training an unusual hound that I had named 'Rexy'. I called the bitch this because Reginy, meaning "queen" in the Latin I was sometimes required to compose in, just sounded awkward compared to "Rexy: King!" Rexy was not like the rest, not a floppy-eared hunting dog. She was twice as big as these hounds, and actually, she did not act like a hound at all. She was more interested in me than any hound I had ever trained; in my experiments with her, I noticed that she, when given the choice between eating or following me as I walked away, would always choose to follow me. This was a characteristic unknown to the usual hounds I worked with. She was a black and brown, with a black snout and black pointed ear that matched nicely and a very broad chest. She was clearly not an English dog.

I had taught Rexy to kill, and she had perfected a very vicious attack upon command. As a way of thumping this highborn girl who apparently enjoyed mocking me, on this spring morning I quietly dispatched Rexy on a kill command in the direction of the noble girl, planning to call the dog back at the last minute as if Rexy had disobeyed me. To my shock, when Rexy approached the girl snarling, this girl issued a loud and authoritative kill command in her Norman French, and pointed directly back at me. It seemed like a dream when the dog eagerly obeyed her. Rexy ran right at me, snapping, and I had to calm the dog at length or she would have badly hurt me. When I looked up, Emma was coming toward me. "Do you mock me, mistress?" I asked with a bow as I began slowly to look up from the still-growling animal.

What I saw standing there stunned me. It has, like a phantom of laughter and sadness, haunted my waking and sleeping hours every day since. First I saw the small leather boots, which covered brown hose that peeked out only a bit from her ankle-length brown tunic. My eyes continued to scan up her form, noting her undershirt protruding slightly from her long, loose sleeves, and another tunic under her overtunic. Her thin leather belt supported a small purse, and her overtunic, quite dirty for a woman of high birth, had small rips in three places. Yet it was edged in exquisite embroidery. Her posture was erect and commanding, and her hands were squarely on her hips. Her neck was covered by her veil, a loose piece of cloth covering head and neck completely, leaving only an opening for her face.

Oh, and that face. Though a bit sooty, her skin radiated with a healthfulness that I had never seen before, nor heard of. The bones of her face held a symmetry and radiance that stirred me to my core. Her eyes were shiny and healthy, the exact green as the apple leaves that framed her from behind. The fact that they were rimmed in blue made her eyes stand out all the more, like flowers in a forest. She was the first art I had ever seen.

Compounding the vision was another amazing truth: my Emma always had her face framed by a halo of butterflies who seemed to follow her through our meadow at some distance.

So there stood Emma. Her tunic, which covered her entirely from her neckline to her ankles, was flapping softly in the breeze. "Do *I* mock *you*?" she began. "Do you attack me, villain?"

"The dog got away," I lied.

"She got away from me also," was her quick answer. She stared at me with pursed lips and I, though she was my better, stared right back at her. Then we burst out laughing and she bid me to follow her to the orchard where she was to do work; I took the dogs and followed her to do my work in that orchard too. She said her name was Emma, and she had so carefully watched me train Rexy that she had decided to work with her some these past weeks, too. "How did I do?" she teased.

"Fine, fine, mistress," I answered. She took me to the farthest stand of pear trees, down in a dell where we could not be seen from the estate. This became our orchard, a place of refuge for us both all that spring, through the summer, and really for a bit too long, on into this past fall.

The first thing she had asked me was where I was from, "with such a polished way of speech for a peasant." She said it was my speaking that had first interested her, but later I came to find out that my well-worked shoulders had something to do with it.

I told her I was from London, and explained that I had gotten that response often; the only explanation I could offer was that those masters who knew me when I came to the guild said that at first, I spoke only French. I do not remember these earliest years at all. Of course, I had since been reared at the guild speaking only Old English, but lately my compositions for the bookkeeper had required more and more French. I admitted to Emma that to my surprise, I had picked French up quite easily, much more easily than Latin, which I hated to write in. Fortunately for me, only a member of the royal court or a rogue monk purchasing a sword that he was not supposed to own required me to write the receipt in Latin.

Around her own manorial household, being part of the broad wave of nobles imported from Normandy that had broken over our countryside since the Norman invasion of 1066, Emma spoke French. But she of course used only Old English when instructing her peasants here on her estate and in her nearby village. The effective lord simply had to learn Old English, and the ambitious peasant simply had to learn Old French. From this marriage, over the next decades, emerged the latinized hybrid that is beginning to be spoken on our streets in my day. Emma and I usually talked in English, but she helped me with my French whenever she got mad.

That first day in the orchard, Emma pointed out that it was highly unusual for a peasant to have such clear diction, such healthy limbs, such good posture. "Even your teeth and eyes," she had declared, "have the clarity of one raised on meat, broth, and all manner of vegetables." She insisted, "Have you not noticed before? Have you not noticed that you have none of the hunched, undernourished peasant in you?" Over the next months one of her favorite things to tease me with was that "You are my little mystery." And sometimes she added, shyly, "Well, my big mystery."

That first day in our orchard refuge, I had asked her the same: Why was her dress torn? Why was a woman of high birth required to work in the orchard? She had no answers for me on that first day, but as the spring ripened into summer, our talks ripened as well. I made her a swing out of a board and two ropes, and we took turns in our orchard. Sometimes I would sit down and she would put her legs through the swing the other way, sitting squarely on my lap with her reddening cheek only inches away from my lips. When we did this she would always insist that we put Rexy between us, "as a chaperone" and she would pant faintly and squint off into her valley as Emma and I would swing away the hours, often in the cloud of butterflies that were never very far away.

Anyway, this was the Emma who loved the dogs as I did, and insisted, on our last day in the orchard, that Rexy accompany me to Jerusalem. She pointed out that she owned the dog, and she had now given it to me; she even had a mock receipt ready for me, anticipating my objections. It was mock because she could not write, as that was a very rare attribute, even among the nobility. In fact, besides the guild bookkeeper, I was the only person I knew who could read and write, a fact that I had not noticed until that moment. Anyway, though I insisted that the dog would die in battle like I would, Emma's green eyes just moistened as she kissed Rexy sweetly on the snout. "She's all I can give you, and you love her," Emma whispered.

"At least we can warm each other tonight," I said to Rexy, breathing visibly into the flurries of Essex. Rexy let out a furious snarl as I became aware that ahead, two bearded men were approaching me from the thick woods on the left, and two more from the embankment on the right. Since the normal peasant style of that day was cropped hair and shaved faces, I could tell from their appearance that these were hill people who were clearly after my purse and, to cover their tracks, they were going to take my life. The blood coursed back into my extremities as I dropped the burlap bag that had been over my shoulder, gripped my staff, and arched my back. What these robbers didn't know was that for as long as I had served as the guild sticking-boy, I had not been allowed to win.

Chapter Four

The Bonfire and the Dead Man

Haley looked up as the reading paused. "Professor, keep reading!"

The Professor stated, "Alright, then, let's get back to the Boy and his awkward situation!"

Since as a villain, or commoner, I of course carried no sword--and certainly never would, that being reserved, except in battle, strictly as a sign of nobility--I could only hope that my staff would do. I saw that the two on the left, one my size and one much smaller, carried wooden clubs and the two giants on the right carried menacing iron maces.

I arched my back again and to my surprise, despite the cold, found my focus easily. As I poised in my balance they arrived, running at me with murderous yelling. I sidestepped the first, one of the giants, and sent him whirling by. Before he could react I delivered a hammering blow between his shoulder blades. As he turned, half-dead already, his fellows could see the blood gushing from his mouth and nose. They froze and looked at me. As I twisted my staff to generate maximum torque, I announced "My name is Boy, and you should now commit yourself to the Lord."

With this, the butt of my staff smashed into the other giant's jaw, projecting his teeth and blood in an arch, while in the same motion I slammed the staff down on the neck of the medium fellow. As he collapsed I turned to see Rexy shredding the bloody clothes of the little man who was now on the ground. I quickly impaled his skull with the end of the staff. Rexy spent the next twenty seconds killing his dead and limp body.

Before the little man went still, I wheeled on the giant with no teeth, who, infuriated, was now staggering to his feet. I heaved back on the medium fellow who had the crushed neck and delivered my staff to his groin with a force that would have felled a tree. The butt of the staff instinctually flew backwards into the face of the now-standing toothless giant, who crumpled motionless to the ground. I commanded Rexy, who suddenly noticed that the medium man began to stir, to "sit" and "stay" as I impaled first one, then the other giant through the skull.

The medium man had been spared for a reason: he could not die until I had stripped him of his clothes. The nobles at the guild had made clear in their war stories that death brings the release of all fluids, and I was in dire need of his stockings, his tunic, and his wool overtunic. After I stripped him, I impaled his skull and quickly dragged each corpse over to the steepest part of the embankment and dropped them, weapons and all, one by one, into the ravine far below. The men had indeed soiled themselves.

I released Rexy from the stay command, petted her lavishly, and proceeded to undress in order to hide the dead man's clothes under mine. While I know this incident may seem unduly violent to my descendants, rest assured that it was the only chance for my survival. I could not have escaped because they knew the terrain and I did not. I had to face them and I had no choice about killing them; had I simply disabled them and they revived later, they would have a blood feud against me and could have come after me with their relatives. More likely, since they were outmatched, they might have reported me to the local royal official, that is, the sheriff, or the local church official, that is, the bishop's priest, or the local feudal official, that is, the thegn's man, any of whom could be either corrupted or misled into arresting me.

In response to Nelson's confused expression, here the Professor added, "'thegn' means lower-ranked knight." He resumed,

Hiding the bodies was also done to avoid my arrest. Robbing the dead was standard procedure in battle, as I am sure it still is in your day. As I finished putting my stockings on over those of the dead man and finished dressing so that none of his clothing was at all visible, I walked up the road and searched until I found the sacks of these robbers. There I found my prize, nine loaves of hard black barley and oat bread, with small crosses cut in the top by some goodwife who would not see her husband again. I also took their canteen of ale. I hungrily ate two loaves, and fed one to Rexy.

I put the other six in my own burlap bag and carefully looked at myself and the scene to ensure that all evidence of the killings had been removed. I had to smear Rexy's snout and whiskers with snow for some time before the blood was completely gone. Satisfied, I walked over to the ravine, rechecked that the bodies were out of sight, and reluctantly threw their bags, their now-empty canteen, and my blood-caked staff over the edge. I knew the falling snow would soon cover over the bloodied and muddied snow on the trail.

Then I knelt in prayer. Pope Urban had promised the redemption of all corporal sin for all who participated in the Holy War. But I was not praying strictly for redemption. Prayer, even as the cold was beginning to bite again, has always been an important part of every day for me as it has been for you.

The dozen or so times a day I stopped for prayer offered me extraordinary comfort that I would never remove from my daily routine, even if I arrived safely in Jerusalem to cleanse my soul by falling to the godless Muslims. For a moment I wondered if the robbers had wanted more than my purse, but, laughing aloud and quite visibly into the loneliness, I realized that I had nothing in this world except a purse filled only with a simple embroidered handkerchief.

With that heart-pounding scene falling farther and farther behind me, I turned again to walking briskly and to thoughts of Emma. The orchard had been a magical time, a time of games and tricks, laughing and innocent kissing. She had slipped away from her family on the feast of St. John the Baptist and had spent that scorching afternoon with me.

I had expected all along that with the end of the summer would come the end of our time together, since my dog training had ended. After all, our stations in society were utterly incompatible. She and I knew all too well that poor peasants did not court noblewomen, no matter how hard the times were for a particular noble family, and no matter how much the peasant had noble markings. And anyway, her family was doing extremely well financially, though they neglected Emma quite shamefully. Now, if I had been a rich and well-endowed peasant, there would have been at least a theoretical chance. Urchins like me, though, did not get the lady. Even in my dreams I could not conceive of a way for us to live happily ever after. This was what hurt the most. This was why I left.

Yet she did not seem to care about these hard facts. When autumn came, in St. Martin's season, she asked me back, every Saturday afternoon. When I objected, she would mutter about her terrible times at the manor, and tell me that she knew I wasn't just a peasant, that I was more.

"I know it," she would say. "I believe in you," she would whisper as she leaned her linen headdress into my chest. And she did believe in me. She so much needed someone to save her from the cruelty of Lady Wallington, who soon enough I discovered was not her mother but her stepmother, that sometimes I let her talk this way. But it was false hope, and our time together removed her from any real chance at escape by marriage, and I knew it. A nobleman should court her, since she was in the flower of her beauty. She must have known the wisdom of ending it, too, but her sweet heart ruled her mind, and she was set on somehow being with me forever. The crush that had colored our playful summer had changed into something more. I had fallen in love with Emma, and she had fallen in love with me.

Finally six days before this cold winter's afternoon I had met her for one last time in our orchard. I was wearing all my clothes, carrying my bag, and carrying my quarterstaff. She knew I was leaving forever. She knew the Crusade would take my life and the tears fell hard to the brown winter grass of our orchard. She felt trapped against a wall. "It is time," I said quietly, "to break this off before someone finds out. If we are discovered, both of us could be shunned by our worlds. Pope Urban has called and I must answer." She gave me Rexy and she gave me her handkerchief, we kissed one last time, and she watched me walk off into the sunrise of my death.

But that was Surrey and this is Essex.

"Surrey is just south of London," said the Professor in response to a perplexed look from Nelson. His laser pointer showed the spot.

The sun continued to drop behind me, stretching my shadow long in the places where the sun still streamed in through the thick leafless trees. I saw my giant shadow in front of me, watching over the unbroken snow. Then I heard a sound that sent my heart racing again. A horse was approaching at a gallop. As it neared, I instinctively jumped into the woods and hid, holding Rexy's snout closed and waiting for the rider to pass. Instead, I drew a breath of disbelief as the rider came to a sudden halt directly in front of the place we were hiding behind a tree. He was tracking my prints in the snow.

He dismounted, looked around a bit, and then yelled in a sharp Essex accent, "I'm seekin the war'n called Boy, travelin with a bitch! I bar'n sent to fetch yar'n to my master name Wulfric of the Dale!"

My first thought was to assume that this was trick on the part of the guild masters to retrieve me, but why would they care enough to go to the expense of a search? What made me decide to trust the man was simply his language. The masters in London would have sent a man speaking the London tongue, and this man here spoke an Essex dialect that was almost incomprehensible to me. So I showed myself.

"Cynewald, they'n call me," he said in his sharp and pointed dialect. "I'm sent by my master to fetch yar'n on a very important errand, war'n that shar'n change your life and leave yar'n with yar'n true inheritance."

"You lie, sir; who are you?"

"I tar'n you now," said Cynewald, "Cynewald they'n call me, and your'n called by your'n great-grandfather to his manor. This is the day your'n been a-waitin', the day when everything gar'n be explained."

To be honest, going with this man was an easy decision. If the man were lying, of which I was almost certain, considering the preposterous things he said, I would still be better off a captive by his fire than remaining in these woods as a meal for bears or wolves or a game for the witches of Satan. What made me like this fellow immediately, though, was the biscuit he threw to Rexy and the large blanket he took out for me to wrap up in. With his help I mounted the horse behind Cynewald, wrapped myself up as well as I could, and we started off at a gallop, Rexy trotting far behind after a while. I remember wondering if my two girls, Emma and Rexy, would sleep well that night.

We rode on for almost an hour, first on the main trail. Then we rode off to the left, up a smaller trail, then to the right, and then up a winding path for some time. I knew the moon was new, and once the sun had completely set, I knew this cloudy sky would block any starlight. I feared it was going to be a night of utter blackness. As the sun began its final dip behind the trees, Cynewald stopped and in a pleasant tone asked me to dismount.

"I'm not supposed to go nar'n farther with yar'n, ar'n orders from the master. Sir, followr'n that path ther'n to the tip top of the cliff and your'n'll see your great-grandpapa Wulfric, whor'n been waiting all his life for'n this night. The bonfire shour'n be blazing when yar'n get there, and I'm told there'n plenty to eat." He winked and flashed his jagged-tooth smile as he said the part about the bonfire; at least that's what I thought he said through his harsh Essex dialect, which I will try to convey in the way I write this tale.

At the base of this steep hill rested a large stone well. Off to the right and up a very steep climb I could see the summit Cynewald was pointing to far in the distance. Some of the stones on this well bore strange symbols of the old religion, which I knew to be against the Church of our Lord. Yet with a knife Cynewald broke the ice out the top of its bucket and drank deeply from the water. Despite my better judgment, I did too, and my body, long-dried out on this frozen day, shivered with welcome.

With a quick and friendly wave, Cynewald mounted the horse and rode back down the trail until I could hear him no longer. The cliff above was sheer, and I knew it would be a dangerous climb once the pitch-blackness set in. After a quick prayer, I threw Rexy one of the smaller loaves of bread, tore a bite off one of my own, and sat down on the ledge of that well to rest a bit. Rexy used the rest to catch her breath.

In the darkening shade of the hill I looked down into the well and saw the rough stones line their way far downward. I could faintly see the frozen floor of the well covered completely in snow. This was a very deep well, perhaps ten feet down to the ice. I remember realizing that whenever the water in this well finally froze solid, it could be broken into pieces and pulled up rather easily by a team of horses. While eating the bread my mind wandered as it does and began building an elaborate underground room that, once constructed, could only be entered by swimming far under water. I promised myself with a half-smile that if I ever had a treasure, that would be how I would secure it. It would be a secret known only to me, a well kept very, very secret.

At this point in the reading Nelson shot a glance at me as if to say, *a secret certainly quite well-kept.*

With little choice, I broke my dream, stowing the rest of my loaf with a quick motion of disgust at having to come back into this world again. As I began the climb up the mountain, a climb that began at a hollow tree, I remember feeling sharp skepticism and burning curiosity, but mainly numbness. I was numb from the cold, numb from the fear, and numb from the loneliness of a new life without Emma.

After thirty minutes of climbing, the night had come. The blackness sank down around us and was complete. I found it easier to find my way with my eyes closed, and I kept Rexy very near me. Finally the ground became level, and I could tell by the breeze that I had reached the top, a summit of some kind, which I discovered by groping had been nicely cleared. But there was certainly no fire, and in fact no sign of any life.

With only the sound of a twig breaking, surely Rexy, my imagination began to take me, to conjure a scene of lurking werewolves. I began to tremble ferociously and was about to bolt down the mountain until I felt the familiar snout of Rexy push my hand up violently, as she tended to do when she wanted attention. After a prayer, my voice trembling from fear and cold, to St. Michael, I found the courage to put the demons and sprites of my imagination aside in the pitch of that summit.

With no choice and no point of reference, I told Rexy to 'stay' in a sharp command and began blindly feeling for twigs in the wooded area next to the clearing. After accumulating enough to get started, I took the flint and steel which I had borrowed from the guild—I would one day return them, I had promised myself—and began to strike the flint hard against the steel, chipping tiny pieces of red-hot steel off until the leaves below began to smolder, but they would not ignite. I had hoped not to have to rip my newly-acquired undershirt, but I had no choice as the temperature continued to drop and our scents continued to waft down the mountain toward what I knew was an array of predators. I ripped some of the linen from under my tunic and made a small bed of loose pieces of cloth. These were more flammable, and soon I had a small fire kindled, at least adequate to produce light enough to find better fuel.

As the faint light suddenly bathed the summit, I jumped violently to see only five feet away the body of a dead man sitting up, supported by the only small boulder on this summit. Though this ghastly sight filled me with dread and demanded attention, the wavering fire demanded even more. In the faint light, I moved around, collecting the small and medium sticks that littered the area. In this dim light I could begin to make out the lay of the summit: it was larger than the light could illuminate, with what appeared to be the strangest arrangement of leather bags laid out very deliberately. In the middle of the design was a pit for a fire, and I could make out that at the far edge of the clearing there appeared to be stacks and stacks of firewood.

I transferred my small fire to the center pit because this area was still faintly warm and because the center was built for a big fire, the size I had in mind building. Over this warmth I constructed huts of wood, designed to burn and collapse, making the fire gradually hotter and brighter. My life was simple at that point: survive, by building a huge fire; build a huge fire by maintaining a flow of air under the burning wood until the ground was coated with a thick bed of red-hot coals. Then load on huts of firewood until the fire was a raging bonfire. Only then would the fire be started, and only then could I turn to the matters of the body, the bags, and this summit.

After the fire was on its way to being red-hot, I released Rexy and moved toward the corpse. He was an ancient man, shriveled and small, and his presence did little to calm my earlier terror. In order to be certain he was dead, I reached slowly for his neck. The wind was strong up on this summit, and the fire was beginning to crackle and throw shadows around the clearing. I reached slowly, closer and closer. Finally, I touched the man but my hand jerked away at the icy feeling. "He is even colder than I am," I chuckled.

As I scanned the clearing in full firelight, I could recognize the pattern that was set up by the placement of the leather bags. It appeared to be three circles, one inside the other, with my now-raging fire at the very center. The outer circle contained eight leather bags, the middle circle contained four, and the inner circle had two bags that seemed to face each other, as if two teams of seven faced off, with the bonfire intervening. What was strange was that at the place of one of the outside bags sat the dead man, with the bag clutched tightly in his dead arms. I include a diagram of this strange arrangement:

Man with Bag Bag

Bag Bag

Bag Bag

Bag Bag

Bag Fire Bag

Bag Bag

Bag Bag

I decided to survey the area. Near the firewood I found a large iron skillet filled with dried beans, several very large black loaves of bread, and several large horns of ale, of course, all frozen. I placed these to melt by the fire that was now quite a blaze. This summit seemed a safe enough place for Rexy and me to spend the night, even considering our rigid companion. I was suddenly struck with the urge to heave the specter quickly off the cliff and be done with his ghastly sight.

Then it occurred to me for the first time that Cynewald might have been right, that this dead man might indeed be my great-grandfather, just deceased. Throwing him off the cliff suddenly seemed, if he were blood relation, like a horrible dishonor, especially considering he was my only relative in this world. I would wait at least until I could determine his identity. Unfortunately, there was only one way I could think of to find out for sure who he was. That was to remove and inspect the contents of the bag which he currently clutched in his dead arms. I knew well that disturbing the dead will bring grave ill-fortune, possibly in the form of the appearance of Satan himself. Yet I had absolutely no choice in this situation.

I gently lifted his stiff left arm and then jerked away the bag, letting his left arm fall limply to his side. I had no intention of ever, ever touching him again. Inside the bag, I found only a small book, which was a thin sheaf of papers, sewn remarkably well to a hard front and hard back leather cover. After searching a few of the other fourteen bags positioned around, I discovered identical booklets.

I brought the dead man's small book over to the fire, sat down, and prepared myself to read the words that I hoped the man had written for me. But I would not allow myself to hope that the words might change the course of my destiny, might take away some of my misery. The first page was loose, not bound with the rest, and was apparently written hastily. I later figured out that this loose opening page was probably a last-minute note written immediately before the man's collapse, which from the warmth of the fire pit must have occurred earlier during the very day of my arrival at this summit. Rexy and I settled in by the warm, bright fire, both of us having drunk our fill of ale and having eaten our fill of beans boiled in ale. Thus I began to read this booklet alone, watched over by a sleeping dog, a frozen corpse, and a crackling fire.

Boy—

I am Wulfric, your great-grandfather, and I love you dearly. I know you will be here soon because I sent my man to London to track you as soon as I heard you were leaving for the Crusade. Your gesture to fight the infidel Saracens is as noble as you are, but, as you will soon learn, your efforts are better spent elsewhere. Cynewald can be trusted completely; I have known him for ten years, since he was a lad of nine. But be wary—no one else can be trusted. Powerful forces may be at work once you arrive here, because until I sent Cynewald to London, your secret had been known only by me. I instructed him to point you to this summit at sunset, and I know that he will do my bidding, as he is a good boy.

Your decision to come with Cynewald was a wise one, because this evening will change your fate. I know you see yourself as a rootless orphan, and I am so happy to be able to finally tell you the truth. You see, I have closely followed the progress of your life for all of its brief nineteen years. It was I that arranged that you be taught to read in the guild, it was I who ensured that you are versed in the fighting arts, and it was I who have been watching over you, waiting until the time that it becomes safe to reveal your secret to yourself. Because your unforeseen departure for the Crusades made me hurry my plans, the time to show you the truth must now be at hand, and from what I am told by your guild masters, I believe you are ready. If I have not lived to see you in person, let me tell you now that I and your other great-grandparents, grandparents, and parents, loved you dearly and have sacrificed gravely for you.

The strange arrangement of leather bags that you see before you has a design. I have laid out the record of your people, your forefathers and foremothers, and what they have given you. In a very real sense, they were all mothers and fathers to you. I only hope I survive to explain, but the cold is biting my old frame very hard. It is imperative that you know this: you must read these records, in order, outer circle first, then middle, then inner, before dawn. Start with mine. Armed with what you will learn this long, cold night, you will survive its perils and you will know the right way to go in the morning. If you can finish these books tonight, your fate will be glorious and your future will be comfortable and fulfilling. But you must finish these volumes before you leave at dawn.

What you see before you is a geometric pattern of your people. The fire in the middle of the clearing stands for you, and it is flanked on one side by a storybook of the life of your mother, with her family behind. This story is in a leather bag to protect it from the blizzard that is coming. This first bag is exactly four feet from the fire. Behind your mother's story and to the right is the story of the life of your mother's mother; behind your mother's story and to the left is the story of your mother's father. Behind each of these two maternal grandparents are the stories of your four maternal great-grandparents. On the other side of the fire is an identical arrangement of seven more bags, each containing the chronicle of your father, his two parents, and his four grandparents, respectively. The chronicles of your closest three generations of ancestors begins to form the pattern of a snowflake, a geometric pattern that goes back infinitely into the lost past. I wish I could tell all these other stories as well.

By this point in my life, my ninety-sixth year, I have traveled many strange roads to learn the stories of all fourteen of the forefathers and foremothers who lived during this eleventh century after Christ. Read these records well, for they will reveal yourself to you. God rest their souls. Through these fourteen books, my lifetime's labor of love, I hope for some measure of absolution in the eyes of God Almighty for my vast sins, about which I regret that you are about to learn. My only hope for salvation lies in these books hitting their mark and setting you on a different course, a course of righteousness for yourself and your family. Perhaps, you too can find your mission in these stories; only the deep roots of family can anchor you through the most trying times of your life. If you are reading this note and not talking directly to me, it means that I could wait no longer. I will try to get to my position in this design before I pass on, but if I do not make it, please put me there, please give me my place. It is my last wish.

Wulfric, your great-grandfather,

Winter, the ninth year of the reign of William Rufus

So much, so fast. I wanted time to think this letter over, time to fathom that I was about to learn about the family that I had ached for all my life. I wanted time to prepare for a feeling of belonging that was already beginning to overwhelm me. But I had heard the urgency in Wulfric's message and knew that I had a long night of reading ahead. The first bound page, headed "Wulfric, Your Father's Maternal Grandfather," was written in a much more stable, much more refined handwriting. Before beginning, I stepped over to the woods to relieve myself, and Rexy automatically followed, standing beside me, staring sleepily into the blackness.

The Professor stopped and silence filled the room. I was the first to speak, the old Haley, before I could stop myself, "What a fantastic feeling it must be, to know that finally the story of your life is about to unfold!"

Nelson responded, "He must have been hoping at this point that he would turn out to descend from nobility, so that he could go back and marry Emma."

This remark somehow brought me back to my own impossible life, and my deep sadness fell back upon me.

I snapped, "You know, Nelson, not all stories have a happy ending."

The Professor asked what we would like to do at this point, and I moved onto the floor and crawled over to sit with my back against the bottom of Nelson's armchair. He moved his legs to make room. I rubbed my open fingers through the minkiness of the polar bear rug. In this arrangement I was facing the open curtains, now still. I simply said, a bit sharply, “Read to me.”

Chapter Five

The Minstrel and the Elephant Gun

The Professor announced, "This section, as the last, and I assume as they all will be, is introduced by Boy in Middle English, then goes into Wulfric's Old English. But children, don't you need to study for tomorrow's history examination? You can stay here tonight and study, if you'd like, and we can read this later. Or I can walk you back to your house and stay with you?"

He still didn't get it. I was a college drop-out. I thought of the impossibility of studying, anywhere, but especially at that house, with so many bad memories of sobbing and binge eating over the past few months. The busted doors weren't very inviting, either. In fact, I had really only rarely left the house this semester, and then only when Nelson badgered me into it. I had been looking into the same patch of stained ceiling over my bed for weeks and I had found nothing. Perhaps there had been nothing there to find, no magical solution to be had. Remembering my real life moved my mind automatically back to its natural setting, dark again, so sad. I hated the thought of that little rental house, I hated this horrible exam, and I hated the Christmas looming only two months off with me as a drop-out.

Let's see, I thought, *Mom will once again force the family to undergo the same lame traditions as every other lame year. She will invite the same relatives over and we will all listen to the same meaningless family stories over some meal. Oh, and once company has gone, on Christmas Eve we'll be forced to sing that same stupid, syrupy, wassailing song. I can hear that cornball tune now, "Love and joy, come to you, and to you your wassail too, and God bless you, and send you a happy new year..." And of course we're only allowed to sing it with the whole family holding hands around the tree as the last thing before bedtime. Then we would simply say 'Merry Christmas' and go to bed.*

Aloud, I simply said, "No, a distraction would be good right now, Professor." As the danger of the stalker loomed less and less here in the safety of the Professor's den, though I couldn't tell at the time, my own grief over my horrible performance in college was gradually overtaking me again.

"Alright, then," said the Professor, looking at me with concern, "Let's go back to a deserted summit in Essex in 1096. But you must understand something right now. We don't know if this Boy is a direct ancestor of yours, but from the location of the find, it is quite possible. If he is, the occasion of reading these chronicles is historically momentous."

"What do you mean?" I asked. At this point I couldn't decide if I was annoyed or interested by this book. Clearly Emma's popularity with the butterfly world suggested she was my ancient grandmother, but that could also just have been a coincidence.

"I mean simply this: as diaries from one thousand years ago, these fourteen texts will make you unique among the inhabitants of this planet. If these journals even approach their promise, you two will be the only existing humans to ever have been offered a glimpse into the daily life of your own ancestors fifty generations back! You will be afforded insight into the origins of your own personal mannerisms, physical attributes, superstitions, and goodness knows what else, as passed down from mother to daughter and father to son through the ages. This is a momentous evening for each of you. My envy for you could not be greater."

I could tell by his tone that the Professor was feeling very protective at this moment. He had no kids of his own, and in fact had made clear to my Dad and us during many cookouts on his patio that he had certainly never wanted kids. The Professor liked order, and certainly liked to be in control of his environment. Sometimes, though, I thought he was protesting too much, that he must have felt, on some level, a deep sadness at having no family. His research had taken him away from the university often, and he had had relationships here and there. I remember when I was a little girl I once talked to a nice lady over here, a woman much younger than him. She seemed great, but she was not here the next time we visited. When I asked him where she went, I remember him brushing aside the subject with, "I just can never find my perfect match." It seems more likely to me that he found her dozens of times and just couldn't pull himself to make the compromises necessary for them to be able to grow toward each other. And now, in his early seventies, it was too late. So we served a special function for him, the kids that he could have had, and perhaps should have had. I liked him very much.

As I looked toward the filling drapes, I was troubled by a sense that my outlook on midterms and grades was about to be brought into question. And then it happened. Leaning on the back of Nelson's chair, playing absently with that bear fur, for one blinding moment I saw my horrible, confused semester the way my foremothers saw it: regrettable, but ultimately simply a glancing blow. I had clarity, only a flash, but there it was. I vaguely understood on some level, far beneath the dread, that what lay before me may just be a clear look down the long well of history, yielding at the bottom a rare glimpse into myself that would change me forever, perhaps even change the color of my world. As the wind pulled the pores of my skin into hardness, I looked back up at the Professor and simply said, for a second time, "Read to me."

So he did.

I could hardly keep myself from quickly skimming the pages of this first book and moving on to the next bag. It also immediately occurred to me that the two bags nearest the fire, those of my parents, were the ones I had really waited for all my life. Could my mother be forgiven? Should she be? Could my father have been justified in abandoning me? Could they be alive, and would God ever grant them absolution for what they did to me so that we could at least be together in Heaven? These were the questions that burned in me as I looked out onto this cliff top arrangement:

Wulfric Bag

Bag Bag

Bag Bag

Bag Bag

Bag Fire Bag

Bag Bag

Bag Bag

But Wulfric had been clear, and trusting that his design indeed had a purpose, I began to read my first of fourteen chronicles, that of my father's maternal grandfather, the man sitting next to me, arms folded, stone cold: Wulfric.

I, Wulfric, your father's maternal grandfather, was born in the year 1000, a year of many frightening signs from God. I was the only son of my mother, Goda, and my father, Osbern. I am told that during the year of my birth a tremendous comet with hair appeared, confirming in the minds of all in our region that the second coming of our Lord was upon us. But the people of my Hereford village needed no such, as you Normans say, confirmation--we English just say "proof." Terror and signs were upon us, in my first years, as we all knew they would be. And we were sorely afraid. I had a little childhood friend, Eadburh, who I remember comforting in her weeping. Our King, unfortunately, made the terror much worse.

The king of England from 978 until Vikings expelled him in 1013 was named Ethelred, whom we in these western parts dubbed "the Unraedy." He earned his nickname well. Unraedy meant "uncounseled," or "badly-advised" and that he surely was. As the Vikings, who had not been seen for ages, began again to attack the shores of England in the 990s and first years of this century, Ethelred adopted an unexplainable policy of listening to those who utterly lacked good judgment. His plan to defend his kingdom from these renewed and very murderous Viking attacks was to try to flee from these invading Danes until they had plundered their fill, and then to pay them off with a ransom of unfathomable wealth. In my earliest years, the constant fear of Viking attack spread terror through our village and through all the villages around us.

The ongoing panic of our village shows the level of alarm in our country in this period because we were as far away from the typical southeastern targets of Danish plunder as you could be in England.

"Where exactly is Hereford?" I asked.

The Professor responded, pushing his glasses up from the end of his nose, "Hereford borders Wales and is a completely inland region. Though without a coastline, you see," —here he shot his laser pointer at the western England portion of the map—"Hereford was still in easy striking distance for any Viking boats interesting in rowing up the Severn River. Vikings were often recorded moving on horseback far inland, once fifty miles from the sea."

The Professor referred to his map again, and then began to read.

The unchecked Vikings, then, worked in our minds as part of the fulfillment of the terror of the new millennium that my parents had dreaded for so long. Through these horrifying days, my little friend Eadburh and I, though both of the lowest possible birth, played together through our first years and would not be seen without each other. My father often remarked that we two were happier than those of the highest birth, and indeed we often played that we were lords and ladies, dressing up with every piece of old clothing we could borrow, making elaborate clover necklaces and crowns. Our world was orderly and fair, and she would always take me to the most special pretend dances. I would build her a house for hours, sometimes days, out of brush and sticks while she made things for it. When we were done, we would just sit inside, without anything to say, because there was nothing for us to say. We were happy.

But our play ended abruptly the day Eadburh's master sold her without warning to Welsh merchants. The scene etched into me much deeper than her fingernails had when they pulled her out of my little hug. My torn skin eventually healed. My jolting moment of helplessness and shame sent me into a shock of—as the Normans say, self-condemnation; we Saxons just say self-hatred—and personal insecurity in which I am afraid I passed the next nine decades. I can still to this day hear her shrill, scratchy outcries and those of her mother. Like the saddest of poems from your darkest nightmare, the shrieks of terror of mother and daughter matched and rhymed so perfectly. Let me assure you, Boy, that neither my father nor I could do anything to stop this hellish scene, one of my first failures. For some reason, though I was only the littlest boy, I felt responsible for not saving her from those men. I cannot write of this loss further.

Boy, the reason I could not reveal myself to you all these years becomes quite clear at the very start of my story: both my mother and father were slaves, and so of course I too was born a slave. I had no power to save my Eadburh. In my wee days, the simple life of a slave was all I knew; it seemed normal enough to do as the master instructed. After the final day with Eadburh, however, I grew up considerably, and I became much more aware of my social status.

My father broke a second very sad piece of news to me when I was about seven. It came out one day as we were alone together gleaning the tiny grains of wheat left behind in the dirt after the harvest. Here in the master's fields, my father told me that my mother had died in childbirth with me. I remember pursing my lips white on this news, and I sped up my pace of grainpicking, though my back was already very achy. Before this admission he had spoken little of her. Now that I understood that I had had a mother, I would ask about her often, and so I came to know her, in a way, through the stories of my father. When he told these stories I was privileged to see my father in the highest spirits he was ever in. I also saw him at his lowest. When I asked him about it, he told me the details of the dark day of my birth, and I came to understand over the course of many talks while cutting trees for the master's firewood or mending fences that the father with whom I was growing up was only a ghostly image of his former self. His sadness struck me on a level I have never understood, but for some reason I took on, at that tender young age, all the guilt of my mother's death and my father's sadness. That it was my birth that killed my mother was something I have struggled with all my life, and I have found redemption to be a very difficult thing to grasp. I told my father I was sorry only once, the day I came to understand that his spirit would never recover from her loss. And I expected that I too would never recover from what I had done to my mother and to Eadburh. Not in this life, and not in the next.

When I was a young child, my elders often noted what a pleasant way I had, and it was true that the lightness of heart cultivated in me in the many days of Eadburh made up the core of my personality throughout my nine decades. I was naturally gifted with the ability to make others laugh. I learned to tell stories, and I always fancied new tricks or acrobatics. My father often joked that I would have made a fine minstrel, or clownish court entertainer, were it not for the little problem of my slave status. I enjoyed pleasing others, and the master was quite fond of me, often calling me to his house to hear the latest jokes.

When I was nine, after we had worked twenty exhausting days in a row at harvest time with only Sundays to rest, my father took ill and died of the fever. For the two weeks leading up to his death, he lay on his musty, damp bed, a simple mattress of decaying straw stuffed into a linen cover. I remember those weeks well, every day of them. I would sit in that smell of must and rotting straw, staring at our bare walls adorned by only a straw broom which hung by a nail. I remember the smell of his dying body, putrid, but still, in a sense, strong. Each sweaty hour brought a new goodwife with a new charm or potion, a new incantation or treatment. At the end they all knew it, and told me it was my Papa's time, and to go in and say goodbye. Boy, before he died he gave me something that I want you to have now. It has been with me every day of my long life since that September day in 1009. Do not be afraid of it, for it does only good. It is an amulet.

At this point I looked over at the frozen corpse, with its left hand dangling down lifelessly. I began to check for some medallion or charm around his cold neck. In my ginger search I touched him as little as possible and found nothing. I knew amulets were charms to ward off evil spirits, but they were forbidden by our Church and had been for many ages. All icons of the old pagan religion were strictly outlawed, on penalty of excommunication. Was my forefather a pagan? Did he expect me to renounce Our Lord? I decided to read his story further...

Do not be fooled. I reject the old religion of the mountain people as idolatrous nonsense, and I embrace the Lord Jesus Christ as the Son of God. Let us not, however, confuse religion and magic. Our religion is a belief designed to bring a better life for our community, and in this you and I are fully Christian. But I view individual manipulations of human behavior and events as completely outside religion, as the realm of magic, a realm separate from our Christian faith. This amulet, then, should not be considered a symbol of Woden, Thunor, or the other ancient pagan gods. This amulet is now fully separate from its original pagan origins.

As you know, our Church has borrowed and changed many of the old ways, and far from being proof that paganism survives, these adoptions are proof of the powerlessness of the old religion. Our Church took the name of the pagan goddess Oestre and borrowed its meaning to ground our festival of Easter in what was familiar to the newly-converted Angles and Saxons of England. Likewise, the church fathers intentionally adopted the Celtic's tradition of Samhain, their pagan bonfire ritual of autumn harvest in which people masqueraded as the dead, to prepare for All Saints' Day. Our Church has shown the wisdom to adopt the pagan feasting at springtime into our colorful festival of Carnival, which leads up to a climax on Mardi Gras, or fat Tuesday. And our Church fathers have chosen to place the date of the birth of Our Lord at the winter solstice, again borrowing the familiar pagan festival of the beginning of the lengthening of the days with our celebration of the coming of the Light. Yes, ruins of paganism can be seen strewn about us, but for the vast majority of us English, they are just that, ruins. The amulet derives its power not from a long-dead pantheon of pagan gods, but from the ways of our folk ancestors, ways long-forgotten but very powerful. I have even heard it said that this Red Amulet holds such power that its possessor will some day save the entire world. William the Conqueror wore an amulet at his victory at Hastings, and if you wear this one, which is known as the Red Amulet, no harm will come to you this night or throughout your life.

Instead, think of this amulet as a vehicle into the power of the old times, when evil doings required a strong magical defense. You can believe in the power of this amulet or not, but either way, it will bring you great security. If your situation ever becomes deadly, simply hold the amulet above your head and recite the following charm: "A charm I know no king can say or any man has mastered; help it is called because it aids at times of sickness and sorrow." Memorize this now. This chant, in combination with this amulet, can repel the mightiest evil. It certainly charmed my life.

One day when I was fourteen I was wearing this charm, snug under my shirts and tunic, while I was watching my forearm vein pop out as I was doing a one-armed handstand. Suddenly, I was visited by one of the master's house slaves, who told me to come to the house quickly. My master, whom I did not see very often, was none other than Bruning, the king's sheriff for Hereford. Bruning was gone quite often, visiting at the court of King Ethelred, trying like every other sheriff in the kingdom to befriend as closely as possible the king. Around this time, King Ethelred had been humiliated so badly by Svein Forkbeard (King of England 1013-1014), King of the Danes, that in late 1013 King Ethelred was forced into exile in Normandy, homeland of his bride, Queen Emma. When this occurred, the Vikings completely occupied the north, east, and south of England, and finally Svein, ravaging city after city with a fierceness that was worthy of a Dane's reputation, was surrendered to and declared king of England! Upon this declaration Bruning came back to Hereford, unsure of his position. After King Svein died the next year, King Ethelred returned to England, and so did the prestige of the master.

Well, on this day in late 1014, Bruning's only son had taken sick and was lying in a sickness from which he could not be roused. He lay there, eyes glazed and barely open, as if his ghost was deciding the best course to take. The sheriff ordered me to try to lift his spirit back into this life. I told him I was no physic, but he insisted that I stay with the boy until the end, trying everything in my power to cure him. So I settled in by the bed and got comfortable. I told him my best war stories, and in between, sang a few silly songs. Behold, he began to stir! So I delivered him my jokes, the very best ones, about shepherds in love with their sheep. The one that got him was the farmer whose nagging wife was killed by a kick in the head from his donkey. At the burial, the priest noticed that the farmer was nodding his head to all the women who approached, but shaking his head to all the men. When the priest later asked why, the farmer explained that the women had been commenting on how lovely she looked and what a fine tunic; the men had each asked in turn if the donkey was for sale. As I delivered this final line hard, the boy bolted up laughing, the sheriff bolted into the room, and although it all happened very fast, by morning I was, as you Normans say, manumitted. We English just called it freed.

Nelson interrupted, "Professor, were there really slaves, and could they really be freed? I've never heard of this in Medieval Europe. I thought in this era Europe only had serfs, who were peasants who were legally bound not to leave their land because of the unpayably large debt built up by their ancestors."

"Oh yes," said the Professor, "in England slavery was the precursor to serfdom, you see, and manumissions, or freeings, certainly occurred. I have some references here on my shelf. Would you like some examples of eleventh-century manumissions of slaves?"

Nelson quickly answered, "Not necessary, Professor! That kind of breaks the momentum of the story! But don't worry, I think that we completely understand that this story is perfectly educational and if we want it, we definitely know exactly where to find more info on cultural, legal, social, religious, literary, political, artistic, linguistic, military, or economic history!

The Professor said, "Very well. Then let us continue with Wulfric's chronicle."

Once Bruning freed me, I did not know what to do. The women of our village, all mothers to me, said to flee, flee far away, before the master thought again. My village family was very happy for me, and said I would make a fine minstrel, just like my father had wanted. They urged me to leave instantly, reminding me that a minstrel did not have to worry about most physical threats, since all sides in battle would welcome the distraction and mirth brought by what was known in those days as a gleoman or a jogler. I pointed out, though, that in Hereford, minstrels were considered outcasts and denied the sacraments and thus salvation itself. And this denial was meet and right because a traveling minstrel could hardly receive Mass every Sunday and could certainly not do the fasting required by the Church. Minstrels also were considered outside the protection of the law. To be a minstrel for one day was to be a social pariah for life. They urged, "Then to the Danelaw with you;" in the east and north—Northumbria, York, and East Anglia--where the Danish had traditionally and still currently controlled. There, minstrels enjoyed more prestige than they did in the west and south of England. "Begone with you," they urged again, and, knowing no better, I accepted the bony hugs of these thin, hard women and I hurriedly left Hereford, not to return for many years.

My amblings eventually brought me to Stratford, on the Avon River, where I had a chance to watch several joglers at their craft. I was taken on as a servant in a local inn, and from this vantage point I saw most of what was new in Stratford. Soon enough, though, I began to feel the pull to return to the sheriff's estate in Hereford. The women who had so sweetly bade me be gone had not thought of my loneliness.

Although it took my uprooting to make me realize it, in my mind, I had existed only as a part of the village community. My place was there, as a slave, and I knew it. The deep, complete sense of belonging that had been a part of me all my days in Hereford had been suddenly ripped away from me. I had no being in Stratford, an outsider to the local peasants, one who could never fit correctly. My thinking was as a villager, yet I was forced to view myself in Stratford as an individual, a point of view that brought with it a hollowness and ache that I cannot describe. Prayer took the pain away only while I was on my knees, which became more and more frequent in those lonely days of Stratford.

But somehow despite all my personal emptiness I made some friends here, and picked up some new talents. It was here that I fine-tuned my skills at joking, storytelling, and wrestling. And more importantly, it was here I learned that trappings were everything. Entering town draped in colorful garb, carrying a harp, on a donkey draped also in bright colors was half the battle. Somehow, as people struggled even to live another day, the minstrel's appearance alone lightened their burden and made them ready to laugh at almost anything that involved crude, base humor.

The Professor interrupted, "I, uh, I must caution you that the very essence of the eleventh century involved a crudeness and baseness that today would make even federal prisoners squeamish. As I have been translating, I have been trying to modernize the language into our vernacular, and where I haven't known an exact translation, I have been approximating and improvising. The joking, however, will be hard to screen because of the nature of a joke. The humor of this era almost always involved body parts, and it was, to say the least, indelicate. What do you think? Should I read this part?"

"Professor," I stared coldly, "you've got to be kidding. Go on."

"As you wish," the Professor smiled and shook his head. "But fair warning: I may be invoking godfather's license and editing lavishly."

He continued,

Minstrels move in circuits, and that is what I began to do, mainly working the manors, villages, and cities of the Danelaw. That is, the northeastern half of England, which includes Northumberland, York, Nottingham, Lincoln, and East Anglia. It was in this circuit that I perfected my routine, which even

I must admit, in its final form, shook the very rafters of a house with the laughter and clapping of the crowds. More than once I have caused parts of ceilings to fall in. And with every uproarious joke, every heart-wrenching song, every riveting epic story, my purse fattened a bit. I learned to focus only where the money was, which usually meant among the Danish lords who only a few years earlier had been the marauding Vikings of another region of England.

At one point, it was 1019, my wandering brought me out of the Danelaw and into Worchester. After my usual performance, I was out walking and I happened on a poor girl. It was past midnight and she was still plowing her strip of the village fields behind a particularly stubborn ox. She looked on the verge of exhaustion, and I was reminded of how hard we worked in the weeks right before my father died.

As I was not one bit tired, sleeping until noon and entertaining until very late, I asked the lovely thing if she would like a little help coaxing the ox. After she made out my minstrel garb, she told me to be gone, but I stuck with it. On my second invitation she accepted, letting her exhaustion overcome her personal revulsion at spending time with a gleoman. The animal pulled much better with me whacking its hindquarters, and in an hour her strip was plowed. At last she told me her name was Ealdgyth, and she told me one more thing before retiring to her father's small rectangular house. By that bright full moon she told me she had one more strip to do the next night.

Here the Professor clarified that though this common Old English name is pronounced "Awld-gith," it is spelled "E-a-l-d-g-y-t-h".

```
This time I decided that I would do the work
by myself, and I made Ealdgyth watch me. Soon,
though, I guess unamused by my technique, she
got up and took the role of whacker, and
between the two of us, our work ended very
quickly. But the whelps I had on my hands! Each
was badly blistered where I had been holding
the leather strap that wrapped around me and
attached to the ox yoke. Plowing, Boy, is
pushing packed soil up that does not want to
budge. Rocks and hard soil will stop a plow
short unless the plower has a will stronger
than stone! I had not worked with my hands in
over two years. We sat for a while in that
moonlight and she made my hands feel better.
She explained as she pushed the gnats off her
face with the back of her hand that her days
were filled with the plowing of the strips of
her lord and no time was left for her own
meager two strips. She said all this without a
smile and in fact I was not sure if that face
even bore the ability to smile. All this was
because of her misfortune.
```

Here the Professor stopped and looked puzzled. He turned back to the previous page and then closed the book completely. "Kids, I…well, I'm having trouble."

"Professor, you're doing great!" we both answered, confused.

"No, it's this damned pluperfect tense. Well," he paused for a moment, "well, I just don't know it. And Wulfric is beginning to use the pluperfect--you know, the recent past tense--far too often for me to be confident any longer about the accuracy of my translation. I cannot go on. I could be telling you inaccurate information."

"But what can we do? We have to finish the book now, tonight. Surely there is someone you can ask?"

"The only person who could possibly help us with the use of the pluperfect in late Old English is the renowned expert, Professor Jameson Page of Yale. And he is my archenemy. And, moreover, he has been dead for ten years. But wait…" Here the Professor began to smile again.

"I've got the solution, but it's dangerous. While I don't have a copy of his book on Old English grammar—never could stand having his works around here—there is a copy in the Special Collections Department of the University library. And, if I don't miss my guess, I still have a key!"

"You mean walk out of here, across the Commons, back to the library, with a madman searching for us?" I asked. "That *is* crazy."

The Professor shot a quick, "Maybe not. Follow me," and explained his idea on the way. As we walked down his basement stairs, he explained, "Tonight is Honors Night at the School of Arts and Sciences. Many professors will be in attendance, in their caps and gowns. I could dress in mine and you, Nelson, could carry the book in my accordion case. We're not leaving it here." At this point he opened a rusty metal cabinet and pulled out an enormous ring of ancient keys, each neatly labeled.

"Kept these from my early days as a Teaching Assistant. While they've changed most locks, I've often noticed that many janitorial entrances still have the same old locks. It's worth a try. Of course, as a full professor with an endowed chair I have full privileges at Special Collections, so we can't get into any trouble. It's just that it seems we can't wait until morning."

Nelson stopped the Professor by the arm on the way back up the steps. "Professor, one question: Why must you wear your academic robes? Is that really necessary?"

"Yes, it is, Nelson. It's the only way I can hide my elephant gun."

Three minutes later we were walking across the Commons, me in my cowboy hat and party dress, Nelson in dreds carrying an accordion case, and the

Professor in his flowing robes that hardly concealed the huge flared-out elephant gun he insisted on bringing.

The Commons was scattered with parties going to and fro, many of which were escorted by at least one professor in his or her gown. The disguise was perfect, yet behind every tree I imaged some small movement that disappeared when we passed the tree. One man sat suspiciously in the shadows at the top of the library steps and seemed to be watching us, but a young lady soon joined him and he lost interest in us. Finally we walked down some remarkably sticky metal stairs to a huge double door. After a little fumbling, we were in the library basement, the same one we visited so briefly earlier that afternoon.

After he locked the door behind us, the Professor turned and walked briskly, mega-shotgun in both hands, straight down a hall and to a door where he stopped. "Special Collections" was painted in a semi-circle on the translucent glass window of the door. We followed him in, waited until he locked that door back too, and trailed very close behind him to a far corner of the department where he instantly pulled the correct volume off the shelf.

A loud boom shook the stillness and my eyes grew wide and fixed.

"Something probably just fell," the Professor volunteered, "I just need to xerox a five-page table and that will do nicely." We followed him into another small room and looked away as the machine flashed bright green light five times, flooding the dark department with light. A crash of shattering glass split the silence and we all jumped together. The madman was here!

Chapter Six

Apache Helicopters and a Trained Bear

On pure instinct we ran in the opposite direction from the origin of the sound. Out in a second hallway we arrived at the main stacks, the millions of bundles of towering newspapers we had seen earlier. In the pitch dark we began to play cat and mouse with our attacker. When we reached the far end of the stacks, without a moment of thought, the Professor whispered, "Push." He leaned the flared barrel of his huge gun on the wall and began shoving the stack nearest him. With all of us pushing with all our might, finally the shelf toppled, beginning a cascade of falling shelves.

"Whut the bloody ell!" we heard, and we knew we had trapped our Englishman under hundreds of volumes, at least for a minute.

"Let's get out of here!" Nelson squealed as we all scrambled for a nearby fire door. The alarm must have been broken, because the door opened silently. We shot across a silent the Commons to the Communications building.

"Quick, downstairs," and we followed the Professor yet again. He took us to a utility closet, unlocked it, and led us in. At the far end of the small closet was another door, and the Professor had this key also. In the confusion I thought for a minute that he actually used the same key here in the Communications building that he had used on the library door, but I must have been mistaken. This door was blocked by boxes of dusty books that we moved as quietly as possible. It opened onto a very long tunnel, long-since sealed off and forgotten about, that we found out soon enough led to the Physics building.

Once inside the Physics building, the Professor spoke more freely. "There. I knew my collection of keys would come in handy one day! This building is always kept locked after hours, so we are safe here. Now, let's go to the observatory on the roof and take a look at the Commons. I want to see exactly where the chap is."

Winded and trying to overcome our earlier fright, we followed the Professor again, this time up four flights of stairs and onto a rooftop with a huge telescope at the center. Light from an upper room in the observatory flooded the roof. The Professor stepped away and made a brief call on his cell phone. As Nelson and I peeked over the side of our building we saw, three buildings over, a shadowy figure that appeared to be slowly searching for someone.

"There he is," we whispered together.

As the Professor returned and leaned over to take a look, Nelson whispered, without taking his eyes off the stalker in the distance, "Professor, shoot him." We both looked at Nelson, who shrugged his shoulders.

I asked, "Nelson, did I hear you squealing back there?"

Nelson changed the subject. "Professor, there's plenty of light up here, and we are stuck for the time being. Do you want to try to read some more? Oh, never mind. I guess we couldn't get the xeroxed pages."

"Au contraire," said the Professor as he stuck one finger down the barrel of the elephant gun and pulled out a rolled-up sheath of papers. After studying the second page for only about thirty seconds, the Professor sat down so that the most direct light was coming from behind him and said, "Ready! Let's get back to Wulfric."

Six weeks ago Ealdgyth's father had been caught under a plow and had lost a leg, which had been so badly torn that the local farmers had sawed it off. He had since been in bed, and last week the thing that Ealdgyth had been fighting against so hard had happened. Despite her best efforts and almost constant praying to

St. Genevieve to lessen the fever, the wound had begun to fester.

She and her aunt had for weeks been cleaning the wound regularly with wine, which the midwife said would help, but her father's pain had steadily worsened. Without his labor, she explained, they would lose their strips, and would be unable to make the required payments to Church, earl, and king. If the payments were not made, she would have no choice but to sell herself into slavery to pay her debts.

Now, because this was exactly what had happened to my father and mother, her situation moved me very deeply. Most of her story I will save until her chronicle, but I will say that sadly, the next night that I saw her, her father had died. Faced with no option other than selling herself into slavery, she accepted my proposal and we were married, leaving Worchester and her indebtedness forever.

It was not long until I learned a simple truth about my calling: minstrels do not have wives, especially a wife as serious as Ealdgyth. What makes the minstrel so welcomed is his stigma of raucous debauchery, which, I discovered, completely vanishes when he introduces the wife. It was as if I embodied an obscenity and a blasphemy that could not be associated with the purity of the sacrament of marriage. As a result, we adopted a policy that I would enter a new town, dressed in my flashy finery and playing my harp, and she would slip in quietly an hour or so later. It was no life for her, I knew, and things became more complicated when her belly began to grow. "This is no life for you," I would say. But of course, we had no choice.

There was no escape from this trap. No one would hire me permanently with a wife, since I would have to follow my lord to each of his holdings and abroad at his whim. So we continued moving in my circuit, Ealdgyth following like a shadow, and soon enough, like two shadows. Little Gunnehilde was born in 1020.

Here the Professor clarified that he would pronounce the girl's name "Goon-hilda" even though in the book the word was written "G-u-n-n-e-h-i-l-d-e."

For Gunnehilde, life was even more difficult. Babies need their sleep, and our life of constant moving wore on mother and daughter terribly. But still, there was no alternative. The pennies I collected were enough to feed us all and to rent a place for each night, but I could save no money, and even if I could, fitting into the closeness of a village family for a minstrel and his wife would have taken many years if it ever happened at all.

This sad state was brought to an end by an even sadder event. One evening, about half way between Lothian and Bamburgh, in the heart of Northumberland, the three of us were camped. What happened I will tell you at length in Ealdgyth's chronicle, but she died and, utterly lost, I left little Gunnehilde—who, Boy, is your grandmother—on the doorstep of a local mill. Although it wrenched me throughout, it was the right thing to do, and any father in a similar situation would have done the same. I never made it to Bamburgh, leaving the Northumbrian region behind me for a long time.

As the wandering lifestyle began to weigh on me, I began to take offers of steady work more seriously. More than once a local thegn offered to hire me on a permanent basis, but I held out for a bigger eel to fry. It finally bit.

As I was wandering one day through territory totally new to me, I was directed to the manor of the earl of Wessex himself, Earl Godwine, who from 1018 until 1053 was earl of this most important region of England. Earl Godwine was so powerful during the reign of Edward the Confessor that Godwine actually wielded more control over England than did the King. This is borne out by the fact that Earl Godwine's son, Harold, was unanimously declared King of England in January of 1066 upon the death of Edward. Had it not been for the October 1066 invasion led by William the Conqueror, Harold might have gained great glory for his family.

So my 1022 arrival in Wessex came at a lucky time for me, the perfect time to attach myself to Godwine's rising star. After years of misery, I had one chance to make Godwine fall so in love with me that he would hire me on as a permanent member of his semi-royal court. I asked around about what he liked, and came up with the ideas that I needed; I just had to gather a few props and make a few arrangements.

The evening was perfect. Godwine had just returned from negotiations with King Canute. These talks expanded the Earl's lands even further. The wine in the main manor hall was flowing freely and the mood was already high. Further, no other minstrel was present. So I was ready for the most compelling show of my life. I entered the outside courtyard on my colorfully draped donkey, catching the eye of every person around the manor house. What really got their attention was the trained bear that was in tow behind my very nervous donkey, which for once was moving briskly. I had rented the bear from a minstrel I met in Farnham who would pass through in a few days to get the beast. The bear was actually a nice enough fellow, but the secret was keeping his belly extremely full at all times, which ran into some expense. I tied him quite securely outside, and made a big show of this. As I entered the main hall, I played my harp and sang one of the saddest tunes I knew, trying to show my full range, but of course my bear outside was all the talk.

After my song I took the center of the room, facing the Earl, and all the people, high and low, encircled me for my show. I opened with a recitation of traditional proverbs, each spun in a very inappropriate way at the end. Then hit them with some of my best jokes. The crowd exploded, and they were eager for more. I recited a few more proverbs, all in the same vein--peasants irreverently poking fun at highborn manners--and the crowd, and the Earl, laughed convulsively.

Next, I asked the Earl and one of his thegns for the use of their swords. They kindly obliged, and I made a big production about how sharp they were, especially the sword of the Earl. Then, with a startling scream, I pretended to slip and threw myself up, walking on my hands with their sword blades as stilts. I held the blades; the handles were what touched the floor. Pretending to be falling the whole time, I ran on my hands all over the room, grown men laughing so hard they were holding their undertunics. I concluded by falling backwards onto, flipping, and walking backwards down the feast table, still on my hands which were grabbing their razor-sharp blades. Falling in front of the Earl, I neatly handed his bloodless sword back. The crowd screamed in hysterical delight.

I asked the Earl how a pig was taken to the physic? By hambulance!

I asked the Earl what they called a fish with no eyes. A fsh!

I asked the Earl what they called a deer with no eyes? A no-eye-deer!

I asked the Earl what a fish said when it ran into the wall? Dam!

After I had them rolling on the floor for long enough, I calmed the mood a bit and then everyone settled in for my version of the great story *Beowulf*. I told it all, with all the drama and running about that I could muster, blowing out many of the candles during the most frightening parts. Nobles and commoners alike were as silent as rats when I told that

Grendel saw that his strength was deserting him, his claws bound fast, Higlac's brave follower tearing at his hands. The monster's hatred rose higher, but his power had gone. He twisted in pain, and the bleeding sinews deep in his shoulder snapped, muscle and bone split and broke. The battle was over, Beowulf had been granted new glory.

When I reached the part about the battle between Beowulf and Grendel's mother, I blew out all the candles, leaving only the flickering light from the great fireplace to illuminate the scene. The effect was new to them, and they cheered wildly for more. I finished the entire epic, and then I excused myself, saying I had to go and check on my bear, which caused much mirth. Outside, I rested up, readying for the closing half of my show, which I knew would have to be even more amazing—always save the best for last, that was where the tips were.

I reentered the manor hall, now as fully lit as it had ever been, to thunderous applause. I immediately opened with my jokes:

A man prepares to leave to go to war with his lord. He asks his best friend to watch after his wife, whom the husband had bound securely in a chastity belt. He gives the key to the best friend. "If I am not back in four years," says the husband, "free her from this belt."

After the wife weeps and swears her eternal fealty, the husband rides off. Before he reaches the next valley, however, he sees a thundering cloud of dust behind him. It is his friend shouting, "Wait!" Wait!" You left the wrong key!

Before the hilarity died down, I struck at them again:

There was an old man who was approached by the doctor. "We're sorry," said this leech, "but as usual, we cannot tell what is wrong with your wife. She either has the dementia of old age or the plague. Our advice is to take her to the middle of town and drop her off. If she finds her way home, don't let her in!"

I then played a few playful tunes on the harp, followed by the juggling of many items in the hall, getting progressively more dangerous, culminating with juggling four swords, which cleared the crowd out of my way very well, especially once I began chasing them while juggling the swords. After a few more of my choicest jokes, it was time for the finale. I told the crowd to excuse me, I had to bring my bear inside now. This was received by a shriek of hilarity that only got more shrill when I led the bear in. I was carrying a jar of honey, and began to slowly make myself less dressed.

The Professor awkwardly broke in, obviously very embarrassed, "Okay guys, this part we'll skip. Suffice it to say that Wulfric got the job and also remained physically intact."

I thought this was for the best as I switched positions. "There may be parts of medieval history," I remarked, "that I just don't want to know."

I looked up at the huge telescope, and frankly I had been so into the story that I had forgotten I was on the roof of the physics building. As I looked up at the telescope pointing off toward the heavens, I remembered learning in some class that the starlight that we see up in our sky actually burned long, long ago, and so seeing the stars is the romantic experience of literally looking back in time. Suddenly I jerked as the roar of a large shiny-white helicopter began to shake the top of our roof. A second and a third helicopter, all exactly matching, each emblazoned with a blue *United States Marshal* star across their shiny-white fuselage, also appeared out of nowhere, and they flooded the area below with light as the first helicopter landed on the smooth grass of the Commons across from our building.

"Our ride is here," the Professor announced dryly as he stood up and walked briskly toward the door. We looked at each other and our jaws hung open in a mirror image of disbelief. Yet the Professor was already heading down the stairs, so without a word we followed him down the stairwell, across the lawn, between armed officers with large rifles, and through the just-opened door of what Nelson told me later was an Apache jet helicopter.

The crouching U.S. Marshals saluted us as we went by and I think they said, "Good evening, Mr. Director."

We put on headphones and the deafening roar was quieted as the Apache took off. Before we could even get a syllable out, the Professor silenced our questions with a finger in front of his lips. In only a few seconds we had shot across campus and had landed on the practice field of the football team. Here we were rushed to a shiny-white Cadillac Escalade with the same *United States Marshal* star on the front door. It took a very roundabout route and then dropped us at the Professor's house. He finally spoke as we walked back down the stairs into his den, but he only had one thing to say about our astonishing helicopter ride, and then he never spoke of it again: "the Federal Marshals owed me a favor."

The Professor settled in quickly to his chair and spoke sharply. "It is imperative that I finish this book immediately so I can know what the stalker is after. I do not want to talk about our little ride. Shall I read it aloud or to myself?

His urgent tone moved us both and we quickly answered, "Aloud, please!"

Nelson and I shot concerned looks at each other--the kind that say, "who in the world is this man?"—but we knew that whoever our godfather really was, he had always watched over us, and that was enough for now. Time would surely tell.

The Professor charged ahead: "Alright, then, back to Wulfric's story."

Once I had secured employment as the court jogler, which the Earl called his "histrio," my life calmed down considerably. The tips were still very good when we entertained high-ranking guests, and I was able to save almost all of it in a safe place. I stayed on as the jogler of the family from 1023 until 1052. As I aged, though, my duties expanded to include those of family scribe. I would be responsible for all epistles to and from the family, a very important position considering the growing power of Earl Godwine in the 1040s. In my free time, I was able to write down the entirety of Beowulf, a feat I was particularly proud of in light of the invasion of Normans of 1066 which began to overwhelm the language of the English. Perhaps my copy will survive and keep this epic pure in its original Saxon power.

In 1048 I was granted the highest honor granted to a minstrel. I was granted seven hides of land in Essex, in Tendring Hundred. And I was given the title "thegn." My holding was a rocky stretch near Ashingdon, a place I have simply called "The Dale."

Nelson objected, "No way. Could a minstrel really climb so high socially, going from scum who was refused the sacraments to a member of the nobility?"

The Professor nodded, "Actually, yes. There are historical precedents. The eleventh century is an era well before the rigidification of European social caste system. For example, records show that Edmund Ironside gave the hills of Chartham and Walworth to his joculator, or minstrel, Hitardus. Surviving records also establish that other minstrels received huge rewards, such as a minstrel who reported a gift given by a nobleman. This minstrel stated that 'six hundred shillings of pure gold were wound to the ring he reached to my hand'. I have more examples on my reference shelf here if you need them."

"Interesting," said Nelson as he waved off the Professor from leaning toward his reference shelf, "kind of an eleventh-century lottery."

The Professor arrested his motion and, looking a bit put out that no one wanted to hear his passage on eleventh-century social mobility, leaned back into his overstuffed chair, adjusted his glasses, and continued.

As a thegn of a small, desolate holding with three peasant families living on my land, I was very secure and very happy. Perhaps the best part was that my decades of social stigma had ended, and in fact I had requested Essex, so far from Wessex, simply because no one there knew of my background as a minstrel. But I must admit, I kept my brightly-colored costumes hidden away, just in case there would ever be a time of need again.

By only the fourth decade of my life, I had developed severe arthritis, which by my sixth decade was already quite debilitating in times of severe cold. This arthritis, however, was made more bearable by the new sense of family that soon grew between my peasants and me. Not since Hereford had I felt such belonging, and I had sorely missed being part of the collective village. Being the thegn did not change that sense for me at all. As I became an established thegn in Essex, my life entered into a new phase. My guilt for the death of my mother and my wife, and my guilt for not somehow stopping the sale of Eadburh, and the abandonment of my daughter Gunnehilde all began to haunt me. I had always been saddened by my role in these injustices, but now I faced the price. I knew then, almost fifty years ago, as I know today, that my end would come soon enough. I felt then and still do that my eternal soul is in peril due to the suffering of these women. They had each in their own way protected me from my own loneliness, and in repayment I had abandoned my protectors.

I cannot tell you how much this weighed on my spirit. One day, praying and grieving on this subject, up on the very summit you are on now, past the hollow tree, I swore the most solemn of vows. I would protect the one who I could still help, my daughter Gunnehilde. I vowed to seek her out and to tell her of the love of her mother and father, and to position her here as the lady of this holding. I would set her right. This was my solemn oath.

After my forty-eighth year I rededicated my life to this oath, having no idea the odyssey that I would have to undergo. Attempting to gather as many as possible of the other thirteen stories of your forefathers and foremothers has essentially filled the past forty years of my life, and has brought me through amazing and harrowing situations. My oath will be fulfilled if you can finish this volume before the rising of the sun. I will end my own story here, because the rest of my life will be revealed in the telling of the other thirteen.

But do not forget that I, like the other thirteen, leave a gift to you. But be warned: the Red Amulet is very powerful and many forces would kill to get it; wizards, especially, have heard of the power of this amulet and would seek it out passionately.

"Wizards?" puzzled Nelson. "Professor, I thought Wulfric said that by the eleventh century, paganism was dead. Which is it?"

The Professor waited a moment and then looked at Nelson. "That question perplexes scholars even today, my boy, but the best answer appears to be this: ninety-five percent of the people of England were fully orthodox Christians by the eleventh century. This did not mean they had abandoned ancient customs and superstitions which had originated in the pagan era, only that they had utterly abandoned the pagan gods themselves and had, generations before, fully adopted all the major tenets of mainstream Christianity."

He continued, "The other five percent of the population, however, could well have still been either fully pagan or a hybrid of pagan and Christian. One leading argument among historians goes like this: if this small minority did not still exist, why did Canute, King of England from 1016 until 1035, make clear in his laws that 'every heathen practice is forbidden, such as the worship of heathen gods, the sun, the moon, fire or flood, wells or stones, or any kind of forest tree, or if one practices witchcraft.' Archbishop Wulfstan similarly condemned pagan sanctuaries around wells, streams, and elder trees."

"Spooky!" said Nelson and me together.

Because its power is well-known to the cult of witches and wizards who still haunt our island, it is best if you never reveal your possession of this amulet openly. Wear it only under your tunic and shirts, against the skin. The risk is small, though, because no one knows that I have possessed it all these years. If they did, the dark forces would long ago have come. Remember, if you are ever in danger, simply hold it above your head and utter the charm of which I have written. Dig deeply and you will find the gift of Wulfric.

So this was my great-grandfather: ex-slave, minstrel, scribe, thegn, and family historian. How full a life! At this point I was both amazed by my forefather and very, very alarmed by Wulfric's reference to dark forces. I decided it would be most pragmatic to believe him when he said I should not worry. Rexy suddenly awoke with a powerful bark that echoed through the valley below. She stared into the woods intently, as if in a trance. Then she curled around three times, lay down, licked herself a while on her bottom and legs, and went to sleep. I froze in silence for at least five minutes more, and then relaxed a little. There was nothing there.

I approached the dead body again, this time getting up enough nerve to dig deeply through the layers of his clothing, but I found nothing. Perhaps robbers had been here. Perhaps Cynewald had taken it. But robbers would have eaten the food, and Wulfric had said that Cynewald was completely trustworthy. And he must be, otherwise, why would he have troubled to find me? But the amulet was simply not present. Finally, I reread the section of Wulfric's chronicle about the amulet. "Dig deeply and you will see the gift of Wulfric." Dig in the ground? I grabbed the iron skillet, and yes, the ground around Wulfric was soft. I gently and respectfully moved his body, which in this intense cold had not entered rigor yet. Two feet down, I hit only rock.

Frustrated and ready to move on to Ealdgyth's narrative, I gave up. Then I paused. I asked myself aloud why the earth was soft down to two feet only to meet a rock. The rock must be a cover! With some difficulty, I dug all the dirt out which had covered the buried edges of the large stone. After some struggling I slid the rock up into a vertical position, revealing the darkness below. I brought over a log that was burning at one end, and before it went out I could discern that under the upright rock was the solid rock of the mountain, but which had a deep groove carved out of it. The indentation was exactly large enough to house a leather bag, one that perfectly matched the fourteen leather bags above.

I reached down for the bag, which required my lying completely on the ground next to my dead ancestor. As I laid there, for a split second, him facing me, me facing him, I had a flash of irony that I would all too soon be in his same position; it might be hours, it might be decades, but we were to be the same. "Are our destinies to be fulfilled?" I asked him quietly. But my fingers found their mark and pulled up a supple leather bag that definitely held a hard object. I pulled out an amulet, a flat disk as round as my large fist, with a pinkish stone embedded offcenter on its face. A loose metal chain was attached. I brought Wulfric's gift over to the fire for a closer inspection. I had never seen such a pink stone before, and I thought that the amulet was the second truly beautiful thing that I had ever seen.

Nelson wondered aloud, “I guess a pagan amulet is not exactly the kind of thing you gave a lady as a present back then, huh?”

The Professor replied, “Probably not. Especially considering that this particular amulet was best kept out of the public eye.”

“I wonder where Cynewald went?” I asked.

And I added, “And you want to know something else I’m curious about? Whether this book is worth any money. The stalker must think so. I know it’s a special history book and all that, but it may or may not be our family record, and our family is hurting with us both in college, and it’s only gonna get worse. Does anyone buy old books?”

Even Nelson was disturbed by this question, partially because it was exactly what he had been thinking.

He said with a venom reserved only for siblings, “You’re a little money grubber, aren’t you?”

He always knew the perfect way to get under my skin, and he had done it again. I glared at him and suddenly wondered why, if he had that much venom, he had never been more upset about the way our parents had always treated us. During so much of our childhood we had been by ourselves, in daycares and after school programs, and then later alone at home on weekends. It never seemed to bother Nelson the way they had raised us. They were the reasons I was dropping out. I remember once, in tenth grade, I wanted so badly to go to the school Valentine’s dance. All my friends were going. Nelson went with his friends, but none of mine could take me. Mom and Dad had to work on that Saturday night and refused to budge. I sat at home all that night as my friends went without me. Mom and Dad had told me that they would try to get off early, and I sat there in our living room all made up, hoping. When Dad finally pulled up it was way too late and my night was ruined.

The worst part about this memory is that I could not rethink that night without my brain involuntarily remembering so many other episodes scattered throughout my childhood, all with the same heavy conclusion about how they felt about me. Anyway, Nelson always seemed to think that they had done just fine as parents.

Nelson must have known that his "money-grubbing" remark had hit home with me, but he didn't seem to care. Instead, he changed the subject: "What I'd like to know, Professor, is how could a great-grandfather know the other seven great-grandparents well enough to write their histories? Their relationship to Wulfric would not be established until the birth of his great-grandchild! And why in the world is it important that Boy finish the book before dawn? He's not in any danger up there—no one in England even knows he's there!"

Chapter Seven

The Bloody Acorn

I had, so far this evening, experienced several unusual emotions, feelings I could not completely account for. First, a strange curiosity about these long-dead characters which were extracting me so fully from the current collapse of my life. But also, there was something about the Professor, something affirming that had brought me into a state in which I could be receptive to these characters in the first place. It was as if the Professor's first assumption was of my competence, of my innate intellectual curiosity. Perhaps what caught me most off-guard was the suspicion that the Professor was right and I was wrong, that lying dormant beneath my surface was a massive intellect, simply waiting to find the proper vent to escape into this world and to its own greatness. Time would tell, I thought.

I hesitated to show my ignorance but quickly decided to throw aside all inhibitions. "Are Old English and Middle English the same thing?" As soon as I asked this question, I knew it had been a mistake. I was now out there, vulnerable, for Nelson or the Professor to ridicule all they wanted.

To my relief the Professor responded, "An excellent question. Let me ask you a question in answer: Are *Beowulf* and Chaucer's *Canterbury Tales* written in the same languages? Absolutely not. While *Canterbury Tales* is written in Middle English, *Beowulf* is written in Old English, which is a language that is completely mutually unintelligible with Middle English."

"The opening page of the Ealdgyth section here, of course, is certainly not written in Shakespeare's early modern English. It is written in Middle English, and not in the relatively refined Middle English of Chaucer, who wrote in 1380s, but in the earliest form of Middle English, I'd say around 1140.

Let's hear about Ealdgyth," began the Professor.

I hung the amulet around my neck, tucked it under my tunics, and felt a strange power course through me. It could have been that I warmed the amulet a bit long by the fire, it could have been the ale, or it could have been the touch of an object that was a family heirloom, from my own family! I looked over at the dead Wulfric, who I had propped back up out of respect. His right arm had now fallen limply by his side like his left. The excitement over this gift added to the thrill of the promise of more information about my origins.

I was aware, however, as I settled in to read the second chapter, that I was physically quite vulnerable on this mountaintop. An amulet and a war dog are all well and good, but a solid quarterstaff would have been nice to have right now, considering that this bonfire was acting like a beacon for every robber within twenty miles. Any weapon would actually do, but in my imagination I hoped Cynewald would return and lend me a battle-axe. Next to a sword, which was not my station to carry, the battle-axe was my first choice.

I remembered the last time I fought with the axe. In the practice barn behind the guild forgery an arrogant nobleman had tried to kill me with his new axe. He was a Norman, a huge man, and an excellent fighter, by far the best I'd ever seen. In fact, I was not altogether certain I could best him in actual combat. In his jesting and leaping he let it slip that he was the heralded hidden prince who was all the talk at that time. I, like every other Londoner, had heard of this hidden prince who, according to the rumors, was an heir of significant import. This mystery prince was said to have had an amazing variety of royal blood in his veins, including Norman, and thus was supposed to usher in a new golden era. Some even said it was our ancient King Arthur himself returned to set things right. From what this man was mumbling, I gathered that he was the hidden prince.

After this day I never saw the man again, nor heard any further rumors about the discovery of the hidden prince. If he was the prince, I suppose he effectively kept himself hidden forever. The rumor was, I later realized, just another legend with no foundation in fact. But this noble, whoever he was, was real; it required real finesse to fight him without killing him or having him feel as if he had lost. Finally I feigned a hurt ankle and he relented, at the urging of my masters, who did not want to see how far I would allow myself to be pushed; I suppose they saw me as a true master of the battle axe who might actually defend myself if necessary. They had nothing to worry about; I was sorely aware that had I even drawn a drop of his noble blood, I would have had my hands cut off.

But I had no such weapon on this windy mountaintop, and would have to make do with Rexy, who apparently was a master at sleeping, gnawing her fleas, and licking herself. So I settled in to get to know my great-grandmother Ealdgyth, who fell into place in her husband's mysterious design:

Wulfric Bag

Bag Bag

Ealdgyth Bag

Bag Bag

Bag Fire Bag

Bag Bag

Bag Bag

Like me, Ealdgyth, who was your father's maternal grandmother, was born in the year 1000. She lived in Worcester, a town in the region of Mercia that was only a day northwest of my hometown of Hereford. Nonetheless, I did not meet her until 1019, the year in which we were married.

She was born the daughter of Aelfgifu and Aethelwald, freeholder peasants who held six acres of the village lands, three long strips of two acres each. By freeholder, Boy, I mean that they were lucky enough to have sole use of the six acres of the master's lands; had they been only cottager peasants, they would have had the use of no land, and would have instead worked the land of other peasants in addition to that of the lord. Of course, like peasants of any rank, Aelfgifu and Aethelwald really had no control over the political decisions that were made in and about their village. Power in those days, as it still does today, rested strictly in the hands of the two higher estates: the clergy, which included the local priest and the regional bishop, and the nobility, which included the local thegn and the regional earl. Your great-grandmother Ealdgyth was not of these ranks.

In years of famine, both paying the taxes and eating were simply not possible for this branch of your family. A horrible famine struck western England in the year 1005, and this hunger carried away Aelfgifu, Ealdgyth's mother. The local people tell the story that she gave up her paltry share to double that of her little one, Ealdgyth. During the two years of our marriage, Ealdgyth spoke to some extent about her childhood but remembered very little of her mother, except her sweet white smile, which was such a rarity then and still is now. I know, though, that Aelfgifu gave herself fully for her young one, and I pray for Aelfgifu daily. She was a good mother to Ealdgyth, and in a real sense, she was a good mother to us all, Boy. She protected us.

According to Ealdgyth, though, her father told her many times that her grandfather on her mother's side enjoyed a particular acclaim: he had been a notorious robber. According to Ealdgyth, her grandfather once robbed the Earl of Mercia himself, Earl Aelfric, who ruled from 983 to 985, of his entire treasury of pennies while they were in transport. This had been the portion of his tax collection that had been paid in coin. She claims that he returned the money to those who had been overtaxed and `gained the reputation of "the merry robber of the wood."`

The Professor interjected, “Remember, now, literally the only coins in eleventh-century England were pennies, often engraved with the likeness of the king, and always about ninety-two percent pure silver. There were twelve pennies to a shilling and twenty shillings to a pound, which in that period actually approximated sixteen ounces, or one pound, of silver. A shilling and a pound, however, were only accounting devices. There were no ‘shilling’ or ‘pound’ coin denominations, just pennies.”

He continued, “A penny in that period would buy about as much as a ten dollar bill today, and a pound in that era would be equivalent to about 2,500 dollars today, roughly enough to buy one good horse. Therefore, any treasure collected in this era would usually take the form of bags of pennies, each penny representing, roughly, a ten dollar bill.”

I pointed out, “Professor, while your information on eleventh-century financial history is fascinating, did you not notice something even more interesting in that last section?”

“I’m sorry, I don’t follow.”

“Could this be the original Robin Hood story?”

The Professor responded, “Ah yes, now I see what you are referring to. You really are very astute, Haley. Actually, Robin Hood is not an historical figure. Historians have tried to pinpoint one progenitor of all the folk legends about Robin Hood, but so far no one has succeeded. My opinion is that no one ever will, because Robin Hood was never one person. All we know is that Piers Plowman in 1377 gave the first reference to “Robyn Hood,” and in his reference he made clear that the legend of Robin Hood was already widespread in the ancient folklore of England.”

The Professor was in his element again. “The literary figure is probably a combination of a number of stories of robbers of the woods. Unquestionably, thieves were, as we have already graphically witnessed, extremely common in medieval England. Balladeers and minstrels no doubt fused the more interesting aspects of several forest thieves into our current perception of Robin and his merry men. The story cited here by Wulfric, then, could easily be one of the many stories that ultimately fused into the modern myth of Robin Hood. But let me assure you, Ealdgyth's grandmother was not Maid Marian," chuckled the Professor. "Let's resume."

While I seriously question whether Ealdgyth's grandfather actually robbed a man of the status of the Earl, and while I cannot believe that a thief gave all the money back to the peasants, I have no doubt that her grandfather was a bandit. I am sure because the mighty bow, quiver, and arrows of this robber of the wood were, upon his death, given to Ealdgyth's mother, who then gave the bow to her husband Aethelwald, Ealdgyth's father. Hunting was strictly forbidden to the peasantry anywhere in Mercia, and so the function of the bow was strictly self-defense, and if necessary, warfare. Her father kept it oiled and kept fresh strings on the bow, and, as you can imagine, it was his most prized possession.

Without the helping hands of Aelfgifu in the fields, the burden fell more and more on Ealdgyth as she was growing up. These years were no doubt responsible for Ealdgyth's serious, somber outlook on life. Her father was a mighty worker, but even he at times had trouble paying the taxes and holding onto his small strips of land. Even when the rains were normal, the threat of foreclosure and even possible enslavement was very real.

I interjected, “I am getting conflicting pictures of the peasants. Were they able to practice handstands like Wulfric and goof off all Saturday afternoon like Boy, or were they near starvation, like Ealdgyth?”

The Professor responded, “Haley, you have such a intelligent understanding of what you are hearing. You are an unusually close listener. The answer is, both. In good times, which means normal rainfall, no plagues, no wars, no Viking pillaging, no raging forest fires, no blight of insects, and no crop diseases, the peasants were able to meet and often exceed the demands placed on them by their various betters. In times, however, in which your father’s leg was amputated, as had been the case with Ealdgyth, meeting the obligations of the household, even for a strong young woman with the support of her peasant community, became close to impossible. Let’s go back.”

When I met Ealdgyth working her fields that midnight stroll of 1019, she was working to overcome an impossible tax load, and the sudden death of her father had meant the beginning of the end of her social status as a freeholding peasant. One choice she had was to become a cottager peasant, who did not own land and sold her labor by the day, but this was a very precarious position, because in the frequent periods in which no work could be found, moving away would be the only choice. This was the only choice facing her when we met, until I proposed marriage to her. Over the next few weeks, I think she reluctantly made up her mind that the security of my purse and my gentle personality outweighed the social stigma of being married to a minstrel. Our talks were always quiet, as she was a very serious, but a very pretty, young girl. Life had taken much from her. I jested for a living, and sometimes I could not make her laugh at all.

I remember the day she finally gave in. We were in her father’s cottage, two weeks after his funeral. The house was a simple rectangle, about fifteen feet across and thirty feet long, with a thatched roof and exposed beams. I glanced at her thatched walls and roof and thought the cottage was very much like my father's had been, only smaller. Just then a rooster ran outside through the low open doorway chasing a chicken. Hanging by a nail near the door was a flimsy-looking curved axe that I knew her hard-working father must have been used for protection, for chopping firewood, for digging in the ground, and for anything else that needed doing. The straw on the floor was not fresh. This house was rotting, and the musty staleness of wet straw and nesting farm animals made me miss Hereford terribly. She was sitting near her hearth, with the smoke rising toward the hole in their roof. She was making my favorite dish, tardpolane. Though she was acting as uninterested in me as ever, I guessed that she was making my favorite dinner for a reason.

I had watched her do this several times in the past weeks, and she was really quite a gifted cook. She had already soaked the quarter of a cup of ground and blanched almonds in water for a short while to make almond milk. I sat down on the straw that covered her floor and began to pet her pig. As I swatted away its flies, I asked her, frankly, what her options were if she did not marry me, if she stayed in this cottage until the looming and very awkward foreclosure. While mixing the two handfuls of flour and one long pour from the honey jar, she pointed out, "There are men in Worcester," and patted the purse which hung lightly at her leather belt.

She was certainly not alluding to her wealth, of which she had none. She was referring to the acorn she always carried with her. When I first asked her about it, she looked surprised and sharply scolded me, "Where were you reared, man? If a lady carries an acorn in her bag, then she will be blessed with perpetual youth." I had not known this before, but it made sense. She blew her hair, which had fallen out from under her veil, out of her face and strained the almond milk through a cloth into the flour and honey and began mixing it. "But I love you, and they don't," I joked.

She looked at me over her floured nose and did not smile. Instead, she simply began to knead the mixture into dough. "If I became your bride, we would save for a cottage of our own and set up as farmers once we had enough?" I thought about this a minute as she patted the dough expertly into a sheet and cut it into four-inch circles, which, when folded, formed into three-sided tart shells. As she began to fill the shells with curds I replied, "We would need to accumulate some money. The tips I can make in a single night you will not believe, Sweetie."

I slapped the pig hard, killing two flies, but the pig did not stir. Nor did Ealdgyth. She said back absently into the dim light of her home, "It would be nice to see someplace other than this one village." She pinched each tart closed, imprinted each with a cross, and then placed the tarts, just so carefully with her delicate hands, next to the fire for baking,

For the next twenty minutes we continued to discuss the matter. She was quick to list the details of a painful life on the road. I made clear to her that we would be spending many nights alone in a strange forest, being far from the peasant companionship she had always known. She snapped that she well knew this. With each of her new vivid descriptions of the humiliation and fear involved in her life ahead, she delicately turned the tarts with her bare fingers. As a result, she turned them very often, achieving an even, golden crust. I may have been more interested in the tarts than the topic, because I knew she had made up her mind. There was really no choice for her. I was, however, mildly curious about my own motivation, other than the obvious.

Earl Eadric Streona had died two years earlier and had been replaced by Earl Eglaf, to whose thegn, I am afraid, we lied. We knew that according to the Church, people were considered married in the eyes of God, but not the law, if they simply exchanged vows pledging before God their intention to be married forever, and then they consummated the vows. Although this would have rendered us married, Ealdgyth insisted on having a priest witness the ceremony and giving the blessing of the Church in order to avoid any trouble later if someone contested the marriage. We well knew the local priest would not marry us without permission of our lord, and our lord would never allow Ealdgyth to leave while the debts of her father were still unpaid. So I claimed that I was going to take up the homestead and help pay the debt, and with such an agreement in place, the priest performed the ceremony.

Our wedding night was not as special as I had hoped. We spent the early evening packing clothes onto ourselves and eating what food there was in the house. In the middle of the night, we packed her few things quietly onto my donkey, and I threw her grandfather's mighty bow around my shoulders. I admit, I had tried it earlier when I was alone, but I could not fully extend the bowstring. I didn't care, though, because I knew that a minstrel traveling alone needed little defense. I kissed the pig, slaughtered and packed it, and we left Worcester never to return.

The birth of our child Gunnehilde moved me greatly, and our days together, my Little Bear and I, brought me utter happiness, as well as an ongoing loss of sleep that I had never before experienced. Although I could not conceive how at the time, I was sure that with Little Bear I would reverse my earlier sins; I would cleanse myself of the pain of my mother and my childhood friend Eadburh. Yet Gunnehilde's life, as I have said in my own chronicle, was very difficult. The situation was really completely miserable, and remained so for many wet, cold days, which turned into weeks. The weeks of filth, fear, and social ostracism turned into months, and on into two years. It rains quite often in England, does it not?

This life ended tragically one night. Gunnehilde was almost two, and we were camped in the deep forest on our way from Lothian to Bamburgh, which I had hoped would be my final show. The night was clear, and we had a fine dinner of dried apples, hard black bread, and an herbed wheat soup that was one of our regular meals. We finished, and the baby had finally fallen asleep from her day of walking and riding the donkey. It was summer, and the crickets played their lullaby all around us, helping keep the baby fast asleep. Ealdgyth and I soon also went to sleep, making sure the fire was roaring before we turned in. We always woke up in the middle of the night to stoke the fire. It was our routine.

Deep in the night, I awoke with a start to the black of night. The fire was out! We had slept too deeply! Worse, I realized that our crickets had stopped. Before I could even throw off my covers, I froze at the low chorus of growls that made my body cringe involuntarily. The growls graduated to snarls and I knew that this was my end. I sent out a silent prayer only to see Ealdgyth dart away into the woods!

"Light the fire now!" she screamed as first six, and then another six wolves materialized from the forest and took off after her. I jumped up and threw leaves and sticks onto the bed of hot embers, and the fire started back up quickly, as I piled small logs onto it.

Then I heard her sad screams, and the furious sound of a dozen attacking wolves. No heavy log was burning enough to use as a torch, and I could do nothing. If I took the baby and went to help Ealdgyth, we would all surely perish horribly; if I left her at the fire alone, she was in grave danger by both the fire and the wolves. Suddenly I threw the blanket into the fire, and it caught quickly. With the blanket burning brightly around my right hand, and my screaming Gunnehilde safely in my other arm, I ran at the furious sound that was still raging. When I arrived, flaming blanket in hand, I found nothing. I continued to grip the searing blanket, though my burns were already severe. As I looked over the scene, I saw all I needed to see.

Her blood and her hair were everywhere, her tunic shredded, her purse spilled, her acorn bloody. I knew that the burns of my hand would already be so severe that they might result in a deadly festering. And I surrendered. Still keeping the blanket afire to ward off the wolves, I rushed back to our campfire and finally threw the blanket down. I put Gunnehilde down to wail. I frantically poured all our ale on my smoking hand, which soothed the burns considerably until the horn promptly emptied, at which time the fire inside my hand flared up again, as if I were still holding that burning blanket. Ealdgyth had acted on impulse, an impulse that saved me and saved her baby. She had been given a choice, and she chose to be generous to her family, to give to us the gift of living on, allowing us to enjoy the seasons as they faded into years. She had used her own life as a shield, and this shield had held death at a distance from us. Though you will never know her, Boy, she was a good mother to your grandmother Gunnehilde, and in the most real sense, Ealdgyth was a good mother to me and to you.

Gunnehilde was shrieking uncontrollably, and I knew I had to calm her with my good hand. I picked her up and began to rock her in my arms, right hand dangling. With a soothing voice I quieted her questions about "Mama?" "Mama?" and told her that Mama was just fine, that she would be back soon to take care of us. All night I shook in fear of those wolves and of the future and I rocked my Little Bear. "Baa, baa, black sheep, have you any wool? Yes sir, yes sir, three bags full. One for master Eadric, and one for my dame, none for the little girl who lives in the lane. Baa, baa, black sheep, have you any wool? Yes sir, yes, sir, three bags full." After a few verses of this sad tune, Gunnehilde was asleep, and all was quiet. The throbbing in my hand made no sound, nor did the fear in my eyes. Only my grief escaped occasionally, the sound of hard sobbing muffled. One day had ended for Gunnehilde and tomorrow a new life was to begin for my Little Bear. I prayed and rocked until far into the night, and then I too began to fall into deep sleep just as Gunnehilde and the sun were rising.

In a state of near exhaustion I approached Bamburgh. I was told of a miller who was wealthy, and knowing absolutely nothing else to do, I hid the donkey in the woods and simply waited until Gunnehilde's nap. Then I left your grandmother Gunnehilde on the doorstep and ran. At the edge of the forest I turned to be sure I had not been seen, to be sure that my stigma of minstrelsy was forever washed from her. The baby lay sleeping, and I had not been seen. In that moment I swore an oath to myself that I would return, and somehow, I would give Gunnehilde a gift so valuable that she would forgive me everything. Turning away from her at that tree wrenched my heart so fully that it never recovered, and it has really never even begun to heal. My mother. My childhood friend Eadburh. My wife Ealdgyth. My daughter Gunnehilde. Lord, have mercy on my soul. Sometimes I feel that God has let me live nine decades because it has taken so long to prepare my special place in hell.

The actual abandoning of the baby I have never regretted; it was the only way. No, my blame lay in getting to that point in the first place. God had given me Grace, a second chance at making up for killing my mother in childbirth and for letting my Eadburh be sold into slavery. I did not deserve this second chance. And I squandered this Grace shamefully. As I led my donkey slowly southward over the next few weeks, my hand began to scar over nicely. The callus would help me to never forget this week. A rough and callused hand might even help my juggling, I thought. One of my curses has always been refusing to accept horror, deflecting it at every turn. For this, too, God will judge me all too soon. So ends the story of your great-grandmother Ealdgyth.

This was my great grandmother, Ealdgyth. Poor woman. She seemed so humorless, so devoid of hope. She was so different from my Emma. Emma, with her sooty face and soiled tunics, shared Ealdgyth's earthiness, but their dispositions could not have been more different. I remember arriving at the orchard one Saturday after having cleaned the guild cesspool. I worried about it all the way to Surrey, since as far as I knew I had literally never taken a bath, and she was nobility, and so of course had bathed dozens of times in her life. But my smell had not bothered her; in fact on this day I remember her face being particularly smeared, and I remember we had a particularly light-hearted and enjoyable afternoon.

For the second time, I noticed Rexy approaching the dead body of Wulfric and licking his face, which I thought odd and a little disturbing. For some reason, she seemed fascinated with him. But she walked away soon enough, only to step over to the cliff and stretch. The other three sides of the clearing went on apparently indefinitely, but the cliff, which was just a little beyond my strangely arranged campsite, looked sheer. Rexy looked off vacantly, and then walked aimlessly toward the woods to the right. Suddenly, she jumped back, her hackles up like a porcupine, her fierce bark continuous.

What then materialized dwarfed the earlier terrors of this evening. There were dozens and dozens of men and women, dressed and undressed in bizarre fashion, edging the woods on the right side of the camp, just staring at me. I knew I had to be dreaming when they started to gradually advance on me. But of course, I was not. These were real men and women who followed the old ways, and someone had told them of my amulet. I turned to flee, only to find the opposite side ringed equally with these ghostly figures, many wearing small pointed hats, some carrying brooms or pitchforks. The circle was closing in on me, and Rexy, standing firmly next to me, continued to bark fearlessly and ferociously. I think she was actually holding all one hundred of them at bay, as if their magic could slay me but not a dog.

Finally, the throng stopped, and one withered-up old man emerged from the masses to speak. “Throw your amulet and we will spare the dog.” My first impulse was to throw the amulet. But the unsavory expressions of many of the women who were framed by the fire, many of whom were carrying only broomsticks, checked my impulse. The scene suddenly put me in mind of the descriptions I had heard back in London of the sabats of Satan that were said to occur on full moons. Our moon, however, was not full. There was no moon at all tonight.

Every puzzle has a solution, that was what I always told myself. Of course, Emma had thrown this back in my face the day of my departure. With no weapon, what could I do? And even if I had twenty swords, this horde numbered almost one hundred.

“Throw the Red Amulet now,” repeated the approaching wizard, who was now infuriated.

"We know now that you have it." Then the solution presented itself to me. Wulfric had prepared me for this. I stood on the rock that Wulfric was leaning on and pulled the amulet out, holding it high in the air.

They all recoiled like a snake. "I curse you," I began, "if you ever lay hands or eyes on me again, after this very moment, your life and afterlife will be forever cursed. Then I began Wulfric's chant, "A charm I know no king can say or any man has mastered;" at this point the throng screamed and ran wildly into the forest. By the time I had finished the line, "Help it is called because it aids at times of sickness and sorrow," there was not one of the specters to be seen, and their sound receded into the forest. I also thought I heard one lone horse gallop off, but through the fading wails I could not be sure. Throughout my life, I was never troubled again about my amulet.

This explains the rush to read the book, I surmised. But I wondered how Wulfric could have known of this ambush—he had claimed that no one knew the location of the amulet. What had the furious wizard meant by "We know now that you have it? How could information have just been given to them? Had I heard a horse? In any event, the threat had been eliminated, and I was very grateful to Wulfric for my gift. I was ready for another story.

"Unbelievable," said the Professor. "An actual account of a witch's sabat. I need to add a sociologist friend of mine to the list of people for me to call when this is over."

I had been absolutely spellbound by the reading, and I found Boy charming. The Professor asked, "Haley, what do you make of all this?"

I had been listening closely to the Professor's commentaries and for some unknown reason I decided to sarcastically mock him.

"Well," I began, "I think that these attackers were believers not in the original Anglo-Saxons gods like Woden or Thunor, but of the much more ancient Celtic gods and demigods that predated the Saxon migration." When I finished, I felt a hot flash of shame as I wondered why I lashed out like this at people. He did not seem to notice the sarcasm.

"You grasp this as if you were a natural born historian," said the Professor. "Are you sure accounting is the major for you?"

I was grateful he had not taken offense and found, to my surprise, that his praise soothed my condition like aloe on sunburn. It was as if his praise was what had grounded me in the secure feeling that I had basked in since early in the evening.

I continued, this time with no sarcasm, "It does make sense that while Boy didn't believe a bit in the power of the amulet, he completely understood that the witches and wizards believed in that hocus pocus completely. No fighter could have beaten up these attackers, but he found the one way to stay alive. I like him."

"Well put," said Professor O'Shea. "Nelson?"

"I think someone sold Boy out. I think that person was the horseman, and I think he is still a threat. If he is not still a threat, then what threat was Wulfric referring to in his opening note?"

The Professor nodded in agreement, stared at one of his stuffed dodo birds, and let himself get lost in thought. Suddenly he snapped back to the present and blurted, "I need to take a quick break. Meet back here in five minutes!"

Chapter Eight

The Legend of the Holy Grail

As I sat on the polar bear playing with its soft fur, I was thinking. Not about the stalker, not about the Professor, not about Boy, but about Wulfric. It was dawning on me that he must have spent years working on this book for his great-grandson, just so Boy could know his story and understand the sacrifices made by his ancestors. Wulfric giving up all those years of his life to create this book was so generous. *Who could do this? Not me.* The darkness fell again as I became more and more sure that I had no such generosity in me. I could never live up to the standard of Wulfric. *How could I, given how we were raised by Mom and Dad?*

The Professor had gone upstairs to the living room to put the gun back on its rack above the fireplace and Nelson had headed for the bathroom. For some reason I could not stop thinking about Mom and Dad and how different they were from Wulfric. Generosity was really not their style. Why could I not stop thinking about my own parents? Maybe being back in the Professor's house was stirring up my childhood memories, and making me compare my parents to Wulfric and the Professor. The Professor definitely had strong fathering skills. I loved his den, which was just like we had left it before going to the library, inviting and comfortable as always. Automatically, I flipped on the TV and immediately began to tune out the CNN reporter, who was harping again on the deadlocked conference of the world's religious leaders at the Vatican. I knelt there on the fuzzy white rug with my knees together and waited on the men. Staring into space I lost myself again in the roulette wheel of my bad memories.

It stopped on the Exxon station. Once, when we had no food in the house and they were working late again, Nelson and I decided to use Dad's Exxon credit card. The plan was to walk down our hill about a mile and buy snacks for dinner at the local gas station. Going this way we had to pass Anthony's, an extremely expensive Italian restaurant where Mom and Dad took us on birthdays if they could afford it. We both looked in the front window to see what people in there were doing and eating. Nelson pointed them out to me in a corner table. I would have never seen them. They were eating desert. Each of them had a desert.

We didn't say a word to each other, just turned and dragged on toward the Exxon where I bought myself three boxes of my favorite pop-tarts and a big root beer. We ate on the sidewalk outside the Exxon and watched down the street until our parents came out of the restaurant, laughing and in one car. When we got home they weren't there, and they didn't show up for hours. Nelson never understood how that had hurt me so much. Denial-boy always insisted, "If they had a dinner break, why shouldn't they eat together? They *are* married."

This state of mind was interrupted by my brother's voice upstairs in the kitchen. He was on the phone.

Bounding down the steps, Nelson snapped off the TV and reported, "I just left a message for Mom and Dad about this amazing book," sounding disappointed. "I told them I'd try back later."

His voice always gave him away. "So what's wrong?"

"Nothing."

"Tell me, Nelson, or I'll hurt you."

"Well, crap. I checked the messages remotely, to try to find them, and they're fighting again. Mom needs two hundred and two dollars for antibiotics for a yeast infection she has and Dad left a very shrill message in response saying the money 'just isn't there.' There are several more very nasty rounds of this fight on the machine, but I don't think you want to hear about them."

"Don't worry, I don't." I hopped up and pushed myself back into a leather chair and pulled my knees up to my chest, wondering again why my mother had held that night job for years, neglecting us completely, so that her daughter could go to college and fail out. *Why did it have to be this way? Nelson belonged here, everybody knew that. But if I just dropped out,* I often figured, *the tuition would only be half.* The guilt of my horrible grades so far this semester had now grown unbearable. Now, the news of our parents' sacrifice costing my Mama, who I did love dearly, her antibiotics was too much for a girl already far too near the edge of hopelessness.

The Professor returned and sat down in his comfortable brown leather chair. There was a pipe in a tray on the table next to the Professor, but out of courtesy he had not smoked it yet tonight. He lit it up now, which was perhaps a sign that the stress of this evening was beginning to affect him.

As the smell of his cherry tobacco wafted through the room, Nelson asked, "Is this book for real? It's interesting, but could such a book have been written in the 1100s, and be about the 1000s? And could any book have survived this long? And did people really live to be ninety-six? I thought people all died when they were thirty back then?"

The Professor, visibly relieved to be back in his chair, crossed one leg over the other and said, "I've been wondering the same sorts of things myself. At first, it seemed quite improbable and I wondered if you two were playing some sort of joke. First, I've been wondering if a book with such strong paper pages and such clear, round script could even have survived. But then, I know of twenty-one that have. Why not twenty-two? Second, to the question of what Wulfric's motivation could possibly be, I remember several references to the urge for older people of that era to record their lives in order to set the record straight in preparation for their judgment by God. This would have been very typical of the period, if writing were at all common, which it certainly was not. Third, could both Wulfric and Boy be literate? Now this is what is so unlikely, but scribes certainly did exist, and a servant at a guild could have learned to write, as long as a noble arranged for the education for some grand purpose. Fourth, could Wulfric have written in Old English two or three decades after the Norman Conquest ushered in the use of Middle English in England? The answer here again is yes, several Old English manuscripts survive which are clearly written as late as the twelfth century."

"Finally, as to life expectancy, you are not correct about everyone dying in their thirties. The average life expectancy in this period was indeed in the thirties, but this statistic is misleading because it reflects only an average. Thirty was the average because up to half the babies born did not survive past age five. If a person did survive past twenty, he or she could reasonably expect to live to be seventy. Anglo-Saxon records prior to 1066 specify that legal obligations of a physical nature—such as fighting and plowing—ended at age sixty, but legal obligations of a mental nature—counseling, for example—ended at age seventy. Ninety-six, then, was about as biologically unlikely as it is today but not historically incorrect. The book, then, is quite possibly historically valid and is, moreover, fascinating! By the way, though I will be pronouncing this ancestor's name 'Reece,' it is actually spelled in the text, 'R-h-y-s'. Let's resume."

Rhys, my mother's paternal grandfather. That means my mother's father's father. That means my maternal grandfather's father. Rhys, though, is a name I've never heard before. It is neither like the English, Saxon names of the guild, nor is it at all Norman French. But at least Rhys has a name, something other than "Boy." My initial hesitation about the name, I soon realized, lay in a vague awareness that the name reminded me of the names of a few Welsh traders that sometimes harassed me down in Southwark, the market across the Thames River. The Welsh, though, are the lowest form of life. I might be an orphan. I might be descended from a minstrel great-grandfather who was denied the sacraments. I might even be descended from his illegal bride who was herself descended from robbers and murderers. But at least I was not Welsh, I thought, as I surveyed the design illuminated by dim firelight on that plateau:

Wulfric Rhys

Bag Bag

Ealdgyth Bag

Bag Bag

Bag Fire Bag

Bag Bag

Bag Bag

Your great-grandfather Rhys was not English; he was from Wales. I know what you must think of the Welsh but before you dismiss this completely as not possible and move to the next chronicle, listen for a moment. First, your great-grandmother described in the next chronicle was Welsh too, so there is no getting around it. One fourth of you harkens from the western mountains that the famous King Arthur was said to be from. The point to be made about Rhys, though, is that he was a very special Welshman, and in fact was nothing like the dishonest scoundrels that trade in the corners of London in my time. Rhys, in fact, never "welched" on a deal in his life, and he came far closer to actual sainthood than I ever will.

Born in 999, son of his mother Rhiannon and his father Gwydion, Rhys seemed different to his parents at the start. It was really quite obvious. While the other boys played at stick fighting in their youngest years and enjoyed war games in their latter youth, Rhys spent much of his time in prayer. He told his parents that prayer was where he found his happiness, and they allowed him this predisposition. They even fostered his path toward the priesthood, once they determined that godliness was simply how he was born. Some of us are lucky enough to know our destiny even from the start.

Rhys was born in Cardigan, the coastal region of Wales at its center west.

Here the Professor brought his laser pointer to bear on the oversized map of Anglo-Saxon England again, pointing out Wales and Cardigan. The Professor continued,

As a boy he served as an assistant, something

like our acolyte or altar boy, in his local parish and then he began assisting the local bishop, Bishop Melan. The bishop was quite impressed, and Rhys was soon ordained a priest. His ministry to the people of western Wales was really a blessing. From the start, he was a natural pastor, tending to the people of the several parishes which were part of his circuit. His life in his early twenties essentially entailed visiting the sick, and the villagers informed me that Rhys would somehow know when someone was sick even before anyone in the village had been informed. Families would spend the entirety of a long night tending to a sick son, only to find in the morning light Rhys praying in their side garden, having been there in the cold, alongside them, through the night. He would come and sit by the bed, chatting with the infirm, relating the news of the district. Toward the end of the visit he would pray with the sick, and finally he would pray alone at the foot of the bed, ending by blanketing the infirm in the blessings of the Father, the Son, and the Holy Ghost. This blessing would often bring tears of comfort to people who otherwise had no hope. The family would thank him for the visit, and for his kind and so comforting words to the one afflicted. Then they would be surprised to find that he did not leave. He would simply pray, out of their way, in the garden, until they needed him. The comfort spread by this man became legendary, and he was considered by many in the region of Cardigan to be the standard of priests.

His brief homilies held fantastic power simply because his message was so genuine, so altogether lacking in hypocrisy. News of his relocation to Powys, which was at that time a separate kingdom in northern Wales, was a heavy blow to the people of the region, who had grown to rely heavily on Rhys. Yet Bishop Melan had a vision, and it included the transfer of Rhys. In his five years in Cardigan, he inspired many people to renew their faith in their hearts, and all the people of western Wales loved him as a good father and bid him a very affectionate farewell.

The first half of the eleventh century was truly a troubled and chaotic period for the Welsh Church, and Rhys took his orders from Bishop Melan as a call to stabilize the northern region of Powys for Christ. As he had hoped, his reputation preceded him, and he more than lived up to it in this new region. When preaching and tending to the sick, his own needs and personal comfort were always forfeited. He always refused all offers of dinner and hospitality in order to impart more powerfully his faith in God to his flock. Before the end of his first year, all the people of Powys already loved Rhys as a good father. Especially one.

Angharad was a beautiful peasant girl, splendid to behold.

Here the Professor interjected, "this next section will be about a woman whose name I will pronounce, 'Anger-rod,' but whose name is spelled on these pages as 'A-n-g-h-a-r-a-d'. Where was I? Yes,"

Angharad was a beautiful peasant girl, splendid to behold. She bore a very round, full face that was utterly symmetric. Framing her unusually smooth complexion and her almond-shaped hazel eyes was a long braid that wrapped around her neck and fell down the front of her tunics. She attracted so much attention from the warriors of Powys, in northern Wales, that she learned early to shun all advances. She was twenty when Rhys was reassigned to her diocese, if such a Roman concept as diocese can be applied to the wild Welsh region where Bishop Melan generally directed Rhys to minister. When Angharad's father, Gwyll, took sick one afternoon, Rhys visited the next day to spend a few minutes. Gwyll recovered nicely. Angharad watched the priest's gentle demeanor and was swept away by him. He was a stark contrast to the bullies that she was accustomed to. In those days, priests typically married, although the practice was disapproved of more and more by the papacy as the eleventh century progressed. In the 1020s, though, it was acceptable for a priest to take a wife, as long as she did not interfere with his duties. She made sure that she did not.

He saw no good reason to refuse her attention. So Bishop Melan married them in a small affair in a squarish stone church on the banks of the River Clwyd, in far northern Wales. Standing under the arched stone doors of the Church, they were wed. Within the year, Mynyddawg was born. This year was 1025.

The Professor interrupted, "I will be pronouncing this name as 'mini-dog,' but it is actually spelled on these yellowing pages in the classic Welsh fashion, 'M-y-n-y-d-d-a-w-g.' I regret, however, that otherwise I can be of little help explaining eleventh-century Welsh history. There is almost no written record that survives, you see, other than some beautiful Welsh poetry and scattered references in the *Anglo-Saxon Chronicles*, an English source that views the Welsh as only marauding criminals. I do know that under the Powys king, Hywel Dda "The Good," who ruled from around 900 until 950, the learned monks of the kingdom were called together to write the laws bearing this king's name. Thus, we know that literate priests existed. I also know that the Welsh

Church had since 768 A. D. agreed with Rome on the date of Easter. Other details are simply do not exist. Let's resume!"

Rhys and Mynyddawg spent much time together, as you would expect from such a sensitive man. Rhys also turned more and more to prayer and meditation. Angharad often watched her husband as he prayed out in their garden. She was very proud of him for being such a good man, and she felt like the luckiest person in the world to be his wife. Many years went by and Mynyddawg grew to be a bright and daring young boy of sixteen. He watched his father retire most late afternoons into the woods to spend the rest of the daylight in prayer. Mynyddawg watched this, but he never fully understood it.

When the two would talk, it became apparent that Mynyddawg was called to be neither a soldier nor a priest. Mynyddawg wanted to roam far from his war-torn homeland of Wales, an idea put into his head first and often by his mother. She had always hated the warring, the raids that brought back such booty from Mercia and Wessex. What were not brought back all too often, Angharad often lamented with the women at the local marketplace, were the boys. Angharad fostered Mynyddawg's notions of himself as a trader, as someone who wanted to learn about and profit from other cultures outside Wales. Throughout the decade of his adolescence, she would send him to the market to volunteer to help any traders who passed through. Mynyddawg gained much knowledge of the world and trading practices from these visits. Mynyddawg would also spend hours talking to the slaves who had been taken on the raids into western England. He even learned some Anglo-Saxon. Finally, Mynyddawg approached his parents with the plan for his life. He would leave, as soon as possible, for the east, and he would never come back until he was quite wealthy.

Now Rhys believed in following your heart, and Angharad believed in getting out while you're still alive. Neither thought much about the extreme rarity of any kind of travel in this era, or why it was so rare. It was rare because it was deadly. Brigands and pirates roamed freely, unchecked by any authority, and they left no witnesses. In fact, of the vast number of social strata in England, really only three groups of people traveled to any significant extent: minstrels, mercenaries, and traders. So at the age of nineteen, Mynyddawg left for London, to seek his fortune, good or bad, never to return to Wales. Before his departure, father and son embraced long and warm, and then he was gone. Rhys tended to stay a bit distant from the family, so no one was surprised that he was able to let go so easily. But Rhys himself was a little surprised, and pleased, that Angharad did not seem more upset at Mynyddawg's leaving.

One day soon after Mynyddawg had departed, as the Normans of your London say--we English just say "left"--Angharad called Rhys inside their small cottage. She was obviously upset, and he gave her his full attention. She told him news that would send his life on a very different course. She stood alone in the middle of the room, hands to her side, and began to cry convulsively. Her face was bloated with redness and her cheeks were sticky with tears. She blurted it out: she had been unfaithful.

Rhys was shocked and disappointed, but on another level, he understood that he was different from the warriors. He had always known this, and so now he somewhat understood the sadness and loneliness that must have driven her to the infidelity. "It was the King, Gruffydd ap Llywelyn," she had admitted, "And I love him." And then the fact that meant the sure end to the marriage: "And I am carrying his child." This was the year 1044. Gruffydd was a powerful man, the king of Powys and also the king of Gwynedd, the kingdom in northwestern Wales that he had conquered five years earlier.

"Well, if this is our family tree, it's just getting better and better," I moaned to Nelson. "Now we descend from a circus freak, a shrew, a holy roller, and a tramp."

The Professor ignored this and continued…

Rhys was not surprised that his wife had the attention of the king, although I think "warlord" might be a more apt description of Gruffydd. Rhys had long known that she had grown up in his attentions, and that Gruffydd had even courted her before their marriage. His loyal parishioners sometimes warned Rhys that Gruffydd asked about Angharad whenever he passed near. But Rhys had never expected Gruffydd to accumulate so much power, and he had never expected Gruffydd to maintain interest in Angharad after all these years. She was, after all, thirty-eight. But then, she looked twenty-three. And Rhys looked all of his forty-four years. He forgave her completely.

As a priest with an adulterous wife, an annulment was the only recourse. In fact, adultery was one of the extremely rare cases in which an annulment would be granted. The bishop granted it freely, and Rhys prepared to begin a new life. The truth would be kept from Mynyddawg, since his parents thought it would be years, if ever, until his return. Rhys then gathered his few things into his bag, said tearful goodbyes to the people of his parishes, and set out southwesterly for a new day. The adultery was a blessing in disguise, he thought; the Lord was working mysteriously again. He was finally going to begin his true life's calling. He was finally going to become a monk.

St. David's monastery in Dyfed, southwestern Wales, was a completely different world from what Rhys had been used to. Most priests could never adapt to the rigid discipline of monastic life; Rhys took to it like an eel to water. Upon arrival, Rhys underwent the ceremony of initiation for a novice, after which a Mass was celebrated. At this Mass Rhys was shaved and given the tonsure, which involved shaving the top of the head to leave a circle of hair just above the ears. In England the lower head is also shaved to symbolize a crown of thorns, but in Wales the tradition is to let the remaining hair fall to the shoulders. It is said that Rhys looked the part perfectly.

Rhys found the unyielding discipline of St. David's refreshing and cleansing. His day was structured around the seven prayer services in the chapel, the first of which was Nocturns and Lauds, observed at 2:30 in the morning. Then, about two hours apart, came Prime at daylight, Terce at midmorning, Sext at midday, None at mid-afternoon, and Vespers before supper. His day was made up of work and prayer, ending finally with the service of Compline immediately before sleep.

His novitiate ended after one year. After the ceremony in which he took his vows for a lifetime of poverty and service, he donned the cowl, a floor-length tunic with a long hood attached. In the first months of wearing it, Rhys was very proud of the cowl and what it represented to all who saw him wear it. It was in this cowl that Rhys spent the rest of his days in the drafts and the cold of a monastery.

He was to put it on under the covers before getting out of bed; he was to use its hood to cover himself when walking inside or outside the monastery. In fact, every aspect of life was dictated for the monks at St. David's. Meat was forbidden. Rhys was expected never to run, under any conditions except fire or the death of another monk. Walking, he was expected to keep his head bowed; standing, he was expected to keep his feet even; seated, he was expected to sit four feet from the next monk. What was most comforting to Rhys, though, was the silence. The brothers did not speak in the refectory during meals. Ever. They did not speak while working in the kitchen. Ever. And they did not speak in the dormitories. Ever. The speech in other places was kept to an absolute minimum. In fact, the silence was so all-pervasive that they developed the use of their own sign language; for example, the sign for beans was to place the tip of the index finger at the first joint of the thumb, making the end of the thumb stick out. And as for contact with the opposite sex, monks were forbidden to talk to or look directly at women for the rest of their lives. The monastic life would never have become available to Rhys but for his annulment.

Rhys excelled at all he was required to do. He sat in the chapter, the communal meetings held every morning, and watched many monks disciplined with beating or even worse. But Rhys was always an observer. He was a model monk, considerate and utterly devoted to his discipline, his prayer, his silence, and his writings. Rhys was taught the reading and writing of Latin, which he had not known at all as a parish priest. The memorization of the Mass in Latin had worked nicely. Here at St. David's, however, literacy was required because in the afternoons he engaged in a variety of tasks including the writing of histories of the lives of saints and, most importantly, transcribing the Bible.

His work was so exemplary that he gained the notice of the abbot, who appointed Rhys to the office of Precentor after only Rhys' eighth year as a monk. The Precentor was in charge of the library and scriptorium, or writing room, and Rhys took on his new position with all his usual vigor and compassion. It was as Precentor that Rhys set out to reorganize a back room of the library one day around 1050. After he had taken books off a bottom shelf, one of the pages fell out and fell through the back of the shelving. Thinking that this bottom shelf rested on the stone floor that made up the rest of this back room, Rhys went for a piece of iron and pried up a flooring stone in order to get the lost sheet.

What he saw in the hidden space below, in addition to the lost sheet of paper, was a loose, heavy, snake-like object. He reached in and picked up the strange link chain, as long as his arm, which he first thought was iron because of its weight, but after wiping the grime off part of a link, he gasped to discover it was made of solid gold. It was worth a fortune. In the dim afternoon light of this back room, Rhys toyed with the object. It had many irregularities protruding from it. He noticed that if the links were pulled apart, they hung loosely like a dead snake. But if each end of the limp snake were twisted in opposite directions with surprisingly little force, and at the same time the two ends were pushed toward each other, the snake snapped into a rigid rod about as long as a hand and forearm combined. Once erect, strange one-inch spikes randomly poked off one side of the shaft, like the teeth of a key. When limp, the eye at one end could be clipped into a catch at the other to form a circle.

The exotic eastern workmanship of the device made Rhys think it was very old, though since gold is the only metal that will not rust or tarnish over the centuries, he could not date the piece from the condition of the metal. It was, however, covered in what appeared to be decades or even centuries of grime. He decided not to polish it, since the gold would then be extremely noticeable even at a distance. The device was definitely very sturdy, he thought, as he moved the piece from its rigid to its limp setting and back. After looking into the hole further, in the quiet of that little closet Rhys found one more thing. A note.

The note, written in perfect Latin, made a claim that agitated Rhys quite a bit, which was a difficult thing to do. The note claimed that the object was "the Grailkey," a device to be inserted into a hole in the basement of the Temple of Solomon in Jerusalem. Once the key is fully inserted up to the final spike, the note instructed, insert an iron bar into the eye of the key and twist to the right seven full rotations. It said to twist to the left brings disaster. It said the keyhole is in the Star of David. It said no more.

"Whoa," said Nelson.

The Professor, almost whispering to himself, said "The monastery that discovered and housed the Holy Grail would be important indeed."

Nelson interrupted and objected, "Wulfric makes it sound like the Holy Grail would be considered merely another holy relic, like the fingers of saints that I've always heard they loved to collect."

The Professor responded, "Perhaps in that age the Grail was perceived in the same vein as the other relics of Christ and the saints. Pieces of the True Cross, for example, were bought and sold throughout the medieval period. Perhaps the fact that the Grail is referred to like any other relic should not be viewed so much as a devaluation of the Grail, but rather should be seen as insight into the inexpressible value our ancestors placed on all relics. They thought of their relics with the awe in which we hold the Holy Grail today. This being said, the Grail even then was considered the premier relic, but it was thought unobtainable."

Nelson also asked, "Was there traffic enough between Wales and Jerusalem for the key to be at St. David's? That seems impossible."

"Yes, again. Archbishop Ealdred of York, for example, in 1058 during a voyage to collect his pallium--the symbol of his authority--in Rome, traveled on to Jerusalem before returning to England. Also, the Welsh at some point obtained the rod of Moses in Rome, and through the same avenue, theoretically, the Grailkey could have been obtained. Additionally, St. David was consecrated Archbishop of Wales while in Jerusalem in the 800s. The Grailkey conceivably could have been brought to Wales at that point. There were definitely opportunities for such a transport to have occurred. Let's resume."

Rhys replaced the Grailkey, the shelf and the books, and, after memorizing it for some time, destroyed the note in the fire on his next trip to the calefactory, which is the room where monks warmed themselves when their hands had stiffened and their inkwells had frozen. Rhys' concern was that he could not be sure that this information would not be exploited, and in fact, with such a valuable find, very few were pure enough to be trusted with the cup of Christ. It was better left safe, he concluded. He told no one of the find for many years, and then, as you will soon learn, your great-grandfather Rhys was forced to break his silence.

The abbot summoned Rhys to his office chamber one day and announced very important news. The monastery at Cluny, in eastern France, had sent word that they desired a monk from St. David's to become a part of their order. Cluny was the premier monastery in Europe, and such a communication with St. David's was a major honor, especially since the Welsh Church was constantly attempting to separate itself from the archbishopric of Canterbury in England. A direct association with Cluny would position the Welsh Church as fully autonomous of the English Church. The Cluniac movement, which had started during the tenth century, had reformed the Church profoundly, and its monks were said to be the purest and most devout in Christendom.

The Abbot continued, "After discussing it among the officers, we are unanimous that you would represent us best. You will depart within three weeks by ship to Normandy, then on by land to Burgundy, where the monastery is located. You will never return to Wales. You and the French will understand each other because they, like us, speak only Latin while in the monastery. They will endow you with a new Latin name."

While this was a great honor, it posed a dilemma regarding the Grailkey. Finally Rhys decided that he would choose the most trustworthy monk at St. David's and impart the secret to him, first exacting an oath that he was never to tell anyone with the exception of his son Mynyddawg, who could be trusted completely. A provision was made to allow the information to be passed to someone who could prove that he came as an agent of Mynyddawg.

Rhys knew that one day Mynyddawg would come for information about his father, and Domnus Rhigyfarch, a monk much younger than Rhys but equally serious, was chosen for the task. Mynyddawg was to be identified by the birthmark under his right buttock. The responsibility for the secret of the Grailkey weighed heavily on the young, earnest monk, who hoped one day to be able to free himself of its awesome pressure. Yet he dutifully memorized the contents of the letter that Rhys had found by the Grailkey and which Rhys had himself remembered exactly.

Rhys drilled the young monk until Rhigyfarch set into his memory the details: that the object was to be inserted into a hole in the basement of the Temple of Solomon in Jerusalem, that once the key was fully inserted up to the final spike, an iron bar was to be inserted into the eye of the key and one was to twist to the right seven full rotations. To twist to the left brought disaster. The hole was in the Star of David. The young monk guarded the secret well for years.

Though he didn't write anything about the Grail, that being secured only in Rhigyfarch's memory, Rhys wrote the remainder of his entire life's story down in Welsh so that Domnus Rhigyfarch could be precise should Mynyddawg ever come. The page was adorned with an elaborate illumination. I include this insert on the following page of this chronicle. With the Grailkey in order, Rhys left Dyfed and Wales, never to return.

Nelson looked at the page written in Welsh, and admired the elaborate and beautiful design of interlaced leaves and flowers surrounding the large, brightly-colored first letter of the page. I could tell from where I sat in my big leather chair that the color was still quite vibrant, but at the same time faded. I barely looked over at the page because I was still dazed and very, very angry that Angharad had betrayed her husband so hurtfully. *Why do people stab each other, and cut each other down? This woman was never to be forgiven. Never.*

The Professor was reading the page as well as he could, considering it was written in medieval Welsh, and when he finished he announced that it seemed less specific than Wulfric's biography. The Professor assured us that "if Wulfric skips anything on this page, I'll let you know."

Eastern France was filled with many sensual delights, few of which ever penetrated the walls of the monastery at Cluny. These monks were Benedictines, and their habits were pure black. The distinctive Cluny bow or salute, effected many times a day, almost touched the floor. Cluny was definitely equipped better than St. David's. The facilities here in eastern France included running water, separate latrines for novices and monks, and several meditative cloisters other than the main cloister at the front gate. The monks of Cluny were accustomed to foreign monks joining the order, staying a short while, and then being expelled for lack of discipline.

"Professor, how disciplined did they have to be?"

"Nelson, if a monk said one word, bowed improperly one time, sat one inch too near another in the refectory, or set one foot outside the cloister without permission, he would be publicly beaten, and sometimes imprisoned."

The Professor resumed…

His Welsh origins at first caused many to question Rhys' discipline and even his faith, but over time he was able to win virtually everyone over. Utter devotion and a gentle kindness win most hearts over time. At the age of seventy-five, his success at Cluny was immortalized when he was chosen as Claustral Prior of Cluny, third in authority at the most powerful monastery in Christendom. Rhys' duties were to oversee all of Cluny's two hundred monks, which he did dutifully until the end of his days.

Now I must reveal how I came to know so many intimate details of a man whose son married your grandmother. In 1078, as I approached the age of eighty, I undertook a very dangerous trip to the western tip of Wales. This was actually not the last journey I was to make to accumulate these chronicles. Servants in the household of Mynyddawg had given me the last known location of your great-grandfather Rhys.

Upon my arrival at St. David's, I explained my errand to the porter, who supervised the arrival of visitors. Domnus Rhigyfarch, now Precentor, would speak to me only outside the monastery. As you might expect, he absolutely refused to share any information with me until I established my identity as an agent of Mynyddawg. Since I anticipated such a need, back in northern Wales I had asked the servants of Mynyddawg for identifying information, and I had been told his favorite foods, a poem his mother used to recite, and the location of his birthmark. Domnus Rhigyfarch was quite impressed with my knowledge, and indeed with my lengthy and dangerous journey at my age. He spent the afternoon with me, telling me the entire story. At the end of the audience, he ushered me into the monastery and into the back room of the library. Here he confided in me the details of the Grailkey that he had memorized years before. And I too memorized them. He had never looked for the device, but showed me where it must be as described by Rhys to him years before. He left me in that room; he said he did not want to see it. I easily found the device exactly where Rhys had left it. I decided to take the device as a gift from Rhys to his son. I sensed that Rhigyfarch went to pray, but he was there to escort me out when I was done in that room.

After some difficulty in the monastery, and many perils traveling from western Wales across the entire girth of Britain to Essex here in eastern England, I finally brought the device to a safe place and eventually one day got up the courage to fully polish the device, which glimmered so brilliantly. Only after I polished it did I discover that the device was more delicately carved than anything I had ever seen. The carvings were of tiny images of various crosses, cups, of Stars of David, of Islamic crescents, swastikas, Hindu pranavas, Buddhist yen and yang symbols, Shinto kamis, strange tikis and totems, and many other symbols that I have never been able to identify in my years of looking into these things. I do not begin to understand why such non-Christian symbols adorn the pointer toward our most sacred Christian object.

At this point the Professor looked up in what was almost shock. He put the book down and walked out of the room. I remember how strange it was that for five full minutes, no one in the room said one word. It was some time before he returned to his still very stunned audience.

When he did return, he said, "Well, that would be impossible, no? As I have been doing all night long, I translated the symbols in a sort of stream-of-consciousness, unedited flood of images and it has so far made sense. But I just used this method on this last passage, and by Wulfric's descriptions of the symbols it came out sounding like the grailkey contains on it a symbol of every single world religion. But that is not possible. No European in the eleventh century knew even of the existence of Japanese Shintoism, Chinese Buddhism or Indian Hinduism. Nor did many know anything of Islam. And of course the New World and its Native American totems and the tikis of Hawaii were still at least four hundred years from discovery by Europeans. This simply cannot be. How can it be? All religions depicted on one device? We must read on. The Professor picked up the book, cleared his throat, and reread the section aloud.

After some difficulty in the monastery, and many perils traveling from western Wales across the entire girth of Britain to Essex, I finally brought the device to a safe place and eventually one day got up the courage to fully polish the device, which glimmered so brilliantly. Only after I polished it did I discover that the device was more delicately carved than anything I had ever seen. The carvings were of tiny images of various crosses, cups, of Stars of David, of Islamic crescents, Swastikas, Hindu pranavas, Buddhist Yen and Yang symbols, Shinto Kamis, strange Tikis and Totems, and many other symbols that I have never been able to identify in my years of looking into these things. I do not begin to understand why such non-Christian symbols adorn the pointer toward our most sacred Christian object.

Domnus Rhigyfarch had been glad to be unburdened of the Grailkey, and now I too unburden myself of it. I urge you, Boy, to tell no one of it or your life may be in danger. I have often thought of turning over the Grailkey to a bishop so he could retrieve the relic and make it safe. But as you may or may not know, relics in this age are looted and stolen constantly. Honestly, I am not certain if even the Pope himself could protect the Grail indefinitely from the many forces who would demand it. I will leave the decision to you—feel no guilt about returning your great-grandfather's gift, if that is what you choose to do, because he would have wanted you to act on your conscience. It was of great importance that you received this gift before your leaving for the great Crusade in Jerusalem, so that all options would remain open to you. The paradox is that if it is ever found, almost any action will result in the Grail's destruction, except perhaps hiding it until this age of lawlessness is finished; that is why I have kept the Grailkey very safe. Ultimately, though, its disposition is now your load to bear. Bear it well.

I have never told anyone of this except Cynewald, and that only because I feared at my age that the secret might die with me suddenly in my sleep. But even Cynewald will not know the location of the Grailkey until the day I have him fetch you here to this summit. Cynewald is like a son; he can be trusted, so you are safe here. Your gifts are in their places. So ends the story of your great-grandfather Rhys.

My first impulse upon finishing this chronicle, I must admit, was to be immediately aware that should I reach Jerusalem, the Grail would be mine. My second impulse was that if I did find it, the discovery would get me killed very quickly. Everyone growing up hears of the fantastic and magical power of the Grail, but even if those stories are not true, the Grail would still be very, very important.

Since exposing the Grail was a monumental decision but finding the Grailkey required no commitment, I began to dig under Rhys' leather bag. Two feet under, I found the rock and finally lifted it. In the leather bag was the Grailkey, very heavy, and very limp. I gripped the ends and twisted, and it snapped into rigidity. I pulled and twisted and it went limp again. It seemed to be half-coated with grime, and I was glad. I called Rexy over and gave her the collar that she deserved for protecting me. It clasped securely and fit perfectly. The grime made it grayish like iron, which hid the gold almost completely. The spikes even looked like they were designed to protect a war dog. I would have to think a long time before I would decide what to do with this new burden. For now, though, it was safely disguised.

Still so many questions. If I am Welsh, why can't I speak Welsh, and why did I speak only French until I came to the guild at age four? Maybe my real name is Welsh. Did Rhys really forgive his wife for the adultery so easily? She definitely did not seem the type to cheat. And it seems that Wulfric knew details of Rhys and Angharad that Domnus Rhigyfarch could not possibly have known.

I then looked over at the space between the amulet hole and the Grailkey hole. Ealdgyth. Could Wulfric have hidden the bow and arrow in her spot? Within five minutes I was counting nine arrows, one of which was slightly warped. Each arrow had smooth feathers and sharp iron points, and they were neatly housed in a hard leather quiver with a leather shoulder strap. The bow was indeed mighty, with a solid pewter grip in the center. It took me some time before I could string it. The arrow rang like a harp when it struck a tree in the shadows at the far edge of this clearing.

"Finally," I thought, as I walked over to retrieve the arrow, "something that I can use." But if I hadn't thought to look beneath Ealdgyth's place, this bow, nestled in solid rock and covered by another rock on this arid hilltop, would have remained undiscovered for a long time. I whipped out another arrow and shot it straight up in the air, slicing some mistletoe that I had spied in silhouette earlier. The arrow landed on its side nearby as the mistletoe slowly wafted down onto me. It reminded me of a saying Emma would use from time to time: "No mistletoe, no luck."

Nelson asked, "Do you think he went to Jerusalem and brought back the Grail? It would have been very dangerous."

The Professor replied, "Well, I do remember reading that in the 1800s archaeologists digging under the Temple of Solomon unearthed tunnels that had been built during the Crusades. If I recall correctly, these tunnels contained a broken Templar sword, a spur, the remains of a lance, and a small Templar cross. Such a find proves that western Europeans were certainly searching earnestly for relics during the Crusades. It does not determine, however, whether anyone actually discovered the Holy Grail. Yet this 1095 adventure does represent the very first Crusade ever, so Boy would have found a virgin surface to explore in the catacombs of the Temple of Solomon in Jerusalem."

I thought it was amazing that the men had not noticed me throughout this entire chronicle. I excused myself and they also got up to stretch. In the bathroom, I closed and locked the door and began to tremble. At least someone in my family could be trusted. In my small world, I did not know where to look for help. I did not yet know to look into the mirror to see the reassuring flecks in the eyes of my foremothers. Instead, my shame made me drop my head. I stared down the rusted drain of the sink, and found nothing. There were no answers here, no character, no bottom to the spiraling and dizzying well of my loneliness. And alone, I knew I could not survive. College felt like a stone wall of despair had crushed me and pinned me breathless underneath. I gave in. In that miserable state I promised myself that when the sun came up tomorrow I would leave this town and catch a bus back to Kentucky.

"There," I said. "My tramp of a grandmother Angharad was a liar but at least I keep my promises."

Chapter Nine

A Secret Cave in Wales

I came back to the den to finish it out. I had little interest in Angharad, and really, I was disgusted by what this "welcher" had done. As far as I was concerned, Angharad deserved the same fate that I did for quitting.

The Professor returned to the den with a cup of hot coffee. "You do understand, don't you, that the office of prior, which was Rhys' ultimate rank, was quite a prestigious position? When a king's court was listed in the legal records of this period, abbots, priors, bishops and archbishops were listed alongside the earls and other barons."

Nelson added, "Yet I can't see Rhys devoting his time to politics. He was really a good guy. It's as if he reached his fullest potential. Maybe all a saint really is is a person hardwired from birth for holiness. I wonder who really is holy?"

The Professor resumed,

So this is my great grandfather Rhys. I was surprised that his Welshness bothered me less than I had expected, but to be honest, I still felt a profound disappointment at the end of his chronicle. Through the first three chronicles I had sustained an unshakable conviction that I would turn out to be of noble blood, that I was the great heir that Emma had created me to be in her mind.

Perhaps the most disappointing thing was that in a sense, she had been right. Wulfric was a minor thegn of Essex, Rhys was a highly revered prior, and Angharad did apparently have a baby of royal Welsh blood. None of these would be close to sufficient, however, to place me as an equal to the family of an established Norman lord. Moreover, in these days of William Rufus, power and prestige was equivalent to landholding. Major landholding, far more than the seven hides of land held by Wulfric, would be necessary. Emma was lost, and this book had given me false hope.

Now Emma's father, Ralph, had indeed been a great lord. He had been Lord of Wallington in Surrey. His lands were vast and they spread out among several regions of England. His dog kennels alone contained dozens of dogs the same type as Rexy, and I have to admit that I constantly fought a strong urge to covet those kennels. When Emma's mother had died, her father had remarried a great woman who already had four daughters and considerable landholdings of her own. Her father had thought this an ideal arrangement, which it continued to be as long as his personal charm kept his wife's cruelty in check. His death, however, changed Emma's situation drastically. Emma became secondary in the family, a ploy by her stepmother to keep her unpolished and unmarriageable. If Emma were sent to a convent, which was the Lady Wallington's plan, the stepmother could administer Emma's lands indefinitely. If Emma married, husband and wife would share her expansive lands, including her kennels.

So for Emma, her stepmother had always denied her the noble social circles to which she belonged by blood. In fact, Emma had been kept on the estate in Surrey as a virtual prisoner. She had been clothed in the least attractive garb the Lady could conceive. It never occurred to the mistress for one minute that Emma might fall in love with a peasant who worked on the estate, and really, she was correct; a lady as high-born as Emma would never have fallen in love with an average peasant. She fell in love, instead, with me.

But as the spring turned to summer, the lady noticed Emma's light-hearted song and elated countenance, and went snooping. She found pressed under the mattress some flowers that I had picked for Emma all the way from London; furious, the Lady insisted on knowing who had been courting her. She got a stone wall for an answer. It was at that point that Lady Wallington made Emma begin to wear a belt of virtue, which Emma told me later was a very painful contraption.

Yet we continued to meet often in the orchard on the far edge of the grounds. Our visits were always proper as a lady and gentleman—whom I fully understood I was not--should conduct themselves. Though I was not, she was reared by a good Christian man who had taught her solidly how to behave like a perfect lady. The tramp Angharad, I thought, my own great-grandmother, had no such upbringing. In fact, I was almost too ashamed to read her chronicle, but I trusted that Wulfric would spare me as much as he could. Angharad took her place in Wulfric's cliff top design:

Wulfric Rhys

Bag Bag

Ealdgyth Angharad

Bag Bag

Bag Fire Bag

Bag Bag

Bag Bag

Angharad, your mother's paternal grand-mother, was born in Powys, in the northern part of Wales, in 1005. She was the daughter of her mother Gwynydd and her father Gwyll. I know nothing of her mother or father except what I will write to you. Angharad's mother's name, however, suggests that her people had originated in Gwynedd, the Welsh kingdom to the west of Angharad's native Powys.

The Professor stopped reading at this point and looked up. With the laser he pointed out Powys again on his map. I looked a little glassy-eyed at this hour and Nelson was, as usual, attentive.

The Professor commented, "It is always interesting to me that proper names are by far the most enduring aspect of a long-dead culture. A name endures centuries after a strong stone building from the same era is in ruins. English place names survive from generation to generation and are roughly the same today as they were one millennium ago. For example, in England today, of all the cities and towns with names of Danish origin, ninety-seven percent are in the northeastern half of the island, the half known as the Danelaw. This fact makes clear the extent of Viking penetration and settlement one thousand years ago. Personal names are equally enduring. People, both Saxon and Norman, in the eleventh century went by only one name. But over time the increase in European population prompted the addition of a byname. People were adjectified, sometimes with their occupation, such as Smith, sometimes with the name of their father, such as Johnson, sometimes with a trait, such as Little, and sometimes with a description of their residence, such as Brooks. As the centuries wore on, these names became permanent and were passed down as surnames and middle names from time immemorial. Sometimes a mysteriously recurrent family name is the only vestige of a long-dead and long-forgotten relative. The fact that such an ancestor was esteemed enough to honor him by reusing his name in a subsequent generation suggests that recurring family names often trace back to an ancestor who was very charismatic in a distant lifetime. Take note of the names as they appear in these chronicles and learn from them."

He resumed,

As a young girl, Angharad once had a very frightening experience that was told to me some time later. One day when she was picking beans in her parents' field, putting them into her tunic as she went, a neighbor came rushing over their hill with his family and screaming, as he was passing, over his shoulder, that Viking ships had been seen up the river Clwyd and the people of the area were fleeing toward the hills.

As he said this, Angharad heard the thunderous hooves of thirty horses moving fast toward her. She broke into a full run, spilling her beans everywhere; then she heard the guttural yells of many men, who must have been drunk because they were extremely loud. They were just about to crest her hill and see her. She realized as she fled that her parents were in the village and she was alone, but not for long, she feared. She lifted her tunic and flew into the woods, moving faster than she had ever sprinted in her life. She heard the thunder moving closer, and she feared she was being tracked. She darted up a mossy glen and began to move quickly upstream, slipping on the moss-covered rocks and leaping from slimy stone to slippery mud. She spied a little creek canyon coming from the left and darted into it, staying in the water as much as possible to hide her trail. "I have escaped them," she thought, as she panted ferociously into her wet hair.

Startling her from somewhere behind, a Viking grabbed her by the throat. Another Viking, also seemingly coming out of nowhere, grabbed her small ankle and immobilized her in an unbreakable iron grip. She broke it like mother had taught her, with her free foot, and wrenched her swollen throat from the other. They roared and laughed cruelly in an indecipherable tongue as she darted deeper up the canyon, leaping from slippery stone to mossy log only barely touching the earth. Her life hung in the balance, and she became pure instinct as she flew like a bird up that glen.

Soon a high waterfall and a sheer cliff trapped her. She managed to slip in behind the sheet of falling water, and noticed that she could see through the translucence back down the glen. They were rushing toward her! She was pinned, but even in her panic noticed a deep hole in one corner, with water falling into it. She moved to it and without a thought and without a sound, jumped, sure she would find herself in a hole from which her life would never emerge. Instead, she landed at the bottom of a long well containing water that came only up to her waist. Light filtered in from a very small opening, a short tunnel at eye level, which seemed to lead to a sort of cave. She inserted herself into the hole by pushing her feet against the slick wall of the shaft, now behind her. She barely fit, but tumbled out into a rather large, wet cave.

No Viking could fit through that, she figured. In her cave she darted up a sort of wide stone staircase to find an entire level that was completely dry. In its center stood a great stone table; on the table was a stone stand that housed a strange, scabbarded sword. She snatched the scabbard up and pulled the blade, as smooth as liquid, out of its sheath with a scrape that struck a pure musical chord, almost singing as it was released into the air. She ran back to the cave opening carrying the sword. With two hands she held the sword over her head and, breathing like a bull, she awaited the Vikings.

I felt a little guilty, but I immediately started digging in the place of Angharad. I found the rock and was soon holding the most exquisite sword I had ever handled. In the guild we had seen nothing like this, nothing so thin and yet so strong. I parried and found the sword rang as it vibrated to a stop. Unbelievable, I smiled. Now I could protect myself and Rexy nicely. I might not have the pedigree, but I sure have the sword!

Angharad heard their voices, and she felt their vibration as one Viking thundered into the well and began to climb through the tiny opening into her cave. She chopped at his neck, expecting to hack for some time before the complete decapitation. Instead, the sword sliced through the Viking's thick neck effortlessly. His body fell back into the well behind. His hideous bloody head landed on her bare left foot, which had lost its flat leather shoe far down the glen. She now felt the other Norseman drop into the shaft as well, roaring in rage at his fallen comrade. It must have been too dark for him to make out exactly what had happened to his friend. When he began to climb after Angharad, the last thing he saw before his life ended was the bulging eyes of his comrade. She grabbed the heavy heads by their long blond hair and threw them back through the small opening. As her panting gradually began to lessen, she told herself that she would find another way out.

All along one wall, the cave had small openings that let dozens of small rays of light come into this strange room. Angharad washed off the sword, careful not to touch the razor of a blade at all, in one of the pools of water on the lower level. She brought it into the rays of light that flooded the upper level near the table. Though she could not read, she saw what she assumed to be words inscribed on the hilt. The weapon was light yet incredibly strong. The room appeared to have been designed to house the sword, since this sword and the table were its only contents.

This singing sword had saved her, and she would give it to her father if he survived. But the room she decided to keep to herself. She contemplated trying to break out the wall that let in the light, but decided that the best way to keep this room her secret haven was simply to go back the way she came. The Vikings' bodies were too heavy to remove, which did not bother Angharad. In fact, they had piled nicely to make a platform so Angharad could easily clamber out to the waterfall. Once back in the dell, she realized that her village was now swarming with Vikings, and that going home in the next two days would be deadly. Her life was ahead of her and she would live it.

So she camped in her secret room, and moved freely in the woods around it, feeling very confident about her retreat plan should anyone spot her. Food was not going to be possible, since, even if she could collect enough edible bark and mushrooms to make a stew, there was no pot and there was no fire. Water alone would have to last her a few days, she understood, but before her vigil was over she longed for just one of her spilled beans from their field.

During these three days Angharad had a chance to look into herself, to the sound of the dripping mosses of that steep green gorge. It sounded like constant rain, a sound that ever after she would find very reassuring. She tried to make sense of the violence of the Vikings whose skeletons would soon enough guard her secret chamber. How could she raise a boy to be more than the slayer, and the slain, that all Welsh boys grew up to be, just as all their ancestors within memory had been? Had we come no farther than this? These were the thoughts that kept away the hunger of those three lonely days.

In the purity of that cooling air and bubbling water, in the stillness of that glen, she would lie on her back and stare through the tops of the forest at the warm midday clouds that passed over her Wales with the slowest dignity. She found the shapes of all she knew in those passing clouds: the billowing masts of the ships out at sea, faces she had known well and faces she only vaguely recognized, and the familiar tools of her village.

But decades afterwards, when she told me of these days, she finally admitted that this story was just her lie. It was only the lie that she had almost come to believe herself about her time in that glen. She had almost convinced herself that this time had been liberating. Although she had lied to me at first, she finally stopped herself and admitted that this had not been a carefree time at all. The clouds took the form of only violent white horses and attackers. And instead of a feeling of pride in her homeland, a tear dripped from the corner of her eye as she remembered why she was here and what she might have already lost back at her village; violence had corrupted even her clouds.

In truth, she had cringed in fear for these three days of horror, knowing that the Danes were excellent trackers and would startle her from behind at any moment. She confided in me that it was while lying on her back, hidden from view for three days under a humiliating pile of wet, wormy leaves in that soft dripping glen, that Angharad had actually seen her clouds. It was here in this early grave, trembling in terror, that she had committed to herself that she would somehow find a way to protect the children she would someday raise from the murderous warring of Wales, at whatever the cost to her. But you must remember, Boy, that trembling and horrified and lying under those decaying leaves, your great-grandmother did not give up. Instead, she made a plan.

On the third humiliating day under her leaves, she thought she saw in the clouds a huge white cross signaling for her to follow. This was the sign that she had waited for to end the hunger cramps of her stomach, one way or the other. So she rose again on this third day, took her sword, and ventured, careful and terrified, back to her cottage.

Her father and mother were safe and had returned. They were of course overjoyed to see their daughter again; they had feared the very worst and they may have been right. Her parents said the Vikings had killed sixteen people and apparently had enslaved about twenty more. The Vikings had moved on in their long boat, laughing and drinking as their new slaves rowed them toward their next terrorizing trip up a river. Angharad never told her parents of the horrors of those three days, and in fact never told anyone but me, Boy.

"Isn't that strange," I slurred. "It is definitely very late for me. Angharad my tramp of a grandmother told a false story of a carefree three days, but then admitted the true version of the horror of what happened. And Wulfric recorded both stories, just as he'd heard them. I'm glad she told the truth for once. I feel very, very sorry for her." Then I realized that I had not been speaking aloud at all; I had only been thinking these thoughts. The Professor was now reading about the sword.

...Gwyll was amazed at the workmanship of the gift that his daughter was so proud to present, and wondered aloud what the lettering meant. Since Gwyll did not know anyone who could read, the lettering remained a mystery for many years, and the sword remained the prized possession of the family, hidden nicely on top of one of the two horizontal beams that supported the roof of their small cottage.

Angharad was, as I have said, very beautiful, and in her early youth, the period in which this Viking attack occurred, she wore her hair in a flirtatious braid down her back. As the men of the neighborhood began to take notice of her, however, the braid was soon hidden beneath a more modest veil. When she was in her late teens, before the arrival of Rhys to the area, one violent young ruffian, Gruffydd ap Llywelyn, took particular interest in her on those days when she was in the village. And

Gruffydd was not just any young man; Gruffydd's father was the king of Powys. Her refusals were unusual for this prince, and this resistance on her part seemed to make her all the more attractive, and not in the purely physical sense. He seems, if his later actions are any indication, to have fallen in love with her because of her purity and her chastity. When she made clear that she would not have him, despite the fact that he was a prince, this seemed to make her even more ideal in his mind; he honored her decisions and decided to bide his time. He married instead a princess of Gwent, further expanding his already growing power.

It was into this situation that Rhys made, as far as Angharad was concerned, a spectacular entrance. She loved him from the start, and with a sweetness and abandon that all men hope for. The fact that he was not a lustful husband actually worked to make her love him more, since his love for her was based on factors other than physical attraction. In the same vein, the fact that he was often gone overnight to minister to the sick and dying made their time together even more special. In the early days of the marriage, she would inquire as to his favorite meals and favorite songs, and she would give him what he wanted. Unlike most marriages, however, her level of consideration and generosity did not diminish over time. If anything, it increased. When her baby Mynyddawg was born, she lavished the same sweetness onto him, since he was the other man who loved her for her. She would see Gruffydd or one of his lieutenants occasionally in the region, and they were always cordial and reminded her that Gruffydd was there when she needed him.

Mynyddawg was carefree from the start, taking after his mother. This made sense, because even on the evenings that Rhys was home, the priest, though warm on one level, always kept his heart at a distance from the family. His strengths lay elsewhere; he knew everything and was infinitely kind. Upon the death of first Gwynedd and then Gwyll, the family sword passed back to Angharad. For the first time Rhys was able to examine it, and although he could read almost nothing, he did suspect that the writing was not Welsh. When Bishop Melan came through a few months later, he examined the sword. He admired the weapon, and remarked that it was a sword for only those of the highest birth. He confirmed that the writing was neither Welsh, Anglo-Saxon, or Latin, and guessed that it was probably Irish since he thought that he recognized two of the words—"king" and "Britain"—as almost Welsh. Bishop Melan was sure that the sword was unquestionably of enormous value, and would have taken it for the Church were it not for the Bishop's admiration and respect for your great-grandfather Rhys. The mystery of this sword would not be solved for many more years.

With Rhys so distant and so often away, Mynyddawg attached firmly to his mother, until she began to make it clear that what she wanted to see was an independent young man. And that is what she got. When the neighborhood warriors would come to insist Mynyddawg join them on that month's raid, Angharad would make excuses. It was not long, however, until the young men of the village began to harass Mynyddawg about his lack of interest in their raids into England. The pressure continued to mount, and Angharad became obsessed with saving her baby from this deadly and immoral activity. So she pointed the way to becoming a wandering trader, and urged Mynyddawg to leave Powys before the neighborhood thugs forced an initiation, a kidnapping in which he might just like the delicacies that marauding and looting had to offer a young man. She understood the potential of her son and she wanted him out of Powys.

Rhys, however, was almost beyond Angharad's understanding. His level of spirituality was far deeper than any of the other priests of Powys. At the age of thirty he exhibited the prayer discipline of a sixty-year old abbot. At first this was a blessing, leaving plenty of time for the independent Angharad to run her household as she liked. But as time passed, his interaction with the family lessened. In its place came Rhys' increasing urge to move to the edge of the back field, one of his favorite spots, to pray the day away. It was while in her mid-thirties that she realized that it was only their marriage that kept him from the calling that was so obvious to everybody. Rhys was born for the monastic life, and instead he was locked into a marriage from which there was no escape. Or almost no escape.

As Mynyddawg grew into a man and prepared to leave, the occasion finally arose in which Angharad was in need of Gruffydd's help. A woman sometimes has to give herself away. Both her men had destinies that could only be achieved if Angharad let them go. She hugged Mynyddawg and told him that she would always love him and to be a good boy. As he walked out of her valley that day and sailed out of Wales that month, she felt the relief of a mother who had reared her baby well. Rhys' chains, she understood, would be even easier to break. She hated Gruffydd and hated what he represented. But in him was the security that she would need once Rhys was liberated. She sent a simple message to Gruffydd through one of his men: my husband is gone all day on Sundays.

After Rhys had departed for his new life, Angharad became the mother of Gruffydd's favorite son. With this birth began a new phase in the life of Angharad, one that she managed with the coolness and caring that were at the core of her identity. The father of her son continued in his warring ways. In 1049, 1053, and 1055 Gruffydd led raids on western English regions from Hereford to Chester. From 1055 until he was slain by his own people in 1063, Gruffydd ap Llywelyn was the first person ever to be able to claim the title of King over all the kingdoms of Wales. It was a long, continuous war, but Gruffydd had hammered a reluctant unity out of the kingdoms of Wales. Your great grandmother Angharad was the first Queen of Wales.

The Professor looked up. "The fact that Rhys and Mynyddawg escaped recruitment into the Welsh bands was probably a strong testament to Gruffydd's attraction to Angharad. Now, back to her story."

Angharad was to live a long and fruitful life, but she never saw her son Mynyddawg again.

I learned about all of this at the same time I visited St. David's in order to learn of Rhys. What must have caught your eye about the previous chronicle was the impossibility of my having a conversation with Domnus Rhigyfarch. He spoke only Welsh and Latin, and I spoke only English and French. There was no common language. But I had foreseen this language gap, and I solved it in the most delightful manner.

On my journey from Essex to Dyfed in western Wales, I found that I passed through my home region of Hereford. Here I tried to find some of the women who had helped me after my parents had died, but they had passed on. The exception was one young woman whom I remembered named Gytha. She was now eighty, I was seventy-seven. When I asked about my old friends, she had little to report, but she was able to tell me that often merchants had reported that my old playmate Eadburh was doing fine as a slave of the master of Gwent, in southwestern Wales. Since I was on my way through that territory, I set it in my mind that I would buy her freedom and take her on as my interpreter, if she remembered any English after seventy-five years. I knew that it was possible that she still lived with other slaves who conversed with her in their English mother tongue.

In Gwent I was directed to the lord in question, who received me amicably when I identified myself as a thegn of Essex. After pleasantries, we transacted the business at hand and I went to claim my property. Eadburh was doing quite well for her age, as was I. She indeed was fluent in both Welsh and English and eagerly agreed to accompany me to my immediate destination, Powys, where I found neither Rhys nor Angharad, both of whom had departed Powys decades earlier. We did learn, though, that the answers that I sought were at St. David's.

Before we left Powys for western Wales, Eadburh and I had a noteworthy experience. We spent the afternoon with one of Angharad's old friends, and she pointed the way to what she called "Angharad's special place." This woman said she had been entrusted to direct Mynyddawg to a gift that was his legacy. We assured her that we would deliver the gift to him, and after hearing our long tale, she fully believed us. That woman told us the way but, after pointing us up the right glen, said she would not come any further.

Following her guidance, we found ourselves beneath a waterfall and climbing down the ladder that the woman had spoken of.

The Professor pointed out, "That ladder may have been in that dampness over twenty years. Even dry, medieval ladders were rickety at best. Our modern superstitions prohibiting certain activities, such as walking under ladders, offer deep insight into the logistical world a thousand years ago. Today it is quite safe to walk under a ladder, have a black cat cross your path, or break a mirror. Back then, however, the profound instability of a ladder made of sticks, a bite from a stray cat teeming with disease, or a nasty cut while cleaning the shards of a broken mirror could very well put you in the grave. That's bad luck. Now, back to Wulfric."

After more climbing than our old bones liked, we found ourselves in Angharad's secret place, and there on a stone table was the sword. I wore it as my sword all the way back to Essex on this winding trip through England, and it made me feel and look very rich indeed. We stopped here in this room, flooded with beams of light from the forest beyond the cave walls, and we laid out our plan to keep my promise to Gunnehilde. That year was 1078, and it was in that secret cave that sweet Eadburh helped me perfect my plan. Since Gunnehilde's 1056 death at the circle of stones, which I will describe for you in her chronicle, I had been keeping the bow and arrow and amulet for her son. Boy, it is too early in the night to tell you the other schemes we plotted in that cave on your behalf—it would give away ancestors of yours that I want to keep secret a while longer--but let me tell you that it was on the floor of this sun-cut room in Wales that we laid out the pattern of your ancestors, what they were to leave to you, and how we could keep it all safe. Boy, be patient. Read every word of all the chronicles in order, me first, then to my left around the outer circle of eight, then my daughter who is in front of me, then to her left around the inner circle of four, then her son in front of her and then his wife. Only reading in order and in full will bring you the happiness you seek.

We had a long afternoon in that cave and in fact decided to sleep in its safety that night. The next day we set out for western Wales, an area these people called Dyfed, which as a slave in southern Wales Eadburh had heard of often. On this circuitous trip through a very scenic country, we told each other our stories, and hers was as full as mine. She wanted to know my plans since I had purchased her. I told her frankly: I planned to marry her and to live happily ever after. She laughed and laughed, but she was my wife for the next five years, until her death at the ripe old age of eighty-three. It was nice to have her to share my special time in Wales and at St. David's, especially considering what I found when I arrived.

Our interview with Domnus Rhigyfarch took place in the wood outside the monastery, since no woman could enter beyond the cloister. She translated beautifully, now that we were back in southern Wales, and afterwards I was ushered alone to the back room of the library. Before I went inside, though, I showed Domnus Rhigyfarch the writing on Angharad's sword; he was able to translate most of it. It is Cornish, said the monk, and a very old form at that. It appeared to say: "He who holds this sword is born king of all Britain."

"That sword is Excalibur," whispered the Professor. "The magical sword of King Arthur that he pulled out of the stone in order to become King of England."

The Professor continued, looking directly at Nelson as he spoke, “Some versions of the story suggest that the sword was originally placed in the stone by the Lady of the Lake, a goddess whose true nature is never fully revealed. She apparently wanted to protect the rightful king, King Arthur.”

Nelson objected, “But that story is simply a legend. Right?”

“Well, yes and no. Historical records show a king-like Celtic warrior named Arthur during the period of the initial penetration of the Angles and Saxons. It was on such an historical figure as this that the legends of Camelot and Guinevere were probably based. Though the legends themselves are fiction today, the King who inspired them was probably a real person and may well have had a sword that was spectacular, inspiring the Excalibur portion of the legend.”

Nelson asked, “Then the sword found by Angharad would have been over four hundred years old. Possible?”

“Have you ever seen a Japanese samurai sword from the sixteenth century? It is still very deadly. But do not be fooled— Angharad’s sword may well have been Excalibur, but it bore no magical properties--it was simply a sword. The inscription on the sword, for example, according to tradition, was, “He who soever pulls this sword from this stone is rightwise born King of all England.” This inscription, however, is impossible! Arthur was *fighting* the Angles, and would never have agreed that his land was called “England,” or “Land of the Angles.” No, Arthur would have used the term “Britain” or some other pre-Anglo-Saxon migration term. In any event, according to legend, Excalibur was finally thrown back to the Lady of the Lake. Historians understand that Arthur was but a man, yet a man who must have had a nice sword.”

He resumed,

As a minstrel, I fully understood the implications of this inscription. In fact, I had uttered a version of it many times in my dramatized recitations of the Arthurian legends. According to the ancient legends, King Arthur's enchanted sword Excalibur was supposed to be inscribed with "He who soever pulls this sword from this stone is rightwise born King of all Bretons." Arthur was said to have died in the first resistance to the Angles and Saxons in the 300s, but the legend insists that Arthur will rise again to bring back Camelot, an era of tranquility and prosperity for all England. This legend has brought comfort to many people over the ages, Boy, so I would not dismiss it too lightly.

I was frightened of the Grailkey, but I was thrilled with the sword, and I was thrilled that it would be my privilege to deliver them both to Mynyddawg, if he would accept them. I will wait until his chronicle to explain why he might reject such gifts, but you may already know. Because of the warring in southern Wales, on our way back twice I had to resume my identity as a minstrel, a performance that pleased Eadburh no end. Our five years together were without question the most fulfilling of my life, partially because of her, partially because it was in this period that most of these chronicles were made available to me. So ends the story of your great-grandmother Angharad.

So this was my great grandmother, Angharad. Not a tramp. I felt very sorry that I had rushed to her judgment. We judge without all the facts, we rush to a decision that is ill-advised. I was really quite touched by the way Angharad had saved Rhys so that his life could end the way it should have. I was no less touched that after all those years of guilt over not being able to protect her, Wulfric in the end saved Eadburh and made her final years, too, so fulfilling. What touched me most, as you, my progeny, may be feeling too at this point, is the fact that I had descended from such nobility. Both Angharad and Wulfric had met their destinies, not being blindly led by fate, but leading their destinies by the hand. Their personal sacrifices, very different but both very important to the course of my own existence, brought the world right again, and I am proud of my family, proud of what I am made of, and proud to pass such a heritage on to a family whom I have yet to meet, but for whom, I already know, I will be extraordinary.

At this point I fell asleep for a while, but I was startled awake by my own nightmare of being devoured by wolves. Rexy was calmly licking herself, and so I settled down to another chronicle.

I excused myself and went back to the bathroom. *They led their destinies by the hand. They all had. Wulfric had. Angharad had. Boy has a chance to live.* Why was I leaving college? Why was I quitting on my own future? This time I looked myself straight in my drooping red eyes, violently snatching the mirror on the wall by both hands and staring. What I saw was beauty and grace dying on the vine. My power and my promise were sinking into oblivion, and I soon would be completely gone, with nothing left on this spinning planet to show for my virgin spirit. My grandmothers knew full well that self-destructive promises were by their nature invalid and ridiculous. My grandfathers knew that my only promise, made long before I was born, was to strengthen myself for the nurturing of a husband and children who I would one day love. Angharad had put herself aside and had made room; Wulfric never gave up on Eadburh. With that, I threw myself to the toilet, looked into it hard at my old reflection one last time, and vomited violently for almost five full minutes.

When I was done, my stomach felt torn, but my spirit had blossomed like a flower that mysteriously blooms twice. I washed my face, really washed it for the first time in months, and prepared to see this out to the end. Something told me Wulfric's work was not finished, I knew Boy's work was not finished, and my own work now needed to begin.

Chapter Ten

Hugh Draws His Sword

"Professor," called Nelson from the kitchen, "I was wondering if I could invite a few of our classmates over to hear the rest of this book. Some of them are over at my friend Bart's apartment studying for tomorrow's final, now only a few hours away. I think they could benefit from this reading more than last-minute cramming. Our medieval history Professor loves to emphasize the kind of social history that this book is all about. Would that be okay?"

"The more the merrier, if you think they would be interested," replied the Professor. Obviously, both men were thinking the same thing: there's strength in numbers.

The Professor called out and added, "Tell them the truth, all of it, up front. If they still want to come, we need to order some pizzas…find out what they want."

I came back out of the bathroom as Nelson was finishing the pizza order. "I… you okay?" asked Nelson over the receiver.

I answered, a little too energetically, "I wasn't feeling very well, but now I'm feeling better. Girl problems."

Nelson ignored me and hopped down the stairs and I gingerly followed. We each picked out a leather chair and settled in as the Professor began. I covered myself with a thin afghan I had found on a nearby blanket rack.

Hugh. A Norman name. Now I am interested. I was quite aware that only this chronicle, a story ripe with the promise of a Norman lineage for me, could make my fantasy a reality. The design was taking shape:

Wulfric Rhys

Bag Bag

Ealdgyth Angharad

Bag Bag

Bag Fire Hugh

Bag Bag

Bag Bag

Hugh, your great-grandfather, that is, your mother's mother's father, was born in Normandy, France, in 993. He was the son of his mother Alice and the bastard son of none other than Richard I, Duke of Normandy (942-996). But like other bastards of Normandy, William the Conqueror being the most famous, Richard was a recognized son who enjoyed all the privileges of his high birth. He grew up in a manner in which it was assumed that he would one day become the count of Evreux. His life was one of power and privilege. When Hugh was eight years old, he was sent away to live at the castle of his cousin, the count of Rouen. Here he began to develop a pastime that would soon become his passion: swordsmanship. It would be the joy of every moment of his life except the final few.

At seventeen, Hugh was excited to see his half-sister Emma back in Normandy. She was staying with her brother, Hugh's half-brother, Richard II, the Duke of Normandy himself, who ruled from 996 until 1026. Her husband Ethelred had sent her back to Normandy because he was not able to protect her, or his country, from the onslaught of the Vikings in this first decade of the new millennium. Hugh enjoyed hearing about the exotic practices of the Anglo-Saxons and the Danish, and Emma was glad just to be speaking French again. He spent less time with her once Ethelred came to join her from 1013-1014, when he was ignobly expelled

from his own realm by Svein, who ruled us from 1013 until 1014, who was proclaimed King of England simply to end the murderous attacks of the Vikings. Once Svein died, Ethelred, with the aid of the Norwegians and many Normans, including Hugh, moved to retake England from the Danes in 1014.

The Professor broke in, pointing out Normandy and London on the map with his laser. At this point I was watching the Professor use the laser pointer as he had done all night, and I noticed he seemed to accidentally click the laser a second time. Suddenly, and only for a flash, the laser beam was ten times more intense and it fried a tiny hole straight through the map. I learned, after a discrete peek later that evening, that it fried a hole through the wall behind the map as well. The Professor instantly clicked the laser again and it turned off, and Nelson never noticed the hole, or the faint burning smell, either. The Professor acted like it didn't happen, and it was so late that I was not sure that it did myself. I remember thinking that only NASA could produce such a powerful yet compact laser. Or would it be the CIA?

The Professor was already explaining, "Yes, this famous battle for London is said to be the origin of the children's song about London Bridge. While Anglo-Saxon sources do not record the battle, the famous *Saga of St. Olaf*, the Norwegian epic that recounts the heroism of their King Olaf, who was an ally of Ethelred in this period, details the scene beautifully. Let's take a closer look at Hugh."

As he matured into young manhood, Hugh enjoyed the typical life of the nobility. As the Count of Evreux, Hugh would hunt on horseback throughout his domains, expertly tracking and slaying deer, carelessly trampling his peasants' precious crops, and dispensing justice as he saw fit. One day when he was in his early thirties, Hugh, who was married, was out hunting at the edge of his domains. He lunched at the hut of one of his peasants. Quite taken with the peasant's young daughter, whose name was Matilda, Hugh took the father into a private conference and demanded that the daughter and her father accompany the hunting party for the afternoon's adventure, and then back to Hugh's castle.

Matilda had not been privy to the conversation earlier, and was delighted at the attention of the Count, who during the afternoon was a perfect gentleman. Soon after beginning the afternoon hunt, Hugh's party encountered a hunting party from the neighboring region of Coutances. These fellow nobles, apparently guests of the Count of Coutances, were hunting in the same vicinity. Hugh haughtily instructed the party to withdraw from his domains, and the leader of the other party, who apparently did not understand a word of Norman French but was nonetheless offended at his tone, stepped down from his horse and drew his sword. The engagement was not so much a duel as a trial by combat.

The Professor commented, "It is not unusual that the two nobles spoke different languages. France, like England, was dotted with many different tongues, you see, all either partially or completely unintelligible to the other. Someone from Devon, in Southern England, for example, would have great difficulty understanding someone from Lindsey, in northern England."

"That doesn't surprise me one bit," said Nelson. "This summer we had a good bit of trouble understanding the English spoken in Essex. Even a girl we met from Australia who was also a tourist told us that there were many times when she could not understand the Essex English at all. We hung around together all afternoon and really had a good time. At one point that afternoon, I remember her commenting that her English hosts' talk of 'soft ', meaning 'stupid', and 'toff', meaning 'snob', was foreign to her. She then taught us some of the words they use in Australia but not in England. And, let me add, that Aussie babe was a hotty."

"You certainly thought so, didn't you," I smirked. I turned to the Professor and asked, "but if the regions of eleventh-century England had totally different languages, how could Wulfric travel?"

The Professor answered, "With some difficulty. As a minstrel, however, you learn the intonations and regional syntaxes over time, and you develop a knack for decoding languages when you first encounter them. It took an intelligent person to move among regions of medieval England, but all successful minstrels had sharp minds."

He resumed,

Hugh was judge and jury on his manorial lands, and in times of jurisdictional dispute, the sword was a standard means of adjudicating the issue. Though the challenger was apparently a nobleman, he was not, Hugh thought, of sufficient rank even to suggest a trial by combat, nor was his training close to sufficient. Yet Hugh had often been forced to admit, when pressed by his subordinate thegns in his manor halls, that he knew of no man whose training was close to sufficient, or in fact of any man who could best him at all.

Hugh dismounted, turned his body to the side to minimize the chance for contact, and drew his sturdy steel sword, which weighed over twenty pounds. Yet his upper body was more than strong enough to manipulate the sword deftly, and, stepping like a cat, or perhaps a lion, Hugh drew first blood. After a vicious onslaught by his opponent, every move of which was countered nicely by Hugh, Hugh tired of the combat and attacked, swiping three times per second, drawing blood here, there, and finally setting his opponent off balance, sending him breathlessly to the ground on his stomach. Hugh then rested his sword heavily on the left kidney of the offender and in Norman asked simply if he yielded. The man indicated that he certainly did, got up, and he and his party rode away quickly. Some communication transcends language; the basic elements of humanity—a smile, a tear, a kiss, a sword to the kidney--are universal and require no translator.

The display had been brief and he knew it had impressed Matilda sufficiently. Over the next few weeks she was assigned to clean his bedchamber, and she remained his "companion" and chambermaid for the next three years, until she informed him that she was pregnant. Far from making a secret of it, he announced the expected arrival as if he were married to the girl. In 1026, when the child was born a girl, Hugh did not seem to mind too much. She would be raised nobly, he said, and that was all he said to Matilda. He had found another chambermaid.

In 1042, things changed for Hugh. When Danish rule over England finally ended in this year, Edward left the safety of exile in Normandy to assume the throne of England as Edward the Confessor, who ruled from 1042 until 1066. Edward the Confessor, as he has come to be known, brought with him a French accent, a French tendency to build castles, heretofore virtually unknown in England, and he brought with him Normans. Boy, your great-grandfather Hugh volunteered to move to England and to control one of the manors on which would be built a new Norman-style castle. This castle was to function as a bulwark against any possible return of Danes or Norwegians. Hugh's fief was granted in Devon, the region between Wessex and Cornwall. Beginning in 1042 Hugh supervised the crushing extraction of labor from his peasants that was required to build the earthenwork castles that began to dot the map of England in this period. When the stone castles would be constructed beginning after William's conquest of 1066, the workload on the peasants would be even greater. He supervised this building while he became used to the new English language, new English legal traditions, and the new English women.

Thus, after 1042 Hugh, whose wife had died a few years earlier, was the local bachelor Earl of Devon. He would while away his days in utter leisure, living handsomely off the toil of his peasantry, but never taking care to give back to the peasants as his office required; alms and bread for the poor were not to be found at his back door, and he was despised by all his people. Instead of attending to his noble duties, he took to a new game brought back by some of his cousins while on their campaigns in Italy. The game was chess, just introduced to northern Europe. Hugh became quite good, and he would teach his chambermaids to play in the afternoon sun. He would lie in his gardens on amorous picnics, explaining the rules of the game to the uninitiated--that bishops can only move one space at a time, and that if that bishop there moved at all, the counselor would capture it—and Hugh's pupil would usually act quite interested.

Nelson pointed out, "That's not correct! Bishops can move as far as the diagonal is open! And there is no such piece as the counselor! What a stooge. Professor, did you know that I was on the high school chess team?"

The Professor countered, "Actually, I assumed it, Nelson. But your chess history is rather faulty. When chess first spread into northern Europe from the direction of both Russia and Muslim Spain in the eleventh century, several rules were quite different, you see, and there was as yet no queen. The 'counselor' was the piece next to the king, and it held relatively little power compared to the modern queen. The queen did not develop her role as the powerful protector of her people--pawns and king alike--until as late as the 1500s."

"I *did not* know that," said Nelson.

The Professor winked and answered, "Knowledge is power, Nelson." As he said this, though, I noticed him glance at the stack of reference books next to him. I looked them over to see if the Professor meant anything by the glance. The only thing I noticed was that the books all bore a faint stamp on their sides that read simply, *Library of Congress.* These books had been checked out in Washington D.C. and it appeared, since the Professor acted like he owned the books, that he owed some serious overdue fines.

"Let's get back," he said, and I leaned back for more of Hugh.

He had an exquisite chess set made for himself out of pewter and brass, and he became, perhaps, even better at chess than he was at swordplay.

Once established in Devon, Earl Hugh arranged for his illegitimate daughter Eleanor, who of course was your grandmother, to take up residence with his cousin, who had married the Lord of Coventry in northern Mercia. She arrived there in 1044 and never heard from her father again. In order to put the matter of Eleanor's mother behind him, Hugh decided to have Matilda admitted into the abbey of St. Mary and St. Elfleda at Romsey, in Wessex. Though a mother who had never been married, Matilda would find a comfortable if subordinate place among the sisters.

A little later the same year that Eleanor traveled across the channel and up to Coventry, Hugh received a surprise. At the age of fifty-one, while he was hunting on his southern lands, he was ambushed by a Norman footsoldier who challenged him to a trial by combat. The soldier identified himself as Roger, the brother of Matilda. Roger had with him ten or so of his fellow soldiers, all stout, while Hugh was accompanied by only two mounted knights. Hugh thought it an even enough match.

Roger then brought out two more people from their hiding places: Matilda, who apparently had come against her will, and a Norman priest, who apparently agreed wholeheartedly with Roger's mission.

"You will marry my sister before she goes to the convent," ordered Roger. "Marry her now, in front of these thegns." Hugh dismounted, excited about killing such an arrogant young man.

"What difference can it possibly make?" laughed Hugh, drawing his large sword.

"There is no difference for Matilda, you have ruined her," said Roger. "The difference lies in Eleanor, my niece. She will be raised as a legitimate lady. If I best you, do you swear to marry Matilda here and now, in front of your thegns?"

"If he bests me," Hugh laughed to his thegns, "I will marry the sow! I swear it!" He yelled this and, without giving Roger a chance to prepare, he lunged crazily at him with his sword flashing.

This treachery gave Hugh a tremendous advantage, thrusting Roger backwards. Roger began to retreat and defend immediately, almost tripping, never having his full balance. Hugh forced him into a dangerous leap onto a fallen tree. From this precarious and vulnerable position, Roger nonetheless got his footing and his confidence. The irate brother, twenty years Hugh's junior, parried all of the Earl's standard maneuvers and spun himself around while jumping high off the log. He somehow landed on his feet. Upon landing, Roger slashed like lightning, drawing first blood on Hugh's cheek, a deep and permanent scar.

Enraged, Hugh lunged again, but found each thrust deftly glanced away by defensive techniques that Hugh had never seen before. The more Hugh sped his slashes, three per second, four per second, the tighter Roger wound his own counterthrusts.

"What is your defense?" Hugh screamed.

Roger grinned, "I have been fifteen years securing Naples for your great-nephew William, our Duke of Normandy! Yet his bastard stain is one that Eleanor will never know!"

Hugh felt his stamina begin to fade only slightly, but apparently Roger perceived this immediately. The two had been locked into cross-curling slashes in a repetitive loop that each had expected the other not to be able to maintain. Suddenly, the circuit was broken by a forward slash that instantly reversed the direction of Roger's attack while maintaining adequate defense!

"The Neapolitan moves have spirit, no?" And with that, Roger began his attack. Hugh went to the standard Maine defense, unbreakable and safe until the momentum could be regained. It was blocked! Hugh was moving backwards, defending with the Brittany defense, but again Roger blocked it, forcing Hugh up onto the fallen log. Forced to deal with the protection of his legs, Hugh wavered for a moment in his Brittany and suddenly found his heavy sword flying through the air. Roger's smaller point pushed up far into the loose skin that hung around the neck of Hugh.

"Will you keep your sworn oath, or will you die?"

"I yield," came Hugh's angry reply.

The ceremony was brief and lacked the magic that Matilda had dreamed of as a child. There was no kiss and no ring, but with his stole, the priest tied the knot that would be broken all too soon. The footsoldiers and priest departed southward for the long journey back to Normandy. After Hugh had kept his oath, Roger kissed his sister and prepared to begin the long walk eastward escorting her to her new life at the convent of Romsey. Instead, he felt a stinging gash in his leg and looked up to see Hugh, mounted, raring for another slash.

"You will now die, you arrogant jackass," snarled Hugh. Roger jumped away, and the two thegns exploded into a laugh as Hugh, now mounted and practically invincible compared to a footsoldier, chased Roger around the clearing. Hugh was commanding his warhorse to stomp Roger's life out, but Roger managed to escape them both for a moment. Finally, Roger leaped onto the fallen log where the horse had less mobility. When Hugh advanced, Roger leapt up, grabbing a branch with one hand, defending against Hugh's sword with the other. While Hugh turned the stallion for better position, Roger dropped down behind him, and placed his sword to Hugh's surprised neck.

Roger whispered the final words that your great-grandfather would ever hear.

"The advantage of your warhorse seems to be neutralized. You know, the problem with courting young girls is that they have young brothers, old man!" With that, Roger sliced long and deep, allowing the wet body to fall heavily into the dust.

The thegns both drew their swords, preparing to fight the vulgar villain. After one step, they heard a commanding voice: "Arrest your actions! By order of the Duchess of Devon!" Matilda was standing in the clearing, with a calm confidence. The thegns then realized that as wife of the fallen Earl, Matilda might now be the premier authority of the shire. Only the birds of the wood were heard as the thegns froze to weigh the legal consequences both if they did and did not recognize her authority. Finally, their calculations were completed. They resheathed their swords, dismounted, and bowed. By her wits and her courage, Matilda had saved herself and her brother.

She instructed Roger to go now, his work was done. She would retire to her castle for some relaxation before she continued on to Romsey Convent, in the Ducal carriage, under the armed escort of all the thegns of Devonshire! She would command these thegns to tell the truth of what happened, about the marriage and the treachery of the Earl that cost him his life. And they would be rewarded. So ends the story of your great-grandfather Hugh.

So this was my great grandfather. What a terrible man. How could a nobleman be so utterly devoid of any personal nobility? Angharad exuded personal nobility, and so did Wulfric, and they were of the lowest births. My days with Emma in the orchard were filled with hearing the wonderful stories of how she protected her peasants, watching over them as if they had been her children. Her integrity was always above reproach.

As I stood in my clearing, I fingered my sword and pulled its blade back and let go. The tone that rang into the still night was very soothing to me. I thought how lucky I was to excel at swordplay in these days of trial by combat. Then I remembered it was not luck, it was the engineering of Wulfric. Good grandfather. Most of my people so far had been admirable, but not this last one.

With a great-grandfather like Earl Hugh, I thought as I looked up into the starless sky, Emma would never take me anyway. Then I noticed a few stars shining through the clouds, and I thought that perhaps the skies still might clear to yield a bright winter morning tomorrow. I thought I could make out the evening star on the horizon, but I knew it was not a star at all. In London I had once overheard a learned man explain that the evening star was really the planet Venus, which in fact was also the morning star. But I also knew enough about the Heavens to know that Venus was not one to be seen in the middle of the night; she would not be seen until the approach of the light. Above me, I knew that the Heavens were following their courses: first the moon, then Mercury, then Venus, then the sun, then the other three planets and behind them the stars, each moving in their perfectly circular orbits, each locked into their crystalline shells that domed above me. The heavenly bodies followed their perfect course just as I must follow mine. Behind them all, though, was Heaven, where my ancestors waited for me now, and where God Almighty knew whether I would ever see my Emma again.

"That Boy can write," said Nelson as he got up and left the room.

I wondered aloud, "Do you think Roger really saved Eleanor from the stain of being a bastard?" Then I answered myself, "Well, if Matilda then became Duchess of Devon, I guess so! I can't wait to hear her side of the story." I laughed to myself that I might actually be able to really understand, after what had happened earlier in the bathroom, how it felt to be saved from a bastard status.

The Professor said that he, too, had to excuse himself. On his way out, he added, "William the Conqueror may have been a successful bastard, but he was still a bastard, known by that byname throughout history for its negative social implications."

"I'm not a bastard at all," I thought.

Chapter Eleven

Steve Joins the Study Party

"Haley, come in here," Nelson barked in an alarmed tone. "Get on the hallway phone." Our mother was on the line, and when we hung up, we were stunned.

"What is it?" asked the Professor as he sat down in his chair to very concerned looks on our faces.

Nelson began, "I just called Mom again to tell her about this book. Don't worry, though, I didn't mention the attack. She would have freaked real good. She was very excited for us, but she didn't understand why I thought these people were my ancestors, just because we found the book in Essex and Wulfric is from Essex and they both have a well. I told her I just had a feeling, and she said she was happy that we were enjoying ourselves."

"That's nice, but not alarming," said the Professor as he earmarked in a reference book a favorite quote that he planned to read to us at some point.

I took over, "Then she put us on hold for another call, which took a while, and when she came on she said it had been Uncle Spencer in England. He had spent the last two days bound and gagged in a closet. The man who had taken the book had come back for it, and beat Uncle Spencer until he told this man where the book was and who we were. This was two days ago. Uncle Spencer says we should call the police right now."

Silence.

"We should have known Uncle Spencer might be in trouble," I continued. "I'm just glad he's okay."

Nelson, thinking aloud and leaning on the kitchen counter, added, "But this doesn't really change anything. This stalker still can't know where we are." In his mind, though, he quickly contradicted this, putting together for himself the fact that he had told one of our neighbors exactly where we were going tonight. *I had told him to be quiet on the Commons, but no!* We all wordlessly came to realize that a determined searcher could definitely find us here. Nelson was about to confide these thoughts in private to the Professor, but his godfather was already getting up and heading for the phone. After calling the police, we overheard a second phone call, this to our parents. He told them everything and the call lasted a while.

Just as he hung up the Professor moved to the front of the house to answer an official-sounding knock at the door. After only a short while, he came back down the stairs and reported, "The police checked the bushes and the surrounding houses. It's still all clear."

I asked aloud, "I wonder what he read that made him want this book so bad? Surely he couldn't've understood much of Boy's Middle English, and I bet he couldn't understand a word of Wulfric's inserted chronicles, since they are written in Old English. He'll need some help if he plans to read all of this book."

The Professor noted, "If he finished the book, he probably could have pieced together much of Boy's narrative, which apparently was enough to initiate felonious activity on his part. Perhaps we had better find out what *is* motivating him."

We gathered our drinks and followed the Professor out of the kitchen. Instead of walking back down the stairs to the den, to our surprise he turned into his living room, so we followed him. He walked over to his front door and locked it. The deadbolt made a loud click as he twisted it and the door hissed as it had earlier.

Just then, we all heard a creaking on the front porch. We went completely quiet, as if the house was empty. All was silence. Nelson and I looked at each other, then back to the door. Suddenly, a shadow fell on the glass semicircle window at the top of the door. I instinctively clinched Nelson's wrist in a painful vise that drained the blood from both our hands.

Nelson jumped and grabbed me as the doorbell split the silence. The Professor peered outside, and then unlocked the door, welcoming four boys and two girls from the history class. I suddenly ran all ten fingers through my hair. One of these boys was Steve.

"Thanks for inviting us over," said Marilyn, a nice-enough girl who Nelson shared several classes with. There in the foyer Nelson explained the situation to everybody, leaving nothing out, and closed with, "We don't want anybody to get hurt."

Hannah, the other girl in the group, took one step back, looked a little disbelieving, and admitted, "Bart told me everything you just said, but I guess I didn't believe him. I think I'd better go. Can I get someone to escort me to my car?"

She looked at the group with a mixture of embarrassment and apprehension. Her concern was real. "Steve, I choose you," she said with a forced smile as she moved toward the door. Steve escorted her out and the door closed behind them.

"Second Dan in Shoto Kan karate," Paul pointed with his thumb as the two stepped out and closed the door.

"I didn't know that," I said. I was really quite relieved that there was a crowd. We were completely safe with all eight of us in the room, since Uncle Spencer had made clear that this was only one deranged thug working alone. And with that English accent, he couldn't hide forever. The police had probably already found him, and they had probably already started the paperwork to have him extradited to England to face a host of charges, including felonious assault.

"Oh, do you know Steve?" Paul asked me.

"Well," I squirmed, "I'm in the same medieval history class that y'all are."

"I must admit," teased Paul, "I've never seen you before in my life. And I'm sure I would have remembered."

Nelson quickly pointed out that there were over one hundred students in our section.

Paul asked Joel's friend, who so far had been quiet, if he'd seen this girl in class. The guy just shrugged.

I explained, "I had a little attendance problem."

Steve returned, and all five newcomers said they would certainly stay, at least until Bart and Shannon, who said they would be by later, arrived.

"We're fine in this big crowd of tough guys," Marilyn smiled. "And I do remember you, Haley. I dropped my books on the quad once and you stopped and helped me get them all up, including dozens of pens from a box I spilled. You spent like seven minutes, until butterflies arrived to help, remember? That was really very sweet. I like what you've done with your hair!"

I shyly thanked Marilyn and we followed the Professor downstairs.

Once in the den, the newcomers were amazed by the wild decor of the room. Nelson and I caught everybody up, describing Boy's cool fight scene and the rest of the stories. Paul asked if Steve used quarterstaffs at the dojo. He said he didn't.

The Professor was settled in now. "The plural form is 'quarterstaves,' not 'quarterstaffs.' Now, let's get back to it," he said.

"Who could know that?" I muttered under my breath to Steve as the Professor began to read again.

I was quite interested as to whether Matilda would be received well at the convent, and so I was ready to dive back in. But I did not. I noticed, instead, that Rexy was licking her bottom again, and somewhat annoyed, I wondered when she would stop doing that. Alone on a dangerous mountaintop with a dead man with crossed arms peacefully in front of himself, it was unusual that I was annoyed by the grooming of a dog. A panic struck me sharply. I jumped up and called her quickly to the fire. After laying her on her back for a quick examination, it was quite clear by her discharge that Rexy would very soon be attracting other dogs.

I knew that this was a deadly situation if wolves caught wind of this. No ointment or potion in England could fully cover this smell, and I had nothing at all that might even begin to mask it. Without any choice, I took off my already ripped undershirt and tied it securely on her like a cloth on a newborn's bottom. She instinctively seemed to agree with me, because she made no serious attempt to remove the cloth after my first scolding when she tried to tug it off. I could only hope that I had caught the problem quickly enough to keep the wolves of this forest at bay. Just in case, I brought the bonfire up to a roaring pitch and settled in to meet another ancestor. The design of my family was well-lit for the moment:

Wulfric Rhys

Bag Bag

Ealdgyth Angharad

Bag Bag

Bag Fire Hugh

Bag Bag

Bag Matilda

Matilda, your great-grandmother, that is, your mother's maternal grandmother, was born in Evreux, Normandy in 1008 to her mother Arlette and father Robert. Her mother and father were typical rural peasants. In her infancy, like most babies, she was kept in a crib near the fire to lessen the cold and the drafts of the harsh Normandy winters. Being so close to the fire could be very dangerous, but many well-meaning parents in their region of Evreux had accidentally smothered their infants while they slept in the same bed with them for warmth. Arlette would not be one of them.

The Professor stopped and pointed out Evreux on the map with his laser pointer. The Professor commented, "Estimates are that eighteen percent of children did not reach one year of age, twenty-five percent did not reach age five, and thirty-three percent of all children did not reach age twenty."

He resumed,

Matilda grew up in the one room of her rectangular cottage. The cottage was about fifteen feet wide and was covered with a thatched roof. Her mother spent the evening hours at her wheel, spinning the shearings of their three sheep into thread, and Matilda and her two younger brothers would sit and listen to her mother tell her tales, spinning her yarns for hours. Spinsters all over this valley did the same thing on the long cold winter nights.

Like everywhere, food was scarce. The Church forbade eating meat on all Wednesdays, Fridays, and Saturdays, and during many religious observances such as Lent. As a result meat was forbidden over half the year. This did not matter much to Matilda and her family, though, because they never had meat at all. And the food they did have was of such small portions as to barely keep them alive during the winter. It was oats and barley, in all their possible disguises—stew, bread, or ale--that kept this family alive between harvests.

The Professor added, looking up, "Because human feces was used to fertilize fields when the cesspools were emptied, no raw vegetables were ever eaten during this era. Their diet was starkly seasonal; Matilda might eat those foods that were easily dried and thus preserved—fish, beans, butter, cheese—all year round if they were available that year. Eggs, fruit, and carrots were seasonal. Also remember, uncooked milk could cause infection before the pasteurization process was introduced during the twentieth century."

He began again,

Their one cow provided much in terms of their sustenance. The milk itself was dangerous, but when the milk curdled and the curds were squeezed in a press, this made a cheese that would keep for a while. And the French do wonders with their cheeses! When the cream rose to the top of a bucket of milk, it would be scooped off and whipped in a churn into butter, which was also prone to lasting a good while. Whey was the extract from the cheese pressing, and like the milk and the cottage curds, could be dangerous to eat. Yet often there was little choice.

Insects and spiders were a part of life for everyone in these days, and as too often happens, spiders brought on tragedy for Matilda's family. Mites and ticks were constant bed companions, and flies and mosquitoes were simply ignored. Wormwood was put into their straw-stuffed floor mattresses to keep away bedbugs and mites. Social grooming for lice was--and of course still is--a common practice throughout France and England. One day as Matilda's five-year-old sister was sitting down to a meal, a spider came along and bit her. She died two weeks later of a raging infection. The family learned a costly lesson from this.

When she was fifteen, Count Hugh took Matilda to be his chambermaid. Her father could certainly not resist; it was only by the Count's generosity that he possessed his land at all. After three years Matilda became pregnant. Hugh, to his credit, did not abandon his child once she was born. The Norman custom of taking care of their bastards was far different from the Anglo-Saxon habit of discarding such children.

When the child was born, Hugh lost interest in Matilda. She understood that her baby, "Eleanor," Hugh had named her, would soon enough be taken from her to be raised with noble cousins. And Matilda was elated for her baby, who would grow up never knowing Matilda's hunger.

She knew that she would have her baby until the age of seven, and she and her baby made the very best of their time. Alone in one of the hunting cabins and having every need satisfied by Hugh, the two enjoyed themselves immensely. One of their favorite pastimes was taking their extra food and distributing it to their fellow peasants who were desperate for any crusts of bread. Another was to enjoy the horses Hugh allowed them to keep in order to teach Eleanor to ride.

Hugh had given Eleanor a gift of a handsome set of stirrups which had belonged to her grandfather, Richard I. Eleanor promptly gave them to her mother, who loved to ride, loved to feel like a lady. Eleanor had presented these stirrups to her mother even though she had known that Eleanor's departure would mean the withdrawal of the horses. Mother and daughter loved each other sweetly every day they were together.

The cleaning woman who was a good source of information on Matilda told me one of the stories that Matilda most liked to tell little Eleanor, your grandmother, in these years before she lost her. I will tell this favorite story in its entirety because it shows better than I ever could how Hugh wounded Matilda:

There was a woman who had made some bread. She said to her daughter: "Go carry this hot loaf and a bottle of milk to your Granny."

So the little girl departed. At the crossway she met *bzou*, the werewolf, who said to her:

"Where are you going?"

"I am taking this hot loaf and a bottle of milk to my Granny."

"What path are you taking," said the werewolf, "the path of needles or the path of pins?"

"The path of needles," the little girl said.

"All right, then I'll take the path of pins."

The little girl entertained herself by gathering needles. Meanwhile the werewolf arrived at the grandmother's house, killed her, put some of her meat in the cupboard and a bottle of her blood on the shelf. The little girl arrived and knocked at the door.

"Push the door," said the werewolf, "it's barred by a piece of wet straw."

"Good day, Granny. I have brought you a hot loaf of bread and a bottle of milk."

"Put it in the cupboard, my child. Take some of the meat which is inside and the bottle of wine on the shelf."

After she had eaten, there was a little cat who said: "Phooey! . . . Evil is she who eats the flesh and drinks the blood of her Granny."

"Come lie down beside me."

When she laid herself down in the bed, the little girl said:

"Oh, Granny, how hairy you are!"

"The better to keep myself warm, my child!"

"Oh, Granny, what big nails you have!"

"The better to scratch my chin with, my child!"

"Oh, Granny, what big shoulders you have!"

"The better to carry the firewood, my child!"

"Oh, Granny, what big nostrils you have!"

"The better to smell the bread with, my child!"

"Oh, Granny, what a big mouth you have!"

"The better to eat you with, my child!"

The werewolf tied a rope to her leg and let her go outside for firewood. When the little girl was outside, she tied the end of the rope to a plum tree in the courtyard. The werewolf became impatient and said: "Where are you?"

When the werewolf realized that no one was answering him, he jumped out of bed and saw that the little girl had escaped. He followed her but arrived at her house just at the moment she entered.

```
This story told what Matilda needed Eleanor
to fully understand: stay out of the devouring
path of both beast and man, and only your wits
can save you.
```

I blurted out, "That is the single most disturbing story I ever heard."

The Professor commented, "The great drive to sanitize the medieval folk tales began as early as the 1500s, but this version delightfully delivers the power of the original prescriptive story, the concrete reality of your flesh being devoured and the terror of your being chased. All the folk tales that originated in the recesses of medieval Europe were functional, not ornamental as they are today. From "Hansel and Gretel," which taught children to stay home, to the "Three Little Pigs," which taught the security of stone fortifications, these stories prescribed a caution that may well have saved the lives of the terrified children who heard them with wide open eyes."

The Professor added, "What stands out most to me about this story is that while our modern story glorifies a woodsman as the hero of the story who saves the helpless little thing, the hero of the medieval original was the girl herself. The original reveals a much more self-sufficient young woman than our modern red riding hood; the medieval riding hood is a woman brave enough, smart enough, and endowed with enough character to extract herself from this very deadly predicament. I also like the fact that at the end of the story, the wolf is still out there, keeping Red Riding Hood on her guard. 'Watch out' was the unmistakable message."

Nelson said, "What I noticed about this story was something completely different. Wulfric said, 'this story told what Matilda needed Eleanor *to fully understand*;' he split his infinitive! He should have said '*to understand fully*.' I have been observing, since it's one of my pet peeves, and Boy is careful never to split his infinitives, but Wulfric seems to often split them. I guess Wulfric is just not as educated."

I looked quickly at my brother. "Nelson, after such a disturbing story, this is all you can comment on? You are officially a freak."

The Professor clarified, "Actually, Nelson, the reason that we do not split our infinitives in English today is that in every Latinate language—such as Latin and the Old French that came into England after 1066 and ushered in Middle English—an infinitive is one word. As a result, since it was impossible to split them in French, it sounded un-French to split them after 1066 and ever since it has been grammatically unacceptable. So both Boy and Wulfric write grammatically correctly; Boy did not split his infinitives in keeping with the rules of his Latinate Middle English, and Wulfric, who spoke the purely Germanic Old English, could split them with grammatical impunity. By the same token, Wulfric could end a sentence in a preposition and generate many other sentence structures that are today syntactically taboo to the purist modern grammarian. Now, back to the eleventh century."

At the age of seven, Eleanor was sent to the castle of some noble cousins in Maine, France to begin her training as a lady. Her kindness and goodness were already firmly in place, thanks to a mother whom she would see very rarely from this point on. Matilda continued to live in the hunting cabin, being provided for still, but in less luxury than before. She missed the horses, and she missed her baby terribly. Eleven years after her Eleanor was taken, she received word from Hugh, who was now an Earl in England in addition to being the Count of Evreux, that she was to join a convent in England. This seemed preferable to life as a peasant, and she prepared to leave, explaining the situation to her parents and her surviving brother, now home from war in Naples.

After the episode in which Earl Hugh lost his life, Matilda became the Duchess of Devon.

Though her title would last her lifetime, her power would last only until King Edward named a new Earl of Devon, but because this took a while, she made the best of it. When she returned to Hugh's castle, all resistance died away when the thegns confirmed her story. Matilda enjoyed counting up Hugh's belongings, which numbered more than she had ever imagined.

She understood perfectly the disposition of his worldly goods; Hugh had three legitimate children by his first wife--she smiled at the phrase--and so Eleanor would probably receive nothing once these daughters began the legal scheming so common in my day. If Hugh had had an opportunity to get his affairs in order, as a Norman, he certainly would have endowed his daughter, whether legitimate or not, with something. As it was, Eleanor would be left with nothing to bring into a marriage. Matilda's duty, then, as current Duchess of Devon, was clear: secretly loot all she could while it was still legal. Knowing that she would soon depart for Romsey convent, and that her baggage would need to be inconspicuous, she took only one chest. Taking only one chest would minimize conflict with the heirs with the better legal claim, and she hoped her simple acquisitions would go unchallenged. She had the chambermaids, strikingly pretty girls, she thought, load a large chest with clothing and tunics that had belonged to Hugh's first wife. In the middle of the night, though, she burned all of these tunics-- except three, which were particularly well-embroidered and nicely-dyed--in the fire in her bedchamber.

She spent the next two hours loading the large chest with smaller treasure chests, each worth a considerable fortune, that she had found stashed in various places around Hugh's chambers. All told, the pennies filled up a third of the large chest and constituted a breathtaking fortune in coins. She made small cloth bags out of torn tunics and so the chest was filled with little bags of pennies that would make no sound in transit. She covered these pennies up with some delicate undershirts and the three tunics for herself, so that she would look the part of a duchess upon arrival at the convent. She also included three pillows to fill the rest of the space lightly and to pack the pennies in so they would shift as little as possible in transit. Before closing her chest, Matilda made one last acquisition. She took the thirty-two chess pieces, which she thought were the most meaningful souvenirs of Eleanor's father that were still quite portable.

After two luxurious weeks as the Duchess, she left the manor behind and set out for the week-long trek to the convent at Romsey. The night before her arrival at the convent, she sent her escorts away so that she could immerse herself in prayer. Before her prayer, however, she loaded the pennies into the hole of a hollow of a tree that was near their encampment. She could hear the bags of pennies fall down to the ground at her feet. The only way to get at them was to chop this tree down, which she thought was a perfect device. She knew that all worldly possessions must be surrendered before entering the convent. It would be years before Eleanor would be in need of a dowry, and this small fortune would remain safe. She also put the chess pieces in, and she dropped her iron stirrups on top of these. Then she covered it all with leaves and dirt. She was ready for a new life.

Founded in 907, St. Mary's at Romsey in Wessex was a Benedictine nunnery, one of only nine in England, six of which were here in

Wessex. There were fourteen nuns in residence, and they were cordial enough to the Duchess. I have already described the rule of Benedict at Cluny, and for the women it was basically the same, except that the floor plan, which is theoretically identical in all Benedictine monasteries, was inverted for nunneries. Another change was the need for quarters for the opposite gender, since men had to administer the sacraments.

Prayer was the center of the day, and Matilda found great comfort in her perception of herself as the bride of Jesus. Her universe was the Lord, and she found herself talking to him most of the time, and composing poetry to him. Her devotion was complete, and she earned the admiration of her sisters. It is said that she attained a position of great honor among her sisters in her latter days. Over time, however, she contracted the coughing and it is said that she finally died of it, I have heard in 1085. A life that had begun in the simplicity of a cottage in Evreux ended in even more simplicity. Matilda spent the final years of her life basking in the love of her Lord Jesus Christ. So ends the story of your great-grandmother Matilda.

So this was my great-grandmother Matilda. What she went through! But she kept her eye on my grandmother Eleanor, and it appears that she positioned her well enough to marry nobly. Now I know a little about my family. I know that either my Saxon grandmother Gunnehilde or my Norman grandmother Eleanor married my Welsh grandfather Mynyddawg. And the two in this union had one of my parents, who then had me and for some reason abandoned me.

At this point a stick snapped far off in the woods, and Rexy let out a series of low, quick, warning barks and then trailed off. We were both a little frightened, and I relaxed. I thought she looked less intimidating with the diaper, but it was better than being devoured by wolves. At least her collar looked formidable.

As I dug up Hugh's gift, I wondered how my noble blood would affect my future. The chess pieces were each as tall as my fist and they were very ornate and very heavy. I did not play chess, which was a noble pastime, but I hoped I would someday learn. I dug up Matilda's gift, and as I expected, it was the iron stirrups, complete with leather strapping. Though the skill of riding horses was reserved primarily for the nobility, Wulfric's engineering had succeeded again. Somehow he had made sure that my training in weapons included combat on horseback, and so I was an accomplished rider. And though stirrups were certainly not common in England, the widespread Norman use of them meant that they were coming into use more and more. Two noble gifts. I hoped that one day I would have the opportunity to try them both out.

Honestly, my hopes were high at this point, high that I might yet win Emma and take her away from her terrible stepmother. But I also understood the near-impossibility. I understood that if anyone knew of my Welsh heritage, my great grandfather's minstrelsy, his previous status as a slave, the brigandage of Ealdgyth's grandfather, or the peasantry of them all, my Norman blood would not avail me one bit. If the good parts of my ancestry were brought to light, how could I hide the rest?

Steve was the first to speak. "Are these the nimble ancestors you were referring to on the Commons? Amazing!"

I looked at him softly and said, "We really don't know. I keep waiting for some clue to let us know either way, but so far we just can't tell. We may never know. They seem strangely familiar to me, though."

"A few more chapters like that one," said Marilyn, "and I can load tomorrow's essay exam with all kinds of goodies. Are the rest of you getting as much out of this?"

They all, except Joel's quiet friend, agreed that it was much more productive than cramming names and dates.

"What about you?" Marilyn asked Joel's friend.

Joel's friend was apparently very shy. Finally, he muttered, almost under his breath, "Well, I'm on exchange from Australia, so I'm not used to your examination system. The story is definitely interesting."

Paul asked if it had all been this interesting.

My brother said, "Yeah, especially the part about the split infinitives!"

Everyone turned and looked dryly at Nelson.

Chapter Twelve

The Vikings Plunder England

I was popping popcorn when Steve walked into the kitchen. "Wild story," he volunteered.

"Yeah," I said.

"Listen to him," mused Steve, as he cocked his ear toward the other room. The Professor was explaining to a crowd that the silver dimple on the cover could not be an hourglass, because hourglasses only first appeared in the thirteenth century, and the action of this book took place in the eleventh century and the book was most probably produced and bound in the early twelfth century.

We both rolled our eyes and I said, "Yeah, he really gets into this. But I have to admit, I am enjoying tonight's little history lesson myself."

Since Steve's arrival at the house earlier that evening, my radar had been telling me that he was interested. *Funny,* I thought, *that he wasn't interested when I wore sweatpants to class every day. He likes my party dress.* But I realized that with the sweat pants had come a surliness that would have turned anyone off. It was designed to. Perhaps I would let my guard down a bit tonight, just to see where it took me.

Steve confessed, "I'm really enjoying the reading myself. The guys I hang around with aren't exactly the intellectual type. It's nice to have a change of pace."

The popcorn was finished and I poured it into a bowl.

Steve smiled a big smile, "Nice job. Very evenly popped."

I carried the big bowl with both hands, and as I passed him I whispered, "You're not a big dork or anything are you?" We both grinned.

We walked back into the den and sat down together on the floor, the popcorn between us, our legs outstretched, almost touching.

The Professor was concluding, "Even sundials were rare. The sun in the sky was their only clock, and so every town had its own noon and so was its own time zone!"

Paul asked, "I know one question that remains unanswered is whether these characters are Haley and Nelson's relatives. But what interests me is where these gifts are now? I guess he would have kept them all and left them to his own children, and so they were lost centuries ago."

Everyone agreed that this was an important question.

At this point Bart and Shannon arrived. They had been visiting a friend at a local bar for a few minutes before resuming their all-night preparation for tomorrow's test. They heard the full story, and had something to add.

I had often thought that Bart, one of Nelson's very best friends, was a little overbearing. He said, in a voice really too blustery for this situation, "Well, I don't know if he's the same guy, but there's this creep with a thick English accent asking everybody in the bars on the Strip where Professor O'Shea lives. I thought it was a weird coincidence that that was where we were heading. Nobody told him where this place was, at least not while we were there, and we split. That was a while ago."

We ten got comfortable, preparing to enjoy another chronicle while the police, who we all noticed were cruising the neighborhood quite regularly, did their job.

The Professor began again in his same smooth, authoritative tone,

I decided to arrange my gifts around me, and I was very gratified by all six so far. The sword and the bow and arrow offered me security, the collar and the amulet made me feel a deep sense of pride in my family, and the stirrup and the chess set kept my hope alive that I might actually come from nobility.

I surveyed the scene and was satisfied. Most of the outer circle had been dug, and Wulfric still leaned against his rock. I worried that the fire might warm him to the point that he started to smell, but I thought he'd be fine until I could bury him in the morning. The fire was still crackling nicely and the immediate area was bathed in light and enough heat. No wolf would get within ten feet of this fire, I thought. Beyond that perimeter, though, was a very dangerous place to be.

I scanned the perimeter, and saw nothing out of the ordinary. I looked up and saw the two hornets' nests that I had noticed earlier silhouetted high in the trees. The mistletoe scattered around the clearing strangely comforted me. It had brought me luck so far. I petted Rexy roughly on the chest and broad shoulders, but she did not wake up. A man was standing beside me.

I jumped in shock and Rexy thundered awake. It was only Cynewald.

"Oh mercy, mercy" he croaked in his coarse tongue as he rushed over to the frozen figure of Wulfric. I ordered Rexy into a "stay" then a "quiet" command. Cynewald knelt next to the body with his back to me and it appeared that he cried for some time.

Finally I called across the summit, "He must have just died when I arrived. He speaks very highly of you in this journal."

Some time passed in silence. Finally Cynewald got up and, taking so much care that his show of diligence was almost awkward, stepped gingerly over the bags to join me nearer the fire.

Cynewald now took a good look at the diaper, and he was obviously quite alarmed. "If tharn dog in heat, your'll need to cover the bitch's stink right now. This'n very serious."

At this point the Professor looked up at the animated movement of the curtains and smiled, obviously enjoying his challenge of translating Cynewald into an uneducated voice. "Do you mind? I don't know exactly how to translate these direct quotes from Cynewald. As far as I can tell, Boy is intentionally using the wrong tense when he quotes the speech of Cynewald. I think the truest modern interpretation would be one in non-standard, non-formal English."

Nelson offered, "You mean 'Redneck'!"

"Actually, Nelson, I don't. Non-standard, informal English—speech that you call 'Redneck'—has a grammar and syntax every bit as consistent and valid as my standard formal English. In fact, since you brought it up, non-standard, non-formal, lower socio-economic southern English is actually far closer to the original Old English than is my more educated speech. 'Redneck,' as you call it, is not cluttered with words of Latinized origin. It is no accident that, on average, the higher one's level of social affluence, the higher the percentage of Latinate words in one's vocabulary. This reality of American social linguistics is directly traceable to the fact that poverty breeds poverty, back through the ages, into, among many other places, medieval England. Therefore the poorest people in modern America, England, Canada, and Australia tend almost exclusively to use words of pure Germanic origin. That is not a value judgment, it is a linguistic fact. Now, let's see what Cynewald has to say."

Looking down at the hard-packed earth, I nodded in agreement as Cynewald's attention turned back to his master. "Hern was a great man. A very good man, and, although 'arm sure you ne'er believe me, very doting on you."

I looked up into the face of this stranger, so like me in appearance, and so good-spirited, but whom I could barely understand. I trusted him immediately.

"What he garn through to protect you!" He said this very loudly as he grinned his jagged-tooth smile before he took a generous swallow from the wine I offered. He wiped his mouth with his soiled tunic and looked around a bit amazed at the leather bags and the holes I had dug. I got the feeling he had never been up here before, and it suddenly occurred to me that Wulfric may have worked for years digging into the solid rock of this mountain all by himself.

Cynewald pointed at the booklet by my side with the flask and gave a prolonged belch that finished with, "But he wants there'an book, not me, to tell the story."

At this point I badly desired to know whatever Cynewald knew about this night and book. "Can you tell me anything to put meaning to this craziness?"

Cynewald looked directly at me, his narrow, youthful face half lit with the moving light of the fire. "I would," he leaned forward theatrically, "if I arnly could. Wulfric tell me almost nothing. He said it'd put me in harm and forbade me ev'ern ask about this book. He'd pass hour after hour, day after day, locked up with it in his rooms. Honest, I'n always wondered myself. I sure ne'er knew about this hilltop. No, he was full of secrets. All'rn know is that the master finally told me a little something about ther'ne book last week. He told me it was written for yar'n and he sent me to the swordmakers' guild in London to get yar'n back here. And believe me, there was no way I could've tracked yar'n lessen yar'n had that bitch with you." He pointed a well-worked finger to Rexy who was sitting bolt upright, faintly growling, and pointing her ears right back at him. Cynewald scowled at the diaper again.

"Anyway, I come up to see if yar'n two needed anything. Shame about his dying. Did yar'n get to talk to the master befar'n he passed?"

I shook my head, and Cynewald nodded and got up to stretch. "I'll be back up right after sunup to take him back dar'n the mountain." He looked at me, "Yar'n be coming back to his manor now? After all, yar'n're our master now."

As agreeable as this sounded, I was firm. "I will be staying up here tonight. It was his wish."

"Alright," Cynewald said as he began to move away, "I told the master I would visit up here tonight from time to time, but unless yar'n cover that stink, I'm afraid I cain't come back til morning. Way too dangerous." He took one last look over at Wulfric's body as he moved away. "He war always so good to me."

Then Cynewald stopped, thought a minute, and turned. He walked back toward me, as if he had forgotten something. "Yar'n read anya these little books yet? Anything worthy o'note?" Cynewald picked one up and looked at it, leafing through the pages. He was holding the booklet upside down.

"Quite boring, really. I'm about to turn in."

"Well, then, I'll take my leave."

With that Cynewald vanished down the trail into the blackness. Rexy gave a final low growl; she never had liked anyone but Emma and me. I was beginning to see why Wulfric had trusted Cynewald so much. Although his frank and colorfully vulgar way of wording things never for a minute let me forget his low station, he seemed sturdy and competent. He might be a great help this night.

I removed the next chronicle from its bag and settled in to read. This chapter was entitled "Neils," a name I recognized as Danish. That meant that I was a Viking. Of all the thoughts that this could have evoked, my first impulse was to hope for an exotic weapon to help protect my Rexy and me. With seven of my ancestors revealed, I did not feel quite as lonely on that mountaintop:

Wulfric Rhys

Bag Bag

Ealdgyth Angharad

Bag Bag

Neils Fire Bag

Bag Bag

Bag Matilda

Your great-grandfather Neils, who was your father's paternal grandfather, was born in 979 in Denmark. His maternal grandfather was said to have been one of those who sacked Constantinople in 941. Neils' father was none other than Harald Bluetooth, the Danish king who had renewed the Viking raids beyond the Baltic Sea after many decades in which kingdoms such as England had been left in peace. Neils, then, was one of the many—perhaps nine--brothers of Svein, who as successor to his father would eventually become king of Denmark. Svein, if you will remember, backed by hundreds of Viking raiders including Neils, sacked England mercilessly from 998 until Svein finally became king of England in 1013.

Neils' earliest days were spent in training for battle, and at the age of thirteen he began plundering with his brothers in the area of Finland. At nineteen, Neils joined the expedition of Leif Erickkson, son of Erik the Red, and visited many strange lands to the far

```
west. One of these lands was so strange that it
was said that the primitives there used
seashells for coin.
```

Nelson whistled slowly. "Wow. Is this the first proof that Vikings discovered America? Didn't American Indians use wampum seashells for money?"

The Professor commented calmly, "Nelson, did you not know that the Chinese discovered America about 45,000 years ago? They crossed a land bridge that later covered over with water and they became the Native Americans. *They* discovered America. Some of these migratory people followed game to the Atlantic shores near modern New England and gradually developed into the Iroquois cultures, some of whom indeed traded in wampum."

The Professor continued, "It has long been established by archaeologists as fact that Leif Erickson was the first European who discovered America. Wulfric is only confirming historically what we have known through archaeology for some time."

"I knew that," smiled Nelson. And actually, Nelson was very curious and did know very many things. So many things, in fact, that, during the course of this evening, as always, he had not minded asking the real questions. While such questions exposed the extent of his ignorance, they were necessary for him to generate the context in which to understand this story fully. He also perceived that others in the room who were not as secure in their intellectual abilities, me, for example, might need him to ask the questions that they were all thinking and were afraid to ask. Again and again he would take the hit for exposing his limitations, but this just made people all the more comfortable around him.

Nelson finished, "Thanks for setting me straight. Now let's go back, Professor."

The Professor pointed out on the map the main areas of England hit by the Vikings and then settled in to read. The newcomers were very impressed by the laser light show.

After his return in 1002, Neils took up with his brother Svein as his gang of Danes began to plunder and slaughter the people of England mercilessly. In this year the English paid the Danes 24,000 pounds to end their assault. But in 1004 the band was back, ravaging Norwich and all of East Anglia. Burning every town they encountered and slaying everyone they met, these Viking invaders had their way with England. King Ethelred could do nothing to stop them, and of course he finally had to flee England in 1013, turning the crown itself over to the vicious Svein.

1011 and 1012 were probably Neils' most profitable years. Neils and his band were able through the treacherous assistance of Eadric Streona, my Ealdgyth's lord at the time, to penetrate Canterbury, the seat of Archbishop Aelfheah, and to seize the archbishop himself. They martyred him. Neils and his cohorts raped and slaughtered from Wessex to East Anglia.

The Professor quickly interjected, "All the sources of the period give vivid accounts of the horror of this era, and I will not dwell on them. One quote will be enough to provide you the glimpse that you need into this nightmarish period, surely the darkest days in English history. Wulfstan, the archbishop of York (1002-1023) lamented in a sermon of the period the violence and loss of dignity associated with this invasion:

And often ten or a dozen [Danes], one after another, insult disgracefully the thegn's wife, and sometimes his daughter or near kinswoman, whilst he looks on, who considered himself brave and mighty and stout enough before that happened."

A silence fell over the room for a moment.

The Professor concluded, "The impact of the violence of these Danes was so severe that not only was Canute allowed to take the throne from 1016 until 1035, but also his two Viking sons, Harold (1035-1040) and Hardecanute (1040-1042), afterwards took their respective thrones completely uncontested. No Saxon king returned until Edward the Confessor (1042-1066) in 1042."

He resumed,

Many good men of Kent were massacred in this hellish year, and the Vikings could not be stopped. Ethelred begged for a truce, which was agreed to for the unfathomable sum of 48,000 pounds, which was promptly collected by Ethelred and delivered. Our Heavenly Lord spared those of your family, Boy, from most of their brunt. In this period I was twelve in

Hereford and Ealdgyth was twelve in Worcester, both regions of western Mercia far removed from the bloodshed of the southeast. Rhys in Cardigan and Angharad in Powys were vulnerable to attack, but they escaped with their lives. As residents of Normandy, both Hugh and Matilda escaped the attacks of Neils, in part because of their southern position, in part because they were allied with the Danes, and in part because Normandy itself originated as a Viking colony, even being named after the Normen. Your forefathers were the lucky ones. Except Neils' wife.

Neils was in charge of the ships assigned to transport this fabulous 48,000-pound ransom from the Isle of Wight, the base of the Danes in England, back to the safety of Denmark. The Vikings gained little by this ransom, though, because the treasure was lost in a storm. Yet the Vikings had accumulated so much booty, and would continue to do so, that this loss was soon forgotten; they attacked again the next year and expelled the king himself. Since Neils was the sole survivor of the fleet of six Viking longboats, each with strong square sails, some suspicion was cast on him that he had absconded with the mountains of pennies, which were said to have filled fifty small, very heavy chests. Since Neils was under the protection of his older brother Svein, however, this rumor was soon forgotten.

Neils joined other Danes as they plundered their way down the Atlantic coast, sacking cities in France and then assaulting the infidel followers of Mohammed in Iberia. In 1020 Neils and his horde penetrated deep up the Tagus river of Cordoba.

Paul looked at the Professor. "Where is Cordoba again?"

"Cordoba is the central region of modern Spain. The Muslims were only expelled from Spain in 1492; in 1012, the southern half of the Iberian Peninsula was completely Muslim. It was still, however, subject to incursions from Vikings and from the Christianizing Spanish who harried the Muslims from northern Spain. Now, Neils:"

It was on one of these raids that Neils first encountered your great-grandmother. Their party, whether on land or, more commonly, in boats, had their way lighted as always by a torch at the front of this roaring wave of murder. Wearing their infamous bronze helmets, Neils and his band ravaged many villages up the Tagus, leaving as few survivors as possible. He would begin his assault with the firing of poisonous arrows, and would always end with the fury of his bronze battle-axe.

On this fateful day for you, Boy, the longboats, rowed by the slaves they had so far accumulated on this expedition, touched quietly on the shore far up the Tagus in the middle of the night. Normally Vikings charge with a mighty roar to intimidate and to destroy most of the opposition, but small villages like this which put up virtually no opposition were best looted if surprise were at work. Neils moved alone into the countryside and discovered an elaborate cottage that appeared to belong to a great Muslim lord. On his smashing down the door, three ran at him, and three fell hard and still to the earth. Neils was looking for the harem, the adjoining structure where the women—grandmothers, mothers, and young girls--resided. By the time he smashed down the door of the harem, all the women had fled but one. Strangely, she seemed to be in no hurry. In the corner, this woman, just putting on her long Muslim veil, was standing next to a crib. She picked up the baby and cringed without looking at Neils.

Here far in the interior of Cordoba, when Neils ripped off the veil, he discovered a sight more beautiful than he had ever seen. A girl with hair of fire was standing petrified here by this crib, holding her newborn baby. The young mother was obviously Irish. The baby had dark hair and dark skin, and was shrieking. It was the girl, though, aglow from the light of the fireplace, that dropped Neils' jaw. Neils approached the girl, obviously a slave of the infidel moors, and snatched the baby violently from its mother. Their communication was wordless, and would essentially be so throughout their marriage to come. Neils motioned that he would throw the infant into the fire, and the mother just smiled her beautiful smile. Neils immediately put the screaming child in its crib. Later she was ashamed to tell me this, but she insisted that with such a wide language gap between her Irish and his Danish, only the most universal human communication would have saved her baby at that moment.

This girl was so exotic and so lovely that Neils did what he had never done before in similar situations—he took her for his bride. At forty, he had been considering retiring to an estate in England, and the discovery of this girl made his decision easier. Though she spoke both Irish and Arabic, no translator was available for his Danish. To a Viking, though, this mattered very little, and his battleaxe flew into all those who tried to stop him from taking his prize back to England. She was put aboard ship, bound, and taken to England where she was set up as Neils' wife. The child came too—the infant assured for Neils not only that this girl would behave as he wished, but also that she would not attempt escape, which would be almost impossible with an infant.

Canute, son of King Svein and nephew of your great-grandfather Neils, had become king of England in 1016 and gladly granted a lordship to his uncle. In East Anglia, one of the centers of the new Danish settlement, Neils settled down in 1020 to become an English thegn under Canute, who was both king of England and King of Denmark, and would soon win the crown of Norway as well. The Irish girl learned the sharp tongue of Norwich over time and assimilated to some degree into the local Anglo-Danish culture. Her name, he came to learn, was Siobhan.

Here the Professor clarified that though this classic Irish name is pronounced "Shiv-awn," it is spelled "S-i-o-b-h-a-n".

Paul asked, "Is it true that the cultural imprint of the Vikings was so permanent that their names of the days of the week, such as 'Odinsday' and 'Thorsday' became our 'Wednesday' and 'Thursday'?"

The Professor looked up and said, "Commonly believed, but not quite true: Odin is the main Norse or Viking god; Woten is the main Germanic god of those who live in Germany ; Woden is the main Anglo-Saxon god of those who live in England. The three gods have many similarities but are a bit different. The days of the week in Modern English are actually derived from the names of the original Anglo-Saxon gods, for example, Woden and Thunor, and not from their Norse god equivalents. Granted, all four—Odin, Woten, Woden, and the Celtic god Lugh--are derived from the same common god that was worshipped in an earlier stage of the evolution of the religions of northern Europe. Their counterparts in southern Europe include Jupiter from Rome and Zeus from Greece. All six of these chief gods trace from a common originating chief god worshipped in the Caucus Mountains before the Caucasian migration that swept Europe around 10,000 B.C.

That does not mean, however, that the Vikings did not exert a profound linguistic influence on Modern English; they certainly did. Many words of Norse origin are in our language today, many at its very core, such as our words 'sister,' 'they,' 'them,' 'earl,' 'law,' and 'die'."

He resumed,

Soon enough, Siobhan bore Neils a son whom he named Roth. Boy, Roth is your grandfather. Roth was of course reared in the murderous Viking way, despite the fact that his Irish mother was very headstrong. Her story will follow and is a tale well worth hearing.

Time passed, and Roth was reared to fight with all the viciousness of his father. Siobhan was a wise woman, and learned to get along with her Viking husband as well as she had her Muslim husband. During one of his voyages to Denmark, Neils had his favorite bronze battle-axe engraved with a curious etching of what appeared to be white cliffs under a broken lighthouse. On the other side, he had an inscription etched in Old Norse rune. Neils retired this bronze battleaxe to a corner of his bedchamber, but he had many more weapons that were still fully functional.

I include on the following page a rubbing of both sides of this axe, in the event that it is taken from me. Considering the value of this axe, I expect that it will not stay in my possession long enough to get it to you. Let me tell you what happened to me one day long after Neils was dead.

After I acquired the battle-axe, I wondered about the significance, if any, of the etching on the axe. I was especially interested in what the runes on the back said, but finding a literate Viking, even in northeast England, took me three years of waiting and inquiring. Finally in a tavern one night I was directed to a tough-looking Viking who, I was told, could read a little. In the dirt of the floor of the tavern I spelled out the runic letters written on the battleaxe, which I had committed to memory in case I ever lost it. I certainly did not tell him about the image on the other side. As a minstrel, I was forced to develop a very sharp memory.

He turned and shouted the phrase aloud in the Danish of his comrades. I did not understand a word, but they did. It brought down a curtain of utter silence on thirty drunken Vikings. It took three hours to convince them that I had only read it from the writing of another minstrel long ago and had memorized it. They would not tell me what it meant, but four of them followed me, tortured me, and interrogated me for the rest of that night. I said nothing, suspecting only my silence would save my life. They finally let me go only to follow me, but I evaded them.

The message of this axe, then, is apparently very valuable. I knew that if I ever told anyone else about this axe, they could sell the information to most any Viking who would then certainly kill to get it. As a result, I urge you to keep it only to yourself—it is very dangerous.

I suddenly understood why Wulfric had urged me to read so quickly. At this point I saw no choice but to remove Rexy's diaper. Then I called her over to the edge of the cliff, which was near enough to the fire to be quite safe, and put her in a stay command with her bottom almost hanging off the cliff into the breeze. Rexy's problem might actually help me. She became comfortable and soon enough went to sleep. I dropped the diaper off the cliff, and dug up my new battle-axe. It was even sturdier than I had hoped. In fact, it was nothing short of magnificent. Then I finished Neils' story.

In 1030, when Neils was fifty-one, an uprising of Saxons in Cambridge required the attention of the local Danish thegns. The uprising was put down, but not before Neils, who was setting fire to the walls of the city, was struck on the helmet and knocked to the ground. Large rocks thrown by the defenders of the city of Cambridge then pelted him. His comrades avenged him murderously and then carried him home.

Of the stoutest ancestry, he recovered well. But soon after his recovery, his household temporarily ran out of ale. Thirsty, the impatient Neils did what he had been warned so many times not to do; he drank the water from his well. Ale was consumed in such heroic quantities in Anglo-Saxon England precisely because the brewing process boiled and purified the drink.

He contracted dysentery which brought on crippling diarrhea and Neils soon lay dying, the flies too numerous to fight. Siobhan was not particularly helpful in suggesting cures for his affliction, but his servants knew the remedy: to cure dysentery, powder human bones, mix with red wine, and give to sufferer. Though they gave Neils several doses, your great-grandfather could not hold out against the fever. Before his death, he instructed Siobhan to take his etched bronze axe and give it to their son Roth. It was his dying wish, and she had absolutely no intention of honoring it. Neils had beaten her and treated her as a prisoner for decades, and she now had a chance to pay him back. Neils had traveled from Finland to Iberia, from the land of the money shells to Norwich, and, as a mighty warrior, he now embarked on his final voyage, sailing to the Valhalla or Heaven of his pagan gods at last. So ends the story of your great-grandfather Neils.

So this is my great grandfather Neils. And I had thought Matilda had had a horrible marriage. I immediately wondered how different my attack on the bearded thugs earlier had been from the warring of my Viking ancestors. This heritage also suddenly explained my atypically large stature and my light blue eyes. Why had I not seen this as I stood a head taller than all the men at the guild? I was a Viking!

I wondered about the huge fortune that was lost. I amused myself with thinking that if I ever recovered that fortune in silver, I would bury it so securely that no one would ever find it without direction.

Bart asked rather skeptically, and a little too loudly, "Where did you get this book? You all seem so sure it's real. Maybe I missed some info earlier that made it more plausible that the thing is authentic. If it is real, we can probably trace it back to this summit! I think it would be worth searching."

I had been wondering how to answer when this question came up, since I did not want to expose the exact location of the setting of this book just yet. But Nelson was ready with a big lie.

"It was mailed to us by an uncle who lives in Wessex. This is a very hilly terrain with thousands of summits dotting southern England. Maybe as we read on, the location of this summit will become clear. Professor, can we read on?"

"By all means."

I could even bring it here and fill in each of the fifteen gift-indentations cut into the stone of this mountain with a stone on top to protect the treasure. That way, I mused, I would seal the gifts securely until I came for them or until I sent my children for them.

I'd tell Emma, though. Emma was probably asleep on her straw mat right now. I wondered if she still dreamed of me, and then remembered it had only been ten days. She loved me still, certainly! I understood, though, that she needed a champion, a male champion in this day of men, to aid her in her resistance to her horrible stepmother. Even with seven ancestors accounted for, so far I could still offer her no release from her painful bondage.

Rexy exploded into barking again, and to my surprise, seven hooded monks walked into my camp and greeted me. They told me that they had come a long way and asked if they could rest a while. I might be a vulgar villain, but I would not deny these men of the cloth whatever hospitality I could muster. I would also very much enjoy the company and security they brought, both physically and spiritually.

After a meal of their dried meat and my boiled beans and bread, the monks got to their business. Only one spoke to me. They were from St. David's and had heard from a fellow monk of my acquisition.

"Domnus Rhigyfarch?" I asked.

"Yes, my son," the monk answered. I looked into the blue eyes of the other monks, who were sitting in a close circle around the fire, talking in whispers. One jumped up and ran to relieve himself. His cowl was frayed in several places, and his hood had a hole in the top where a little hair stuck out.

"Now, what can I do for you brothers?" I asked, absently pointing my index finger at the first joint of my thumb.

"Domnus Rhigyfarch has sent us to collect the Grailkey. We have come to take it into our custody, to be returned to St. David's to be destroyed. Our abbot has determined that its destruction is the only recourse that will ensure the safety of the Holy Goblet. If you will yield the Grailkey to us, we will protect it. It is what your great-grandfather, Mynyddawg, whom we all knew, would have wanted."

I moved over and pulled out the counselor from Hugh's chess set. It was pewter and might be mistaken for the Grailkey by an imposter. I walked over and put it down at the edge of the clearing.

"Go in peace," I said.

All seven jumped up and ran to the counselor, examining it closely. While their back was turned, I silently fired two arrows high into the tree directly above where I had placed the counselor. Then they turned back to me.

"Are you sure this is the key, my son? I thought it would be larger."

Suddenly first one, then a second hive of furious hornets landed in the midst of them, both cracking open and exposing hundreds of stirring hornets, preparing to swarm out from their winter resting state. As the monks fled in disarray from the fallen nests, I began launching deadly arrows as fast as I could load. "This is for eating meat," I said as the first monk fell. "This is for not knowing the monastic sign language that I just used on you," I fired, "this is for running," "this is for being able to speak English," "this is for sitting too close," "this for breaking your vow of silence," "this is for having blue eyes in Wales," "this is for confusing my grandfather Mynyddawg with his father Rhys the monk," "and this is for not having shaved heads." I was out of arrows and one "monk" remained, and he drew a menacing sword from under his cowl.

"You read your book well, my boy. But you must die now. I was afraid you might figure out that we did not know what the key looked like, but he never told us of your cleverness. We were also told that you were unarmed, but all the better that you killed these thugs. Saved me the trouble. But your arrows are spent, as you soon will be too."

"Before I die, tell me what you are going to do with the Grailkey. I assume that when you mentioned destroying it you were lying?"

"You assume correctly," said the false monk. "I am going on the Crusade! In Jerusalem, I will gain the Holy Grail, which I will sell to the highest bidder."

"Do you know where the keyhole is?"

"No," said the false monk.

"Do know which way to twist the key? The other way brings disaster."

"No."

"Do you know how many times to twist the key?" I asked.

"No."

"Do you have any preference whether I kill you with this sword, or this battleaxe?" I held one in each hand weighing one, then the other.

"You are full of surprises," said the false monk.

"And I never expected that you would actually think hornets remain active through a frozen winter like this. They would never have swarmed. Surprises abound."

With that I approached, reinforcing Rexy's stay command that she was still honoring with her bottom hanging off the cliff. The weapon that he chose was my new battle axe, and the engagement was only brief. It felt wrong to sink the axe into his back, wrong to watch a monk slump so slowly to the earth. But of course, they were not really monks, only bandits who had purchased the secret of my Grailkey from someone. Rexy's collar had been the perfect disguise. None of them would ever have found it. After salvaging all my arrows and cleaning them with the imposters' cowls, I took all I could from their belongings and hid these items behind a tree in case of more unwanted visitors, which I really could not imagine. Then I stabbed all seven of the monks through the heart—I do not like surprises popping up again later—and dropped all seven bodies off the cliff. I also heaved all four halves of the hornets' nests, just to be sure the heat my fire did not eventually wake their winter slumber. Then I released my Rexy. She and I ate their dried meat ravenously.

Steve said, "Wow! Nice scene!"

"Which one, dude? Neils and the redhead, or Boy and the monks?" said Joel, a classmate with hairy sideburns and a hemp chain around his neck. He had so far remained quiet.

"Show us that etching," said Shannon.

They all gathered around to see the first etching page. It was a picture of white cliffs with a sea below, with a broken lighthouse still shining its light.

"I know where that is," blurted out Steve.

"So do I," said Marilyn.

"Me too," echoed Joel with an animated nod of the head.

"The white cliffs of Dover," they said in unison.

Nelson added, "And you can see by the Professor's map that Dover is on the way from the Isle of Wight to Denmark. That must be where the treasure is buried."

"You mean was buried," I corrected. "Boy obviously lived after the events of this book, otherwise how could he have written it? He obviously figured this out too, and so he took the treasure long ago. But wouldn't he secure it someplace? And wouldn't the most secure place of all be just what he was joking about, this summit?"

"But man, where in Dover could it be?" asked Joel. "I was there on our high school choir trip two summers ago. The cliffs have to be at least thirteen miles long."

"Finally, I'm needed," scowled the Professor. "At the castle of Dover today there are ruins of an ancient Roman lighthouse. Only a large brick circle still exists there now but it can be plainly seen where the structure used to be. It must be the exact landmark for the treasure."

Bart objected, “Must *have been*; the treasure has certainly been discovered by now, after one thousand years in a place that is today a major tourist attraction. If the silver is still located at Dover, we have no hope. But if it was removed to Wulfric’s summit, the land might be for sale. I’ll admit I have been skeptical of the authenticity of this book all along, but it does provoke the imagination, doesn’t it?”

I thought to myself, *or we might already own the land.* Without speaking, Nelson and I had come to the same conclusion early on in the evening. It would be best to keep the fact that we owned a summit in Essex to ourselves, and in fact we both avoided even the fact that we had found the book in Essex, and identified its place of origin as “near Wessex.” This was quite true enough, I supposed, since they were both in England, and England is so small! I wasn't worried that anyone in the room might be untrustworthy, but I did want to control the flow of information. Mainly, I didn't want everyone to get all worked up over what was almost certainly a dead end.

"Let's look at the next page, the runes on the reverse side," suggested Shannon, "What are runes, anyway?"

The Professor clarified, "Runes are simply ancient Germanic phrases written in an obscure Germanic lettering. The runic script is based on the Roman letters we still use but has slight differences. Runes tend to be associated with ancient spells, but can also have very practical functions. There are examples of runes on swords and examples of runes that worked as treasure maps. Let's see this etching."

"What's the rune sketched here say?" they asked in unison.

"I'm sorry, but I cannot read the runic script. Runic is just too obscure. I have a friend in Germany who can read it, but it will take some time to reach her."

"I bet its translation will come to light soon enough," said Nelson. "Whatever it says, it sure got those Vikings in the tavern excited. I bet it gives the exact location of that treasure. I bet that those Vikings knew what treasure, but just never saw the lighthouse and the cliffs that were on the reverse side. Had they been able to combine what they knew together with what we know now, pow! Fabulous wealth!"

At this point four pizzas arrived, and they were eaten very quickly, except Nelson's anchovy pizza, which he got all to himself.

It was such a beautiful night that most of us decided to eat on the front porch. My stomach still hurt so I passed on the pizza, but I sat on the porch swing next to Nelson as he talked non-stop to his friends about tomorrow's test. I gazed out into the street as a police car cruised slowly by under the strong moonlight. I recognized Sargeant Thackerson's bushy mustache come into view as he silently rolled down his window and waved to me. I remembered his whispered promise to me earlier that afternoon that he would hunt down my attacker. Somehow I had believed every word of his promise and I still did. He had to be our university's most inspirational rent-a-cop. He cruised on and his police car turned the corner, vanishing into the blackness of this night.

I thought about the events of the evening so far. For about the past hour it had been dawning on me that lying beneath the hurt that I felt over this horrible semester may have been the life-long hurt I had felt from Mom and Dad. Glimpses kept coming to me that perhaps my confusion about school was really only a symptom of the betrayal that I had been feeling all my life from parents who either didn't love me or didn't know how to show it in a way that I could recognize. Had Mom and Dad really been the greedy, selfish, negligent parents that I had come to resent so deeply, or had my warped perspective just resulted in my reading their behaviors and actions incorrectly?

Or was this the wrong question completely? Perhaps what I should be asking was, given the crappy hand I had been dealt so far in life, whose responsibility is it to fix the problem? None of Boy's ancestors had had it easy, but all of them responded the same way. They each understood that whatever our starting point, we can and must reinvent ourselves as soon as we are mentally strong enough to stand up to the weaker parts of our personalities. Instead of harboring resentment against my parents forever, I imagined for a minute that the approach that would actually build me up and allow me to break free of my past would be to forgive them and make a new promise to myself, a promise that I would not pass such uncaring tendencies on to the next generation. Instead I could watch over my children and protect them like the best mothers in all the ages. Did I have the power inside me to reinvent myself, to rise up above my past, and force a strong and happy future onto myself and the family I would one day have?

My concentration was broken by the sudden realization that the crowd was moving inside. Steve, however, lagged behind the rest. I decided that I, too, would not get up just yet, to see if I couldn't just start reinventing myself right now. The door hissed closed and we were alone in that moonlight.

Chapter Thirteen

The Greens of Ireland

"I know you probably hear this a lot," said Steve, walking over alarmingly close to me and leaning on a column of the front porch, "but your eyes are so beautiful that they disorient me, as if I were a compass and you were a magnet. Looking directly into your eyes is like the first step off a roller coaster."

"I've definitely never heard that before," I said as I stood up and leaned on the railing.

"Seriously," he continued, turning to look at me, "I can hardly look away. I can't believe you're not dating anyone."

"You're sweet," I said, as I turned away from his strong gaze, looking off the porch but moving myself slightly closer to him.

I asked out into the cooling night air, "So, Steve, you're really not afraid to be on this porch at one in the morning, with a stalker on the loose?"

"Honestly? Not one bit. Are you?"

I took a moment to get my answer to say exactly what I meant. "Honestly? I feel completely safe here with you. I've never felt so secure." I turned and looked at him a bit too long.

"While we're being honest," he continued, "I'll admit that I want the guy to come try to assault us right now, so that I can end your worrying about him right now. You don't need to worry anymore." He looked at me a bit too long. The stars above twinkled in anticipation as our gazes intertwined and I moved toward him.

"Hey hey!" said Nelson, as he burst out onto the porch. "What'chall doing? Don't forget, buster, I invented the porch maneuver, too. Storytime! Let's go, people!"

I smiled at Steve and he smiled back at me, and we both frowned at Nelson as we walked by his puffed-out chest through the threshold of the front door back inside. Steve had a substantial torso, and the contrast with Nelson's almost concave chest as we moved by his mock-disapproval was sharp. As we slid by Nelson, though, I interlaced my warm fingers into Steve's strong, sweating hand. I led him firmly back to the den and then uncoupled as we entered the room.

Soon the discussion turned to how Boy could possibly get Emma at this point.

"I know they will be together," I said.

"Not every story has a happy ending," winked Nelson. I could tell he was very happy that I was feeling better.

The Professor added, "Well, the best argument for them getting together is not found in the book, because given the social standing of Boy at this point in the narrative, eleventh-century Anglo-Norman society would never accept his marriage to Emma. Unless something develops here. No, the best proof that I can think of that they live happily ever after is simply your eyes, Haley."

"How's that, Professor?" I laughed, beginning to redden.

He continued, "When Boy described Emma's eyes, I thought he was describing yours. It made me lose my concentration. Do you think that's only a coincidence?"

The Professor was trying to be nice to me, and I felt a blinding flush of embarrassment. "Let's read," I said. All the eyes were on me, and my charm was back, my inner light. The room and the boys were beginning to revolve again, the movement of my life accelerating back to its former happy speed.

The Professor resumed,

I was still not entirely sure that the wizards and the false monks were the threat that Wulfric had warned of. But how could there be three? Looking over at the cross-armed corpse, I could not help but admire him. I decided the best approach was simply to read on, since the night was advancing.

Wulfric Rhys

Bag Bag

Ealdgyth Angharad

Bag Bag

Neils Fire Hugh

Bag Bag

Siobhan Matilda

Your great-grandmother Siobhan, who was your father's paternal grandmother, was born in 1000 in Cork, Ireland. Her father was a rich and important landholder, the counterpart to our Earl, and early in her life she was betrothed to O'Brian, son of King Brian of Dublin. Brian was the first king ever to style himself as "King of the Irish," and the union promised to be fruitful and to stabilize relations between Dublin on the east coast and Cork in the south.

Brian was the hero of the 1014 epic battle of Clontarf, one of the most heralded Irish battles ever. It was here that the Vikings who had ruled Dublin and the eastern region for so long were finally and permanently expelled. But it was also here that Brian died, leaving the throne for his son O'Brian. And it was while escaping after this battle that Vikings captured young Siobhan, his princess bride.

Before her capture at the age of thirteen, Siobhan was a precocious young lady. She rarely listened to her father, and instead whiled her days away riding her favorite mare through the gray-green heather of Ireland. Of course, as the future queen of Ireland, her confidence and spirit were as high as any young girl's could be. And the grass in Ireland, she often remembered, was the greenest in the world. She would unravel the long braid of orange hair that her ladies in waiting had worked so long on and would ride hard, her green eyes outshining the grasses, her coppery hair floating timelessly in the air behind her hard gallops.

It was this flowing orange hair that had first caught the attention of Viking raiders as they rode through the heather looking for booty. When she saw them riding wildly toward her, she shot away like a rabbit. She told herself that this was one race that she would win. From the left, more Vikings closed, and she was galloping hard for a cliff that opened onto the Lee River far below. It was jump or stop, with the barbarians screaming on either side. Papa had told her not to ride here. She braced herself for the hardest jolt of her life and brought her mare to a stop. To win this race would mean to run it another day. A Viking's wooden club matted her hair with blood as she was rammed onto the ground, where her world went to black.

When she awoke she was chained on a Viking slave ship in the middle of the ocean. Huge blond Danes were talking to each other at the front as rowers, almost all with the red hair of Ireland, strained to avoid another stroke of the whip from a very angry foreman. Siobhan's eyes, bright green, strained to scan her surroundings for some sign of hope. In her weakness, she collapsed again, and as she fainted away she heard the shaky voice of one of the slaves say, "Your turn soon, missy."

The Professor apologized, "Sorry about using the word 'missy,' but, remember, I have to improvise often as I translate this. Some words do not translate well, but I'm doing the best I can."

Joel asked, nodding his head as he spoke, "You are awesome, Professor. But did the Vikings really sell slaves? Irish slaves? I never heard that in my life."

The Professor answered, "Oh yes. For example, the Icelander Hoskuld Dala-Kolsson of Laxardal paid three marks of silver—three times the price of a common slave—for a pretty Irish girl; she was one of twelve offered by a Viking raider." Professor O'Shea added, smiling, "It is good to have a view of Ireland before it began its historical phase as subordinate to England. In these first decades of the eleventh-century there was virtually no interaction between England and Ireland yet. Now back to our Irish lady."

Siobhan fetched a very high price, as the Vikings had expected she would. She was bought by one of the most important imams, or religious leaders, of the caliphate, or kingdom, of Cordoba. From 1014 until 1017 Siobhan lived as one of the wives of this imam and learned the Moorish tongue. The green in her eyes, she often thought as she looked into the reflective silver at the women's chapel of the mosque, had faded some.

Siobhan, though, was not like the other slaves. Perhaps it was her royal upbringing, or perhaps it was her natural personality, but she resisted this new culture and this new land at every turn. She cursed her beauty for resulting in her enslavement, but she knew that charm might well be her only passage back to her home, the green fields of Cork. Escape became her obsession, and she knew it would come at a price.

One day a trader came through and met her as she was alone washing clothing at the creek. Years later she commented to me how the Muslims cleanse themselves almost daily—"a vast waste of time," she would sing to me in her Irish accent. Yes, Boy, I met Siobhan and I spent much time with her. She and I have a grandson in common since her son married my daughter. Yes, our mutual grandson is your father Thorkel.

There it is. So Wulfric and Ealdgyth were the parents of Gunnehilde who married Roth, whose parents were Siobhan and Neils. Gunnehilde and Roth had Thorkel, my father. I was thrilled. And that means Rhys and Angharad were the parents of Mynyddawg, the Welshman, who married the Norman Eleanor, whose parents were Hugh and Matilda. Mynyddawg and Eleanor, then, were the parents of my mother, still unidentified by Wulfric, who somehow married Thorkel and had me. I felt as if my very soul was being colored in as I gained knowledge of my family, ancestor by ancestor. I remember looking over at the corpse of Wulfric. I was very grateful, very moved, and very impressed by his skill to compose what was for me such an interesting narrative.

Immediately the trader noticed her exotic beauty and the wisps of red hair escaping from her long black Muslim veil. He showed her his compass, which was a device which, he said, always points toward Ireland. We have no such device in England.

Siobhan asked, "Always points toward Ireland?" and he assured her that it did. This trader said he would give both the compass and the lodestone to her. The compass was only a small piece of steel slipped snuggly inside a reed, but touched on one end by the lodestone carried by this trader, the compass pointed exactly to the right of her setting sun every single time it was floated in a bowl of water.

The Professor repositioned himself in his chair, crossing his other leg. "Fascinating. For them, there is no north. I had forgotten that even the notion of north had not developed in the eleventh century. What a foreign mental universe our ancestors lived in compared to ours! The Chinese thought the compass always pointed south, and eleventh-century European maps of the known world always had east at the top; Arabia was at the top, with Jerusalem at the center, Gaul on the left and Egypt on the right."

The Professor looked at the wall clock and declared in his lecture voice. "Let's get back."

She purchased the compass with silver candlesticks that she had stolen from the master. She bought the compass not simply because she knew she would need the device on her daring escape to come. She had a more sentimental reason as well. She knew that the thought of always knowing which way her family was would bring her great comfort every day until she could leave this place forever.

She made a plan to sell herself to traders if they would take her back to Cork. She knew they could not be trusted, but then, neither could she! She was waiting for the right opportunity when her plans were delayed by her pregnancy. She gave birth to her son Ali, who was the only light in her life. Yet she knew that travel until he grew older would be impossible, and this discouraged her terribly. It was into this situation that Neils exploded, and she soon found herself both a slave and a wife in Norwich, East Anglia.

The Professor pointed out Norwich on the map and made clear that it was in the heart of the Danelaw, that northeastern half of England that had for centuries been dominated by Danes and Danish culture. He resumed,

Once established in England, her compass still afforded her great comfort, even after several of her household explained to her that here in England, as opposed to Spain, Ireland was in the direction of the setting sun, not right of it. Her status was strange; Neils referred to her and treated her as his wife, and she held the social position of the wife of a thegn, but it was still clear in the way he spoke about her to his friends that she was technically considered a slave. With each rudeness and each insult, the green of her Irish eyes faded further. Perhaps the actual differences between the wife of a Viking and the slave of a Viking were only theoretical.

Before long Ali developed a toothache that soon became infected. It began to ooze yellow liquid, and finally a barber was called in to pull the tooth, but too late. Despite continuous prayer to St. Blaise to cure this deadly toothache, Ali simply worsened. A few more weeks of an excruciating infection and the boy died.

Your grandfather Roth was born in 1022. Neils and his fellow warriors reared Roth from the crib to be a ferocious, murderous Dane. Roth would accompany his father on all raids and into all battle conditions, and early on Roth would share in a percentage of the spoils. While the men were away, Siobhan would spend her time, as did other English wives in the region, spinning thread out of piles of wool in the corner. Near the hearth in her manor house was a loom for weaving this thread into cloth, and Siobhan became very good at the production of fine linen.

One day in 1030, when Roth was eight years old, Neils was brought home from battle in Cambridgeshire. Though he was badly hurt, he recovered only to die of dysentery. Roth, whose violent disposition had always been an obstacle between him and his mother, had already begun his training as a warrior, far away with fellow Danes who ruled in Northumbria. When Roth returned to East Anglia for the funeral, Siobhan did not recognize her little boy. In his skin was a rude, surly, little warrior. He was his father's boy.

After 1030 Siobhan's legal status was clarified quite quickly: she was considered a slave, but one of some position. Because she was the mother of Roth, a neighboring Dane, Guthrum, took her in. Guthrum was a small and evil man, often venting his bad tempers on his slaves and peasants. Things became far worse for Guthrum and thus for his slaves after 1042 when Edward the Confessor took the throne of England, ending three decades of Danish rule of England. Edward reassigned many earldoms and lordships, but quiet and compliant, Guthrum managed to retain his lands in the Norwich area.

Siobhan was spared the worst of his moods, though, because apparently Guthrum very much feared Roth, even though he was only an early teen. Her fourth decade was spent under the authority of this man, which only made her yearning for her homeland stronger. Finally, in 1047, when she was forty-six and Roth was twenty-five, Siobhan received a perfect stranger as a guest. That stranger was I. I was forty-seven.

She asked me into her house, which she shared with four other high-ranking slaves who were not present. She was combing fibers of flax that she had grown and picked. As I sat down and got to the nature of my business, she was combing the fibers expertly so that they were all completely parallel.

I began, "My daughter Gunnehilde and your son Roth were married eight years ago, in 1039. Did you know Roth was married?"

"I did not; the murderous lad tells his mother nothing," she said as she tied her clump of fibers to a drop spindle and gave a terrific spin. The fibers spun and compressed nicely into a thread. She tied this off and tied it on a spool with other threads that had been prepared in the same manner.

"What prompts my visit," I continued, "is the birth of their son Thorkel." At this she looked up from beginning to tie her threads onto the vertical loom that sat near her hearth. "A grandson? I have a grandson?"

"He's six now, and quite a lad. Very smart, sharp really. And extremely kind, just like his mother." I picked a tick off myself and began smashing it with a stick.

"His mother sounds like a wonder," Siobhan said as she finished tying off her threads vertically to her loom and laid a crossthread horizontally across these vertical threads.

There were some moments of silence.

"Where is Thorkel now?" she asked as she pulled one lever of the loom down while pushing the other up at the same time.

"He is with his mother in Northumberland. Roth is currently off defending one of his Danish comrade's landholdings. Even at six, Thorkel's disposition seems very different than his warrior father. I spent time with him recently, and he does not like or respect his father's manner at all. I hope that is not offensive to you."

"That makes me very happy," said Siobhan as she wove another thread in. "I could never stomach Roth's warring ways, and I am so sorry about this because I am his own mother."

As she continued her weaving, I explained the purpose of my visit. This required telling her my story, which took some time. She listened attentively to the tragedies of my mother, Eadburh, and Ealdgyth, and of course she had just heard that I had been forced to abandon Gunnehilde. I had resolved that since I had failed all of these women, I would watch over the boy Thorkel and see to it that his life was charmed. I told her about the amulet and bow and arrow that I had been saving for

Gunnehilde, and was now saving for him too, and told her that if there was any little thing of hers or belonging to his other grandfather, I would see that he received it.

"I have got very little," she said, "but I'll think on it." By this time she was finished weaving the cloth and had cut it off and was sewing the edges in a very fine pattern, almost like embroidery.

"Perhaps a shirt that you made would be very special to the boy when he is of age?"

She ignored this question and I began to think I was pushing too hard.

She changed the subject and warned me that I'd better be careful around Roth, that he would not appreciate any interference, and I told her that I had already experienced this.

"You know, I don't know you at all," she said as she teased the surface of her new cloth up and trimmed all the loose edges to leave a smooth, water-resistant surface.

"Yes, I know. But I have not come here to ask for an heirloom. What I have actually come to ask of you is that you offer your grandchild his heritage. I have decided to accumulate a series of stories for the boy. I already have enough information to compose my story, Ealdgyth's, and Gunnehilde's. I also know much about Roth from my discussions with Gunnehilde and from talking with Roth's housekeepers. What I need, though, is the story of the life of Neils. And the story of your life, and the story of Roth, as much as you know." As far as I knew then, these were all the stories I would ever need. Little did I know that the eventual marriage of Thorkel to your mother would require the accumulation of seven more stories!

"And how do you plan to remember these stories?"

Then I explained to her why the household staff was usually so generous with information about their masters. I told her my occupation, and proved it with some eye-popping juggling and a few jokes that amused her greatly. She liked me, and she thought that accumulating the six stories of Thorkel's people was a very kind gesture.

For the next three days she told me everything that had happened to her, and I logged it duly in my memory as if it were an epic story. We began to meet in the woods to avoid being either seen or overheard, and while she spoke, her powerful yearning to return to Ireland became abundantly clear. As we spoke, in fact, I had an idea that gripped me more and more.

Finally, I said to Siobhan, "I have a proposition for you. The best present that I could ever give Thorkel is to deliver you back to your people in Cork."

She looked at me sideways for a long time and finally said, "That is the most kind thing I have ever heard. Thank you. But escape is impossible. These Danes will torture and murder an escaped slave and anyone who tries to help her. They actually like that sort of thing."

Yet as we talked more, and as I continued to ask her questions to flesh out the full details of her life and the lives of her men, we came back to the notion again and again. Boy, between your great-grandmother Siobhan's bravery and my drive, there is very little that together we could not do. It would not be until the following year, 1048, that I would become a thegn of Essex, and so this plan would require some cleverness.

Norwich is not on the sea, and so we had to get ourselves to Dunwich, and then somehow onto a boat bound for southern Ireland. I left for

Dunwich immediately, and returned in three weeks with good news. A boat was to sail in two weeks, and I had booked passage with my wife. I then wrote a letter summoning Guthrum, Siobhan's owner, who was in his sixties, to Dunwich for the retrieval of "his inheritance"—I said nothing more. He was to arrive at the office of the King's sheriff in Dunwich on the day of the sailing. We knew that meant he would arrive at least a day before, which would give Siobhan time to familiarize herself with the Dunwich docks. I would go ahead and set up the berths on the ship, and I would carry with me whatever she wanted to bring back to Ireland! It was her job simply to convince Guthrum to take her with him to Dunwich. She said she might be forty-four, but she could still "convince a dead man to dance."

On the night before Guthrum's departure, Siobhan paid her first visit ever to her master after living on his lands for over seventeen years. When asked, he said his wife would not be joining the party to Dunwich, and she asked if she might go, since she had never seen Dunwich. She had told him that she would not take up much room, and in fact could sleep in his chambers on the floor. At that point the wife entered, and Siobhan excused herself. The next day she was summoned to pack for a trip: "You are to clean up after the master in Dunwich."

She was determined to do what she had to, and equally determined to do *only* what she had to. They arrived the day before the ship was to sail. Upon the arrival of the party, which included several of the thegns of Norwich, Guthrum gave them all a tour, Siobhan with him at the head of the loose procession. She slid her arm into his and let him show her the town, the shops, the massive city wall, everything.

She was memorizing. She asked to see the dock and he showed her a large ship that someone in the party said was being loaded for departure for Ireland. The sight of the rocking ship brought big drops to her eyes. Siobhan immediately choked these back and resumed pretending to listen. Every rope they unhooked from its moorings, every sail they hoisted, made her long for home more and more. She walked on by, heading back toward the marketplace, and then her eyes bulged. This was her ship and her ship was leaving! In a flash she replayed the scene in her mind and it was definitely leaving. Somehow she had gotten the date wrong.

Without a word she wrenched her arm from Guthrum and began running, her English veil flying off and her red hair flowing behind. She could hear him chasing her, angry, confused. She took a wrong turn and had to backtrack, and two of his thegns were chasing her now, in full recognition of her plan for escape. She suddenly realized that if they saw her get on the boat, they would easily have it stopped by signals. Because of this threat, though against all her instincts, she ran back toward town, overturning applecarts and slamming into people, moving farther and farther from the docks. One thegn gripped her shoulder, but she wrenched away, running as fast as she could. She turned a corner and ran smack into a fish cart, spilling the fish everywhere. She had started this race decades earlier, and it was a race she would now win.

Now she had positioned herself correctly in the town, having misdirected them into thinking her escape was by land. She began to fly back toward the dock, completing the circuit she had constructed. She ran at full speed with the curves of these stone streets, moving farther and farther away from the thegns. They followed, but this was a race she had to win. She broke into the quiet port side street at which the now-moving ship had been berthed.

It was silently moving away, already just out of reach. She ran at the dock at a ferocious speed and jumped with all the life in her body. As she sailed through the cutting ocean breeze, she looked straight at me with such a fierce look of determination that I will never forget it. As she flew toward me I was the only witness as the green flame of her eyes blazed silently back to life in the greenest fire I had ever seen.

She landed with a thud partially on me and partially on the shipdeck and I quickly stood up and lifted one foot over her prostrate, panting body. I cocked this leg up on the low rail, peering calmly at the waves, slowly waving at people on shore. As she pushed herself as closely as possible into the low rail that encircled the shipdeck, I leaned in my most leisurely manner over the rail. We were still only twenty feet from the dock and I had a heaving woman lying prostrate beneath me. Just then, three furious thegns ran breathlessly onto the street.

Before they could catch their breath and yell "Seen a redhead?" which would have gotten the attention of the crew, and would have ended our very lives, I pointed frantically and silently up a street. They shot away out of sight. The crew still worked on their rigging.

As we gained speed away from the dock, I became acutely aware that if any of the crew saw this scene or saw Siobhan lying on the deck in such a suspicious position, we would be foiled. I snapped, "Get up quickly." I firmly spun her to the other side of the boat where the cabin concealed her from the dock. Just then another thegn emerged and I gestured wildly, pointing up the same street, and he too disappeared before a sound escaped his lips.

A sailor walked by with a heavy rope; "The wife barely made it, eh? Glad to have you." His was an Irish accent.

Just then the captain called out in Irish something that Siobhan quickly interpreted for me as, "Heave to! Sheriff signals for all boats back to the dock!" Guthrum had gone straight for the sheriff, and he had ordered the harbormaster to signal the return. The fact that both she and the ship were Irish had not escaped him for a minute. The boat was turning sharply back toward the dock and in the distance I could see the thegns gathering, swords drawn. We were doomed. The only good thing about this situation was that in their fury they would probably kill us immediately.

Suddenly, Siobhan was on her feet, speaking loudly in Irish with a startlingly commanding voice. The captain and sailors gathered around to hear her words, and spoke back intensely. The word "Clontarf" was all I could make out of their foreign tongue, and the discourse became more heated. They seemed to ask one last question and then paused, all of them waiting excitedly for the answer. She responded with one lilting word, an Irish word that catapulted them into action: "Siobhan."

Immediately, they ran for their rigging, the captain barking furious orders. I could see the whites of the eyes of Guthrum when the boat heaved about again. Sails were hoisted full. A smile stretched across the face of Siobhan, now a legend in Ireland, it turned out, a legendary lost princess for whom her brother, the Earl of Cork, still offered a kingly reward. The sails popped full of wind, violently lurching the boat forward toward Siobhan's true destiny.

Our voyage southward through the Channel was blessed by clear skies and strong winds. I was very gratified that Siobhan had possessed the wisdom to employ her authority as the princess bride of Ireland to rescue us both. Honestly, I had given up at that point. In Norwich I had tried to rescue her from captivity, but she ended up rescuing me from execution. She also rescued me from something far worse: failing another woman. But I did not fail her, because she wouldn't let me. She ultimately saved herself, which may have been her real destiny all along.

With England barely visible on the right, I showed her first East Anglia, where she and Roth had lived, then, to the south, Essex, to which I always hoped my master Godwine would one day send me for retirement. We passed the White Cliffs of Dover and were awed by their sheer massiveness and majesty. At one point—it was when the ruins of an old lighthouse came into view--Siobhan became very excited and even asked if we could stop here at this place. I told her that that would be unspeakably dangerous and she seemed to calm down and agree. She pointed at the lighthouse with a knowing look and simply told me to note it well, but would say no more.

As the cliffs receded behind us, I eventually showed her the bay that the Thames flowed into, and she told me the story of the falling down of London Bridge, which apparently Neils had witnessed as a defending Dane. I would not hear anything else about this until years later, and then only from the maids who were good sources for the life of Hugh.

We rounded Kent, the southeastern corner of England and began sailing day after day toward the sunset, passing southern Kent, then Wessex, then Devon, then land's end at Cornwall. On the fifteenth day we came into sight of the land of her dreams, and on the seventeenth day we sighted the Lee River and the church of Cork at its mouth. Siobhan was very quiet as we approached. The sailors said they would go spread the news and summon the local Earl, her brother. She granted them permission to do so and said she would go first to the church to pray. Her brother was to meet her there. Before she entered the church she said her goodbye to me, and she gave me her compass to give to your father. As you will see, this would not be possible. It is yours now, Boy. Siobhan said, "I shall not be needing it any more and he might need it still. Tell the lad I love him."

Then she said one more thing before she turned away, a thing I will never forget until the day I die. I had brought her large chest from Norwich to Dunwich and had stowed it safely in our cabin for her the day before her amazing arrival on board the boat. "This," she said as she dug into the chest and clumsily hoisted from the bottom a menacing bronze battleaxe, "belonged to my murdering husband. Note the lighthouse." So ends the story of your great-grandmother Siobhan.

So this was my great-grandmother Siobhan. Finally someone of whom I can be proud. My foremothers never knew each other, but were somehow alike. Ealdgyth gave her life to save little Gunnehilde; Angharad gave up her happy home to remove her son to safety and her husband to his rightful calling; Matilda hid a huge dowry for her daughter at great peril. Siobhan kept her battleaxe as a gift for a grandson she would never meet. Yet while they were certainly all good mothers, I sensed more at work.

These women had all seized the pivotal moment in their lives and had directed it. Instead of sitting by, they took action and changed the course of their destinies. Ealdgyth forestalled the death of Wulfric and Gunnehilde. Angharad prevented a dangerous life for her Mynyddawg and a false marriage with Rhys. Matilda reinvented herself as the Duchess of Devon and averted the arrest and execution of her brother Roger. And Siobhan as the princess bride took control of the loyalties of her crew and saved herself and Wulfric. These women bravely redirected the course of their lives in order to save a loved one and themselves. Are they telling me something from beyond the grave? Can I redirect my own destiny, lead it by the hand and get my Emma? I did not understand.

I got up to stretch, and looked out into the night and wondered if this battleaxe was a protection or a threat. "Probably both," I chuckled to myself. I looked at the axe, at its etched cliffs and lighthouse, and I could see, even in this dim light, that it was good workmanship. The lettering on the other side meant nothing to me; some of the letters I did not even recognize.

All was quiet. Rexy was asleep, Wulfric silently guarding his place. Here at the edge of the cliff, nothing could be seen, not even the morning star. But the breeze on me felt good, cooling a face that had been too long near a fire. I moved to relieve myself again and Rexy woke up and followed me, as constant as the morning star.

I said, "Professor, I could listen to your Irish accent all night. Nice touch. You might want to work a little on your Cynewald, but you nailed Siobhan."

"Really," he said, "It was nothing."

Nelson wondered aloud, "Will Siobhan live happily ever after? Will she be heard from again? Will she gain the crown of Ireland lost thirty years earlier? She was the princess bride when she was thirteen, but then was captured and taken away for thirty years or so. How exactly would it be possible? And can she possibly help Boy if she does? Fitzy, what do you think?"

I answered, "Well, if it can be done, Siobhan's headstrong nature and fabulous attitude will get her the throne. I think it's clear the way she looks at her life: she will never give up, never even consider it, no matter how bad things look."

Chapter Fourteen

The Richest Man in England

Joel sat back down after the break and said, "Check it--it's the middle of the night in 1096 just like it is in this room right now!" He smiled, threw his hands up, locked his fingers behind his head, and continued, "I definitely think we have the better end of the bargain—let's see, we have a police force, we have central heating, we can all read, and we have cable TV!"

The Professor, standing by his chair and stretching, seemed to take offense. He turned to Joel and stared at him for an awkwardly long period, as if trying to decide whether to explain fully just how wrong he was, or to give the abridged version. "Young man, there is a good argument that Wulfric's people were less lonely, were in less emotional pain, were more morally consistent, and were more together psychologically than we are." Joel squirmed in his chair and absently tugged at his hemp choker, well aware how close he had come to a lengthy aside on psychological history.

I looked at Steve with one eyebrow up as the Professor picked up the book and resumed,

My eight great-grandparents had taken their place and I could not help but admire the fact that Wulfric's plan was unfolding exactly as he would have liked. Four grandparents and two parents to go. I surveyed the mountaintop with a strange and deep satisfaction, and I launched right in.

Wulfric Rhys

Bag Mynyddawg

Ealdgyth Angharad

Bag Bag

Neils Fire Hugh

Bag Bag

Siobhan Matilda

Your grandfather, your mother's father, was Mynyddawg. He was born in Powys, Wales in 1025 to his father, the priest Rhys, and his mother, the peasant Angharad. Angharad was a very gentle mother, reciting the old poems of Wales rather than sending him off to train for battle with the other children. A source told me Mynyddawg's favorite poem. This was the poem that, when he was only a wee lamb of three and four, he would beg his mother to recite each night until he fell off to sleep:

Oian aparchellan llimy vinet!
Kyuuely anwinud panelhute y oruet
Bychan a wir ryderch hael heno y ar y wlet
Aportheise neithuir o anhunet
Eiri 77 pid impen clun gan cun callet
Pibonvy 30 imblev blin wy ryssett
Ry dibit div maurth dit guithlonet
Kywrug glyu powis achlas guinet
Cwbl mewn un melyn dyfrgi blwch

I am afraid I can offer no translation, but perhaps if you will read just a few lines aloud to yourself right now, Boy, you will see that it needs none.

From a very young age, Mynyddawg was a natural trader. He had an eye for the true value of a good, and he had a knack for buying the good cheaply and moving it to a place where it would be bought at the highest price. At first his trading was limited to selling fruit to the other children in the village, but after some time Mynyddawg began to make some profit, always in the form of extra food he brought home to his parents.

As Gruffydd's raiding parties grew more numerous in the 1030s, Angharad pushed Mynyddawg to volunteer his services and free labor to any merchant who stopped in the village. From this and from his long talks with slaves who had been born in England, Mynyddawg began to speak some English. One trader was a Welshman, Caradog, who traveled the circuit from London to Powys, always by ship. Mynyddawg took great interest in him, and decided that soon he would follow him out of Wales. Mynyddawg learned many things from his conversations with Caradog, including that while pirates were a serious threat to his trade, a land route was out of the question for carrying valuable cargo. The chances of being sunk or caught on the ocean by pirates, usually Vikings, were slim compared to the near certainty of being robbed in the deep forests of Wales or England.

The Professor stopped reading and pointed at the region of Powys on the map absently. He pushed his glasses up from the very end of his nose, and asked, "Can I make a comment at this point?"

"Of course," came a chorus of replies.

"Translating Wulfric tonight has been the most fun I have had in a long time, perhaps ever."

I asked, "More fun than translating Boy's part, Professor? Why?"

"Well, here's why. Translating both Boy's Middle English, which is a Latinate language, and Wulfric's Old English, which is a Germanic language, have been fairly simple. In the case of Wulfric, however, in the interest of maximum authenticity, I have been forcing myself to first translate into Modern English, then to retranslate back into words based on Old English."

"Now, what?" said Joel.

"Let me explain. When I translate a line of Wulfric's Old English into my mind as, for example, "he excitedly anticipated departing immediately," which is how I personally would say the phrase in question in my common speech, I realize that each of these words is of Latinate, that is, Old French, origin. But I cannot allow myself to translate Wulfric using modern English words of Latinate origin! That would be cheating. Therefore, tonight I have made myself retranslate all of the Latin-based phrases of my mind—for example, "he excitedly anticipated departing immediately"—into Germanic-based phrases such as, "he eagerly foresaw leaving at once." They mean the exact same thing, but Wulfric, who spoke and wrote in the purely-Germanic Old English, deserves our Germanic-based words. They make the tone of his speech more authentic. With Boy, it is different. With him, I can in good conscience translate using the Latin-based words that I use so often in everyday speech, but with Wulfric, he requires a double-translation, which I find, as Boy would say, exhilarating, or as Wulfric would say, thrilling! Now, let's get back to it."

"By all means, Professor," said the crowd as we gave each other knowing and impressed looks that suggested the Professor was indeed the man for this job.

He resumed,

At the age of fifteen, Mynyddawg said good-bye to his parents and left Powys forever for Gwynedd, where he went in search of and eventually found Caradog. Caradog had dismissed

Mynyddawg's initial offer, which Mynyddawg had foreseen. Caradog had laughed, "Work for your food and passage? What kind of businessman would that make me?" So Mynyddawg did what he had to, he enslaved himself, agreeing that if he were not able to pay one pound of silver in exactly one year's time, Mynyddawg would become Caradog's slave. Caradog agreed to this deal mainly because he had known Mynyddawg for a long while, and he knew of the reputation of Mynyddawg's father Rhys. Mynyddawg was quite confident that he could meet this deadline with ease.

In London Caradog spent his time at Southwark, the market immediately across the Thames River from the city of London. Mynyddawg began to intensively learn the language, the English language, and at the same time wandered the city, discovering its better parts, and longing for a stable household like those that he watched from a distance. When he tried to interact with the established English elements of London, he discovered an entrenched hatred for the Welsh. Some Londoners hated the Welsh so fiercely that Mynyddawg was physically attacked and chased out of neighborhoods. It was his accent and his name that were the focus of this prejudice, and he recognized at once that they were markers that would forever keep him poor, and probably get him enslaved to Caradog. He began to practice an English accent and was getting pretty good when he decided to change his name.

The choice of a new name was very important, because Mynyddawg planned to work his way into the highest ranks of Saxon society. He would pretend to have been an orphan of London, who fought his way to the top. Since the Saxon King Edward the Confessor had just replaced the Danish King Hardecanute on the English throne,

Mynyddawg had to predict the wave of the future in England. If he chose a Danish name and the Danes fell out of favor, he would be sunk. Yet the Saxons had not ruled for three decades until Edward took the throne two years earlier, in 1042. Mynyddawg's intuition sensed the future, though, and it was not Viking. As a result, he made his choice. He chose the most reputable Saxon name he had ever heard: Osgod.

Osgod took his wares to the richer neighborhoods and tried out his new accent. Some were fooled at first, but others could detect a foreign twang. What he brought to sell, moreover, they did not want. Finally, his clothing set him apart from the people with whom he wanted to do business. He had hard work to do.

For the next four months Osgod worked without tiring, perfecting his accent, learning what the rich Saxons consumed, and saving enough money to invest every penny into clothing. In a few months' time he could stroll slowly and fashionably down the finest streets of London, being greeted by London's best. By this point he was working in a shop that sold embroidered tunics, and he was in a good position to overhear the conversations of the richest men in London. One day Osgod overheard that there was to be a gala function to open a new building of Westminster Abbey, a monastery that under King Edward the Confessor was beginning to undergo massive new construction. Part of Westminster was to be royal chambers; the undertaking was King Edward's pet project, and of course he would eventually be buried there. Osgod understood that this dedication was his chance and he would seize the day.

Entering through the delivery entrance with a tray of baked fish, Osgod walked straight into the crowded banquet hall, placed the fish on the table, and ate one. He began to chat with the crowd of thegns, bishops, and earls. The king himself was to arrive later. Osgod introduced himself as Osgod, the international trader, and made friends quickly as the wine flowed. But after charming one circle of businessmen with elaborate lies about his holdings in tin and lead, and his wool enterprises in Bruges and Flanders, he made sure to leave this group before they had tired of him in order to meet more people. He was an absolutely charming man, a man who knew how to listen and who knew how to flatter. Every time he would revisit a group of drinking magnates, they would feel as if they were seeing an old friend again, and they would introduce Osgod around. Many would boast that they had long known Osgod, and that no introduction was necessary.

The evening became truly festive only after the entrance of King Edward the Confessor, to whom Osgod was eventually introduced. At one point a high magnate called Osgod over to a group of men who appeared to be on the road to drunkenness. The magnate slurred, "Odda here produces chainmail, and is very short on his supply of tin. I told him you might be able to help him out."

Osgod said "Certainly," and the two talked for a while. Osgod said that he would be around tomorrow to conclude the bargain. Several other business connections also emerged before the evening was finished, and your grandfather was on his way.

At the meeting with Odda the next day, Osgod demanded a deposit to ensure his investment in the delivery of fifty tons of tin, which after all, would require ten ships. Your grandfather walked out of that meeting with a letter of credit for the staggering sum of one hundred pounds sterling, and this letter was from one of the richest men in England! Though he couldn't read the letter, Osgod could still have run off with the money and been a very rich criminal if he had chosen to, but dishonesty never entered his mind. His life goal was reputability; he was going to establish himself. He had promised his mother.

First, Osgod bought his indenture from Caradog so that he could devote every second of his days to this new deal. He gave Caradog a substantial tip, five shillings, and the two parted on the best of terms. Contacts were very important to a trader.

On the boat trip from Gwynedd to London, Mynyddawg had stopped in Cornwall at Hingston Down, where he had overheard a great supply of tin was to be had very cheaply by miners who were in desperate straits. Because in this early period Cornwall was only to a slight degree under English control, the vast Cornwall deposits of tin, lead, and iron had yet to be fully recognized. Exploiting the lack of interaction between Cornwall and London, Osgod parlayed his knowledge of both cultures into enormous profits. The political stability brought by Edward the Confessor made possible a climate of constructive trade for the first time in many decades.

Arriving very soon in Cornwall with a letter of introduction from Caradog and letter of credit from Odda, Osgod made the first of many deals in which he made an enormous profit. He had agreed with Odda to deliver fifty tons of tin in exchange for a price of two hundred pounds. He purchased the fifty tons of tin here in Hingston Down for seventy-five pounds. After paying the cost of the transportation and his laborers, Osgod netted fifty pounds and bought himself his first cargo ship.

Though Cornish and Welsh are completely different languages, they are somewhat alike, and Osgod's Welsh helped him greatly as he learned over time to haggle with the Cornish miners. He became the regular supplier to Odda, reaping huge profits with each new contract. He soon began providing Odda with lead and iron as well, and within two years, though he kept his relationship with Odda healthy and growing, Odda was not even one of Osgod's ten biggest accounts.

Around 1048 Osgod branched out further into the international wool, tin, lead, and iron markets. In fact, he decided to take the enormous step of relocating himself and the center of his business to the most vibrant economic center in the world, Constantinople. If he were going to excel at commerce, this was the place to go. His decision being made by cold reason, Osgod packed his few things and personally escorted a fleet of twenty of his ships first to Rome, then Venice, and finally on to Constantinople, the capital of the Greek Empire. Before he left he placed his English concerns in the hands of several talented managers, who continued to operate Osgod's business at a huge profit while he was away.

Once settled in his new estate in Constantinople, Osgod's English wool, tin, lead, and iron, as well as goods acquired in Italy and Iberia, generated for Osgod enormous profits. King Canute had secured good terms for traders during his reign and now Osgod was the beneficiary of this foresight. He directed an ongoing trade empire between his concerns in London and Constantinople, gaining wealth with every transaction, building relationships and contracts with every new social engagement. His fleet of armed ships could repel any Viking pirates, and in fact Osgod accumulated a fine collection of Viking weapons, none of which he knew how to use.

One weapon delivered to Osgod by his captains was a strange iron spear with Greek letters down the shaft. It was quite heavy and his men informed him that it was the famous Byzantine weapon, "Greek Fire." Osgod had heard of this and insisted on seeing it function. The next day a showing was arranged.

His man instructed him, "Just hold the shaft with this blanket, and put the flame to this string at the end. It is currently loaded and the load is sealed in with wax, so there is no spilling until discharge."

"Why the blanket?" Osgod asked.

"It gets pretty hot when you fire it. Now, simply bury the butt into the ground, point, and ignite that string on the butt."

The iron spear had been pointing at a barn and when he touched the string, a mighty hiss turned into a roar as the spear blasted fully-ignited black goo all over the barn, and the barn was instantly afire! Several men threw water on the liquid, and this only made the fire spread faster.

Osgod thought, "Horrifying invention. It would win a naval battle very quickly."

He simply said, "Load it again and bring it to me." The Greek letters written down the shaft were the ingredients for making the black goo. Osgod added it to his collection, and it was definitely his favorite.

The Professor looked up. "Greek fire, the secret weapon of the Byzantine Empire, has long been a mystery to historians. We do not know how it worked or what was in it. It was used centuries before the introduction of Chinese gunpowder to Europe. All we know is that this invention kept the Muslims at bay until 1453 when Constantinople finally fell to them and was renamed

Istanbul. It is in Turkey today. If that formula could be uncovered, it would be a major find for military historians. Of course, this book is equally a gold mine for political historians, psychological historians, literary historians, legal historians, intellectual historians, economic historians, social historians, art historians, religious historians, and cultural historians. Now, to Constantinople."

In the 1050s the political situation in Constantinople began to crumble because of the ongoing break-up—or schism as they call it—between Rome and the Greek Emperor. In the fateful year of 1054, the Pope and the Byzantine Emperor would excommunicate each other, beginning a rift into the Body of Christ that I hope will be healed very soon. But before this, in the first years of the 1050s, things were still quite economically stable. Because the Byzantine Emperor, Michael VII, was greatly in need of the military assistance of Pope Alexander II, the situation was not actually threatening to Osgod's trade empire; after all, Osgod had been aware of the severity of the rift for a long time, but there had still been profit to be made. Emperor Michael, who theoretically was sovereign over the area of Naples, had just lost Naples to conquering Normans. The Emperor pleaded with the Pope to intervene and require that the Normans withdraw. Osgod understood intuitively, however, that the Pope would eventually use this leverage to force his view of church doctrine on the Greeks, whose doctrines had been irreconcilably different for centuries, and who could not acquiesce on such a matter.

Osgod sensed that without a unified Christianity, Constantinople would eventually become vulnerable to the Muslims now swarming the Holy Land. Therefore, before others were even aware of the changing climate, in 1053 he began a strategic sale of all his holdings in the east. Finally he had liquidated all his diverse assets into the most portable form: pure gold coins. The amount of gold coinage that Osgod transported back to England was really nothing short of staggering; I have since discovered that the amount aboard his twenty ships would have been enough to badly devalue the price of gold in England had it been allowed to enter circulation all at once. He departed, as you Normans say—we English just say "left"—Constantinople in 1053. This was one year before the mutual excommunications made it clear that the rift would be very long-lasting. On Osgod's final trip home, he was guarded by his entire fleet that carried one last precious load of cargo—silks, purple dyes, precious gems, cottons—to England.

Once in England, he continued to liquidate his assets, moving farther away from commerce, becoming more and more interested in starting a family and living a life of noble leisure. Within a year, Osgod had established himself as a major landholder in Cambridgeshire.

Joel asked, "Surely Mynyddawg—a very cool name, by the way--would not be accepted as a nobleman? Don't you have to be born into the nobility, isn't it a bloodline thing?"

The Professor was in his element on this question. "That question taps into a complex phenomenon. Different eras of European history and different geographic regions of Europe allowed different degrees of social mobility. While the fourteenth through nineteenth centuries in England were very rigidly socially stratified, with social mobility taking three or more generations if it occurred at all, the eleventh-century far predated such rigidity. Being knighted on the battlefield was still common, and economic success could vault a person into the elite of society as well.

The Professor used one finger to flip down a small olive book from his little shelf. "Let me read you an original anonymous Old English code, written between 1002 and 1023:

And if a ceorl [peasant] prospered, that he possessed fully five hides of land of his own, a bell and a castle-gate, a seat and special office in the king's hall, then was he henceforth entitled to the rights of a thegn…And if a trader prospered, that he crossed thrice the open sea at his own expense, he was then afterwards entitled to the rights of a thegn.

Osgod was destined for a life as a noble as soon as he returned to England. Which we should now do as well. It's three-thirty in the morning."

Once the fleet arrived in England, the disposition of all his wealth was quite a problem, considering no place was safe from thieves and liars. But of course, Osgod's foresight was as usual incredibly precise, and he staged a very showy production involving the movement of his wealth to a secure site in London. All those who had been eyeing his riches attacked the train of covered wagons, as expected. This convoy was actually robbed three separate times. The train had contained fully five percent of his wealth, and he thought it was quite worth the price to get the wolves off his back. Actually, long before this scene was staged, he had had some digging done on a portion of one of his properties to "increase productivity." No one knew the location of this vast wealth, or even that it existed at all. I discovered much later from a completely trustworthy source a secret that people will kill for: that buried somewhere on his estates was no less than sixteen tons of pure gold. And he certainly did not bury it all; his standard of living remained high throughout his life.

At one point in 1054 Osgod was invited to an exhibition of sorts in Coventry. It was to be a gala show of battle talents—what was beginning to be termed a tournament—for a few well-connected friends. Coventry was a beautiful part of England, and Osgod enjoyed his first few days there. The ladies knew of his station in life, and he was introduced to several eligible maidens; however, he was not attracted to any of them. He said they seemed too flighty.

One afternoon, while strolling the grounds of the estate, Osgod heard a sound behind some hedges and peered around the corner. There was a mature woman of twenty-eight sitting in the grass, petting a cat, talking to it, and picking its fleas. He watched her for a while, eavesdropping delightfully as she carried on lovingly with the cat. The lady's purr was very endearing. Then he spoke, making both cat and lady startle. Osgod and the lady talked for a while, and he asked her if she would sit near him at dinner that evening. It was obvious from her reaction to him that she knew nothing of his riches, and he liked it that way. She said she would certainly join him for dinner and she did.

As the days passed by at the Coventry estate, Osgod and Eleanor fell in love. Her cousins were quite glad of this, because Eleanor was well past the prime age of marriage, and they had worried that she had missed her chance. Soon enough, her cousins with whom she was staying explained to her that her suitor was one of the richest men in England, and at only twenty-eight!

His hosts in turn explained that she possessed an amazingly large dowry and that her grandfather had been Richard I, Duke of Normandy! Everything about her was right; her father had been both the count of Evreux and the Earl of Devon and her mother, the Duchess of Devon, was now a respected nun in the convent at Romsey.

Everything about him was right; he had risen from an orphan to a rich businessman possessing enormous wealth and now sat as a Lord of Cambridgeshire. He was handsome, with a sophisticated continental accent acquired from years among the Greeks. They were married in 1055 and their daughter Margaret was born in 1056.

I finally get to know her name. My Mother is Margaret. My mother is forty. My mother is still alive, she must be. My mother is the third cousin of His Majesty King William Rufus. I am of royal blood.

Rexy looked directly at me for a long time.

The silence was broken by my throaty bellow off this cliff, a scream that echoed softly back when I was done with the one, sustained word: "Emma."

"My work here is finished," I thought, but I decided the darkness dictated that I wait until dawn to begin moving quickly back to Surrey in triumph.

What I did not know at the time was that back on Emma's estate at Surrey, the inhabitants of that estate, noble and villian alike, lay butchered on the ground in large pools of cold purple blood. When the bloodshed had finally subsided and the attackers had departed, behind them at Surrey they had left no one alive.

The wedding of Osgod and Eleanor was a great feast, and Matilda traveled from the convent in Wessex to attend, stopping by the tree with a local peasant that she hired for the day to collect the dowry that was Eleanor's gift to the marriage. After the peasant boy finished chopping the tree and had left, Matilda removed the coins and rehid the stirrups and the chess pieces in another tree on her way north.

In the Norman tradition, grains were thrown as the guests shouted, "Abundance!" After the festivities, the couple traveled by covered wagon to Cambridge to begin their new lives.

Margaret came along the next year, and Osgod settled down to a gentle life of fatherhood.

Osgod taught young Margaret many things, and quizzed her often on where the kingdoms of the world lay and even on how to get to Constantinople! Your mother Margaret learned many things from her father, including the traits to look for in a man-- kindness, intellectual curiosity, and industry--and the two spent many hours together. There was a farm at the corner of his Cambridge estate that he named "Wild Dogs" after some dogs he had seen there once. Boy, "Wild Dogs" is a very special place to your family. He and Eleanor and Margaret often picnicked there, naming all the pigs in the sty, picking apples, and hiding in the hay. There was one pig, with very sharp toe nails, that they loved to name and rename every time they visited this farm. Somehow, they always managed to include the sharp toe nails in the name! Life was slow and good, and Margaret, your mother, grew up happy and secure. At the age of eighteen, in 1074, she was married to Thorkel, your father. Her dowry was quite sufficient.

Unfortunately, two years later both your father Thorkel and your grandfather Osgod were struck by the wave of Normanization that swept all England. Thorkel and Margaret were stripped of their titles and lands in Kent, where Thorkel's estate was located. They were expelled from their estate and were forced back to Cambridge to live with Margaret's parents. Osgod, as a much more established member of the nobility, was allowed to keep his Cambridge estate and his title, but only because he paid a fine that rendered him and Eleanor practically penniless. Although Eleanor and Margaret were both Norman by blood, their marriages had put them very much out of favor with William the Bastard, who needed good, loyal, Norman Fitzgeralds and Fitzsimmons to keep his militaristic state working at full efficiency.

"Fitzgeralds?" I asked. "What does that mean?"

Steve fielded this one. "Oh, Wulfric is just listing common Norman names to show that it was only Normans that William wanted in power. The prefix "Fitz" is a unit simply meaning "son of" in Norman French. The same device exists in all northern European languages: the word for "Johnson," for example in Russian was and is Ivanovich, or son of Ivan, or John; the Irish equivalent is O'Sean; the Scottish, MacIan; the Swedish, Johansen; and the Norman French, Fitzjean. All these names have the exact same translation into English: Johnson. Names are probably the most lasting holdovers of ancient cultures; they would have been applied in the eleventh century very much as they appear today. Only these days we all have a surname."

I informed Steve, "The Professor said that same thing before you arrived." I added with a smile, "You, sir, are a genius!"

The Professor read again,

Three years after the marriage of Margaret and Thorkel, I learned the secret that no one else in England knew about your grandfather; that he was Welsh. I learned the secret when tragic circumstances, which I will tell you of soon enough, forced me to approach Osgod's household in Cambridge in 1077. I did so in my capacity as a minstrel and gleaned some important information in this way. I spoke at length to an old servant woman whose father—whom she had only known briefly, she insisted—had been Welsh. She had of course kept the stain of her Welshness a secret, and so Master Osgod never had any idea. One day, when Osgod stubbed his toe on a rock, he had let out a tirade of cursing in Welsh; she concluded her statement to me by emphasizing that these Welsh words were "the same exact words that my no-good father would use."

Quite surprised, but now suspecting strongly that Osgod was originally from Wales, of all places, I left Cambridge. I hoped that I was about to go on a very long trip that would have me returning to Cambridge very soon. I decided to begin in the Welsh section of London. For a week no one would give me any information that helped. Then one day the people I had befriended in the main tavern directed me to the house of Caradog, who, they said, knew most everyone. This Caradog, I found out later, was the son of Mynyddawg's deceased friend, and when I explained the good intention of my errand, Caradog told me that he might be able to help me for a price.

After I paid the man, he said his father had told him that once he had brought a young boy named Mynyddawg to London from Powys, northern Wales. The lad Mynyddawg had made good over time, had even become a rich noble, and had promptly abandoned his own people. Rather than be bitter, it seemed from the son's story that the father Caradog appeared to admire the lad for this. As we talked, I understood that the lad had actually paid Caradog for years and years to watch over his western concerns and to keep the secret of his blood safe. And he did. Caradog went to his grave suddenly, and so though he had always promised to divulge the name of the rich noble to his son, he never got the chance. The son of Caradog tried to pay me to tell him his name, but I would not.

So I left for northern Wales. First I journeyed to the region of south Wales known as Gwent, where I found my Eadburh who acted as my translator. Then I traveled north through Wales to Powys. In Powys I did not find the parents of Mynyddawg but I talked to some old women who said that the person who I sought was Rhys, now a monk in Dyfed at St. David's monastery. These women told me many of the stories of Angharad and Rhys that I wrote of earlier, and it was here that Eadburh and I visited Angharad's secret place. Let me say again that I was amazed at Angharad's spirit and Rhys' spirituality.

By the time we left St. David's monastery I had received both Welsh gifts. These were of course the sword and the Grailkey, which I was so excited to be able to soon present to their rightful owner, Osgod, whose original name I now knew to be Mynyddawg. It was not until after the death of my Eadburh that I was finally able to return to Cambridge in 1083. Your grandfather Osgod was still alive and well at that point, only fifty-seven years old. He being of such a high station, I decided that the best approach was to go again as a minstrel, this time performing for the lord and lady. I was a very old but very coordinated and enthusiastic little minstrel.

I performed for Osgod and Eleanor, and they were delighted. Since this was seventeen years after the Norman Conquest, minstrels were now performing almost exclusively in French. I had learned many French epics, such as the "Song of Roland," in my earlier days, and my French was good enough, as it had to be to get along with our new French lords. When I asked, Osgod made clear to me that he wanted his stories in English, not French; in fact, the very mention of Norman French set him mumbling for a good while about the "confounded robbery of the Norman taxation in this day."

When I stopped for a short rest, another minstrel, very young, came in to play his vielle, the new harp brought from France that was plucked with a large disk. The tone of the new instrument was very dream-like. He sang, rather off-key, of a poor girl who had been ravaged by wolves but who was saved by a light of unknown origin. In the tune the girl suffered severe and permanent scarring to the face. She was finally taken to a village and had learned a good lesson about being careless in the deep woods. When my turn came round again I frightened the wits out of everybody with some of my sword juggling. I still had the gift. That was certain.

Afterward, I took Eleanor aside and explained who I was and that my grandson had married her daughter. Then I told her all about my quest. After she recovered from her surprise, she was very forthcoming. This will be related in her chronicle. But she told Osgod to give me his ear, and, sitting all alone, we talked all through one long night. I told him everything; I could see no alternative. He could not believe his father was a monk, probably now long-dead, nor could he believe the Grailkey that I then handed him was his property. He could not believe his mother's infidelity nor could he believe the story that the old women had told me, that she had been disgusted by the act and had done it only to free Rhys. I handed him the sword, which he had loved during his childhood, and he could not believe the translation of the engraving. It was he who was finally able to completely identify and translate the Cornish that had perplexed him as a child. He confirmed that it read, "He who soever pulls this sword from this stone is rightwise born King of all Britain." He sat, very satisfied, with Excalibur in one hand and the Grailkey in the other.

Then I told him what I had not anyone else in the world. I told him that I had kidnapped his grandson, Margaret's son, two years earlier and I was keeping him indefinitely. He completely understood why I had done it and thanked me with a long embrace. He told me that he wanted me to give the Grailkey and the sword to you, Boy. If he kept them, he explained, they would expose his Welshness. He told me that he wanted to keep his true identity quiet until the death of Eleanor, who would be the most embarrassed. "And the gifts are Boy's heritage," he added in his musical Welsh-Greek accent which he had cultivated for years. Margaret's royal blood would save her from the shame of their Welsh background, and of course Boy was only a quarter Welsh. In fact, in this audience Mynyddawg, as he asked me to now begin to call him, told me specifically that he was ashamed that he had been ashamed of his people. "I simply had no choice," he had said as he shook his head.

He handed me the sword, which I now understood was Excalibur, not magical, but nonetheless very special. I gingerly put it down. Then he handed me the Grailkey and told me to guard it well. This I have done. Mynyddawg at that point told me that he had something for you also. He left and returned, handing me your gift. Then he told me his story. Everything. He told me that at one point he had buried one full ton of gold on his property, but the tax collectors had taken it. "They were too smart for me," he complained.

He was referring to the bookkeepers who produced the *Domesday Book*, that inventory of all land and chattel—every pig, horse, and barn-- in England. After 1066 William the Conqueror had ordered the book to be compiled as a tool for taxation in order to satisfy his lust for money. Mynyddawg pointed out that this thirty-four-volume book, not finished until 1086, was the perfect symbol of how no one could escape the crushing taxation and the random confiscations of William and his army of bookkeepers. Mynyddawg seemed very animated when he explained that the Norman tax collectors had outsmarted him.

And then he told me everything he knew about his father Rhys, everything he knew about his mother Angharad, everything he knew about his wife Eleanor, everything he knew about his daughter Margaret, and everything he knew about my grandson and his son-in-law, Thorkel. Then he told me that he wanted me to write down a poem that his mother always sang to him. He made me write it in Welsh. And he made me promise him that you, Boy, would hear the poem translated into your English one day. He said that because of King William, he could leave you no wealth, but this poem was all the gold you would ever need. It is the poem cited earlier, but I cite it again:

Oian aparchellan llimy vinet!
Kyuuely anwinud panelhute y oruet
Bychan a wir ryderch hael heno y ar y wlet
Aportheise neithuir o anhunet
Eiri hid 77 impen clun gan cun callet
Pibonvy 30 imblev blin wy ryssett
Ry dibit div maurth dit guithlonet
Kywrug glyu powis achlas guinet
Cwbl mewn un melyn dyfrgi blwch

He refused to translate it, and in fact insisted that no translation was required. He would not explain why this made no sense, and frankly, a few times I worried about the health of his mind. As a poem of your heritage, I include it, but it is gibberish to me.

In 1086 the plague devastated England, and both Eleanor and Mynyddawg, as I will hereafter call him, as was his wish, gave up their ghosts to God Almighty. So ends the story of your grandfather Mynyddawg, the richest man in England.

So this was my grandfather. At this point I had a strong feeling that Wulfric, or perhaps it was Mynyddawg, was trying to tell me something. I liked the name "Wild Dogs" that he had given to one farm on his estate, and I decided that if it turned out that I really owned this estate, I would name the area to the right of this cliff as I look off it "Wild Dogs."

I was excited to dig up the present from Mynyddawg, which reminded me that in my haste I had forgotten to dig up Siobhan's gift. First thing first, I dug up Siobhan's compass. Compared to the others, it was unspectacular, but I knew the sentiment that lay behind her gift and it was very precious to me. Enough sentiment; I wanted the weapon.

I then dug up Mynyddawg's gift, and found that my guess had been right. The stone was the usual size but the carved out area was seven feet deep! I grasped and slid out the entire length of a long iron pole. Digging this trench had taken Wulfric or his men some time, and I noticed what appeared to be candles waxed onto the sides of this tool. I suppose they were lit and then the vault was sealed with stone and earth on top. Inside the vault, the candles had obviously used up the air before they burned up, leaving no air to rust the iron of the weapon! Ingenious! Wulfric had thought this out!

The stick was iron, without any rust. It appeared to be hollow but corked with wax. At the other end was a small string. This was not a weapon that had been seen in England before, I felt almost sure. It should frighten any Vikings who happened by, I thought. I wanted to test it, but realized that until I found someone who read Greek, I would not be able to replenish its fuel. Best to save it.

Nelson began, "Now I'm getting the distinct feeling that Boy is trying to tell us something. Hmm."

I agreed. "It's as if some readers were supposed to know what is being said, and some were supposed to be left out."

Bart again objected, "Has Mynyddawg successfully removed the stain of Wales? I don't think so. Then why in the world has he authorized Wulfric to tell his family that he is Welsh after Eleanor dies? The whole premise of this book is ridiculous."

Steve added, "Maybe Wulfric thinks that even if he tells Boy and Margaret, it can remain a family secret, since it would hurt them all equally for the secret to get out."

Nelson said, "Fitzy?"

I answered simply, "Maybe there's even more than that at work."

At this point Bart changed the subject. "Professor, can I mention something to you?"

The Professor looked directly at Bart and said, somewhat warily, "Go on…"

"Well, did you know that in the past, you have been something of a sensation around my fraternity house? Of course everyone knows who you are around campus, being a full professor and an endowed chair and everything. But did you know that you were actually the subject of a strange fraternity prank a few years back? Apparently, there was a story floating around that was started by one of our fraternity brothers who is the son of a U.S. Senator. He pranked the whole house really good, especially our pledges. He circulated some wild story to trick our freshmen pledges back then and it really worked! The gag involved a document he produced that looked like an official top-secret U.S. Senate document, one he said he stole from his dad, which seemed to indicate clearly that instead of seven articles in the U.S. Constitution, that the founding fathers actually included eight articles, and one was removed and hidden in the early days of our history! The story went that the eighth article described a fourth branch of government, one of oversight. Our pledges were all apparently completely fooled into believing that this branch was said to coordinate the judiciary, executive, and legislative branches behind the scenes and that it wielded immense governmental power. The very existence of the eighth Article of the Constitution was said to be kept a secret by all three branches of government as a failsafe against attacks domestic and foreign on our government. Well, a few years back it was all the talk around the frat house that you, Professor, were actually the Director of this secret branch, or something to that effect, and that the President, Senators, and Supreme Court Justices looked to you for guidance as 'The Director.' Strange, though, that even his faked document was unable to identify the name of this fourth branch of government. Then abruptly the Senator's son admitted that he had just made all this up as a gag! He dropped out of school soon after that and we heard no more from him. Someone said he joined the CIA. Wild, huh?"

The Professor looked unamused. "You kids should spend a bit more time studying, do you not think? Who wants candy?"

Chapter Fifteen

Daybreak at Stonehenge

The Professor reached up and placed a big metal bowl on his kitchen counter. He loaded the bowl until it overflowed. He arrived down in the den with a big bowl loaded with dozens of Reese's Cups and everyone dug into the treasure ravenously.

Everyone except Steve and me. We were on the front porch again. Steve had suggested we keep the lights off "to reduce visibility." As a result, the deep shadows of the porch were illuminated only indirectly by the light from inside various windows, and by the moonlight that now completely bathed this neighborhood.

Steve was saying, "Are you prepared for the exam tomorrow?"

I pulled my shoulders back against the column I was leaning on and asked back, "Are you ready?"

Steve leaned in, "Are you?"

Gazing steadily into my eyes, with a quiet and provocative confidence, Steve kissed me and ended my lonely days forever. We did not speak at all, but when the silence was finally broken, and that took a beautiful eternity, I smiled radiantly at him. We interlaced fingers again and both floated back into the house, bouncing down to the den. Apparently the Professor had abandoned the wait for us and was just starting to read.

...since I was to begin my return trip at dawn, my thoughts of course turned to Emma. She would be so surprised to see me, so elated at the news that I had been noble all along. What would come next, we would deal with then. But we would definitely go to our orchard, and she would kiss Rexy's snout a thousand times, and we would frolic like children. We would be children again.

Though I was eager to get back to Emma, I suspected that, given the twists and turns that these booklets had already brought me through, it would be wise to finish my stories before I left this place. And that is what my great-grandfather had told me to do. For the first time in my life, I was grateful for England's fourteen-hour winter nights.

Wulfric Rhys

Gunnehild Mynyddawg

Ealdgyth Angharad

Bag Bag

Neils Fire Hugh

Bag Bag

Siobhan Matilda

Your paternal grandmother, my daughter, was named Gunnehilde and was born in 1020 in the region of Holland, which is in the heart of the Danelaw, the area of England traditionally ruled by the Danes. She was born into a life of dreadful travel, and she never knew a crib at all. Ealdgyth and I would take turns carrying her on our way from village to village along the east coast of England. As you know, Gunnehilde was almost two on that night of horrors when the wolves came and I forever scarred my right hand by carrying the burning blanket. Fortunately, Gunnehilde later told me she had no memory of that night.

Here the Professor's laser pointer was put into action again, this time at the region of Holland in eastern England, right across the English Channel from the country by the same name.

After I dropped her off at the mill in southern Northumberland, Gunnehilde was taken in by the miller's wife and was raised better than I had hoped. I chose a mill because millers tend to have bread even in the worst times. Gunnehilde finally slept in a crib, and the miller's wife, until she died, would feed little Gunnehilde a rich wheat porridge from fine pottery. It turned out that during our traveling my Little Bear, as I always called her, had contracted flukes, but this kind woman knew the herbs and liquids to clean these large worms right out. We had tried our best to keep the head lice off of Gunnehilde, but this miller's wife was able to do a much better job, since Little Bear now had a stable home. The miller's wife kept Gunnehilde in very unclean clothes compared to what I have become accustomed to as a thegn, but she was cleaner than most peasant toddlers. Her new mother would even occasionally scrub her teeth with hazel leaves. And so, thanks to God Almighty in Heaven and perhaps as well to her new mother's grooming, she avoided any serious childhood infections.

Because Gunnehilde and her adopted family were a good bit richer than most of their neighbors, Gunnehilde was much better fed than most peasants. Her adopted parents were proud to describe her as "plump." As millers, it was the job of this family to take the wheat of the local peasants and grind it, using a waterwheel, into flour. Because there was no way to measure how much flour would be yielded from a given quantity of wheat, this process was subject to being abused by the millers. Such abuse was so common that in England, as you know, millers were generally considered to be inherently dishonest. This was not true of all millers, Gunnehilde would object when the subject came up with her playmates. But she understood that it was certainly true of her adopted father Wigmund.

The neighborhood boys noticed Gunnehilde as she was growing up because she was the only girl in the village who was not gaunt or downright emaciated as you French say—we English just say "thin." Instead, her face and arms were filled out so nice and round!

The Professor interjected, "I am always amazed at how relativistic our conceptions of beauty are. For example, to this day the Chinese revere tiny feet as the hallmark of a beautiful woman, while in America, a muscular abdomen is currently what is considered beautiful for women. What was "beautiful" in the middle ages, though, and well into the Renaissance period of the 1500s, was plumpness. Just as today trim and *fatlessness* is equated with heathfulness, in the eleventh-century *fatfulness* had the same association. Those who had stores to burn would be the most fit mothers, and as a result, were perceived as the most beautiful. This is still quite true in near-starving countries such as India. My friend Professor Chandra always laughs when she tells me that back in India she is revered as beautiful, but here in the South she is pitied as fat. Beauty is and has always been in the eye and the caloric intake of the beholder."

He resumed,

Part of the reason for Gunnehilde's beauty was the abundance of bread in the house, but another explanation laid in their abundance of ale. With so much grain on hand, the miller's wife was usually busy brewing ale. From infancy

Gunnehilde consumed plenty of ale, which added to her glow.

"Very, very cool," said Joel. "Beer formula."

The Professor looked over his glasses, obviously annoyed again at Joel's flippancy. "I hate to burst your fantasy, but let me remind you of a few facts. First, there was never formula, children all breastfed until they were about two, and some breastfed much longer than that. Second, Gunnehilde did not consume beer as a toddler, she consumed ale. Beer is made with hops that give it that bitter flavor, and hops would not come into wide use until subsequent centuries. Third, ale was necessary precisely because it had been boiled and so was free of disease-causing impurities. It was actually the safest drink available, much safer than either cow's milk that carried infectious microbes or water that often contained dysentery. Fourth, the consumption of alcohol, then and now, was responsible for a great many accidental deaths from falling out of boats, falling on knives, and so forth. Many such cases are documented of alcohol-induced fatalities in the eleventh century. Fifth, the very production of ale was extremely dangerous, since it meant many tedious hours leaning over a twelve-gallon cauldron of boiling ale. It is estimated that of the deaths of women in the eleventh century, fully five percent were caused by falling into or being burned or scalded by such vats. And finally, let me assure you that the alcohol content of ale was far lower than modern beer; that is why the records often show daily allowances for beer in terms of gallons."

"Thank you, Professor," said Joel a bit sheepishly as the Professor pulled the book up to begin reading again, "for sobering me up."

Gunnehilde did more than her share of the work around the place, I must say, but her disposition and attitude were always very cheerful. She would sing while she worked, and her voice was quite lovely. It was so lovely, in fact, that little Gunnehilde soon enjoyed the reputation as the prettiest singer from Bamburgh to Lindsey. Gunnehilde's voice sounded even lovelier as she grew into a young woman.

As the years passed, and her voice continued to impress listeners, it was becoming clear by the accidents in her adopted family that some curse was upon them all. I often wondered if it was my doing that had cursed them. For instance, when Gunnehilde was twelve, her older sister had been out gathering honey from the family hives one day to prepare a cake. She did not take the proper precautions and as a result was killed by the bees in a horrible death. Not long after this, the handle of a big cauldron of ale broke. The mother was doused by the boiling ale and severely scalded. This infection was very painful, and Gunnehilde could do little to help in her final days before this kind woman gave up her ghost. Though these were difficult experiences to get through, they did not kill Gunnehilde's spirit. In a matter of months after this accident Gunnehilde was taking on many of her mother's duties and beginning to sing again, but now with a lilting sadness behind her songs that added a new, richer quality. The older folks often asked her to sing for them, and being the kind girl that she was, she always obliged.

One day a very important lord, Lord Roth, came riding through and was eating the noonday meal at the home of the local thegn. The thegn mentioned Gunnehilde's singing and the lord wanted to hear for himself. He was amazed at the lovely voice of this rounded young girl and summoned her to sing at his manor outside Bamburgh. One song led to another, and the Lord decided to marry the girl.

The miller eagerly agreed and provided a tiny dowry, but Roth accepted it graciously enough.

The wedding occurred in 1039, when your grandmother was nineteen, and within two years your father Thorkel was born. Roth liked the violence inherent in the name, which meant "Killer like Thor," in Viking, but Gunnehilde had plans to raise her boy in a loving and peaceful home. She could not keep Roth from taking Thorkel away to train for battle, but she thought she might just be able to make the boy opposed to senseless brutality. And she did exactly that.

Now Roth had been greatly in favor with the king while Canute's son Harold, who ruled from 1035 until 1040, had held the throne. Roth held an even higher position in the court of Hardecanute, who ruled from 1040 until 1042. Hardecanute was at the same time king of Denmark, and he did not juggle his resources as well as had his father Canute, who had been the only king ever to rule over England, Denmark, and Norway at the same time.

When Hardecanute died, however, the fortunes of Gunnehilde's family changed abruptly. Edward the Confessor, who ruled from 1042 until 1066, was a Saxon, the first in thirty years, and as a result he slowly began to replace Danish earls with his own Aldermen, as we Saxons called earls. The first nobles to be replaced would be those closest to Hardecanute; that meant my daughter's husband, Roth. He was given a new position of much lower rank as a simple thegn in the region of Lindsey. Roth, like his father Neils, had quite a temper before this, and this insult, this lowering of his social rank, made him an angry, angry man.

As the 1040s advanced, Roth was more and more excluded from Edward's reign, and he turned more and more to his fellow Danes in York and Denmark for patronage. Since he was gone often, Gunnehilde had a free hand at raising Thorkel.

In this new region she made friends, and as the wife of the local thegn she enjoyed a relatively prestigious life. She felt very connected to her peasants, and thought of them as her extended family. In every real way except by blood, they actually were her extended family.

It was when your father was six, in 1047, that I visited Siobhan and told her about our mutual grandson. By the time I had returned from Ireland and from resuming my position as minstrel to Godwine of Wessex, a year had passed and I had been given a most gratifying honor by my lord: I had been granted land in Essex. Now free to follow my own pursuits, I visited Gunnehilde often. The initial reunion was awkward, but when she heard the horrible story of her mother's death, she understood. She also understood that my position as a minstrel was to be kept strictly between her and me since it would permanently cripple Thorkel's social position.

Roth came and went, and finally gave up trying to take the reluctant boy to battle. But he was insistent that Gunnehilde have another child, which they were unable to do for a long time. In 1053 Roth was called to York to confer with none other than Siward. Siward was Earl of Huntingdon and Earl of Bamburgh and was also Earl of York, and as a triple-Earl was very powerful. He had been appointed by Canute and was of course Danish. Because Siward had cooperated to some extent with Edward's accession to the throne, and because he was too powerful to remove in this pre-conquest era of limited monarchial control, Edward had allowed him to maintain his earldoms. Siward had for several years been hosting the exiled Malcolm, son of the Scottish king Duncan, who had been murdered by his kinsman MacBeth. MacBeth, who ruled from 1040 until 1057, was now king of Scotland, and Siward was thinking about invading Scotland and helping Malcolm to regain his father's throne. In 1054 Siward did just that, and Roth was a leader of one of Siward's divisions. The spoils of that war are legendary.

When Roth returned to Lindsey in 1056 after more extended campaigns which I will describe in his chronicle, he was infuriated to find that Siward had died and Edward had replaced him with Tostig, the son of Godwine. The Earl would now be a Saxon! Livid, your grandfather Roth barely noticed that Gunnehilde was much plumper than usual. Finally at dinner, in the middle of one of his angry fits of yelling, he stopped short and looked at her. She smiled and told him that she had enjoyed his break from battle eight months earlier.

This pregnancy changed Roth's plans a little. He told her that they were leaving for Norway, where his reputation and bloodline would result in an appropriate level of honor and titles. They were leaving England forever, or at least until he returned as part of a Norse invasion force! Grumbling, he agreed to wait for the birth of the baby, but he would begin arrangements for their departure immediately.

She did not tell Roth how she felt about this. Thorkel was now fifteen and knew without having to ask how his mother felt. Roth never suspected. Put simply, Gunnehilde was not going to move to Norway. She was a part of her community, and it was part of her. Norsemen would not raise Thorkel or the new baby! Although it defied all common sense, Gunnehilde just fled.

She took her boy, and she took three horses, one of which she packed with supplies. She also snatched up a massive gold ring that Roth had said he found in the castle of MacBeth after this king had fled. Eight and a half months pregnant on the dangerous roads of England in the middle of December was a punishment I would not wish on anyone. Nonetheless, the two left one cold morning after Roth had gone into Lincoln on business. She was trying to reach my land in Essex and she got terribly turned around. Word reached me through a friend in her village, a friend who had risked travel to come and tell me of her departure and of Roth's furious reaction. Roth was following, and he swore he would kill her and take his sons to Norway. I knew Thorkel well by this point, and he knew me. With the help of Gunnehilde's friend from Lindsey, I finally picked up their trail in Wessex of all places. She had ridden on the wrong road for many days without her or the boy knowing it.

When I finally found her, it was in the middle of a plain broken only by a circle of huge rocks, some of which were stacked neatly on each other far above my head. To this day, I am not sure how this was done, but it was done long before Saxon times, local people said.

By the time I found Gunnehilde, the sun was setting, and in fact it was the shortest day of the year, the winter solstice. Tomorrow would bring a new year in which the days would lengthen and lengthen. On this longest night she had already begun her labor. Thorkel was very glad to see me, and I was glad to see him. I told her that this journey had been insane, and she agreed. I comforted her the best I could, and she kept telling me that she was afraid of Satan. I calmed her by praying, and we prayed Satan away most of that long night. My fire blazed brightly in the middle of that ring of huge stones, looming silently like ancestors, watching over us all.

At one point Gunnehilde noticed Thorkel crying, and she called him over. The emotional tendencies of Thorkel had always infuriated his father; the two had very different constitutions. She told him it would be all right, and asked if he wanted a song. Her songs were her gift to him. He said yes and put his head on her chest as she began to sing a cheerful Christmas song that was sung in their part of England. She could see that I was very sad so she called me over too. I sensed that this new year would not begin well. She held my hand and she held his hand and she sang us one last song there by our ancestors. Generous as always, she sang many verses to us as we comforted each other near that fire, each verse ending with her light, sweet voice singing Here we come a-wassailing, among the leaves so green, Here we come a-wandering so fair to be seen, Love and joy, come to you, And to you your wassail too, And God bless you, and send you a happy new year, and God send you a happy new year.

Nelson looked over at me to find me dripping with silent tears. Nelson understood that Wulfric and Gunnehilde and Thorkel were doing what Nelson and I had done as our family Christmas tradition every Christmas of our lives. Others in the room were deeply touched by the scene, but not like me and not like Nelson. The others did not know.

Nelson and I both knew now, and we knew the other knew. Before this scene, little intangibles had already piled up to the point that there was no longer any doubt that this was our story, our family tradition unfolding for the first time. We looked at each other and felt the exact same emotion, one of utter thankfulness and belonging.

"Let's finish this scene," said the Professor.

In the middle of the night, we were joined by a strange woman who said that she always came here at midnight of both solstices. She was of the old ways, and said with weird certainty that she had always known this day would come. She took out a strangely-carved knife that had a handle that looked as if it were carved out of the same huge white stones that towered around us. She said to Gunnehilde that she had birthed many babies, but none from so special a family. As the hours of the night passed, she said little else, and Thorkel slept. When it became apparent that Gunnehilde was going to have trouble, the woman said she had to get fresh cow's milk and left.

When she returned, she had Gunnehilde drink the milk from the cow, and then spit it into water being poured from a horn that she had also brought. She said that this would bring on the baby. With the same hand, Gunnehilde was to scoop up a mouthful of the water and then drink it, and then walk around. Gunnehilde did this twice, but it did not work. Gunnehilde knew me well, and knew my guilt was rising up again. She motioned to me to come closer. My blood ran cold when she told me not to worry, that she would take this baby with her. And she told me that in order to atone for my part in her current situation, I had to watch over Thorkel. She told me very plainly that if her Thorkel survived and prospered, then her story would be happy. And she told me that if I saved Thorkel, then my guilt for my mother and my wife would also be cleansed, completely gone. In the midst of those large, silent stones she made certain that I understood this. She gave me another chance at salvation. One last chance.

As the sun began to tip above the horizon, the baby began to come. It was a breech, and the baby would not dislodge. Its cord was tangled and the situation was terrifying for Gunnehilde. The old woman was very confident that she knew exactly what to do. But her chants and charms did not work. As I listened to her incoherent chants I realized that she must be some sort of Celtic priestess, an adherent of the old Druid religion. She could not understand why all her measures had no effect, and ran about frantically pulling at her light gray hair and screaming, that "this was the bloodline, the promised bloodline," and that "the baby girl had to live." Through her raving, in both Celtic and English, I understood very little. The one notion that became clear to me as I watched her with amazement was that she seemed utterly sure that the baby would be a girl, and she was equally sure that only a girl from this family could fulfill the prophesy.

The sun dawned on us, illuminating the birth perfectly through the main passage of these huge stones. But it was not to be a live birth. Finally it became obvious that the baby was dead, and it had to be removed quickly. I tried everything but could do nothing. The old woman said that the only choice was the knife. Gunnehilde said, "do it," and the lifeless child, a tiny, tiny boy, was removed after cutting Gunnehilde severely. The amount of blood a woman contains is unnerving. Gunnehilde was becoming weak, and I knew something was wrong. The old woman shook her head, looked at me very sadly, dropped the strange knife on the ground, and began to walk away. "Is this boy hers, too?" she asked, motioning to Thorkel with her thumb.

"Yes, he is hers."

As she walked through those huge stones she turned back and said something very faintly. I think she said, "Then he is our only chance."

She vanished over a hill and I never saw her again.

I called Thorkel over to say goodbye to his mother, but it was I who needed the consoling. My eyes stung and stung again as I watched the life pour out of my daughter, and Thorkel sat numbly and held her hand. Finally he cried with me as the sun finished its rise and her body went limp. This new year had not begun happily.

After a long, long silence on that windy plain we heard the thunder of Roth's horses and men, and I told Thorkel I had to go. I promised him through my stinging eyes that I would take care of his little brother, and I would take care of his mother's body, and I would always watch over him. I swore this to his face, I kissed him, and I ran, carrying the stillborn with me.

I finally stopped behind some rocks. The woman had brought salt and I had put some in my purse. I put the salt in my grandson's little mouth and sprinkled his head three times with water, baptizing him in the name of the Father, and of the Son, and of the Holy Ghost. I knew that a stillborn was to be buried in an open grave, and that is how I laid my grandson to rest. I waited alone behind these rocks for most of the day, and then I returned to the circle of stones. She still lay there, but Thorkel had been taken away by his father, as I knew he would be. I buried my Little Bear in the middle of those protectors, the winter winds tearing at my tunics. I took the ring from her purse and the knife on the ground and put them in my bag. Then I moved over and leaned on one of the enormous columns. I tried to gather myself together and I began to weigh my sins. I had so far lost my mother, Eadburh, Ealdgyth, and now Gunnehilde. But I had saved Siobhan, and now it fell to me to watch over

Thorkel and protect him from all the perils of this life. In that circle of rocks I swore this on my very soul. So ends the story of your grandmother Gunnehilde.

The Professor offered, "Sadly, the general perception among the inhabitants of eleventh-century western Europe was that the average person had very little chance of going to Heaven."

He resumed,

Now the reason for Wulfric's urgency was becoming clear. It was not only that he wanted me to survive this night and prosper; he believed that if I did not prosper before he died, his soul would be damned for his many failures and, more importantly, for breaking his solemn oath to take care of Thorkel. Somehow by saving me, he would fulfill his oath and receive full absolution. Or at least that was how he saw it.

But Wulfric is already dead. I looked over, and there he was, still perched by the stone, still with one hand dangling down. Perhaps his soul was currently undergoing excruciating pain because this matter had not been finished. But surely even Almighty God would wait to see this night through to its resolution, to see if Wulfric had engineered this night so that he might keep his oath even in death. I knew I should proceed at once, but that I must still read carefully and understand fully. I applied my energy to determining what I was supposed to learn from this chronicle.

So this was my grandmother Gunnehilde. She reminded me very much of Emma, and I looked forward to reading this story to my new noble bride. I wondered how Lady Wallington would react to my arrival and my announcement. She had been so cruel for so long to Emma that surely she would assume that I would try to punish her for how she had always treated my Emma. And she would be right: my family has taught me not to associate with cruel people.

Emma's four stepsisters would surely be jealous of her marrying me, and perhaps her mother would scheme a way to keep Emma, and I guess me, from inheriting the property at Surrey. It was only then that I realized that with a male champion, Emma would inherit everything of her father's immediately upon our marriage. I did not think that Lady Wallington would allow this.

No, a public and vindictive reunion would not be my best approach. The best approach was to discuss the new development with Emma in private and formulate a plan that would use our element of surprise to forestall any chance of her thwarting us. I suddenly became extremely worried that Lady Wallington was so evil and so versed in the ways of the nobility that she might well get the upper hand in this new situation. I could not think of any way that I could legally outmaneuver her since she personally knew the judges, none of whom I could have known, and she knew the law, none of which I understood. Further, I had, at least so far, very little proof of my nobility. Often Emma had wished for a fairy or a sprite to come along and save her from her evil stepmother. Perhaps the next chapter, the story of either my grandmother Eleanor or my grandfather Roth, would light the way toward living happily ever after.

Steve asked, "That was Stonehenge, wasn't it?"

"Yes," answered the Professor.

Steve looked a little embarrassed to ask, but said, "What exactly is Stonehenge, anyway?"

The Professor took a very deep breath and said, "Stonehenge is a ring of enormous stones that sits on a plain in Wessex, southern England, today. It dates from about 2900 B.C., which is long before people began to write in England. It was constructed by the earliest Celtic peoples who used it as a ceremonial place and as a calendar. The huge stones are aligned with the rising of the sun at the summer and winter solstices, the latter occurring on December 22. And such festivals did not go unnoticed by the Church fathers who made up the earliest Christian calendars. The Christian festival of the birth of Christ was placed on December 25, precisely when it becomes apparent that the days are beginning to get longer again. This date was carefully picked in order to associate Christ with the coming of new life and with pre-Christian rituals. In modern times, the solstices draw thousands of people to Stonehenge each year."

The Professor continued, "It's the 'Wassailing Song' that arrests my attention. The song is the perfect example of how Danish, Roman, Celtic, and Saxon traditions were beginning in the eleventh century to fuse into a culture that can be identified as "English." Wassailing was actually a Druid custom of toasting to the good health of apple trees. In the early Middle Ages—perhaps 500 or 600 A. D. —the tradition was adopted by Roman Christians and became incorporated into Christmas traditions. The word itself is related to both the Norse "ves heill," and the Saxon "weshal," both meaning "good health." This carol is very old. Like the apparently Celtic knife and the site at Stonehenge itself, this scene crystallizes the ongoing fusion of cultures into what could now begin to be called English culture. A culture, I might add, that exactly one decade after this 1056 scene at Stonehenge would have French added to the stew. William the Conqueror, after all, wore a Saxon amulet when he conquered the English at Hastings and, according to the depiction on the Bayeux Tapestry, had Celtic hand bells rung at his funeral. Even the language I am speaking right now is a symphony of these various impulses."

He concluded. "Let's take a break. I need to stretch."

Chapter Sixteen

Lady Godiva Takes a Ride

I sat on the floor in the den waiting for the others to get back from the bathroom and kitchen. With my knees pulled up to my chest, I was wondering how different tomorrow would really be. I was thirsty and the late hours may have been making me a little irritable. Certainly I had found a second wind in terms of schoolwork, and I knew I would have a very different view of hard work from now on. But even if I did well enough on tomorrow's history exam, and even if I changed my major to something I could get the fever for, my family's financial problems were still overwhelming, and I might have to drop out of school, leaving Nelson, leaving Steve, and leaving learning behind forever. I thought the answer might appear in the pages to come; at least I hoped so.

Just then Steve arrived, handing me a big, fizzing glass of coke with plenty of ice. He beamed with his broad white smile, "Here you go, Haley FitzArthur Stuart!"

"You know my name and you know my favorite drink! Just like I like, with a tall glass and lots of ice! How did you know?"

"I asked Nelson. You know, when he's not inventing frisbee maneuvers and porch maneuvers, he's an alright guy."

The group was reassembled and Joel asked, "Isn't anyone a little worried about stalker-man out there? Honestly, it's giving me the creeps a little. They should have caught him by now."

Steve had been giving everyone's nervousness a lot of thought, and he was ready now with his answer. He spoke softly. "I don't want this to come out wrong, but nobody in this room needs to worry. I will soon be promoted to fifth Dan in Shoto Kan and I have never lost a match, even to true masters. If this guy shows his face, I will make it so that he won't ever get up again. He's so crazy that I know that I'll have no trouble with the police. It is against my training to say any of this, and I apologize, but I have no choice: I will not have this man frightening anyone, especially you ladies."

No one knew what to say to this, but everyone felt infinitely more secure when Steve had finished. I thought "you ladies" sounded a bit sexist, but I thought I could fix that later, maybe after he saved my life.

The Professor resumed,

I must admit that the idea of leaping ahead to my mother's chronicle was very tempting at this point, but I knew it would have references that I wouldn't understand. I decided to abide by Wulfric's instructions. After the lifetime of work he did arranging this evening and this mountaintop, I felt he deserved to have his instructions followed exactly.

Wulfric Rhys

Gunnehild Mynyddawg

Ealdgyth Angharad

Bag Bag

Neils Fire Hugh

Bag Eleanor

Siobhan Matilda

Your grandmother Eleanor, who was your mother's mother, was born in 1026 in Evreux, Normandy. Her Mother was Matilda, the peasant, and her father was Hugh, count of Evreux, bastard son of Richard I, Duke of Normandy. As I told you in Matilda's chronicle, Eleanor and her mother were very close as Eleanor grew. This bond was perhaps made stronger by the certain knowledge that Eleanor would have to leave at the age of seven. All parties agreed that Eleanor should be raised as Hugh's noble daughter. She would soon enough leave behind her peasant roots, her peasant life, and her peasant mother forever. Eleanor loved to ride horses with her mother, and she listened to her mother's stories for hours. The kindness that Eleanor showed throughout her long life was kindled, fostered, and fully rooted in these earliest seven years.

At seven, in 1033, Eleanor said goodbye to her mother and was taken to the castle of distant cousins in Maine, France, for training in the arts of noble womanhood. She learned to ride like a lady and she learned to be graceful. She became well-skilled at embroidery. It was in this period that your grandmother Eleanor gained a refinement that throughout her life matched well with her kindness.

In 1042 Hugh was granted the earldom of Devon, and this elevation prompted him to decide to move Eleanor in 1044 to his cousin's estate in Coventry, England. The Lady of Coventry was Hugh's father's sister's daughter, who had married the Lord of Coventry, a Saxon. The other young ladies at Coventry were therefore second cousins to her, and they treated Eleanor well, almost like a sister. The death in 1044 of Eleanor's father Hugh at the hands of her Uncle Roger did not trouble her at all. Matilda explained the entire episode clearly enough when Matilda soon after called Eleanor to Romsey to break the news; it was then that Matilda told Eleanor about the dowry and its exact location, in case Matilda should not live to see her daughter's wedding, God forbid it!

Eleanor made good friends with a fellow noblewoman, Godgyfu, who became her best friend. Godgyfu was wife of Leofric, Earl of Mercia, of which Coventry was a main city. There were many advantages to being best friends with the Duchess and having a mother for a Duchess also, the very best of which is that no one told you what to do. Eleanor and Godgyfu became so close, both bracing each other against all the storms of this age. They hated cruel or even unkind people, and built up an emotional wall at their respective estates so that none of the viciousness of this era seeped in and affected them or their charges, the many peasants who depended on them.

We all turned our heads to see as the Professor pointed out Mercia and Coventry on the map.

These two women understood their role to be simple: function as the protector of the peasant families in their care, and expect loyalty and service from the peasants in return. In times of famine, both took special care to ensure that their vassals were provided for as much as possible. In times of legal dispute, the ladies would watch over the proceedings and ensure that no one was treated unfairly. In times of serious sickness, they would tend to the peasant, and ensure the timely arrival of the priest for the last rites. In 1044, the year of Eleanor's arrival at Coventry, the area was struck by a horrible famine. The price of wheat soared from ten to sixty pence per barrel. Through this terrible time the household at Coventry kept bread available at their back door as much as they could. While they lost some of their peasants to starvation, the many survivors were touched by their lords' great kindness. Eleanor's family truly understood the reciprocal nature of nobility, the covenant in which they were bound by their privilege. In 1047 the winter was so hard that fish and birds perished, and again Eleanor and Godgyfu met their obligations. The following year, a huge earthquake struck England, collapsing many of the peasant cottages. Again, Godgyfu and Eleanor supported their respective peasants as much as they could. When Edward finally abolished the heregeld--the tax to bribe off the Danes-- in 1051, this was a mighty relief for their peasants.

Well, Eleanor sounded truly noble, all right. Exactly the way Emma perceived her role! Let us see, how noble was my grandmother Eleanor? In other words, what was my exact relationship to the current king? I mapped it out: Rufus, current King of England, was fathered by William the Conqueror who was fathered by Richard II, Duke of Normandy who was fathered by my great, great grandfather Richard I, Duke of Normandy. My mother was Margaret, her mother was Eleanor, her father was Hugh, and his father was Richard I, Duke of Normandy. So Hugh and Richard II were half-brothers, my grandmother Eleanor and William the Conqueror were first cousins, and the current king William Rufus is second cousin to my mother Margaret. That makes me the second cousin once removed to the King of England, and third cousin to his children.

Since the friendship of these two ladies happened to blossom in the 1040s and 1050s, they enjoyed the period of prosperity ushered in by Edward the Confessor, who ruled from 1042 until 1066, the same king whose economic stability made your grandfather Mynyddawg prosper. He was also the same Edward the Confessor whose replacement of Danish nobility with loyal Saxons made your other grandfather Roth furious. For Eleanor, though, the prosperity of the period simply meant that during these decades her peasants and those of Godgyfu experienced relatively mild taxation, at least compared to the post-conquest period.

It must be remembered, though, that while Godgyfu was the lady of her expansive manor, Eleanor until her 1055 marriage certainly was not the lady of her smaller manor. Yet Eleanor watched over her cousins' peasants of Coventry, people who were technically not her vassals, waiting for the day when she would be asked to marry and would begin the administration of her own estate. That day did not come by twenty, and it had not come by twenty-five. Though she had a considerable dowry, marrying a Norman, which Eleanor certainly was, was as yet not considered fully appropriate to the minor thegns of the area, all of whom were of Saxon stock. The fact that she was opinionated and firm in her dealings with unscrupulous men who came to the court of Coventry also hurt her chances a bit. It was feared that after some time she might be required to join her mother at Romsey.

Instead, in 1054 a man of vast influence named Osgod descended into her life and she fell in love with him. What providence had brought a high nobleman with no fear of Normans and no patience for cruelty was beyond Eleanor's understanding, but there she was, getting married in a Coventry church in 1055. I suppose you have sensed the truth about your grandmother: her life was blessed from the day she was born in 1026 until the day she passed on and proceeded directly into Heaven in 1086. What is so very happy about her story is not so much the extent to which she was blessed. What is so happy is simply that she knew she was blessed, and this knowledge radiated through her in the form of kindness and concern in all her dealings with everyone she encountered for all her days. Your mother has much of this in her, too. Perhaps even more. Godgyfu was elated for Eleanor at the wedding and Matilda traveled to the ceremony, telling Eleanor how proud she was.

They rode off toward the east at sunrise to begin a new life at Osgod's demesne. The Cambridge estate was opulent, and with the birth of Margaret the next year, Eleanor's life was truly full.

The Professor remarked, "The word 'opulent' is not one that I would employ to describe anything in Western Europe in the eleventh century, but to Wulfric I'm sure the estate certainly was. Everything is relative. For him and his contemporaries, Gunnehilde's roundness was exquisite beauty, and for him, she stayed very clean. No one noticed the smell—the skin-deep soaking of sweat and urine--that accompanied each person, noble or peasant, through their daily lives. We can glimpse the hygienic quality of the eleventh century today by taking one long, deep breath while hugging a homeless person. With no frame of reference, though, inhabitants of the eleventh-century could not recognize the filth that they lived in every day: open sewage running in the middle of town streets and flies constantly on their faces. Another example of their lives that they assumed was adequate which would bother modern Americans is interior lighting. The lighting in even noble houses was extremely dim, and smokiness was ever-present since few houses had fireplaces; smoke escaped through a hole in the roof. They could not see their own filth, just as we cannot see ours today. By our modern standards, this estate is rather simple, but by theirs, truly 'opulent'. Let's continue."

Every Tuesday morning the family would go to the little farm they called Wild Dogs and frolic, naming the pigs something sillier every time, playing half-penny prick, and enjoying the day together.

In 1057 Eleanor returned to Coventry to visit, and her stay was scheduled to last the length of a typical visit, six weeks. She brought the beautiful one-year-old Margaret to show off as a prize. But what she discovered on her arrival in the city of Coventry very much embarrassed her. The entire shire had gathered for what was rumored to be the Duchess of Mercia riding completely naked through town on a horse. Now, Godgyfu was Eleanor's best friend, and Eleanor would have nothing of this. Eleanor located the Duchess preparing to go on exactly such a ride.

"Have you lost your mind?" snapped Eleanor. "Why in the world?"

"I have a reason that you will find so convincing that you will ride with me too!"

"Tell me your reason, my crazy friend."

Godgyfu explained, "Well, my pig-headed husband Leofric and I have made a wager. He was scoffing my attempts to spread the love of ancient Greek art to my peasants. He would always tease that they had no business learning such abstractions when there was plenty of work to be done. He jokingly said that if I thought the ancient Roman and Greek nudity was really all that noble, then I would have no trouble riding through the town of Coventry showing only what God had given me. I told him I certainly had no such trouble and, to indicate my seriousness about art and about the welfare of my peasants, I told him that if he released all peasants in his earldom from taxation for one year, I would take the ride nude."

"The fool agreed, and here we are. He doesn't think I'll do it! Now, I need ladies to ride behind me--don't worry, fully dressed--to ensure the dignity of the occasion. I have one. Will you be the other, as a gift to bring great happiness to my vassals?"

Your grandmother answered, "It would be my honor."

With only the brooch in her hair and the flies on her back, Godgyfu rode through the streets in all of her glory. She was in no way ashamed, and instead sat proudly with the excellent posture of her upbringing. When the ride was finished, she offered as a gift to Eleanor the brooch that she had worn to keep her hair up. It was the only thing she had worn during the ride, and Eleanor gladly accepted it. The two then traveled on to Godgyfu's manor and had a long vacation together. As I heard this story from Eleanor during our interview, I sensed that at least part of it was not exactly true. But she claimed it was, and I am writing it down.

Nelson asked, "Well, did the Lady Godiva ride actually occur or not?"

The Professor had been waiting patiently for someone to ask this. "The answer is: historians do not know. She definitely lived and she and her husband Leofric were definitely very magnanimous givers to the churches and convents in the area. That much is historical fact. She is even listed in the *Domesday Book* in the Coventry volume. One more historically indisputable fact exists. Unexplainably, the Earl of Mercia did not collect any of his usual taxes in the year 1057. The rest is unverifiable. Eleanor might have concocted this story in order to make her point about the duty of a noble, or she might be the first ever to record the true events of that day. Since Wulfric himself was not sure how much was true, we may never know. Perhaps a clue awaits."

This experience would stand out for Eleanor as a superb example of the responsibility that true nobility brought. To be noble was to act nobly; ignoble acts were proof of a lack of nobility. This is the way she reasoned.

Around the manor house at Cambridge, peasants came and went, often bringing grains to satisfy their tax obligations to Eleanor and Osgod. Eleanor became excited when I asked her about her life on the manor. She explained that the manor, with its main house for the lord and all its smaller cottages, was a large family, with many silly fights and much mutual admiration. The families of the manor usually had two or three children, and adults with their own children only rarely lived with their older parents. She explained, "The families who held more freeholding land on our lands tended to have more children because they could feed more mouths." Before their planting each season, Eleanor would have the local priest sprinkle the fields, both the peasants' own freeholds, and the demesne lands that the peasants would work for their lord, with holy water. Everyone of every station would attend church on Sundays unless they could not walk, and even many of those were somehow able to get to the service. The women always wore their darkest colored tunics to church. Many women of all classes worked on their embroidery in the evenings by the fire before they retired. If they spilled salt on the table, they were careful to throw a pinch over their shoulder for good luck. They were just normal people of high and low station supported by a web of mutual helping, living this life out with as many comforts as possible.

After the Norman Conquest of 1066, as part of his new tax obligation, Osgod was required to provide two mounted knights each year to King William the Conqueror. Since Osgod was no warrior and he had no sons, this requirement meant keeping up smaller estates for his thegns to occupy in exchange for their military duty. Osgod had managed his money superbly, and was able, until the political winds shifted, to sustain sufficient estates to meet his military obligations to King William.

William's taxation of the peasantry, however, was another problem. He required peasants in all quarters of his England, which was spreading rapidly northward toward Scotland and westward into Wales, to provide labor. The building of numerous stone castles was begun in the period after 1066, and this was the general period in which the Tower of London was begun as well. Peasants experienced much hardship meeting the royal demands for labor while paying the local church and nobleman taxes as well. When the tax burden became too much for her peasants to bear, Eleanor had her husband suspend feudal taxation for a while, a move that was shocking to both the peasants and fellow nobles who soon learned about it, but which was in keeping with Eleanor's outlook on life. She would not allow William, "her scoundrel of a cousin," as she would say, to starve her people into their graves.

In 1074 Eleanor's daughter Margaret married a nice boy named Thorkel—my grandson! But when King William in 1076 stripped Thorkel and Margaret of their holding in Kent, in an embarrassing reversal they were forced to move back in with and live with her parents in Cambridge. King William also took most of the holdings from Osgod, but allowed him to keep his primary estate at Cambridge in exchange for a "loan" that left Osgod virtually penniless. Events that I will relate soon enough brought me on a visit to this Cambridge estate in 1077, when I learned from the servant woman about Osgod's Welsh heritage. The next year I went to Wales and was of course married to my Eadburh until her death in 1083.

While I was married, I kidnapped you, Boy, from Cambridge in 1081 and set you up in the London swordmaker's guild, a move whose cleverness I do admit myself. You had had four good years with the sweetness of your mother at this point, and your disposition was already set. After Eadburh's death in 1083, as I have earlier disclosed, I traveled a second time from Essex to Cambridge, this time doing my act and learning the full stories of Mynyddawg and Eleanor. It was true that Eleanor was of such a dignified state that she simply did not deserve the scorn that would be heaped on her if it were discovered that she was married to a Welshman.

I did not have to keep the secret long. Three years afterwards, many people contracted fever and chills and took to the bed, never to recover. Boy, Eleanor and Mynyddawg both died in the plague of 1086. This plague affected thousands of us, but somehow I escaped. I suspect my amulet had something to do with it.

Joel asked, "In the plague, didn't the people after the plague sing 'ring around the roses, pocket full of posies, ashes, ashes, we all fall down' to remember it? I think I heard that in a Bob Marley song."

The Professor responded, "Wrong plague. Your reference is to a completely different plague, the devastating Black Death of 1348 in which the bubonic plague wiped out thirty percent of western Europe. The bubonic plague was characterized by large black growths on the groin and underarms, which were called buboes. Posies were thought to repel the miasma, or evil cloud, which spread this plague."

"The eleventh-century plague was not a bubonic plague, which was first introduced to Western Europe only in 1347 and still emerges from time to time. No, prior to 1347 plagues were usually pneumonic, spreading a viral pneumonia that recurred every few decades to ravage the already undernourished population. Now, back to Eleanor."

But before she died, our talk in 1083 revealed Eleanor's entire story to me, and she gave me a gift to give you, a token very special to her that once was given to her by her friend Godgyfu. Eleanor's comments not only revealed her entire happy story, but also shed light on the lives of Mynyddawg, Hugh, Matilda, Margaret, and my grandson Thorkel from a wonderful new perspective. In fact, it was this talk that prompted me to visit her mother at Romsey the following year. Matilda was aging but still quite lucid and quite spry. She told me her story and she told me where to find two gifts that she had kept for Eleanor. Eleanor died two years later before I could return to Cambridge, and so the chess set and the stirrup became Thorkel's and Margaret's. Your mother Margaret's position is currently too dangerous for her to hold such valuable property, and so I keep it in trust until a champion can emerge and save her in her time of peril.

In 1086 the horrible plague swept central England and it took both her Osgod and then soon after herself. She was caring to the end, protecting those in her care like a shepherdess. She had told me during our interview her simple outlook on life, and she insisted that I deliver it to you from her. It is your grandmother's voice from beyond the grave, and I urge you to listen to it well. She told me to tell you, "From those to whom much has been given, much will be expected." So ends the story of your grandmother Eleanor.

So this was my grandmother Eleanor. What an elegant, noble woman. I will remember her words.

Her gift was exactly where and what I thought it would be. It was the first thing that I knew I would have no use for this night: the brooch of Godgyfu. While it was ornate and would be a beautiful gift for Emma, I must say that I had preferred the razor-sharp knife that had been the gift from Gunnehilde. I then realized that the brooch might help keep my cloak closed on the trip back to Surrey. But its symbolism did not escape me: Godgyfu had given beyond measure for her peasants, as is our duty in our station in life.

I wondered, "I guess after the death of Mynyddawg and Eleanor, the peasants no longer enjoyed their support. I wonder who received the lands? Margaret may have still lived there with Thorkel."

The Professor offered, "Though an estate in this period was not hereditary, it typically passed to survivors once a huge tax was paid. Margaret and Thorkel may still have held the Cambridge estates."

Steve objected, "But Wulfric made it sound like Margaret was not in any position to control any property, even a chess set, much less a huge estate in Cambridge. He said she needed a champion desperately. And we know from earlier that Margaret and Thorkel were stripped of their titles and lands in 1076 and were forced back to Cambridge to live. If she is holding onto the estate in Cambridge, she is doing it only barely."

I concluded, half-thinking about how I had won the Homecoming crown, "If Margaret is holding on, I bet her peasants are helping her."

Chapter Seventeen

MacBeth Hath Murthered Sleep

It was four in the morning. No one was fading. In fact, the group was more focused than we had been at eleven. We all felt comfortable that with ten of us in the room--Bart, Shannon, Paul, Marilyn, Joel, Joel's friend, Steve, Nelson, me, and the Professor—we were in no danger whatsoever.

Joel said, "The problem with having stalker-man outside somewhere is that even if he is busted tonight, won't he just come after the book when he gets out? If he came all the way from England, I get the feeling that he won't stop until he gets the book. So far, his crimes have not been very violent—he'll be out of prison before long."

The Professor said, "Let's worry about that later. I have a few friends in the State Department who owe me favors, so I'm not too worried about that. Roth awaits us, and I suspect that he will be criminal enough for now."

Nelson and I shot each other the look again: *the State Department and Federal Marshals have virtually nothing to do with each other. No one has connections in both. Or almost no one. Time would surely tell.* The Professor had begun…

…I was feeling tense. Maybe it was the hour, or maybe it was because I was beginning to miss Emma terribly, since all my ancestors were choosing mates. Rexy's diaper had been off for a while now, and I was beginning to doubt the wisdom of my removing it. But at this point I decided to tie her as closely to the fire as possible, in case there was any problem. I tied together the thin leather belts that I had removed from the false monks and made a short leash. Using this rope, I tied Rexy by the Grailkey firmly to the boulder on which Wulfric had been leaning throughout this dark night. I assumed that Rexy did not mind too much, since she soon lay down so that she pressed against his stiffening leg. I was sure he did not mind. Roth took his place in the design.

Wulfric Rhys

Gunnehild Mynyddawg

Ealdgyth Angharad

Bag Bag

Neils Fire Hugh

Roth Eleanor

Siobhan Matilda

Roth was your grandfather, your father's father. This will not be easy for me because he drove my Little Bear to her death, but as your ancestor he deserves his place, so I will do my best. He was born in 1022 to his mother Siobhan and his father Neils. Half Danish and half Irish, Roth was destined to be a hothead, and that is exactly what he was. Growing up in Norwich, East Anglia, he was given free reign by his father to terrorize the local peasant boys with no punishment, and that is exactly what he did.

Once when he was six, the boy Roth came down with a fever and many were sure he would not survive. A physic was summoned who explained that according to the teaching of the ancient doctor Galen, Roth's humours--the four liquids which regulated his body—were badly out of balance. The physic explained the Roth's dominant humour was sanguine, and it was being badly overcome by the phlegm. The only cure was bloodletting. The largest leeches were employed, but this did no good. Frustrated,

Neils told the boy to hold still and Neils quickly sliced his arm, leaving an eye-catching and permanent scar. The boy did not flinch, and in fact he laughed heartily, which impressed the gathered Danes tremendously. If he survived, they joked, he would be joining them on the raids. He survived.

He was taken early from Siobhan for battle training, to which he was naturally suited. At his father's death in 1030, when Roth was only eight, he was already in battle training and residence with some of the Danish nobility in Northumbria. His ability with the battle-axe and the mace won the admiration of the burly Danes who would gather to watch the games. Their favorite game, though, was to trump up charges against a local village and to ravage, plunder, and murder these innocent people. At only sixteen, Roth's prowess won him a respectable landholding as a thegn in Northumbria, and as his warring increased, so did his prestige and his lands.

In 1039, when he was seventeen, Lord Roth heard Gunnehilde sing and for some unexplained reason decided to have her as his bride. She and her adopted father were certainly amenable, as you Normans say—we English just say "willing" —and she was wed. In this year Roth, despite his young age, was already moving with the royal party of King Harold, who ruled from 1035 until 1040, and this gained for Roth added lands and titles. When King Hardecanute, who ruled from 1040 until 1042, acceded the throne, he included your grandfather Roth in his royal court. Despite Roth's disposition, you should really be proud of him; your grandfather was, after all, a first cousin of Hardecanute's father, King Canute, who had ruled from 1016 until 1035. Moreover, Canute's father had been King Svein, who had ruled from 1013 until 1014, and King Svein had been a brother of Roth's father Neils. That means that King Svein, boy, was your great, great uncle, and it means you are of both royal Danish and royal Norse blood!

Because he was born a male, Thorkel's 1041 birth was excellent news to Roth, and was heartily celebrated by the royal court. Such a bloodline in conjunction with his prowess on the battlefield meant a bright future for Roth, at least until Hardecanute died suddenly at a party one day in 1042. This event was momentous in your life, Boy, because it brought the Saxon Edward the Confessor, who ruled from 1042 until 1066, to the throne. Roth was out of favor, and he was relegated to a second-rate landholding in Lindsey near the town of Lincoln.

As usual, the crowd paid close attention as the Professor pointed out Lincoln, Lindsey, Bamburgh, Northumbria, and the other places of this chronicle on the map.

Gunnehilde did not overly-object to the move because her roots at Roth's manor in Bamburgh had not grown very deep in her two years there. In Lindsey, she made a greater effort for her and her infant Thorkel to become a part of the village community. This was made hard, though, because of the rocky start they had in Lindsey. They happened to arrive the week before All Saints' Day. Every valley in England celebrates different regional traditions and festivals, and this region, far to the south of Northumbria, had a peculiar custom on All Hallows' Eve. They would dress in the garb of the dead and visit the local manor houses, demanding grains in this harvest time. It was said that the custom traced back to the old religion, but I have heard conflicting explanations. Since there was plenty of excess so soon after harvest, the demand was not unreasonable. If the local thegn did not provide a small payment of grains, the peasants would then badly vandalize the manor later that night under the cover of darkness. It was either a trick or a treat, and the thegns in Lindsey always prudently chose to treat their peasants.

But not Roth. Unused to the local etiquette, he ran the begging peasants away with his sword, thinking that there could be no retribution. The family then went to sleep as usual. It was the middle of the night when the coughing woke them. The entire north wall was aflame, which happened to be the wall with the hearth, and so it was where the one-year old Thorkel was sleeping. Your father was not badly burned, but he spent his life very much afraid of the flame, a fear Gunnehilde was sure originated here in the first hours of this November. The house, however, did not fare as well. With one wall aflame, there was no hope; the manor house burned to the ground. It was six weeks before life was back to normal, and the nobility of the entire region had received their ageless reminder that the function of the nobility was to protect, militarily and economically, their peasantry.

Roth was often gone on campaigns back in Northumbria in this period. He would return from time to time, hoping Gunnehilde had finally become pregnant with a second child. Though still very young, it was becoming apparent that Thorkel had no interest in the manly arts, and this irritated Roth to a degree that I cannot explain. He would tell Gunnehilde to try again, since the first one was a girl. When Thorkel was six, he was informed that his grandmother Siobhan had run off back to Ireland; since Roth had spent no time with his mother Siobhan and since Thorkel spent little time with his father, her leaving affected Thorkel very little.

Siobhan's idea of running away from brutality, however, seemed to be planted inside Thorkel from a young age. Poor Thorkel longed to take his mother away from this tyrant, and his only solace was that she loved him dearly simply for not being his father. In the days after my 1048 move to Essex, I would come up, without Roth knowing, and visit. I had some trouble with the Danish-influenced eastern language of England, with me coming from Hereford in the western lands. In Hereford, we pronounced our tops "shirts," while those in Lindsey would sharpen the word to "skirts." In Hereford, we had said "church," but in Lindsey they said "kirk." Despite the language difference, I got to know the boy very well on my long stays, and saw him at least once a year from the time he was eight until the terrible day when he was fifteen and his mother ran away.

In 1053 Roth thought his fortunes had changed when Siward, one of the few remaining Danish earls, summoned him for military advice. Roth was very attuned to omens, and he thought this one boded well. Gunnehilde told me that he would never pass a well without throwing a penny down it for good luck, a custom of the old religion that almost everyone in Lindsey still observed when they could. Gunnehilde would laugh when she told me that whenever Roth found a hairy caterpillar he would have to throw it over his left shoulder for luck. He could not resist such impulses, although he fully and sincerely embraced our Christian faith, unlike his pagan father Neils.

The issue that Siward wanted to discuss was Malcolm, the son of the deposed and murdered

```
Duncan, king of Scotland. MacBeth, who ruled
Scotland from 1040 until 1057, had murdered
Duncan and now had been king in Scotland for
some years. The question was to what extent it
would benefit England in general and the Danes
in particular if Siward led an army that saw to
it that Malcolm replaced MacBeth. Roth's answer
was that Malcolm would then be a close ally and
there would no longer be fear of attacks from
the north. Siward could then redirect energy to
the south in case Edward ever tried to remove
him as Earl of Northumbria, York, and Huntingdon
by force. The decision was made to attack
MacBeth, loot all of Scotland as only Vikings
can, and dethrone MacBeth, and in early 1054
Roth, as an important lieutenant of Siward,
mobilized his battalion and marched north of
Hadrian's Wall, the ancient Roman wall that
traditionally divided England and Scotland.
  The battle was pitched, and finally the
Northumbrians together with Malcolm's Scots
broke through and routed MacBeth, forcing him
to flee.
```

I asked, "Is the play *MacBeth* about this Scottish king?"

The Professor responded, "Absolutely. And happily, Shakespeare's *MacBeth* does not deviate too radically from the facts as recorded in his best source for information available during this period, the *Anglo-Saxon Chronicles.* Shakespeare, who wrote his play in 1606, probably made use of sources that had referred to the *Chronicle* when beginning to compose his play. According to the 1054 entry of the *Anglo-Saxon Chronicles*,

In this year Earl Siward proceeded with a large force to Scotland, both with a naval force and with a land force, and fought there with Scots, and routed the King MacBeth, and killed all the best in the land, and carried off a large amount of plunder such as had never been captured before."

The Professor continued, "Shakespeare used these core facts and wrote a story of an overly-ambitious MacBeth who was told by witches that he would be king. Consequently, he murdered the King, Duncan, his kinsman, and was then overthrown by the invasion by Malcolm and Siward from Northumbria. What is so interesting about this play, you see, is that the greed for the throne exhibited by MacBeth should be viewed less as a brilliant invention of Shakespeare, and more as simply an overriding characteristic of the times. MacBeth is by no means unique in his ambition; throughout the eleventh-century, kings were often attacked by their kinsmen. For example, war was declared on both Harold (1066), and William Rufus (1087-1100) by their respective brothers, Tostig and Robert, Duke of Normandy, in order to gain the throne. Such aggression was common because the concept of primogeniture—the passing of all property to the first-born son—had not yet taken hold in England. The result of such fabulous wealth being available to the strongest claimant was that succession to the throne was practically always disputed in this period. Let's continue; it's getting quite late. Shakespeare was right again: 'MacBeth hath murthered sleep'!"

Though he fled, MacBeth was not killed and in fact maintained the title of King until three years later. Malcolm retook this region of Scotland in this 1054 engagement. Roth and his men pillaged the surrounding countryside mercilessly, and were the first to reach MacBeth's castle. Roth's men entered first, and the gold that they found in that royal residence was considerable. MacBeth's bedchamber was found, but all his personal treasure had already been removed during his flight. At least that was what Roth's men had concluded, and they had moved on. Your grandfather, however, was an excellent soldier and looter, and he understood that MacBeth had

had little time to flee. Roth also understood the difference between a manor and a castle. A manor was simply a large house made for residential life. A castle was built to defend against military attack. As a result, castles tended to have secret passages to help defenders escape and stop attackers from looting.

MacBeth lived in a stone castle, which Roth understood was exclusively a Norman architectural concept. MacBeth had ruled for several years before this battle with the assistance of Norman mercenaries who had been thrown out of Wessex when Earl Godwine, my master, returned from exile in 1053. Earthen work castles were common in England until the 1066 conquest, when the material changed almost completely to stone. Knowing the military tendencies of Normans, which included ransoming rather than killing their captives, Roth thought there must be a secret room very near the royal bed for hoarding the wealth. It took much searching before the stubborn Roth hit his mark. He finally stood on a chair and pushed on an upper corner section of the closest wall, very hard, and it moved slightly. He could have called for help with this heavy wall, but instead used a section of the wall to pull it back in place. He moved on to other rooms in that castle, and received his share of the loot. When Roth announced that he would sleep in MacBeth's bed that night, it seemed perfectly natural to his men. In the middle of the night Roth went exploring and found incredible jewels and gold, including a massive and ornate ring of gold. It was of exquisite workmanship, and Roth knew it was perhaps the most exquisite ring ever made in Scotland.

As Roth began in the next days to secure the region militarily, his knowledge of the various battle tactics of his enemies stood him in good stead. In fact, the battle techniques employed in this war were quite varied. Roth and the other Danes led by Siward were fond of the battleaxe, and the Yorkish English that accompanied them enjoyed the iron mace and the axe. Their Scottish adversaries tended to favor the use of spears and, to a lesser extent, the sword. The Normans, allied with the Scots, used a weapon no other group employed: the warhorse. Although all sides rode horses to the battle, the Normans were the only ones to engage in battle from a mounted position, and their leverage and height gave them tremendous defensive and offensive advantages. They understood that weight applied properly in their stirrups—stirrups being strictly a Norman war secret in this day--would transfer the force of the horse directly into the thrust of their weapon. In fact, Boy, in my opinion the stirrup made the pivotal difference at the Battle of Hastings at which the Norman Conquest of 1066 took place. You must learn its use well. Additionally, the horse itself would attack, producing an overwhelming effect. The sheer numbers of Siward and Malcolm, however, won the day, but admittedly at great cost.

Roth continued his conquest of Scotland long after Malcolm was reestablished, returning home to Lindsey occasionally to tend to affairs. Once, when pillaging a village near Carlisle, Roth encountered a strange old witch. As he prepared to slay her, she told him something that saved her life. As he rushed at her, she looked into her cauldron of ale that she was brewing and screamed that it was the will of the great god Thunor that one of Roth's descendants would save the entire world. With a strangely confident air about her, she instructed him to be patient with his children, because their seed was that of greatness. Roth, being very wary of magic, decided to leave the woman alone, and her words haunted him for several years. He would tell the story whenever his Viking buddies were drinking and telling the warrior tales of conquest. The old woman certainly knew how to save herself.

The Professor paused to cross the other leg and Joel blurted out, “Their seed was that of greatness! Extremely cool! Then Boy will definitely live happily ever after!”

This passage, strangely inserted by Wulfric in the middle of his description of the Scottish Wars, had set me tingling in my stomach. By reflex, I suddenly looked over at Nelson. Though he had spoken less and less as the night had advanced, he was preparing to speak now.

“Hang on a minute,” Nelson began. “Earlier, during Gunnehilde’s tale, hadn’t the old Celtic priestess at Stonehenge said that Gunnehilde had the ‘promised bloodline?’ Yet she was also sure the stillborn would be a girl, but it was actually a boy. She must have been wrong. Or just plain crazy.”

The Professor responded in his usual calculated tone, “Yes, she was Celtic. But the witch in this current scene is described by Wulfric as being of the ancient Saxon religion, which originated, of course, in Saxony, Germany, long before the Saxons and Angles invaded Britain starting in the 300s A.D., an invasion of “Angland.” which gave the country its current name.

He continued, “The priestess at Stonehenge was clearly of the Celtic religion, the original religion of the British isles. The red-haired, green-eyed Celtic people had been practicing their polytheist faith thousands of years before the blond-haired, blue-eyed Saxons invaded beginning in the 300s. These two religions are totally separate, yet they both—Roth’s Saxon witch from Scotland and Gunnehilde’s Celtic priestess from Southern England--seem to be pointing, independently, toward Thorkel as being the fulfillment of some major prophesy. That makes no sense."

Bart added, "It makes about as much sense as what came from his other side, the mother's side, of Boy's family. From this side Boy received Excalibur, the lost sword of King Arthur. Doesn't the legend of Arthur say that one day Arthur will return, and Camelot, his court of gentility and grace, will rise again, bringing in a golden era of greatness and peace? And wasn't that a Welsh and Cornish story? And then there's the Grail itself, a purely Christian legend, whose discovery will bring powerful change. And of course the Grail's owner, Jesus, according to all four Gospels, will return to usher in an era of one thousand years of peace. Maybe the Second Coming of Christ can occur only once some prophet establishes a peaceful world that can receive Jesus correctly, like John the Baptist prepared the way for Jesus on his First Coming. Could it be that all these prophecies converge with Boy's combined bloodlines, and that he is on the verge of ushering in a new golden age?"

The Professor had been packing another pipe and now lit it up. "Yet no golden age came to Europe in this era." He puffed and thought a minute. "Nothing even close. Perhaps Boy's bloodline alone had not been enough to trigger the Welsh, Celtic, Saxon, and Christian prophecies. Perhaps even sweeter bloodlines, encountered in unions later in the family evolution, would be necessary. Let's read on and see if a clue emerges."

Siward died in 1055 and with this death died Roth's hopes of establishing himself as a prestigious lord, perhaps even an earl. His looting in Scotland increased. He was home in March of 1056, this we know for sure because your infant uncle died nine months later in the ring of rocks in Wessex. Since Tostig was a Saxon and not a Dane, the naming of Tostig as Siward's replacement as earl of Northumbria was a hard blow for Roth, who then swore he would leave for Norway and return only with a conquering Norse army. He actually did leave in 1060 and returned in full battle array in 1066, the year of his death.

The afternoon he returned to find that his family had fled he had been furious, and he rode with his men immediately for Essex once he beat the servants into confessing Gunnehilde's destination. Of course, she was lost and he did not find her for several weeks. I also barely escaped him in Essex. Roth arrived at the scene of the circle of rocks to find his grown son, who was fifteen, weeping beside his dead mother. He lifted and dragged his boy back to Lindsey.

Complications arose in Norway, which had been his intended destination, and Roth could not depart immediately. He trained Thorkel for battle more than ever, and Thorkel had natural talent, as his bloodline would suggest. But Thorkel's greatest strength was strategy; he enjoyed outthinking his enemies and using their own strengths to defeat them. Thorkel eventually resigned himself to a life of battle and allowed himself to learn from his father. Associating with his father and his father's friends for these few years, Thorkel heard the stories that Roth had been hearing so long. The legend was that Neils, Thorkel's grandfather, had hidden a vast fortune and had left a map of it on a bronze battle-axe. Though Roth vaguely remembered seeing such a thing, neither Roth nor Thorkel knew where it was to be found. Because the treasure represented by far the largest ransom ever paid to the Vikings, the lost treasure had achieved legendary proportions. Every new Dane who came to our shores asked your father and grandfather about this when their lineage became known, but the treasure was never found.

Despite Thorkel's compliance with his father's wishes, do not be fooled. Thorkel never forgave his father, and never stopped despising him. He was simply a captive who had no means of escape. Finally, when men of Edward the Confessor, the new Saxon king, had visited the area and asked for volunteers to return to London, Thorkel suggested that he go "so he could learn the secrets of the Saxons and defeat them with this knowledge." Roth thought it an excellent idea, and he never saw Thorkel again until the day he died.

In 1060 Roth left for Norway and spent six years about which I have never received a report. What I do know is that in 1066, after Edward the Confessor died childless, this vacant throne was the target of great commotion in our part of the world. Three kings ruled England in this fateful year: Edward the Confessor until January 1066, Harold, son of my master Earl Godwine of Wessex until October 1066, and William the Conqueror until 1087. Harold ruled well for his ten months and appeared to be a very promising choice for a king. He was intimidated, however, by stories of a massive invasion force that was gathering in Normandy. It seems Harold had sworn to God that he would support William as King of England after Edward, and now the Pope backed William because of the sacrilege of Harold seizing the throne of England despite his oath to the contrary.

The Professor interrupted, "I've got pictures. Let's use the jumbotron."

He picked up his remote control and pushed one button. Gradually the lights dimmed and an oversized projection screen lowered from a recess in the ceiling as a projector also hummed into view from its ceiling recess. Huge slides began to fill the long 20-foot wall with amazing crispness of image. This room suddenly took on a feel of a government operations center. I would look at that remote later. The Professor must have set up the slide show during the break.

The Professor began narrating the images: "This tapestry is one long continuous depiction of all 230 feet of the famous Bayeux Tapestry. This slide show depicts all of it. The Bayeux Tapestry can best be understood by comparing it to a newspaper cartoon that is a football field long. The Bayeux Tapestry contains approximately seventy discrete scenes, leading up to and including the Norman invasion at Hastings in Sussex, the southern coast of England. As you can see, it is probably the single best source for information about the clothing, manners, arms and armor, architecture, folklore, and events of mid-eleventh century England. This tapestry essentially is laid out as a description of Harold's broken oath and its consequences." He narrated briefly but thoroughly, emphasizing the parts of the tapestry that portrayed the glorious Norman victory at Hastings, a battle that he explained occurred nineteen days after the battle of Stamford Bridge, which he emphasized must be treated first.

The Professor pushed a button that ended the show and retracted the jumbotron and continued,

With such pressure mounting in the south, King Harold received disappointing news from the north. His brother Tostig, who had earlier been named earl of Northumbria until his own vassals had expelled him, had returned. Tostig had declared war against his own brother and had returned with Harold Hardraada, the King of Norway, and a massive Norwegian invasion force. Tostig had secured York and would soon begin moving southward toward London. King Harold, decisive as always, chose to ignore the huge and impending invasion of Sussex from Normandy. He gathered the forces of all his earls as he moved northwards to repel this final Viking invasion of England. In the ranks of King

Harold was none other than your father Thorkel, whose story will be related in time. In the ranks of Tostig and King Hardraada was your grandfather Roth, who was convinced that a star with hair foretold his and your family's great rise.

The Professor stated, "from February until May of 1066, Halley's comet, referred to at the time as 'the star with hair', was plainly visible in the European skies. This omen was widely interpreted as a harbinger of an entirely new era, which it certainly was."

He resumed,

And waiting in Normandy for these two sides to wipe each other out was your cousin, William the Conqueror, whom I will turn to shortly. But for now, the matter at hand: at the epic English Battle of Stamford Bridge, the matter of the death of my Little Bear would be settled.

Stamford Bridge is just north of the city of York, and the Vikings led by King Hardraada and Tostig were not expecting a direct, immediate assault because they expected that the even larger invasion force about to pounce from Normandy would keep King Harold in the south of England. King Harold, however, though he only ruled England for nine months, was a great leader. In only four days, he moved his entire army to York and attacked, gaining the full advantage of surprise. King Harold's army slew the Norsemen and Tostig in devastating manner. Both King Hardraada and Tostig died at this battle but many of King Harold's people died as well.

Thorkel did not move with the main body of Harold's troops, but instead led a battalion around the right flank to ensure that the

Vikings did not withdraw to their boats, a position from which they were almost invincible. Thorkel waited for several hours for the retreating Norsemen and soon enough, they appeared. After hard hand-to-hand combat, the Norsemen had fallen and only one, their leader, remained standing. He defeated, one, two, and then a third of Thorkel's band. Thorkel moved to assist against the marauder, and it was none other than his father Roth.

There was no warm embrace. Roth ran at Thorkel with a murderous yell and Thorkel deftly sidestepped the onslaught, sending Roth slamming into a tree. Several Saxons arrived to aid Thorkel, but he called them off. "The old man is mine," he said. He did not want anyone to know that this was his father, because they might try to stop him from what he was about to enjoy.

"Always the womanish tricks, is it not? You and I both know you can not defeat me." And with that, Roth rushed at Thorkel, who had repositioned himself at the edge of the woods. As Roth pounded toward Thorkel in a thunderous run, the boy let his sword slip to the ground.

Surprised and pleased by this apparent act of surrender and cowardice, Roth screamed, "There will be no mercy!" as he raised his battleaxe above his head and thundered even faster toward his own son. Five feet from the boy, the ground gave way under Roth and he fell into the spike pit that Thorkel's men had dug earlier that morning. Roth's leg was fully impaled and broken in many places. He was trapped. Thorkel reached behind a tree and brought out a long spear. He told me later that he had seriously considered leaving Roth to the ants, yellow jackets, and maggots to finish, but that would not bring the certainty and closure that he wanted. With the spear he skewered his father

```
with one hand. Thus ended the battle of
Stamford Bridge, and thus ended the life of
Roth. I am sure he would tell a very different
version of his life, but then he is not here
and I am. I was very proud of your father when
I heard this news. So ends the story of your
grandfather Roth.
```

So this was my grandfather Roth. Interesting life, interesting death, but not a very savory character. At this point I looked up from my seated position by the baking fire and saw a star that caught my eye. I walked over to the cliff and there she was: the morning star, now clearly on the horizon. It was Venus, the goddess of love. I thought of Emma. And there she was. This time, though, it was not my imagination.

Rexy, from her tied position at the rock, let out a furious series of barks as nine large Vikings came crunching through the underbrush into sight, surrounding my campsite. The biggest one, and he was ugly, was roughly holding the arm of none other than my Emma! She was more beautiful than I remembered, but with the anxious face of someone doomed. Her hands were tied in front of her with what looked like very painful knots.

The ugly one spoke in a northern dialect of English or Danish that I could barely understand.

"So we found you, you rat! It took seven days, and we thought we would have to settle for this one"—he shook her arm painfully—"but we got a little help from your friend!"

The ugly Viking approached a bit, while the others held back, each holding a battleaxe much like mine. "Give us the battleaxe and read us the inscription, or we will finish her right now. We plundered her manor already, and killed every soul on the place. Her mother and sisters lie in their own blood tonight. But we saved her, to ensure that you would tell us the location of the treasure. We thought you might need some prodding, since it's rather clear that you are going to die no matter what you do. She has been a warm comfort riding in front of me all the way from Surrey."

The ugly Viking continued, "Now we kill her. You may watch, or you may talk." With this, he pulled out a heavy knife, but his movement was arrested by the screams of his men. They turned their backs to us to find huge, foaming wolves lunging at them. The wolves had got Rexy's message! Romance was in the air!

The Vikings swung at the nimble wolves, but cleanly missed these beasts as they darted agilely in and out. There were twenty, maybe thirty, all snarling and dodging the Viking blows, then ripping at the flesh of their attackers after their swings. Emma knew what to do; she had apparently thought it out. She darted away, toward the fire, and sat down, hands still tied in front of her, next to the viciously barking Rexy, who was very glad to see her. A big Viking chased her immediately, but ran face-first into Rexy's flashing teeth, which dislodged part of his nose. He staggered backwards, looking up to see me give him the axe that he wanted.

I knew that we were safe from the wolves if we stayed here by the blazing fire, although quite a commotion raged around the perimeter. I quickly cut Emma's ropes with my Celtic knife and gave the knife to her. Every time a Viking escaped the wolves and reached the safety of the firelight, I showed them the axe that they came for. None of them seemed happy to see it. Rexy remained tied, since she was no match for these male wolves and since her presence ensured that the wolves would stay until their usefulness had been exhausted. The wolves had already dispatched four of the Vikings, and I had taken four. Finally, only two huge wolves survived and one Viking. This man, the ugly one, was a great fighter, and swung his axe furiously. I knew that if he bested the wolves, I would never be able to beat him in battleaxe combat. But then, I was armed rather thoroughly.

Emma watched my shoulders tremble with effort as I waited patiently with the mighty bow fully drawn. Finally, the Viking killed the last wolf and turned to claim his prize, the battleaxe. The arrow flew into his bronze helmet and stayed there. As he slumped so slowly to the ground, I heard the sound of a horse riding away quickly. I let another arrow fly into the Viking's heart.

Emma jumped up to hug me, but I said quickly, "Not yet. Better not watch this."

She did watch, though, from the safety of the fire, as I took Excalibur and stabbed each of the nine Vikings in the heart, heaving them off the cliff one by one, counting all the time. I then stabbed a total of twenty-one wolves in the heart, and threw them off the cliff also. I kept all the Vikings' axes and many of their belongings behind the tree where the false monks' gear had been stashed. I kept these weapons in case there was a need later, which I feared given that I still had no idea who gave my location to these Vikings. I was so covered in blood that I discarded my outer-tunic, hesitating because of the intense cold, but hoping for an even more comfortable source of heat.

Then came the embrace. We kissed long, as only the young can. Finally, we released Rexy and wrapped her bottom up well. I gave Emma plenty to eat and drink, and asked her to tell me what happened. She said they were all dead, all of them. Servants, her stepsisters, and even Lady Wallington, all were killed out in the courtyard. Emma explained that she had confided in one of the stepsisters —she knew it was a horrible mistake—about me and the fact that I was off in the direction of Maldon to join the Crusade. After all, she thought she would never see me again, and thought it might help things when this sister broke the confidence and told Lady Wallington that the suitor was gone. This sister gave up my location very quickly to a small Viking who tortured her with a torch and a rope around her ankle. Emma told me that the Vikings had actually lost my trail when they were approached by the young man who had originally struck the deal to tell them where I was. On the way up the mountain, there had been no sign of the wolves; they came out of nowhere.

"They always do," I said.

I then told her about what had happened to me so far that day, the robbers on the road, Cynewald, Wulfric, Ealdgyth, the attack of the Wizards, Rhys, Angharad, and Hugh. At Hugh I had her attention. Then I described Matilda, Neils, the false monks, Siobhan, Mynyddawg, Gunnehilde, and Eleanor. At Eleanor I really had her attention. Then I told her about Roth, and what I knew about the Vikings and the wolves. But I bet you can guess the thing that by far stirred my heartbeat the most that night.

I said, looking over at Steve, "I was wondering what good the ring and the brooch might do on this dangerous night, but now I'm beginning to get an idea."

Steve wisely ignored this comment for the moment and observed, "Well, now we know for sure that the bronze axe is a treasure map. All we need is someone who can decipher runes, and the treasure can be recovered, if someone hasn't beaten us to it in the last thousand years! Of course, it would help if we knew where that summit was."

Nelson looked puzzled. "Maybe Wulfric meant for Boy to know the exact location of the treasure by this time, so he could use the information if Vikings arrived. If so, Boy was not reading fast enough, because he did not know at this point."

Everyone agreed to take a break but to make it quick, as we prepared for the final two chapters. Steve and I went outside again. Steve asked, "Speaking of medieval linguistics, have you ever noticed heteronyms, which are words like 'b-o-w' which people cannot pronounce until they see them used in context?

'Bow,' for example, pronounced 'Bō', could mean the arrow-shooting weapon Ealdgyth left as a gift for boy, or, pronounced 'bou', could be Rhys' ceremonial bending at the waist. They are spelled the same, but pronounced differently, and have totally different meanings."

I answered back, "You mean like 'w-i-n-d,' which could mean 'wind a clock' or 'wind through your hair'?"

"Right," said Steve. "Discovering these words is one of my hobbies. Want to take me on? Let's go."

I answered, "Bring it on, tough guy: 'refuse and refuse'."

"Nice one," said Steve. "Sow and sow."

I countered, "does and does."

"Ouch," Steve winced, but countered with the combination, "dove and dove," "minute and minute," "supply and supply."

I sucker punched him with an untoppable heteronym: "unionized and unionized, as in 'an un-ionized particle'!"

"Kids, kids, break it up!" said the Professor as he came out on the porch. "I invented the heteronym treatment. Did you know that the reason we have heteronyms in our language is because some of our Modern English words are of Germanic origin and pre-date the Norman conquest, while other of our modern words are of Latinate origin, entering through the French that came into English after 1066? Heteronyms are the perfect daily reminder that our language was the purely-Germanic Old English from 600-1066 A.D. Then in 1066, the Normans invaded our language with enough French influence to shift our language to Middle English. And with the standardization of spellings that was brought on by the introduction of the printing press, Modern English was born, cementing the spellings of our two-origin language and often establishing the spellings of Germanic-based words without regard to the fact that those spellings happened to be identical to the spellings of Middle English, French/Latin-based words.

Steve got in a last jab, "Yes, Professor, like "number" as in "numeral" and "number," as in 'more numb'."

"Exactly," said the Professor. "While 'numb' as in 'desensitized' comes from the Old English 'nimen' through the Middle English 'nome' to the modern 'numb' and 'number,' 'number' as in 'numeral' derives from the Latin to the Old French 'nombre' and developed through the Middle English 'noumbre' to our current 'number.' Heteronyms are definitely a glimpse into the linguistic dualism that characterizes the history of the English language, a dualism that has its roots in the year 1066." At this point the Professor went back inside and closed the door.

Steve said, "Yeah, and 'sewer,' as in 'one who sews,' is from Old French while 'sewer,' as in 'underground conduit' is from Old English, and 'bass' as in 'fish' is from Old English while 'bass' as in 'low note' is from the Old French."

"You really are a tough guy," I said.

Steve struck a muscular pose. "Yeah. At the beach, I kick sand in linguists' faces!"

Chapter Eighteen

The Great Fire of London

As we began to come in from the porch, Steve asked, "Listen, would you like to come over to my house tomorrow morning after the exam and take a nap with me in my hammock to recover from this all-nighter? It's a really big hammock in the front yard, a doublewide, and I could make you my special "Fungi Steve" afterwards? It's steak with sautéed mushrooms. Don't worry, though, I have six roommates and, just like Emma and Boy, my big sweet black dog will be in between us; we would be thoroughly chaperoned."

"Well, since we're chaperoned," I answered excitedly as we moved down the stairs, back toward the den, "I guess I have no choice. I'll see you after the exam in the doublewide."

Marilyn and Joel were returning from the kitchen, and they settled in to hear the story of Boy's father. "Finally, answers!" said Nelson.

The campfire had never glowed brighter than now, since Emma had joined me. I was so excited that I could read the final two chronicles—the stories of my two parents—pushed up against the woman I loved. I was also happy that the threats were finally over, and that we could settle in without a worry in the world. Wulfric had done his work superbly, warning me well enough so that I had Rexy "invite" the wolves to protect my perimeter. His soul was secure. All was well.

Wulfric Rhys

Gunnehild Mynyddawg

Ealdgyth Angharad

Thorkel Bag

Neils Fire Hugh

Roth Eleanor

Siobhan Matilda

Your father Thorkel was born in 1041 in Northumberland. His mother was Gunnehilde and his father was Roth. As I have made clear earlier, Thorkel's relationship with his father was one of animosity, as you Normans say—we English just say "hate." Really, "loathing" may be the best word. For so many reasons--Roth's inept bungling of the Hallow e'en incident in which the house burned down, his insistence that Thorkel train as a warrior, his insensitivity to Gunnehilde which ultimately caused her to flee and consequently to die giving birth--Thorkel had little love for his own father. His mother Gunnehilde, however, could do no wrong. She sang to him often as a child, and defended his softer nature. He was incorporated into the village family that became his own family as he grew into a young man of fifteen. I think he had a lot of me in him; he was clever and warm, worried too much, and looked at life through the eyes of others perhaps too often.

The incident at the circle of stones, however, changed your father. From this point on his mother could no longer protect him from his father's temper or from his father's bent on training him to be another in a long line of murderous Danes. Boy, never forget that this is your line, too. Roth did not care that Thorkel was actually only a quarter Danish, with another quarter Irish and Gunnehilde's half, of course, all Saxon. Thorkel left Lindsey when he was eighteen and never went home again. In 1059 he followed some thegns of Edward the Confessor to London where he began to fight in the armies of Edward, earning quick advancements because of the techniques of death that his father had known and taught so well. Your father's pedigree as a direct descendant of King Harald Bluetooth of Denmark also helped his position at Edward's Saxon court somewhat.

If you want to really know your father, there is one incident that stands out. In 1063 his bravery established Thorkel firmly in the court of King Edward the Confessor. King Gruffydd ap Llywelyn of Wales had been harassing Mercia during the years before and King Edward determined to send a force to stop the Welsh king once and for all. Edward charged Harold Godwineson, who would as Harold II take the throne of England in 1066, to attack and defeat Gruffydd. Your father was an important captain in the ground assaults of Rhuddlan, near Gwent, a major center of support for Gruffydd. After Rhuddlan was destroyed, Harold and your father led men by ship from Bristol around to Cardigan, from which Gruffydd was forced to retreat repeatedly.

Finally the weakness of Gruffydd's loose coalition of Welsh kingdoms was his own undoing. His own men killed him and sent his head to your father. This was a high moment of glory for your family, Boy. Your father Thorkel then relayed the head to Harold who in turn relayed the gruesome object to the king. What makes this story so pertinent for you, Boy, is that at the time, Gruffydd was your mother's grandfather by marriage. That's right, Angharad had married Gruffydd and was now Queen of Wales. After this 1063 incident, as the mother of the new king, she would be Queen Mother of Wales until her death some time after. Of course, in the year 1063, Thorkel was still nine years from meeting your mother.

The Professor stopped and showed these locations on the map.

Another aspect of these Welsh campaigns that affects you is the honor it bestowed on your father, and on you by blood association. Boy, Edward the Confessor knighted your father after this campaign. Perhaps even more importantly, your father soon became a close confidant of Harold Godwineson, and the two were actually best friends. Harold saw to it that Thorkel was granted a very attractive demesne. His holdings were granted in Kent, on an estate that is known as Wickham, in Ruxley Hundred. The estate at the time was large, with twenty-four villagers and thirteen slaves associated with it. At the time your father took over the estate, 1064, it was valued at eight pounds; by the time of the 1086 completion of the Domesday Book in which it is listed, its value had increased to thirteen pounds, partially because of a castle that was built in the 1070s. Today, for reasons that will be revealed soon enough, its value is quite a bit higher still. Let me tell you boy, that these estates are now yours. You currently hold the sprawling and extremely valuable estate of Wickham in Kent. You also hold your grandfather Osgod's expansive estate in Cambridgeshire. You also hold the small tract of land you are currently standing on here in Essex.

Bart whistled. "He owns it! He could have transferred all the chests of silver coin to this mountain. It could still be there!"

Joel added, "Or, he could have left the gifts in their mountaintop grooves, and they could still be there. If only we knew exactly where this place in Essex was. There has been absolutely no hint yet. Read, on, Professor!"

Emma looked at me and hugged me. She said to me, "You are a great man! And Wulfric did not know of my vast holdings in Surrey, all of which will be yours the second that we are married."

I could hardly believe any of what I was reading. The day before, I had been a poor runaway servant from London. There was a catch somewhere, and I read on, braced to discover it.

In 1066 the accession of Harold Godwineson as King Harold II, who ruled England from January 1066 until October 1066, required Thorkel to join Harold at the royal court in London. Harold was a good King, and had it not been for the dual invasions only nineteen days apart, he would have ruled long and justly. As it was, Harold and Thorkel were forced by Harold's brother Tostig and King Harold Hardraada of Norway to abandon their defenses in the south. The Battle of Stamford Bridge was an epic battle, and it constituted the final attempt of Vikings to take over England. Though your father and Harold won it, the victory was very costly. Harold's army was badly depleted, and stood little chance if the huge invasion fleet should sail from Normandy to begin the Norman conquest of England. To the horror of your father, William the Bastard did exactly that, and landed a huge invasion force in Hastings, in south Sussex, only nineteen days after Stamford Bridge, which had been, up until that point, perhaps the most epic battle in English history.

The English rushed toward Hastings. Your father Thorkel made a special point to throw a penny into every well between York and Sussex, trying to muster as much good fortune as he could. He even stopped by here, my estate in Essex, both because it is on the way and because my grandson wanted to say his good-bye to me before he faced the horrors of this dreaded war for which he was bound. Yes, your father threw a penny down the well at the base of this cliff, the well you saw as you began to mount this summit. And indeed, the English put up a heroic fight against the assortment of French-speaking peoples and mercenaries led by William. In fact, the bravery of men such as your father at many times appeared likely to win the day.

The Professor looked up and laughed, "Yet actually William the Conqueror won this day, and with his victory died the fledgling reign of Harold, died the language known as Old English, and died Anglo-Saxon England. Let's see if Thorkel died this day."

Your father fought valiantly but at last had to flee. Many of the English, your father Thorkel included, and honestly me included also, felt that the star with hair had been a clear indication that change was ordained by God. This divine blessing very much aided William in his earliest days of gaining control. William took the field and was crowned King of England on Christmas Day, 1066, at Westminster Abbey. His policy regarding his restructuring of England was to move slowly at first. So, for several years your father kept his lands at Wickham without any problem. As William consolidated his position, however, this Norman king began to place his own loyalists in the strategic earldoms of the country. Soon the Normanization began to trickle to lower levels, and it became obvious that a great Saxon hero such as your father Thorkel, despite his Danish blood, had no place in the highest levels of the hierarchy of this new Norman order.

During the early 1070s, life at Wickham on a day-to-day basis was normal enough, despite the constant threat of dispossession faced equally by all Saxon thegns. The members of Thorkel's household urged him to marry, and to marry Norman, but at first the unstable climate meant that this was out of the question. It seemed, however, that Thorkel's demesne had escaped the notice of William's restructuring. As time went by, Thorkel began to consider the possibility of marriage. In 1073 a mutual friend suggested that Thorkel visit Cambridgeshire to attend some of the pre-Lenten festivities. The festival was Carnival, the week leading up to the Fat Tuesday that precedes Ash Wednesday and the beginning of the fast of Lent. Thorkel enjoyed the gala parties of this week, and there he met several eligible ladies, the most striking of whom was a young girl named Margaret. Thorkel by this point was thirty-two years old, and Margaret was seventeen. The age difference was just about perfect, as was everything else in their courtship. Your mother and father were instantly attracted to each other, and Thorkel was very young at heart, while Margaret was quite mature. Your grandfather Osgod often joked that she was the older.

The 1074 marriage was grand, in the Norman style, and there was the usual throwing of grains and shouts of "Abundance!" Margaret moved from Cambridge to Kent where they started their new life. Your mother gave birth to an older brother of yours, who I am sorry to say died at the age of two years. Two years after the marriage, unfortunately, Wickham was hit by the Norman wave. Your mother and father were stripped of their lands, which were granted immediately to a Norman named Adam, who had four very vicious and unruly sons. Your father had no choice but to accept Osgod's kind invitation to move back to Cambridgeshire.

Margaret was glad to be back at their estate, and her peasants were so happy to see her. She could play now at Wild Dogs again, and she and Thorkel named the pigs more than once. They would often pray for the health of the pigs to St. Anthony. It was in these days that Thorkel sat down to draw a detailed map of the world as he knew it. He had been amazed at how little knowledge of the lands of the world people in England possessed. His grandfather Neils had visited several lands to the west and to the south, and Roth had traveled widely in the Baltic Sea area. Roth's great-grandfather, if you remember, had traveled down Asian rivers to sack Constantinople. Information about all these places had been passed down through the generations of attackers and now resided intact in the mind of Thorkel. Thorkel's father-in-law Osgod was extremely knowledgeable about the lands of southern Europe, Constantiople, and Italy and was a great help to Thorkel in this effort. So your father drew an elaborate, detailed map of all known lands. To my knowledge, no map exists like it anywhere.

While Thorkel tried to settle into his new existence as a father in Cambridge, the entire family of Adam down in Kent was still mad with greed. Having talked to the local peasants who had been extremely fond of your mother and father, Adam and his sons became obsessed with the possibility that Wickham might revert to Thorkel if the political winds shifted. I am very sad to say that these four sons of Adam rode one day to Cambridge to kill Thorkel and his boy. At the time, Thorkel was not at the estate, but your two-year-old brother was, and they killed him.

When he returned to discover the tragedy, Thorkel was furious with rage, but the law and numbers were on the side of the sons of Adam. As a result, your father, always a thinker, bided his time for the opportunity both to avenge the death of his only son and to regain his estate in Kent. He decided that his best hope was to go to London to plead his case to the court of King William. William was almost always hostile to those who had been generals of Harold, and so the attempt appeared unlikely to succeed, but your father was determined to try. Your father's plan was that once his lands were back in his hands, he would turn to the subject of vengeance on the sons of Adam, and believe me, boy, he would have done so.

In London, Thorkel met with a legal brick wall. The court would not hear him, which was an answer he was unwilling to accept. William the Conqueror was a new kind of king to England; while the Anglo-Saxon and Danish kings had functioned as loosely controlling overlords, almost figureheads at times, William was lord of all England. His requirement that each estate supply mounted soldiers, and his systematic accounting of the property in England by means of the *Domesday Books*, were unprecedented moves toward full control of England. With stone castles popping up and old Saxon nobility losing sway, the French manners and the French tongue began to rule the day. Even your father's Wickham had been part of this movement; during the year 1075 Adam and his sons had begun the construction of a stone castle at Wickham. It was still being built, I was told, when Thorkel made his fateful trip to London.

One day during this trip when Thorkel was visiting a friend, attempting to gain support that might break the legal deadlock and let him into this new day, your father looked up sharply from his ale at the sound of cries that could be heard in the streets. Thorkel stepped out into the sewage of the street and was assaulted with the horrifying stench of the city on fire. He knew exactly what his priority was: he had to retrieve his purse, which was hidden in his room near the wall of the city close to where Westminster Abbey was still being built. Unfortunately, this path took him directly toward the baking flames, the one thing of which he was most terrified. But he was even more afraid of losing any chance he had at buying his way back into Kent. Your father knew well what many had learned; William the Conqueror would sell and resell land to the highest bidder. Thorkel finally got to his room, which was engulfed in flames, and he found his heavy purse.

I was also in London at this time doing what I could behind the scenes to further my grandson's cause. When the fire started, I hurried as fast as my old legs could take me to Thorkel's room. I was there as he left the building, and I saw the thick beam fall. It struck him heavily on the top of one shoulder and he was crushed horribly onto one of his knees. He fell onto his face and lay still. As the buildings all around us baked hotter and hotter with heat, ready to burst into flame, I dragged your father as far as I could, but my legs gave out again and again. The heat was scorching and chapping. I found some cobwebs nearby and put them on his burns, which soothed him some.

I knew that this was the end, and I knew it would be one more sad scene for me. I tried to save your father here in this great fire of 1077, but I could not. As he lay dying, he whispered to me. His final words to me were: "Bring this gold to Margaret." Then he added in a whisper, "She is pregnant. Teach the baby the song of Gunnehilde and keep him safe. Do this, and you will have done your duty for me."

Then I kissed my grandson, took the purse, and I ran as fast as I could out of that oven. I heard his screams recede behind me, and they intermingled with the screams of Gunnehilde, the screams of Eadburh, and the screams of Ealdgyth into a nightmare of guilt and heat. When I finally plunged into the safety of the Thames, I promised him as I swam across that freezing river that I would teach you the song my Little Bear sang to your father the day she died. I have written this song to you in her chronicle. You must learn it well, and you must sing it at Christmastide, when the days begin to lengthen again with the promise of new life. So ends the story of your father Thorkel.

Emma was deeply moved by the story of my father, and it made me realize that I was also deeply moved, by his story and by those of my other fathers and mothers. She loved him for running full out at his worst fear, fire, and dying in order to bring my birthright back. I told her that I loved my father, too, and that it was now up to me to avenge his death and the death of my older brother.

We then turned to lighter thoughts, and I gave her a tour of the camp. I decided to wait to tell her about all the gifts, although I knew that under Thorkel's place there was a map still buried, and I knew that in Roth's place there was an exquisite ring. I hoped there would be time for these later.

Everyone said, "Professor, show us the map!" It was very detailed, with no words on it since Thorkel could not read or write. England was drawn extremely accurately in the middle of the map. It included lands from Maryland to Moscow to Morocco, with east at the top, and the Professor said that it was definitely the best map to survive from this era.

As the group finished examining the map, Joel's friend, the Australian, suggested they just launch right in to the final chapter, and Nelson and I both agreed that this was the best approach.

Chapter Nineteen

The Norman Cross

"Wow. Final chapter," I said aloud. As the rest of us streamed in and began to take our places in the chairs and on the polar bear rug, I looked back over the events of the long night behind me and all the emotions that I had felt. I wondered if people could change so radically in only one night. Was there really such a thing as an epiphany, a breakthrough into a higher state after which you never go back? *Of course there was, I smiled to myself, but epiphanies can only come to those who are ready. Not only am I ready to move on from what I had been, it is becoming clearer and clearer to me that school may never have been the real problem. Sure, my classes had been confusing, but that was all they were. I was the weakling who let them cripple me. I was the idiot who never went to class and never asked for help. I was the liar who pretended that my classes were my problem, when I knew deep down that my own self-destructive anger at my parents was what had kept my grades so low. And maybe my parents didn't raise me with the attention that I thought they should have, but that is them, and I am me. I will make my own rules for my own family and I will follow them loyally. Maybe I am ready for my epiphany to come to me. Maybe now I can let the truth in.*

For the final time, I said, "Professor, read to me, please." And he began to read Boy's story again:

Preparing to read my mother's life story with my Emma by my side made me as happy as I had ever been in my life up to that point. Even in this darkest hour before dawn, I could see Emma's face with perfect clarity by the light of our roaring fire. I saw the blue-rimmed greenness of her eyes sparkle when I told her that somewhere nearby I had a present buried for her. She told me that she wanted it right now, so I dug up the remaining gifts, including the ring, but instead of giving the ring to Emma, I simply placed it on one of the leather bags on the perimeter. I told her she would have to wait for her present.

From her tied position, Rexy whined her objection every time our laughter turned to silence as we kissed each other into the stillness of time. The dog thought we were wrestling, and I got the feeling that she was on Emma's side. But Rexy, the ring, and my mother's story could wait a few more minutes. As my reunion with Emma became more romantic, I actually thought in those few exquisite minutes that a kiss could last for all eternity.

Wulfric Rhys

Gunnehild Mynyddawg

Ealdgyth Angharad

Thorkel Margaret

Neils Fire Hugh

Roth Eleanor

Siobhan Matilda

Your mother Margaret was born in 1056 in Cambridge to her mother Eleanor and her father Osgod. As I have told, her childhood was very happy, growing up with a loving father and a dutiful mother who taught Margaret her responsibilities as a noblewoman. In many ways Margaret was very much like her mother, a fact that in itself is a powerful endorsement of Eleanor's mothering. Margaret was collected and poised in good times, as when she gave food to her peasants at All Hallows' Eve. She was equally poised in the bad times, such as her embarrassing removal from Wickham in 1076, only two years after her wedding.

With the 1077 death of Thorkel, Margaret became very depressed. She had not recovered yet from the death of her first son, and now she was pregnant and widowed. She would not be granted the charmed life that her mother Eleanor had lived. In fact, her situation would soon turn from bad to worse. She understood that if the sons of Adam discovered her pregnancy, they would be back to Cambridge to end any chance at her child's claiming the family lands. As a result, the years after Thorkel's death were not only filled with grief, they were filled with acute apprehension that her child would be located and murdered. You, Boy, were kept a secret.

One day in 1081, when you were four, a local thegn stopped by the Cambridge estate unannounced and saw you. The secret of your existence was suddenly out. I had arranged for one of the servants to notify me in Essex if anything were ever to threaten you, and I received the news at once. I was able to seize you two full days before the sons of Adam arrived. I took you, Boy, in the middle of the night without Margaret or your grandparents even knowing I had come. My friend who was Margaret's servant made clear to Margaret and your grandparents that you were being looked after and would be returned at the right time, when you could stand on your own.

Margaret put together a rather convincing act for the sons of Adam. When they arrived, they were told that you had just died. Margaret showed them the body of a peasant child who had also only recently died. Margaret was superb and the plan worked. The sons of Adam left Cambridge believing that you were dead and that there was no future threat to their possession of Wickham. I suppose they were wrong about that.

Your mother understood perfectly that to search for you was to kill you. Though it broke a mother's heart, she could only trust that you were in good hands. Then, as today, it was still imperative that I remain anonymous because the stain of my minstrelsy and former slave status would taint you permanently. But no one will ever know, because I know you will destroy or at least hide very well this book as soon as it has served its purpose. Your Welsh heritage, since it is four generations removed, and since both your Welsh great-grandparents arrived at such high stations—a holy monk and a queen—is certainly not a bar from the highest social rank in Norman society. And of course, in the veins of great kings always courses the royal blood of many peoples. It is my minstrelsy and your Ealdgyth's peasant status that must remain buried forever. I know you will guard the book well, Boy, as you will guard the Grailkey.

While you were being reared after age four in the guild, your mother eventually began to recover from her grief. After mourning the death of her husband and son, and after learning to live with the removal of her only other son, Margaret eventually regained some of her old vigor. She began to plan, just as Thorkel would have done. Though she had spoken French exclusively to you to prepare you for Norman society, around the manor it was still usually Saxon that was spoken. She began to polish her Norman French and had perfected her court demeanor when her parents were both taken by the plague of 1086. The plague, however, also took Adam, leaving his sons with even less restraint than they had had before, but reducing the number of family enemies from five to four. The news that Margaret had been awaiting came in 1087, when it was announced that William the

Conqueror had died, and his second son William Rufus, who ruled from 1087 until now, would succeed him. The political winds had shifted.

In 1088 the entire region of Kent, led by Bishop Odo of Bayeux, revolted against the kingship of William Rufus and recognized instead his older brother Robert, Duke of Normandy. The Bishop's men plundered the area of Kent. The sons of Adam of Wickham, and almost all their neighboring thegns, were some of the staunchest supporters of the Bishop in this treasonous activity. In this year of 1088 Robert schemed to invade England, as his father had done, and he fully expected to seize the crown of England from his own brother.

Now Margaret had taken it on herself to visit her former lands of Wickham in disguise. The villians on the estate still loved her and excitedly took her in. They told her of the evils that had been done by these new landlords. At one point her former peasants showed her hidden tunnels and actually took her inside the new castle and showed her some secret passages. This castle had been built over the same floorplan as her old manor house. She used this access to get to an old hidden storeroom that lay to the side of the hearth in the manor hall. Here she found what she had really come for: a gift for you, one that she did not want to fall into the hands of the sons of Adam.

Her former peasants, who insisted that they desperately needed her to return, revealed the plot of Robert's impending invasion to her on this visit. Margaret was delighted with their loyalty and basked in the mutual generosity that is associated with feudalism when it functions correctly. She moved straight for London and demanded an audience with her cousin, which she received. King Rufus was very grateful for the information and dispatched troops immediately. Robert's invasion force was intercepted and most were drowned. The revolt in Kent was suppressed by 1089 and Odo was expelled permanently as Earl of Kent in 1090, being exiled to his see in Normandy. Rufus allowed the earldom of Kent to remain open.

The climate, then, was perfect to bring legal action against the sons of Adam for murder and for illegal possession of another thegn's demesne. The possession charges held little legal merit, but Margaret had put politics heavily in play. Though they were allowed to keep their lands, the sons of Adam were fined heavily for their involvement with Odo, a penalty that they simply passed on to their peasants. These peasants still were worked almost to death, spending half their days constructing the stone castle, which was now having the finishing touches applied. I saw the finished castle once and it is so massive and elegant that it takes the breath away.

It was in 1092 that I decided that I no longer had any choice; I had to confide in someone about the gifts, the book, and your status. I chose Cynewald because he was young enough and strong enough to keep the information as long as was necessary. The only elements that I withheld from him were your location and the location of the summit. These I plan to tell him only the day I dispatch him to end your long separation from your mother.

In 1093 Rufus fell deathly ill and Margaret feared that he would not survive. He did recover, however, and afterwards swore many oaths that from this point on, he would right all wrongs and begin to treat his people fairly. The climate was perfect and Margaret asked for a second audience, this one easily granted since the first had alerted Rufus to

```
his brother's impending invasion. After much
debate among his court, finally Rufus granted
Margaret's petition for a trial and agreed to
hear her pleas at Dover in the late spring of
1093.
  This trial was attended by people from far
and wide because it had repercussions on all
those who had been associated with the revolt
of Odo. The entire royal court was present,
including earls from as far away as Devon,
Chester, and Northumbria.
```

The Professor here pointed out Kent, Devon, Chester, and many other places referred to in this chronicle so far.

The weakness of Margaret's case was not so much that the sons of Adam owned the land legally; this was assumed, but certainly not stipulated to, by all parties. No, Margaret's real problem was that she had no one of position to support her claims. She was alone against a social element that everyone present except Margaret understood to be too high for her to fight. Her status as an unaccompanied woman also hurt her chances. The trial began poorly for Margaret. The sons of Adam put on an eloquent case, calling three bishops to vouch for their reputation and for the clear authenticity of their claim to Wickham.

It was then Margaret's turn, and she had no one to speak for her. King Rufus asked the assembly who would stand and speak for the Lady Margaret, daughter of the deceased Lady Eleanor and Lord Osgod. Again, no one came forward. I sat in the very back of the gallery, seething over my low social standing, a standing that meant that with one word from me her petition would be immediately denied. Again, Rufus, presiding and now becoming a bit impatient, asked again who would represent the Lady Margaret. Finally, after a prolonged and awkward silence that brought smirks to the faces of the sons of Adam, one voice broke the silence.

Henry, the brother of Rufus and the next in line for the throne, stood. "This woman is my second cousin, and I will stand for her."

The gallery buzzed at the apparent unfairness of the judge's brother acting as prosecutor, but Rufus seemed pleased. Henry began at once, moving to the front of the hall so that all could hear him. Henry explained that the property had originally been hers until his father William the Bastard had seized it for no cause. It rightly belonged to the Lady Margaret.

At this point, an old hag who had been sitting near me was looking very confused. I moved over and asked her in English if she would like a translation, since she spoke no French. She was ancient, and bore scars that crisscrossed the wrinkles of her face. She replied, in a tongue very difficult to understand, "Thank you." She seemed to be holding a small nut of some kind in her old trembling hand.

Henry had finished stating the essential facts, and he asked your mother some questions. She comported herself with the dignity of a queen.

"Why do you want the land? Are you not satisfied with your holdings at Cambridge?"

"Sir, my holdings at Cambridge are subject to the same seizure if this matter is not soon rectified. And it is not for me that I fight, but for my heir."

The gallery buzzed, because Margaret was childless.

Henry continued, "I had heard that you had a second son, but that he had died. Is that not true?"

"No, sir, it is not true. My son was born in 1077 and has been hidden from these murderers and from me ever since. Even he does not know his own identity." She scowled at the snickering defendants. "They killed my first-born son and came for my second two days after he was taken away to safety."

"Where is the boy now?" asked Henry.

After a long pause, Margaret said, "I don't know!"

The gallery exploded with cries of "liar" and "a mystery heir!"

She continued, "The boy is now sixteen and is approaching manhood. When he reaches full maturity, both these estates, Cambridge and Kent, will pass to him, unless they kill him first." She pointed an accusing finger.

One of the sons of Adam jumped up. "Yet your claims are unsubstantiated! Who can support these lies?" He looked around the room. There was a long silence. Then the door in the back of the manor opened slowly, and in walked a figure carrying a crosier, the hooked staff of a spiritual leader. She wore a habit with a heavy ornate gold pectoral cross. Behind her were two more nuns. "I can," came an authoritative and firm voice.

Rufus welcomed his honored guest. "Matilda, the Abbess of Romsey! Do you support this woman's claims?"

"I do. Lady Margaret, as some of you may remember, is my granddaughter, and that means the Boy is my great-grandson. I know for a fact that he lives. His claim to Wickham is valid. Who would call me liar?" She looked at the sons of Adam, who looked away.

She bowed courteously at William Rufus and left in all the dignity with which she had entered.

A son of Adam stood and stated, "Still, only one. We have three bishops. Can anyone else support the fact that she has a boy who still lives? I think not." There was silence.

Suddenly, the doors flew open with much more force than they had for the abbess. Strangely-dressed soldiers lined the aisle down the center of the room, and the Norman soldiers prepared for battle. Rufus waved them off and waited. Into the room strode none other than Queen Siobhan of Ireland. Her red hair and crown made that quite clear, though no words were spoken. Nor could they be. No one in that room knew one word of Irish. There was one, though, who could translate: Siobhan herself.

In a soft Irish accent, musical as ever, Siobhan began in her Norwich English, "The Boy lives. I know it. I know it because he is my great-grandson as well. His father was Thorkel, whose father was Roth, and I was the mother of Roth. Roth's grandfather was King Harald Bluetooth, and as such, Boy has royal Danish blood coursing through his veins today. And much more importantly, he has my blood in his veins. Boy is alive and well and he is the rightful heir to Wickham. Who would call the Queen of Ireland liar?"

Again, the sons of Adam looked away. Siobhan did not acknowledge me as I sat in the back, but I noticed that she saw me. Now Margaret knew nothing of this lineage, and was delighted with the unexpected support. Siobhan had received my message, and had honored an old debt. She was a good mother to you, Boy.

After such a jolting turn of events, Rufus declared a break, and the hall cleared out. I went outside and sat with the abbess for a good while, catching her up on your story and thanking her for answering my summons. It was in this audience that Matilda was finally forthcoming about all the details of her story, most of which I had received from secondary sources. She, like me, was in her final days and was eager to cleanse her soul in preparation for her death. Believe me, Boy, she had very few sins to atone for. She was a good mother to you.

I then went for a stroll on that chilly summer day along the cliffs of Dover and found Siobhan exactly where I knew I would find her. She was resting on the green grass that had grown inside the old foundation of an ancient Roman lighthouse. Her soldiers were surprised that she ordered them to let me pass. "You remembered our spot!" she called as I approached.

We talked as the cold July gusts blew in off the sea, and she told me the rest of her story. After I had left her at Cork, she was put into contact with O'Brian, second King of all Ireland. He had married but his wife had died some time prior. She explained that, "Since the same political advantages were still available if we wed, we were married, and he died soon after. There have been several kings since, but my title as queen is of course permanent. These Norman fools do not have to know that I am not the current reigning queen. Who in all England speaks Irish? No one. Our secret is safe," she said as she brushed away the flies.

And she had one more secret as well. She told me that Neils had told her what the runes on the battleaxe meant. He only told her so that she would tell Roth. She said she was glad she never did. She told me that the front of the axe represented the very spot we then sat on, and I said that part I knew.

She then told me what the runes on back said. "'The treasure of Svein is 77 feet 10 inches toward home.' The angle of ascent is about 30 degrees. And to them," she continued, "home is Denmark. That puts the treasure somewhere halfway down this cliff. There is probably a cave not visible from the top or the sea."

"Shall we go exploring?" I asked. We laughed and laughed, two old fools in their nineties. Her hair was no longer as brightly red, but her eyes were vivid green.

She told me that at her age she had absolutely no use for the treasure, and I laughed and said that I also had no need of it. I tell you all this, Boy, to let you know that the treasure belonged to your great-grandfather Neils and so is rightfully yours. We talked a bit more and it became apparent that she had had a happy life. She asked about me, and I told her about finding Eadburh and atoning for my part in her enslavement. I also admitted that if my chronicle could save Boy from these sons of Adam, then that would atone for my mother, for abandoning Gunnehilde, and for leaving Thorkel in the fire of London. Then I would have only the death of Ealdgyth to weigh me down at the Judgment. She wished me Godspeed, said she would pray for me, and assured she would stay for the decision by Rufus.

The trial was called back into session, and a son of Adam jumped up and addressed Rufus. "This trial is preposterous. We clearly own the land, given outright by your very father! Who can refute that? Who can?"

He looked around the room. Slowly, the door at the back opened again. Another crosier came through, this time held by a man in all black. "Anastasius, The Prior of Cluny! Here in England!" The bishops present moved to him and bowed, and the abbots in the room kissed his ring.

Rufus greeted the Prior. He exclaimed, "This is indeed an honor!"

I explained to the old hag that this was one of the highest-ranking men in Christendom, and his renown as the holiest of men was widespread. Anastasius, formerly named Rhys of Powys, had accepted his Latin name Anastasius upon arrival at Cluny. His name was often mentioned as a candidate for the papacy, and even sainthood was whispered about. This was indeed a blow for the sons of Adam. The Prior spoke in Latin, which was translated, line by line, by the abbots in the room.

The Professor broke in. "Oh my word. Rhys is Anastasius XX, Pope and today a saint! Oh my word." He waited in silence and looked in turn at me and then at Nelson. "Oh my word." He resumed.

Rhys explained, "Before I became a monk, I fathered the child Osgod, who is the father of Margaret. She speaks truly when she says that her boy, my great-grandson, is alive."

The three bishops then spoke up one at a time and recanted their earlier testimony. They spoke to the court and made clear that they felt that the Prior was without capacity for error. The sons of Adam were alone.

At this point the door in the back opened one last time. In walked another woman of some years, this one escorted by soldiers who were immediately recognizable. They were Welsh. The Norman soldiers that lined the walls drew their swords again, and again Rufus, throwing back the long flowing hair that fell to his shoulders, indicated with a coarse laugh for them to stand down. The woman wore the exquisitely embroidered robes of a queen. This queen, however, had brownish-gray hair and hazel eyes. She walked slowly and regally, with the posture and flowing grace that spoke of the highest nobility. Her walk was so beautiful that it made one think of a dance. She reached Rufus, looked him in the eye, and, surprisingly, did not bow. He continued sitting behind his enormous oak table and he slowly looked her over from head to foot. She spoke a strong sentence filled with sharp and lengthy words, but her speech was utterly incomprehensible to anyone in the room. Except to one person. The Prior walked up and smiled at his former wife. Though they had not seen each other in over forty years, the warmth was still there. She smiled back lovingly.

She spoke loudly in Welsh, and he translated it into Latin, which the abbots translated in the Norman French of that court, which I translated into Saxon for the old woman beside me who was still playing with her acorn. The queen proclaimed, "I am Queen Mother of Gwynedd, and my influence over my son, King Gruffydd ap Cynan, is considerable. Your consideration in the matter of Margaret would go a long way toward smoothing the conflicts that our two peoples still have in Gwynedd."

Now, the Normans had conquered most of Wales by 1093, but the northwestern corner still fell outside the control of the marches. "The marches" was the term applied to the southern and eastern areas of Wales that had been to a significant degree Normanized since 1066. Rufus probably did not seriously recognize any influence she might have with her son King Cynan, but our king was touched by the woman's sentiment. Angharad continued, "The boy in question is my great-grandson; I was the wife of the Prior long ago. I am now Queen Mother of Wales, and I say the boy lives." She turned with great dignity and slowly left the room, her green dress flowing sumptuously.

The Professor paused to look at the next page for a minute.

Although I had no concrete proof, there was no question at all in my mind at this point in the evening. I knew I was a direct blood decendant of a saint. I knew it. And now I had something to say. "Guys, over and over we've watched the same thing happen in this book. Mother after mother in this story has sweetly sacrificed herself for her baby. And the fathers too. It's like all this family does. I'm starting to feel that I'm only here today because of the sacrificial love of hundreds of generations of my foremothers and my forefathers. Isn't it sweet that generation after generation, down through the ages, all of us in this room have been protected, and that's why we made it this far? Maybe way back in time, those who did not love intensely did not have babies that survived. I'm beginning to understand that the parents whose babies' survived were the parents who could make that hard commitment, you know, take the leap, to selflessly trade their happiness for the security of their children. And this in turn cultivated children who themselves grew up selflessly enough to raise their own kids. It's a chain of generosity that has remained unbroken for ages for those of us alive today. What's really cool is that it seems like all the different ancestors of Boy each made their sacrifices in very different ways."

Then I thought of Mom and Dad, working nights for years to save enough to get us twins through college. How miserable that must have been for them. *Why couldn't I appreciate what they had done for me? Why can't I appreciate what they are still doing for me? Why did I have to make it so much worse for them? They had not raised me the way I would have raised myself, but they never abandoned me, and they sacrificed their own way, maybe the only way they knew how.*

I continued to speak to everyone. "What I'm saying is that those families whose parents did not sacrifice for them, over the generations, did not survive. The process of nature rewarding those parents who protected their children purged many of the ungenerous each generation. We are the ones who made it through the great strainer of historical generosity. We are the all-stars. We are the protectors. We have a responsibility."

"Amen to that," joked Nelson.

The Professor remarked, "This trial is definitely very moving for all of us. It does speak in a touching way to what each of our ancestors went through so long ago to be sure we are here today. Let's hear how the King rules."

Rufus declared a break for the noonday meal, with final statements to be given in the afternoon. Outside, I found the abbess of Romsey and asked if she might translate some Latin for me. She agreed, but when we saw the tender moment that Rhys was having with Angharad, we hesitated. We instead went and had our meal, and I told her the story of Rhys and Angharad, the two parents of Matilda's son-in-law Osgod. After our meal we approached Rhys a second time, and he was still talking with Angharad in Welsh; he was very emotional. I discovered over the course of our conversation that she had just told him that her infidelity had been staged so that he could follow his call. He was very grateful. It was obvious that she had never stopped loving him, and that she wanted him to hold her one final time, but that would have been a violation of his discipline and vows as a monk, and as such was inconceivable to him.

I had the abbess introduce me properly in Latin, and asked that Rhys in turn introduce me to Angharad. When they realized that it was I who had sent the messenger through such dangers to summon them to this trial, they smiled kindly. With Matilda translating for me, I learned what Rhys had been doing since he arrived in Cluny, and I in turn told Rhys and Angharad all I knew. Is it not a great wonder, Boy, that though you were not present at the trial and knew nothing about it, these strangers who knew nothing of each other were brought together by you, and it was they who won this cold, gusty July day for your mother, for you, and for your many generations to come.

I then asked Angharad her story, and she told me that Gruffydd had married her, and their third child had become the current king of Gwynedd. Life had been very difficult with the encroaching of the Normans. I then asked her about the poem that she used to tell her boy Mynyddawg. She asked, "This one?" She recited in Welsh:

Y theiaf addod helfa!
Sefyll ar y dirgel ffynnon
Wynebu cywir gogledd
Deintyddion awr
Adio un awr
77 troed deg modfedd hwnt
Llethr 30 gradd
Tarren goruchelder addod
Cwbl mewn un melyn dyfrgi blwch

I said yes, that was exactly the poem, and asked if she could translate it for me, that it was her son Mynyddawg's last request. She said of course she would try. From Angharad's Welsh to Rhys' Latin to Matilda's French to the

English of my mind, line by line the poem, stated, roughly:

Greetings little pig!
With the sharp toe nails
Indelicate in your lying down
Little know soldiers
In the blizzard of the night
77 will be honored tonight
Snowy for 30 days
Icicles on my beard, my way weary.
Amongst Wild Dogs of the woods

Angharad said, "It's really just a silly poem he loved. He was a good son."

Boy, Mynyddawg had said years earlier that it was "all the gold you'd ever need," and somehow I think your grandfather was right.

I thanked them all and told them I would see them in the hall for the ruling. The trial, however, did not resume in a timely manner. Apparently Rufus had decided to hunt for a while, and many people milled around the bailey, or courtyard, inside the outer wall of this castle. I noticed the scarred old woman sitting alone and went to her and asked her what brought her to this trial. She said that she was a simple midwife from Northumbria who had accompanied the party of the Earl. The Earl's pregnant daughter had come, and though she was only seven months, they wanted to be sure she was taken care of in case labor came early.

She said the trial was fascinating. I finally got up the nerve to ask her how she had received the terrible scars on her face, and as she told me my heart began to fall freely through space. She told me that she could not remember, but that shepherds had found her after she had been half-eaten by wolves. She had never been able to remember anything from before the attack. I asked her if she remembered the wolf attack itself, and she said no. All she remembered was a strange light that came and scared the wolves away. A light that saved her. Nothing more.

And then I knew: by coming after her with my arm afire, I had saved my Ealdgyth. I had thought she was dead, and here she was, returned to me by the Grace of God. I ran my fingers over my scarred right hand, and noticed how the scars seemed to match those of my Ealdgyth. I told her what happened to me one night in 1022 to get the scar on my hand and she said it was truly amazing. We talked for some time, and by the end of our conversation, she still had no memory of me. The name Gunnehilde, though, gave her a start and made her quiet for a long while. She said she did not know about all of this, but that she believed me completely. I asked if she still made tardpolane with almond milk and she was quiet again. She stared off that Dover cliff into the distance.

I ask her if she had ever heard the old saying, "If a lady carries an acorn in her bag, then she will be blessed with perpetual youth." She snapped her head toward me with the energy of a twenty year old. We stared into each other's eyes a long while, and I simply asked her if she would like to come back to Essex and be the wife of a thegn. She ran a finger over my scarred hand and asked, "Your hand on fire was the light that saved me. Oh my Lord in Heaven."

She simply said yes, and just that suddenly, I was married again. I told her what I was doing there, and she thought my actions truly noble. I hired a midwife to take her place both here in London and back to Northumbria, and we remained married for two years until her death last year. In these two years she lived like a queen compared to her Northumbrian conditions, and she died happy and gratified. I had to win her all over again, and it was a pleasure doing so.

Finally Rufus returned, and we all came into the chamber. The two queens sat on a back row, and soon the abbess joined them. The prior came in and sat with them to make a very impressive group of forebearers. As the proceedings began, Ealdgyth quietly got up and moved to their row. She was blocked by both Irish and Welsh soldiers, but a nod from me had the queens allow her her place. When I was sure no one would notice, I also moved over to this back row and sat at the far end next to Ealdgyth.

Henry was making a closing statement. He eloquently defended his cousins and I was grateful. I was very surprised that when he was finished, he walked to the back of the hall and sat on our bench with all of us. In my mind, he represented all that was good in Hugh.

Rufus was ready to rule. "Not only is it clear that you four sons of Adam have committed murder on this family, for which I hereby forfeit your frankpledge, but also, the entirety of the estate of Wickham is now ceded to Margaret in keeping for her Boy. Moreover, because you have shown no regard for my reign, I hereby forfeit all five demesnes that you hold in Kent, and I cede them all as now and forevermore part of Wickham. All members of my royal court will mark their X on a document setting forth this judgment.

A stir erupted in the hall as the sons of Adams stomped aggressively out. Many people hugged Margaret. She greeted all her supporters and then went out to the bailey.

Once the hall was almost emptied, I experienced one of the most gratifying moments of my life. Your four great-grandmothers, very different women all, came before me and bowed, one at a time, and then left; I never saw Siobhan, Matilda, or Angharad again. Two queens, an abbess and a midwife all thought that I had been a good man, and that was the worldly judgment I had waited for my entire life. Saving you is my only duty left, Boy, and this I will do. Then I will stand and face my heavenly Judgment with confidence that my life served its purpose and trusting in the mercies of God.

Margaret was elated with the outcome of the trial, but as you would expect, the four sons of Adam were infuriated. Because they could not even vent their anger on their peasants, which were now Margaret's peasants, it just worsened and worsened as they continued looking for you to kill you. In fact, my source in the guild told me that you fought one of them with a battleaxe in the guild. I have protected you until you were ready, and now, my boy, your departure for the Crusade has sped up my timetable. But do not worry; I believe you are ready now to eliminate these threats to your family once and for all. Margaret has had trouble of late coordinating so many estates, each of which annually require a number of mounted knights as service to Rufus. She is ready for you, now, Boy.

At the end of the trial, King William Rufus had asked only one more question: "Margaret?"

"Yes, your Majesty?"

"This boy is now a powerful landholder indeed, and he seems to have more royal blood than I can measure. Your son possesses Norman, Welsh, Irish, Norse, and Danish royal blood, which is more royalty than I have ever heard of in one man. His bloodline is absolutely amazing. Does this hidden prince have a name?"

'Yes, sir," said your mother Margaret. "His name is Arthur."

So goes the story of your mother, Margaret, but it is my hope that this story will not end for many more years.

So this is my mother. And I am Arthur.

"Arthur!" screamed Emma, "The savior of all England come to usher in a new era! I had no idea!"

She was kidding, but then she slowly realized, "So you are the missing prince everyone in Surrey was talking about two years ago. You are indeed full of surprises, Arthur. Tell me again the part where marriage is valid in the eyes of the Church if the two swear an oath to be together forever and then consummate the marriage. Tell me that part again," she teased, looking over at the ring of MacBeth that lay on one of the leather bags at the perimeter.

Instead of responding immediately, I told her that I needed to show her my gifts, and she was eager to see everything. I laid the knife by Wulfric and showed Emma the compass, the bow and quiver, and everything. She was amazed at the rich legacy that she saw before her.

Emma said Margaret sounded like a lovely woman, and she was eager to see her at Kent. It was time to dig up the final gifts. Emma watched as I dug up first the map of the world. She wondered how Wulfric had been able to dig into the solid rock to make the indentation in which the gift rested. I told her that he had been at this for a long time, since at least 1047—forty-nine years earlier—when Wulfric first escorted Siobhan to Ireland.

The map itself was encased in a leather tube, which was in turn encased in, of all things, a solid block of wax. The wax seemed old and it was obvious that the map had been buried here for years. On cracking the wax case open I discovered that Wulfric had used layer after layer of wax, and had again employed his trick of burning a candle inside to use up all the air. The leather tube had a slight burn mark on one end, but the map itself was in perfect condition, as I had expected. After marveling at the map at length in the firelight, we placed it back in the leather tube that housed it.

Finally, I dug up my mother's gift. I had no idea what this one was, or even if anything was down there, since she was still alive. After digging, I determined that it was one very long rock that covered this gift. Like the bow and the Greek fire, this hole was amazingly deep. Using both hands and most of my effort, I finally slid up the contents of the hole. It was a solid battle shield, almost as tall as I was, trimmed in iron. It was solid white and had one very distinctive marking on its front in the form of a crest. The marking was an imposing curved blue cross in the center, which I presumed comprised my family crest. I later discovered that it was indeed my family crest, and it was also the royal crest of England! The cross was the famous Norman Cross! It was a rich gift, and one that I would enjoy for many sons of Adam to come. They would soon enough feel its weight.

Emma watched me handle the shield and practice with it, and she finally asked, "Why are you so preoccupied with the shield when you have a Grailkey right here?"

My answer was simple. "There are hundreds of relics, but I have only one family. My mom risked her life to go back into that manor and secure this shield for me."

And with that Emma kissed me softly. When we separated I could tell she was about to say something important. Instead, we were abruptly interrupted.

At that moment Rexy, still tied for fear of more wolves, growled another alarm, and crunching into view on horseback came four of the meanest-looking Normans I had ever seen. I instantly recognized the one I had fought at the guild, but, as I expected, he seemed not to recognize me. From their stirrups and their armor, it was obvious that they were Norman knights, each trained in the deadly art of war.

One of them stated, "Your mother and your family have stolen our lands, and we will now avenge the insult. Your pretty shield cannot help you now!"

I knew that I could probably not defeat even one mounted knight, and I had thought about this eventuality at length. Wulfric had prepared me well! I simply put down the shield and picked up the Greek Fire, held it with a shirt in which I had wrapped it, and told Emma to light it. The Normans seemed to want to add more to their speech, but I interrupted them with chaos and a sickening smell as the device ignited and covered the four warhorses with burning tar. All four knights were thrown immediately, and all four horses screamed and ran away in terror. One horse fell dead as he ran away. I remember wondering if his heart had just given out.

The two Normans who were hit point blank dropped apparently dead to the ground. The other two, however, stood, slapped out their burning clothes, and drew their swords. Expertly, one moved around so that he was behind me. I moved away from the fire and stood with my bronze battle axe in my right hand and Excalibur in my left and prepared to defend, and to attack, as best I could. I flashed the axe as I spun it fast on my wrist while I did the same with my sword. I was ready for this. I knew that I would have to keep my head snapping back and forth constantly to be able to have the full vision to repel both attacks. I would take out the weaker first and then turn to the other. But both were huge, and neither looked at all weak.

Suddenly, though, my plight lessened. Emma had cut Rexy loose, and she herself smartly darted off into the woods. The war dog flew into the closer of the two Normans, arresting my attention and that of the other Norman for just a moment. I left Rexy to it and turned to see that Emma had somehow run up behind the other Norman. She was just pulling the knife out of his back and stabbing it in again. She jumped out of the way as he swung his sword at her with a might force, and when he turned back to me I sliced through the front half of his neck with Excalibur. By the time he had crumpled to the ground, I had wheeled to see the other Norman rearing back to deliver the deathblow to Rexy. With every muscle in my back and shoulders, I flipped my battle-axe through the air. It lodged deeply between the shoulder blades of the other Norman, who sank down and dropped his axe in the snow. I let Rexy loose on him because she had been tied up far too long. It took five minutes before she had completely finished this mighty warrior. Telling Emma not to look, I went over to the other two Normans who were badly burned. I stabbed the one that was rousing through the heart, and then I stabbed the other apparently dead Norman in the same manner. After all four were very dead and neatly dumped off the cliff, I turned to Emma.

"Nice fighting," I said. "You are very handy to have around." I hugged my two war girls, one on each side, and felt like the luckiest man in the world. My women had protected me when I had sorely needed their aid. Wulfric had prepared me well for my challenge, and I had met it. My mother would be very happy with me, I thought, and I smiled a smile as broad as one face can support.

Then we both heard the sound I had come to dread. A horse galloped off into the distance. Dawn would break soon enough, and we both knew we had one more challenge to overcome.

I began, "Wow. Emma was smart enough to let Rexy go and brave enough to stab that Norman. It was as if with this family around him, Arthur did not even have to try."

The Professor commented, "Perhaps that is what Wulfric is trying to tell you, my dear."

Bart added, "Perhaps he is telling us several things, Professor. On the subject of treasure, perhaps what he is trying to tell us is not about the silver coins of

Svein at all, nor is it about the silver dowry of Matilda that was also an immense fortune in silver coins that seems to be unaccounted for so far. Maybe instead these clues are about the gold coins of Osgod. Wulfric and Osgod together are definitely hiding something, and I think I know what, I think I know why, and I think I know from whom. One clue is that they include this unintelligible Welsh poem twice. Nothing else is repeated in this entire book. Why that poem? I'll tell you why, it's because its translation must mean something! 'It's all the gold you'll ever need' is stated twice, and I think I now know what that means: buried in that poem must be the exact geographic location of the gold!"

"Here's how I figure it," Bart continued. "Neither Wulfric nor Osgod could stand the thought of the Normans knowing the location of the immense stores of gold that must have still lay hidden somewhere in Cambridge. They didn't even want the gold's existence discovered, much less the extent of its value. If William's tax assessors had found out about it, Osgod understood from experience that they would have taken the lion's share. In fact, with a prize that tempting, they most probably would have arrested Osgod and taken it all. The gold, then, was actually a danger to him. Osgod had to hide his immense treasure from King William the Bastard or these tons of gold would have been as good as forfeited to the crown. And it would need to stay out of sight for a good long time, until this treachery against the crown—that is, the hiding of this immense treasure—was completely forgotten by history. So, sending the secret location of the gold through a Welsh poem would be the perfect device for avoiding the Norman bookkeepers who were systematically looting England in the period in which Osgod lived. Only a family member would read this book closely enough to piece together the clues, and, moreover, most of the book is written in Old English, which few French-speaking Normans would stoop to read. And you have to hand it to Wulfric and Osgod; the Normans would certainly never have gone to the trouble of translating a poem written in Welsh! And they couldn't even if they wanted to! Perhaps this is what explains why Osgod was so quick to reveal a Welsh heritage which he had hidden for many decades."

We all thought that this was quite plausible. We also thought that Bart fit in perfectly in pre-law, and that his ultra-realistic perspective on this book was serving a useful purpose. Bart finished, "But the location of the gold is still a mystery."

Joel added, "It's extremely cool that so many people in this family started as nothing and ended up as something; this family is ever-impressive."

Chapter Twenty

A Clever Little Trick

The Professor cornered us twins in the kitchen and told us quickly that he was going to test the group with a few questions, and for us not to speak until after the questions were over. “I’ve got a very strong feeling.”

He got serious and said, “This is important.” We were a little puzzled, but agreed.

When we three returned to the den, Bart was speaking. “Hmm. Steve, hand me that newspaper—let’s see what forty-eight thousand pounds of silver would fetch today.” He dug into the paper.

The Professor asked the exchange student, “You don’t happen to know the price of silver in Australia, do you? It might be even higher than here.”

The exchange student shook his head without looking up.

The Professor persisted, “Maybe you don’t move in the same social circles as precious metal owners. Do you, like me, find these people to be such soft toffs?” the Professor inquired as he chuckled at his foreign usage.

“Yeah, mate, I do. Rich people really bust my bum. I’m just a regular bloke, on exchange for the term.”

I went dizzy and turned white. Nelson, too, was biting his lip and looking strange. I composed myself immediately and saw the same composure come over Nelson. I needed time to think. As if in answer to a prayer, the Professor then launched into a comparison between the various uses of the semicolon by the Benedictine monasteries of Dorset and Wessex. Even Nelson was not listening to him.

I thought deeply. *This Australian guy is a friend of Joel's, someone said. But Joel hasn't talked to him once tonight, and this "bloke" hasn't spoken at all unless somebody made him. It's amazing how people study for college exams with perfect strangers. Marilyn and Bart said they saw the English stalker-boy at the bar, but in that dark, smoke-filled room, I bet they didn't get a good look, if they saw him at all. Before this Australian came here with the others, Nelson had mentioned to the Professor that Australians do not understand British words like "soft" and "toff"...but this Australian just understood them perfectly! The Professor asked him that because he suspects, too. But I may be wrong. There is only one way to know for sure.*

Mustering all my courage, I leaned near the Australian to reach for Nelson's drink, and that sickly-sweet cologne that I had smelled out on this afternoon's balcony, faint though it was by this point in the evening, hit me hard like concrete into my stomach. I was sitting in the room with the stalker, and he was absorbing all the information about our summit, and possible treasure.

Then my thoughts turned to what to do about it. If I excused myself and called the police, they would surround the place, and the stalker would panic. Steve would surely subdue him. Then I remembered, *the Australian had been in the room when Steve had calmed everyone! He knew of Steve's karate expertise, which I doubt this guy would want to deal with, unless he had a gun.*

I decided that now was the right time for a peek to see if anything was bulging out of his shirt. *Under his thick cotton shirt, yes, was a strange bulge! It's pretty big! Why had I not noticed that before?*

I calmly reasoned, *so if the attacker is found out, he will pull that gun and shoot Steve immediately to eliminate the threat of his karate. But we are all safe as long as this bloke doesn't figure out we're on to him. Now the Professor knows who he is, Nelson knows, and I know, but no one else does. The two men will not give this away, and neither will I.*

Knowing that the wrong look on my face would alert the "Aussie," and Steve might die instantly, my palms began to sweat. *Calm down, Haley*, I ordered myself. I focused and tried to get myself under control. *Everything was okay as long as he thought he had the element of surprise.*

The Professor was just finishing up on the semicolon. "I have a black and white video in German with subtitles on the use of the semicolon in the Gutenberg Bible all cued up on the jumbotron, if anyone is interested?"

"Maybe later, Professor," several people responded politely.

Bart finally said, "Here it is. At today's price, seventeen dollars and eighty-six cents per ounce, sixteen ounces to a pound, if it were really 48,000 pounds, the value of those fifteen boulders would be…" Here he borrowed the Professor's pencil and calculated for a minute. "The total before taxes would be a cool $15,033,280 and change. That's fifteen million dollars!"

As we settled in for the final section of the book, my mind was racing. *Are these people really our ancestors? Boy's name is Arthur and hers is Emma; there could be a clue there somewhere. And how did all his enemies find Arthur this long night? Surely they were not working together. There is still danger here: danger for Wulfric's soul since his solemn oath to Thorkel that he would protect Boy was so far unkept, danger to Arthur's and Emma's life, and danger in this very room.*

As the night had advanced, it had become obvious to me that the Professor had at some point done extensive linguistic or decoding work for the government, and it seemed more and more likely that he may well have been some sort of agent in his prime and might still be. He certainly wields enough power to summon three Apache helicopters on a moment's notice. Who could do that? My godfather, who had spent so much time mysteriously out of the states as Nelson and I were growing up, really was full of surprises.

But I looked over at the Professor at this point and could tell that he was out of tricks. When this story ended, the Australian would have to reveal himself in order to obtain the book, and this might well cost Steve his life. Though Steve thought he was going to save me, I understood perfectly that it was up to me to save him.

Joel spoke, "It's six-thirty in the morning and we have to leave to walk to the 8:00 exam, across campus, in about an hour. We better get a move-on, Professor sir."

At this point Emma and I made the decision that we would one day combine the fourteen booklets into one book, and to insert the etching of the axe, the Welsh biography written by Rhys, and Thorkel's map. Angharad's poem, Gunnehilde's song, and Matilda's story about the girl and the werewolf would be included in the text itself. We were very excited about the project, and planned to keep the book in a very safe place for our children and grandchildren yet unborn. I had the perfect place in mind.

Wulfric's body had lain here patiently throughout all fourteen stories, arms outstretched in a somewhat ghoulish pose, and now we read the second half of his chronicle, which was inserted into the leather bag of Margaret as a separate book. It obviously should be placed in this scheme at the spot of the fire, but the fire was ablaze. It appeared to be very brief. Before I began, though, I surveyed with great pride the layers of family that spread before me.

Wulfric Rhys

Gunnehild Mynyddawg

Ealdgyth Angharad

Thorkel Margaret

Neils Arthur Hugh

Roth Eleanor

Siobhan Matilda

Arthur, you are yourself and you were born in 1077 to your mother Margaret and your deceased father Thorkel. You know your life better than anyone else and so I'll leave it to you to write your own chronicle. What you may not know, however, is that for the past two years all of England has known of your story and your position, and even your name. All that they did not know was the location of this missing prince of the blood. The common understanding has you associated with the original legend of Arthur, that you will rise and usher in an era of new prosperity. They don't even know you possess Excalibur! I suggest you simply be yourself and let your destiny be your guide. But do not forget: the earldom of Kent is currently an open position; it is probably yours for the asking. I need not tell you that it is a stepping stone to kingship, as are your multiple royal bloodlines.

If you are wondering about me, I can give you a quick summary of my life since the 1053 date when my chronicle, the first one you read tonight, ended. In 1047 I had helped Siobhan escape back to Ireland, which I wrote of in her chronicle. In 1056 I went to the circle of stones and saw my Gunnehilde die, and gathered the ring and the knife. I already had the amulet and the bow from my marriage to Ealdgyth and already had the axe and the compass from Siobhan's 1047 return to Ireland. In the 1060s I worked on their stories. In fact, I assumed I was done when I finished the chronicle of Thorkel's two parents, Roth and my Gunnehilde, and his four grandparents, me, Ealdgyth, Neils, and Siobhan. And of course this history originally was written for your father, not for you. I never imagined until Thorkel's 1077 death that I would need to research Margaret's two parents and four great-grandparents as well. Yet as he was dying he informed me that I did, after all, still have one living descendant, the unborn child of him and Margaret. So I set myself to researching your mother's side of the family, Arthur, to be sure you knew your full story.

In 1077 you were born. I had to watch your father, my grandson Thorkel, die earlier that year. He never saw you. But the knowledge that you had been conceived, Arthur, set me into motion. I visited first Cambridge and then Wales in 1078 and received the sword and the Grailkey. I kidnapped you in 1081, when you were almost four years old, and set you up at the guild. I visited Cambridge again in 1083 where I heard Margaret's parents' stories and received the brooch and the Greek fire. The following year, 1084, I went to Romsey and received two more of the fourteen gifts, the chess set and stirrup from Matilda. Your mother entrusted the final two, the shield and the map, to me after the 1093 trial. I told her that I had engineered the witnesses to arrive and that I had been the one keeping her Arthur. A weak old man outwitting the four sons of Adam! She understood both that knowledge of me would stain the boy and that her knowledge of the boy's location could potentially cost him his life if she leaked the truth through error, torture, or trickery. Your mother Margaret, too, told me that I was a very, very good man, and at one point kissed me on the hand. This was another of my most gratifying moments.

I was married to Eadburh from 1078 until 1083 and was married to Ealdgyth again, a second time, from 1093 until 1095. Since 1093 I have completely rewritten these chronicles, a task which took fourteen additional months. I had to insert all the new information that I gained at the trial, and I had to stress certain parts of the book differently. You have made it to the end of the book, and I am impressed. In fact, I can now tell you that one function of this book was to point you to your family fortunes. Another was to direct you to the Grail. I knew only a family member would be able to stay interested long enough to glean these facts from the previous pages.

The Professor smiled at this as he reached for his cup of coffee and one of the cookies he had brought from the kitchen for all of us. During this pause I wondered, *could it be that Wulfric, Arthur, and my other family members are trying to save us across the ages by giving me the idea and the confidence to win this struggle with my attacker by outthinking him? Can I overcome my fear and finally triumph, like Wulfric did with his summit, with his book, with his trial at Dover, and with all his ingenious scheming? Can I overcome my past, like Arthur did, and find the inner strength to conquer my enemy, just as he defeated the wizards, the false monks, the Vikings, and the Sons of Adam? My grandmothers and grandfathers never gave up. Are they the only ones in my family who can outthink their enemies?*

The Professor read on.

The last thing I want to say, Arthur, is this. I don't even know if it has really been you who has been reading this book all along. I cannot be certain. The responsibility that I bear is heavier than you know, and so I have had to be unclear about certain aspects of this book in order to defend its secrets from those who would be poor guardians of the information contained herein. Even at this last section of my chronicle I cannot explain this clearly, but if you are truly Arthur, then you must have read every word of your people's story and you must have been struck, as I was, by the most important part of it. I refer to the eerie similarity of the prophecy of the ancient

Celtic religion, the Old German religion, and our True Faith. For the sake of security, I will leave it to you to discern the meaning of this strange coincidence, but mark it well.

"What?" blurted Bart.

The Professor read the passage again but no one in the room said they had any idea, or even a guess, at what Wulfric was talking about. I, however, understood it so completely that with a jolt from long ago I was electrified by what Wulfric was telling me. But I was not saying a word just yet. Wulfric was telling me that it was up to me to shatter my own draining hourglass, that it was time for me to take my place in the long and noble history of the men and women of my family who saved the people they loved.

I gave the Professor a strange, arresting look and asked, "Professor, don't you figure that Boy, that is, Arthur, lived a long life but died suddenly, so that he was not able to deliver this book to his children? It's not like anyone else could have written the book, right?"

The Professor began to reemphasize how few people could write in this period, but for the first time that night, I interrupted him. "But is it possible that someone else could have written this, such as Emma? Is it possible that Arthur died on this summit and Emma took up the task of writing the book? After all, she did know the entire story and as a noble may have learned to write later?"

The Professor smiled a little and turned his head to one side. "It is, I guess, possible. Let's get back to the narrative." His mind was racing now.

My rheumatism has been very bad in these past few years, and honestly, Arthur, my time has nearly come. Lately, I have begun carrying a piece of mountain ash to cure the aches, and it has helped a good deal. Believe me, Arthur, I hated keeping you in the guild and I always planned to send for you as soon as I could.

When you arrived up here at this summit I hope you found fourteen stories, fourteen gifts, and fourteen ancestors who loved you, each in their own way—God bless you and if this record has sufficed to save you, then perhaps, after all, I will see you in Heaven. It is my hope that so ends the story of your great-grandfather Wulfric.

Emma was very moved again, and it was so nice to be able to be there with her. She put the knife down by Wulfric and tied Rexy to the rock. She was getting ready for something, and I let myself begin to hope. She brought over the ring of MacBeth, the stirrup, and Godgyfu's brooch. "Can you make this my size?" she smiled coyly. Pure gold is very soft and I had no trouble slipping the ring onto the top of the stirrup and squeezing the ring so that it now fit a woman. I slipped it on her finger and I knew that it was time.

She knelt and began. "I swear to God on my soul that I am now married to you and will remain your faithful wife all the days of this life and my afterlife."

I went next, getting on my knees, facing her. "I swear to God on my very soul that I will watch over you and protect you as my wife all the days of this life and all the days of the next." And just like that we were married in the eyes of God. Then we kissed so intimately that even the sun stayed away for a while longer. The darkness and moonlight played for a long, long, time with us, and then finally began to fade. But of one thing I am certain. Venus would never shine that brightly for me again.

The sun was illuminating the edge of the sky to a faint white glow as we prepared to depart. Rexy was sleeping soundly, still tied. With Excalibur in my hand I walked over to the edge to take one last look off the cliff, trying to see the bodies far below. When I turned around, I stood horrified.

Rexy was still asleep and Cynewald stood with my bow fully drawn and an arrow pointing at my Emma. Rexy snapped awake, but she was tied and out of range.

"Shut thar'n dog up," he commanded.

I did.

"So, Master, it looks like you'rn out of tricks. Now, this is how it's gar'n be," he began. "Either yar gar'n throw yar'nself on yar'n sword right now, at my count three, or I'm gar'n kill you with this'n arrow and make good friends with the little lady thar'n. If yar'n do stab yar'nself all the way through, then Ar'll set her free. Ar'll only ask her for one thing. That'd be an oath that she nar'n in her lifetime tell the tale of what I did her'n this morning."

I asked, "What is it that you want? The Grailkey? You can have it. I have treasure. You can have that."

"You fool yar'nself, Sir Arthur. Yeah, thar'n's right, Wulfric told me a whole bunch of the story after all, including yar'n name. It was enough to sure get mar attention! Who you think sent all'rn the attackers this long night! I made me a bargain with the wizards, thar'n monks, the Vikings, and thar'n Normans, and yar'n beat em all! I was sorry that I sold away the pleasure of killing yar'n myself, I so wanted to pay yar'n back for taking my Wulfric's love away from me. But this turned out better'n I could ever'had hoped. I got thar'n money, and I get to kill yar'n myself. But Arthur, I don't wont just yar'n things, grand though they is; I'rn after the biggest prize of em all! I'm after yar'n very identity!"

The Professor paused, "I had not thought of that. In this period before fingerprints, photographs, or birth certificates, it was quite easy to assume someone's identity if he had been absent for an extended period. In a case such as this, when no one had ever seen Arthur before and Cynewald would be in possession of all the family heirlooms, no one would ever even suspect he was an imposter. They would just be disappointed with Arthur's character."

He resumed,

Cynewald was enjoying himself now. He had the mighty Arthur trapped; Arthur was far away from Emma and from Cynewald, and could never approach before the damage was done.

Cynewald sneered, "My mama Margaret is gar'n be so happy to see me, war'n't she? Until the night I slit harn throat, taking all hern lands for myself. How'll I look as an earl? How'll I look in a room filled to the beams with gold and silver?"

"Wulfric old man," Cynewald yelled toward the dead body, "You shard never have chose him over me. Are you ready to hear'n the screams of yar'n great-grandson mixing with allr'n the others you failed? And of course, yar'n own screams'll be in the mix as you begin to freeze in the corners of hell for going back on your'n oath!"

He continued, "How yar'n want it, Arthur, arrow for you, death for her, or sword for yar'n, freedom for her? You'rn out of tricks, Boy. I will give you until my count of three, and then I'm gar'n kill yar'n and make her suffer. Stab yourself all the way through, and she'n leaves right now, after her oath, no torture, and no suffering. I swore it."

"What's it gar'n be? One." Cynewald pulled the bow taut again and aimed it directly at Arthur's torso. "Two...

At this, Arthur did the only thing he knew to do. He plunged Excalibur deeply into his stomach, its point piercing his kidney and coming out his back. He muttered, "I love you," which came out of his mouth accompanied by some blood. He slumped and was dead. My mighty Arthur had fallen. Cynewald had sworn my freedom, and so I left that place after taking his oath and after he made me spend hours and hours telling him every bit of the story. He had needed Arthur to read the books because he of course was illiterate, as was I at the time. Tears streamed down my face as I heard him throw the body of Arthur off the cliff, and as I heard the yelp of Rexy as she too died by Excalibur. I turned for one last look as he was taking her collar off. As you can now tell, it was I, Emma, who wrote this book in order to tell our descendants of their excellent father and his people. Our son was born nine months later, and his would be a new day. And so ends the story of Arthur.

The Professor closed the book and put it down.

"That is the worst story I have ever heard," said Marilyn.

"A truly lame ending, and a colossal waste of time," said Joel.

Bart objected, "No, it just seems realistic to me. Times were not pretty back then; that's where the phrase 'going medieval on someone' comes from. Oaths were simply not broken in those days, so she could only record the story in a book and then hide it, and never do anything to reveal his bogus life, even if she ran into him. Not all stories have a happy ending."

Bart continued, "Cynewald must have found all the treasures and killed Margaret, claiming the life Arthur could have had. It really is a good story. Cynewald was a genius for figuring out the simplicity of it all, and for sending the wizards, the false monks, the Vikings, and the Normans to try and kill Arthur, since Cynewald knew he could never defeat these enemies of Arthur in combat, but thought perhaps Arthur could. Cynewald had nothing to lose by trying to use Arthur to eliminate as many enemies as he could, since Cynewald was going to impersonate Arthur and inherit his enemies."

Paul added, "This impostor must have been delighted that Arthur had killed every enemy, leaving a smooth life ahead for Cynewald's impersonation of Arthur. It was the same brilliant strategy as when Arthur had the Vikings kill the wolves and the wolves kill the Vikings. Cynewald definitely needed Arthur to stay alive long enough to defeat these foes, but he also needed Arthur alive for his other rare talent: reading. Arthur had to read the book for him, in order that Cynewald could learn the entirety of the story and locate the exact position of all the gifts.

Nelson added, "So that means that any treasure that had been around then—tons of gold, tons of silver, the Grailkey, Excalibur, everything-- was located and squandered by Cynewald a thousand years ago. There is no chance it has survived. That is really very sad." Everyone began to stand up and gather their things.

The Australian just sat on the floor, stunned. He was muttering, "I cannot bloody believe it. What a bloody waste." He eventually stood up with the rest of us and I watched as he stood frozen with indecision. He must have been deciding whether it was worth anything to him to blow his cover and assault us.

Joel was saying, "No joke. Let's go. Thank you, Professor, for such an unusual and entertaining evening." The students all began looking for their backpacks and saying their good-byes. The Australian looked at the Professor one last time and, fists clenched, shook his head in disgust. He slammed Joel, who was walking ahead of him, out of the way as he was storming out of the house. "What is your problem?" Joel yelled menacingly, but the Australian kept on moving. A few minutes later we heard a motorcycle roar to life down the street, then fade into the distance.

I walked aimlessly toward the kitchen, away from the crowd, trying to regain my composure and calm myself down. Before I could do either, Steve caught me in the hallway, spun me around, and gave me a very affectionate kiss. This calmed me down quite well. He said he would see me after the exam in the doublewide, and we shared a silly look. I watched him closely as he walked into the living room to join the crowd who was by now spilling out onto the porch and down the steps. Joel and Bart said they would run home before the exam, and most of the others said they were off to grab a bite of breakfast. Finally, everyone was gone except Nelson, the Professor, and me. We walked out onto the porch too, and stretched as we watched our companions move off in various directions through the dawning night.

There was no doubt that a mist of crisp coolness had come and settled over the South, and the earliest leaves were floating excitedly toward autumn. The sun was still under the eastern horizon, but it was beginning to cast pink up into the reluctant black sky. The morning had begun to raise itself up.

"Professor," I began, "That was brilliant. It was absolutely brilliant. But Professor," I smiled into his smirking face, "Arthur couldn't have committed suicide; such a thing would be unthinkable in his era. You know that."

"You are correct."

"In fact," I continued, "Arthur didn't die at all."

"You are correct again, Haley."

"And Wulfric had not been dead at all during this long, cold night. His hands kept changing positions throughout the night, and Rexy kept licking him."

"You are correct."

Nelson leaned on the railing and listened in disbelief. Apparently he had not followed all of this.

The Professor grinned broadly, "Shall we retire inside and finish the book as it was actually written? I hope you enjoyed my made-up ending!"

Chapter Twenty-One

Wulfric Takes His Place

"Yes, I did, Professor. Come, Nelson," I called, as we moved back inside.

As we walked down the hall I walked ahead of the men. Turning and walking backwards I continued explaining to them, mainly to Nelson, "Am I correct in assuming that you, Professor, made up an alternate and very unhappy ending because you knew the stalker was among us? My guess is that as a linguist, you must not have been fooled for a minute by the stalker's fake Australian accent. You realized that Australian people could not possibly have understood either the word 'soft' or the word 'toff', and so you set up the stalker to expose himself linguistically, which he did by understanding vocabulary that no Australian could have known, but every Englishman would have. You figured out from his speech, as I did from his cologne, that the Australian was actually the stalker, and that Steve's life and all of us were very much in danger. Am I right?"

"You are exactly correct," said the Professor as we walked back into the den in which we had spent the past thirteen hours.

"And so you generated an ending in your mind and pretended to read it as if it were written on the pages. Very ingenious."

Nelson muttered, "You're freaking me out."

I resumed, "The stalker was utterly convinced by this, and he couldn't believe he wasted his time on such an ancient dead end. He will not be bothering us again."

The Professor said, as he moved toward the kitchen, "You are correct, again, Haley. Now hang on a minute while I telephone the police to apprehend the stalker at the airport. I can now indeed give a very specific description of the bloke."

While he was gone, we twins sat side by side and examined the penmanship in the book. Nelson said, "Well, I can't tell if the writer of this thing is a girl or a guy. I can hardly tell if it's right-side up!"

The Professor returned and settled into his chair one last time that night. He perched his glasses on the end of his nose in his usual way, retraced a few lines, and, with one of his big smiles, began to read again.

Cynewald continued, "How yar'n want it, Arthur, arrow for yar'n, death for her, or sword for yar'n, freedom for her? Yar'ns out of tricks, Boy. I will give you until my count three, and then I'ma gar'n kill you and make her suffer. Stab yar'nrself all the way through, and she leaves right now, after her oath, no torture, and no suffering. I swore it."

"What's it gar'n be? One." Cynewald pulled the bow taut again and aimed it directly at Arthur's torso. "Two...

At this point the ghostly figure of a frail old man appeared silently behind Cynewald. It was Wulfric, standing, alive and ready to finish his story the way it was destined to end. With a power that I cannot explain, Wulfric drove the Celtic knife solidly through Cynewald's neck. The arrow shot harmlessly into the distance as Cynewald and Wulfric both slumped to the ground. Emma and I rushed over to Wulfric, and Emma looked away, when I asked her to, as Excalibur made sure Cynewald did not ride away from this final scene. I quickly flung his evil body off this holy summit.

Wulfric lay dying, and we all knew it. He motioned me closer, and breathed his dying words into my ear. They were exactly what I had expected, as much as Wulfric himself had been exactly what I had hoped for in one of my fathers. He breathed, "Put me in my place," and then he gave up his ghost. We heard the ghost leave his body, and we even saw it, in the chill of that morning, as it rose higher and higher toward the Heaven for which he had fought all these years and which he had now won so lovingly.

I interrupted, "With that one motion, that one stroke of a Celtic knife, Wulfric saved all three stories; he won his salvation, won Emma for Arthur, and won the book and its treasures for us."

And I continued, "And when dawn had broken, it was the day of St. Valentine, which in that era held no association whatsoever with love, but that was okay, because the scene could not be any more romantic."

The Professor smiled. He was very, very, pleased with how much better I was feeling, and he understood fully how much he had helped me over the course of this night. He began to read one last time, his voice radiating with the pride of a very satisfied father.

It seemed very fitting to bury him up here, which Emma and I did together off to the left of the cliff.

Emma and I agreed that this summit was a very special place, and that it would be the perfect small manor to hold in secret to keep all the family treasures safe. Wulfric had dug the grooves in this mountain with love, and it would be in them that these gifts would be stored until we needed them. We would take them all as we departed now, to protect us and to prove our story. But we vowed to return some months later, and bury them with many burning candles, as Wulfric taught us, to use up the air and preserve each gift as well as possible. Most would preserve for a very long time--the amulet, the sword, the Grailkey, the chess pieces, the stirrups, the battle-axe, the compass, the brooch, the Greek Fire, the ring, the Celtic knife and the shield—because they were metal. Since only the grip of the bow and tips of the arrows were metal, they would not preserve as well. Thorkel's map of the world we would put in our book. I suspected that because of the level of humidity in the place I planned to build to house this book, it might be best to protect the book by using Wulfric's wax encasement idea.

And we agreed that if we found the treasure of Neils, we would fill the empty spaces of these fifteen grooves with a ton of silver coin each. And if we found Osgod's gold buried deeply under the pigsty at his little farm called Wild Dogs, as his poem had promised, we would bury all that gold up here until we needed it as well. Since it was hidden from royal tax officials and the Domesday survey, it is best that we let it rest here for many years to avoid legal confiscation. We agreed to make the book and keep it as a marker in case the location of the gifts is someday lost. Wulfric was again right: no French-speaking royal tax official would be patient enough to read through these fourteen Old English books closely enough to determine the location of the gold and silver, nor could they ever even tell whether the buried treasure were actually real, or if it were just part of a made-up story; in fact no one in their right mind would ever finish this story, except the heirs to our glorious English history.

As we prepared to leave, Emma and I were both glad we would be back again some day, perhaps many times. One more look around, and we left Arthursdale, as she would later take to calling it. And so Emma and I heard Cynewald's horse ride off once more, but this time we, the happy newlyweds, were riding it, dripping with gifts and being escorted by a war dog wearing a diaper. Of course we rode Cynewald's horse, which actually belonged to his master Wulfric, and so was mine now, along with so much more! I sat proudly with the amulet around my neck, with my sword and battleaxe dangling by my sides, with my shield hung over the other side of the horse, with my quiver of arrows and rolled map across one shoulder and bow across the other shoulder, with my chess set and compass in my bag, with my fourteen booklets in another bag, with my Greek Fire spear in my lance sheath, with my dog wearing the gold Grailkey running ahead, with stirrups--attached by the leather straps that had earlier worked as Rexy's leash--supporting my weight, with Emma snug in back of me wearing the ring on her finger and the brooch in her hair, and with the Celtic knife in its sheath under my braiel. Emma, green eyes shining with the lights of morning, gripped me hard as we galloped into our new day together. And our life together would thereafter be happy.

"Wow," uttered Nelson. "Arthursdale has been shortened over the centuries to Thursdale, and we own its summit and all the minerals buried there, and that means our parents are going to live happily ever after. And this much gold today is worth something like twenty million dollars. Professor, will you fly with us to England today, after the exam? We need a guide, and we need a loan for the trip."

I, too, looked pleadingly at the Professor.

"You have to be joking. Of course I will. We can fly out late this afternoon; it'll take me some hours to make the arrangements. The boys over at FEMA owe me a favor. Haley, Nelson, can you two find some way to entertain yourself after your exam for a few hours?"

I thought about the doublewide hammock, the only place on earth that might be better than tomorrow's summit. I responded a respectful "Yes, sir," exactly at the same time as Nelson's response.

The Professor added, "But Nelson, on the subject of the value of the gold, you are quite incorrect. I looked this up in the newspaper when I was on the telephone on hold with the police and did some calculations. At the current price, $1211.40 per ounce, at twelve gold ounces per pound, two thousand pounds per ton, and calculating fifteen tons, the current value of what Wulfric describes is $701,024,000.00, approximately. Seven hundred million dollars! Unless you just want to, you and Nelson don't ever have to get dressed again in your life. Here on out, it's slippers and robes for you. And for your parents and your friends as well!"

I let that sink in a minute, and said to myself under my breath, "And Steve still likes me even though he thinks I'm poor."

The Professor looked serious and added, "Let me tell you something about Steve. You understand, dear, that with your solution, you saved us all. With your one comment you suggested to me that Emma might plausibly have written the story, and that we could trick the stalker into leaving empty-handed if he thought Cynewald had beaten him to the loot a thousand years earlier. At the point where you suggested this approach to me, I was totally out of ideas. I had completely resigned myself to losing the book; by that time I was just hoping that no one would get hurt. And that was not really a possibility considering that we knew exactly where the treasure was, just like the stalker. In order to get the treasures for himself, he was clearly going to have to kill every last one of us. I thought your solution was pure brilliance. You sitting calmly next to your attacker, arriving at the idea to fake-translate Arthur's death, and passing it to me unnoticed in conversation was not only heroic, it was inspired genius. There is no question in my mind that you saved us all. You especially protected Steve, because he was the real threat to that criminal; he surely would have been attacked first."

The Professor thought for a while about his remark, and then snapped his head toward me in excitement as if he had just received a revelation. "Haley, your middle name, 'FitzArthur,' means 'son of Arthur' in Norman. Could it be? Could a girl, I mean a young woman, be the Arthur that history has awaited all these centuries? Is there something you will do to usher in a new era of peace for mankind?"

The Professor continued, "And could it be that the Grail, if it is ever located, will be carved in matching fashion to the Grailkey and will depict the symbols of every single world religion, and depict them in equal stature, revealing and proving what many in all of our world's faiths have long suspected, that all religions express the same truth? That there is really only one religion? Does every religion contain the same core message: "Peace be with you?" One object of perfect sacredness revered equally by all world religions will both incontrovertibly prove the very existence of God and will also instantly unify our planet's people into an new era—no, a new epoch—of peace."

My posture was erect as my eyes burned into his. He continued, "Could it be that you have already done it, that fooling the stalker into leaving us unharmed and in possession of this book has already set the future off on its rightful course? Could the old witch in Scotland have been right one thousand years ago? Are you the fulfillment of her prophecy?"

I responded instantly, "I don't know, Professor, but I do know what Wulfric must have been trying to say at the end of his story. Even at the time you were reading it I understood his mysterious remark about the similarity between the German, Celtic, Welsh, and Christian prophecies, but I didn't want to speak in front of that crowd."

I thought a minute, moved onto the rug, and began playing with the polar bear again. "I think I know what Wulfric was trying to say. Maybe we all do. When Siobhan first told Wulfric the part of Roth's story where the witch foretold that Roth's offspring would one day save the world, it sent a chill right through me, and it must have sent the same chill through Arthur and Wulfric alike. Alone, of course, the witch's prediction was meaningless. Especially since it only came from a desperate witch, an adherent of the old Anglo-Saxon religion of Woden and Thunor. What was alarming to us all was that at the circle of stones, when Gunnehilde died, the Celtic priestess had also said that Gunnehilde's blood would fulfill a prophecy. And the priestess was certain it would be a girl who would do it. These prophecies represent two totally different and unrelated religions. When I heard this, I didn't understand how this could be possible, so I dismissed it as the coincidental ramblings of two insane pagan women of two very different religions. And as you remember, Wulfric's father also told him the same thing, that the possessor of the amulet that he wore would one day save the world. For much of tonight I pushed these comments aside as the kind of off-hand predictions that must have been made routinely in that era. But once I discovered that Arthur's mother's side of the family possessed both Excalibur and the key to the Holy Grail, the truth became apparent to me. It was at that point that I began to realize that Wulfric was saying that someone in my family will eventually save the world, and I was suddenly overwhelmed with the feeling, no, the certainty, that he was talking about now, and he was talking about me. That was what gave me the adrenalin rush of confidence that allowed me to sit calmly and figure the way out of our danger. It had to be a girl.

My confidence built up more as my imagination fleshed out the meaning of these prophecies. According to the legend, Excalibur will surface again one day in the possession of a great hero who will usher in a new era of prosperity. That day is today. And when the Grail is located, it is said, this will herald an entirely new age of man. That age is upon us now. So Wulfric's quest had not been simply to save his own soul nor had his story been written only to secure Arthur. The fact that Arthur finished the fourteen books in that one night not only secured Wulfric's soul to Heaven, it also kept the hope for the fulfillment of the prophesy alive. My confidence was wildly boosted again as I realized that whatever prophesy Wulfric was so sure about would only be fulfilled if the information in the book remained safe. Wulfric could not come out and plainly declare that our family would one day usher in a new age for fear that the information would fall into the wrong hands, diabolical hands that could stop the prophecy from being fulfilled. That, ultimately, is why his story was cryptic in places; his book was a puzzle that could only be solved by Boy. And with his solution came my solution."

The Professor added, "Boy was aware enough to understand that the revelation of the Grail during his era would have been disastrous since there was no way to protect it back then. Perhaps that is why he never made an attempt to go to Jerusalem and acquire the chalice."

I interrupted the Professor. "Professor, I think you are exactly right, but there is one aspect that I believe even you have overlooked. Didn't Arthur repeatedly say that he planned to take the already dug fifteen holes and fill them with the family gifts, with silver coin, and with gold coin?

"Yes, he said this several times."

I drove my point home, "But he only received fourteen gifts. Two parents, four grandparents, eight great-grandparents, that adds up to only fourteen. His spot in the middle should not be counted because he never gave himself a gift. But he has a gift for us, doesn't he, Professor? The cover of the book shows an hourglass, but it's no hourglass. And it is no butterfly. It's a goblet. At the center of our summit, right now in England, is buried the Holy Grail, probably surrounded by tons of gold and silver coins! Arthur went on a Crusade after all! He was a man of his word. He was another good father to our family."

The Professor was excited again. “I had not noticed that he said fifteen gifts, well, I had noticed, but I hadn’t thought anything of it. Of course, you are right. Obviously you are right. There is another gift.”

The weight of finding the Holy Grail was on us all, and we were silent. A new era was beginning with this morning, and it had only been made possible by my intuition at the well, my triumph over despair, and my scheme to trick the stalker.

At this point the Professor went to the kitchen to answer the phone, and came back shortly. “That was the police,” he remarked. “While the stalker was being apprehended at the airport, he pulled a gun on the first officer on the scene. The officer reports that he had no choice but to shoot the stalker in the chest six times. Our stalker is quite dead. The officer on the scene was a senior Secret Service agent and is a very deadly shot.”

“Oh, and Haley,” the Professor added, “This officer, Agent Thackerson, sends his regards.”

Nelson blurted, "Secret Service? They protect the president and other high officials! Thackerson told us he was campus police. What in the world? Who sent him to our house in the first place?"

No answer was forthcoming from the Professor. He simply said, “Just call me if you need me” and handed me a business card that simply read:

Flannagan O’Shea, Ph.D.
Library of Congress
Director of Circulation

Nelson and I looked at each other with looks of complete understanding. The senator’s son in Bart’s fraternity had been right the whole time, there actually was an eighth Article of the United States Constitution, and the Professor was actually the Director! Our godfather wielded immense power over the Presidency, the Supreme Court, the Senate, and all the U.S. Government. The space-age security seal around the house was to protect this den, which by the looks of the jumbotron and intense laser pointer was obviously a government command center. Sergeant Thackerson was actually Agent Thackerson, assigned to the security detail of the Director. The house was decorated with dodo birds and prehistoric giant polar bears because the Professor oversaw the Smithsonian Institution as well, and so got to browse through their basement storage bins for his decorating needs! The Apache helicopters of the Federal Marshals finally made sense. Nelson handed the business card back to the Library of Congress Director of Circulation and we never spoke of the Professor's real job again. Some secrets are kept very well.

As my confusion about how the Professor could know so much about the officer faded, the horror of such a brutal killing began to overwhelm me. Nelson and I were both sorry that it had come to the extreme that someone had to die. But I said a silent prayer of thanksgiving that Agent Thackerson had been watching over me tonight. *A prayer, the first one in so long. And this single true prayer dislodged so many others, quiet prayers, for the Professor, for my Daddy, for Nelson, for Mama, for Steve, for all those here last night, for Wulfric, for Arthur, for Ealdgyth, for Rhys, for Angharad, for Neils, for Siobhan, for Hugh, for Matilda, for Gunnehilde, for Roth, for Mynyddawg, for Eleanor, for Margaret, for Thorkel, for Emma, for Rexy, for all those who work or watch or weep this morning, for myself, and for all my children and my children's children yet unborn.* It felt so good to be able to pray again. A new age was surely dawning, an age in which prayer could be pure again.

The Professor's calming voice broke my thoughts. "I can't say that I'm very sorry the bloke's dead, since the publicity on this matter is going to be world-wide. Of course, I suggest we tell no one until any treasure and any gifts are physically secured in a bank and legally secured by a statement from the British government regarding ownership. You are going to need the finest barristers, which means lawyers, in England."

He continued, "The Grail, however, is another story. If it is up on that summit, once the discovery is publicized, no museum or vault will be able to safely hold it. Before the media circus begins, we must quietly and personally deliver it—I know we're not Catholic, but it is the right thing to do--to the Pope in Rome. Only he has the resources and wisdom to protect the Grail. Maybe we can even get it there before this conference of world religious leaders is over. The reporter last night was saying that the conference was not going well but it's supposed to last for nine days. Perhaps the arrival of such an object at such a time would be the sign for which they are all searching. Even the faintest hope for the unification of humanity is a gift in itself."

We got up and walked up the stairs, through the living room, and onto the porch.

I stopped and looked the Professor in the eye. "This is way too heavy for me to take in all at once," I said, sounding a little overwhelmed.

"I now know my family and I know my roots, I found a love and found a fortune, I've discovered a new major, I have found the Holy Grail, and what's more, I've discovered that I am a very smart girl after all. And now, it appears, I'm going to live happily ever after."

"You are correct. Haley, is there anything that you don't understand?"

"No, Professor, there is nothing that I don't understand."

"Then I'll leave you, my dear, to your destiny." And with that, he kissed me on the cheek, shook hands firmly with Nelson, and said, simply, "Good night." He closed the door and left us on the porch.

We were alone now, just the two of us, just as we had arrived here. Our closest moment was at hand. I leaned over the porch railing to let the new cooling air wash over me, and I was still for a moment, letting myself feel the morning chill of a new season wash over my face, my arms, my legs, and flow into my sandals. The pinks and greens of the morning sky had come to be with me, and this time I let them in.

The thoughts rushed in like a cloud of butterflies landing, *Nelson has always been there, always there, always watching over me, and this night, for the first time, I had watched over him and kept him safe.* I looked up and he was coming over. We fell into a hug, and finally, after damming and damming for months, I let myself begin to convulse in sobbing. I collapsed into him in an embrace of the ages.

My hands finally slipped from around my beautiful brother, and I took one last look at the house. With a hard look at Nelson, who I knew would be along soon enough, I stepped down from the porch and out onto the earth. I began to move down the street, feeling more in control than I had ever felt in my life.

As I prepared to cross the street to the Commons, I saw them. Turning in front of me onto the Professor's street were my parents in their car. The party dress and hat fooled them completely, and they kept on driving. But I knew they had come. As I walked on, I thought about their long night, and how they must have been very scared for me after I was attacked. The Professor had called them and my sweet parents had driven all night long from Kentucky to be with me, to watch over me and keep me safe. I stopped walking toward my test under those oaks and rested a minute, closing my eyes to let what they had done, all that they had done, begin to sink into my heart's memory. *Remember. Remember.*

A cold chill shook me awake and I walked on into the first true frostiness of autumn. This cold meant I would have no butterfly escort until the Spring, and I would wait loyally for their return. With my building up ahead, I turned and looked back across the Commons once more to admire the immense lone oak tree that Nelson and I had sat under yesterday, now so long ago. As I admired the timelessness of that oak tree, so alone but never lonely, the chimes began echoing out eight long, knowing tolls, each followed by an eternity of silence. Just as the eighth chime was struck, four helicopters in tight formation buzzed the Commons. They were only above me for a few seconds and then they were gone: the dark blue of the U.S. Navy, the bright orange of the U.S. Coast Guard, the dull black of the *F.B.I.* and the deep green camouflage of the U.S. Army. I could not hold back the smile that spread across my face as my suspicions had been confirmed. I was being escorted to class by every agency of the United States government. The surrounding buildings were swarming with Navy Seals, C.I.A. snipers, and, knowing the Director of Circulation as I did, probably the National Park Rangers as well. My suspicions had been correct. I understood and the Director understood that my business in England later that day was going to change the course of human history, and so my physical protection and safety as I completed my destiny that day was now the highest priority of the United States government. *Would the prophecy be fulfilled? Time would surely tell.*

I had come so far, as we all had. The well had silently kept its secret over the ages, and my family secret was now mine. I now understood the secret that had been coursing through my veins every minute of every day of my life, the pulsating anchor of my own ancestry of redemption and belonging. My secret, so well-kept from myself for so long, is that I have never been alone because it is impossible to be alone. I cannot be alone because all the greatness of all my ancestors is in my bloodstream. My yellow-wings can taste it in my sweat. I descend from greatness and my ancestors have silently showered me with all their best traits. I cannot ever be alone. We are together.

I admired the dignity of my oak for one more moment. Then I turned and walked on. The coolness of an autumn orchard had turned to a winter of loneliness for Arthur, and he had triumphed over change. And he had lived. The snowflakes of winter had thawed into spring for Wulfric, and no one can say that he had not lived. The butterflies of a spring day had turned to summer for Emma, and she had lived. And the wishing wells of summer have now turned to fall for me, true fall, and I knew that this day, yesterday, and tomorrow would soon fold into years, and the years would rise into decades, and I too would live.

Thoughts kept fluttering and lighting. *This has not been about me all along. This is not about me; this was never to be done alone. Who will drop a penny down the well that reveals us at the bottom, and wait, take time to wait, until all is clear again?*

With my back a bit arched, I felt the chilled air begin to stir my blood. I knew Nelson understood more than I did, and I knew he would tell me in time. I knew what I would find on our summit. I knew that no one could have revealed my own secret to me except me, and I had finally revealed my well-kept secret to myself: I am a FitzArthur, with roots driving me deep into my planet, fusing me into the perfect motion of my whirling mother earth. My mothers and I would walk together now, keeping step with each other like the sisters we had always been. And I would be a mother for the ages, a protector goddess to my children yet unborn. As the force of my chilled air swirled around me in this early morning, I surrendered to the soft glow of a cooling sunrise that would stir our sweet, sweet blood with a bold new age.

Chapter Twenty-Two

The Well Kept Secret

As I finished my story in our big flannelled bed, the sun was already up. It had been for her, for my baby Emma so coming apart last night from her break-up, that I had decided to finally tell my story. My teenage daughter had come to me once again, she had needed me one last time, and it was a time for one last act of mothering. I had snuggled her up and had told her lovingly throughout the night about the night I first kissed her father on the Professor's porch.

I had told her everything. Finally, in the early glow of dawn I turned my moistened eyes and triumphant half-smile to look on my daughter, only to see her form rise and fall with her gentle breathing. She was asleep now, and she had been deep in slumber all night long. Her father, my Steve, also slept in his usual timeless oblivion on the far side of the bed. Even our German Shepherd Lowey sprawled motionless at the foot of our big flannelled haven. In her sleep, Lowey kicked out once, her mind wildly chasing the bunnies of her ancestors. I had been ready to walk Emmy over to my college diploma that hung on the bedroom wall and to show her the secret elevator behind it that led down to the fully restored room under the wishing well where the waxy box and the book had first been found, a room that now secured so many important family heirlooms. I wanted to show my Emma her family treasures, to tell her about her beautiful name, and to finally share our powerful family secret, our amazing well kept secret. But not this morning. My family, my beautiful family, had been here all night, but none had heard my story. Our Thursdale groundskeepers droning their lawnmowers far in the distance had not heard it. The chauffeurs waxing our Rolls Royces in their garages had not heard the story. The people of our beautiful planet earth, a planet now finally at peace after the end of its final war ten years earlier, had not heard the story. Our government, busy redirecting trillions of military dollars into helping the people of our beautiful planet, had not heard the story. And my daughter, absorbed in the tiny world of a seventeen-year-old, had not been ready to hear her own story and slept through all of it.

But the story would one day be heard. Those who turn toward the butterflies that flip their elegant acrobatics through the sunlight of summer gardens can begin to hear the story. Those who stop and listen down a wishing well, if they wait long enough, can begin to hear the wishes and lessons of the ages begin to echo. Those who sit alone, turning into the familiar breeze of their own summit, can begin to hear the story. And of course, I now know the story that courses through my veins every minute of every day. And I know all too well that the time will come when my lovely children will be desperate to hear their own story. And on that day when they finally long to hear it, we will all be here to tell them of the well kept secret.

Made in the USA
Middletown, DE
06 May 2015